Wizards

Stories of
Magic, Mischief andMayhem

Wizards

Stories of
Magic, Mischief andMayhem

edited by
Jennifer Schwamm Willis

Thunder's Mouth Press
New York

Wizards: Stories of Magic, Mischief and Mayhem

Compilation copyright © 2001 by Jennifer Schwamm Willis
Introductions copyright © 2001 by Jennifer Schwamm Willis

Published by
Thunder's Mouth Press
An Imprint of Avalon Publishing Group Incorporated
161 William Street, 16th floor
New York, NY 10038

A Balliett and Fitzgerald Book

Book design: Michael Walters

Library of Congress Cataloging-in-Publication Data is available.

ISBN: 1-56025-320-7

9 8 7 6 5 4 3 2 1

Printed the United States of America
Distributed by Publishers Group West

For Harper and Abner,
who prove to me that magic is real

Table of Contents

Introduction

As a girl playing at the beach in the summer I dug in the sand for psammeads, the sand fairies I'd read about in E. Nesbit's *Five Children and It*. During games of hide and seek with my younger brothers and our friends I kept an eye out for rabbit holes like the one Alice fell through in Lewis Carroll's *Alice in Wonderland*. And if I stumbled upon an old wardrobe in someone's house I would peer inside, on the chance that it might lead me into the magic world of Narnia. After all, that's how Lucy had gotten there in C.S. Lewis' *The Lion, the Witch and the Wardrobe*.

Although I never found a wardrobe like Lucy's, I did discover other worlds in my bedroom closet. One of its walls was lined with bookshelves that held volumes and volumes of fairy tales, folk tales, myths and fantasy stories. I spent many evenings on that closet floor, transported by words.

That's where I began to learn that good stories are like magic spells. They make time fly by. They make us forget where—or even who—we are. They help us to find unexpected worlds in our own imaginations. In those ways they help us to become magicians ourselves.

Some of the stories I read in my closet—and many of the stories in this book—are old. Many of the best stories are old ones and the best new ones often come from them. Have you ever noticed that sometimes a new book you read or movie you watch reminds you of some old story you've already read, or one that your parents read to you when you were little? When you read Margery Williams' *The Velveteen Rabbit*, think about its connection to a movie like *Toy Story*. When you read *The Once and Future King* notice how the wizard Merlyn teaches magic to his young pupil "Wart," the future King Arthur of England. Does Wart remind you of Harry Potter at all? When you read *Half Magic*, notice what the children in that story are reading.

Magic in stories—and in life—often comes as a surprise. Maybe you are following a thought or a feeling, or maybe, like Alice, a rabbit in a waistcoat, and suddenly . . . you are somewhere else.

The story that starts in that moment is a true adventure. You may overcome terrible obstacles, may find that you are stronger than you thought you were. You also may learn that things you thought were true are not. Such discoveries occur because magic lets us peek beneath the surface of our days often showing us things that feel more true than what we learn in school or see on television. An old rocking horse in *The Velveteen Rabbit* offers this definition:

> Real isn't how you are made. It's a thing that happens
> to you. When a child loves you for a long, long time,
> not just to play with, but REALLY loves you, then you
> become Real.

Better yet, the world of magic invites us to create our own definitions of reality. When Alice falls down the rabbit hole and finds herself in Wonderland; when Colin in *The Secret Garden* enters a mysterious garden; when Lucy finds Narnia—they must rely on their wits and their hearts to tell them what is real.

It may seem strange to say that the best magic stories are about the way things really are, but that's the truth. Such stories are about the way people really feel, about their true hopes and fears, including the ones they sometimes are afraid to talk about. Ged in *A Wizard of Earthsea* learns to become a wizard, but he also learns how to grow up. He makes mistakes and fails, but he eventually succeeds in changing from an apprentice into a wizard, and from a boy into a man. Both transformations are magic.

Children are good at magic because they are less likely than adults to doubt what they see or experience. This gets them into trouble and leads them to wonderful discoveries. The people in these stories don't always look for magic, but because they are open to the world around them they find it. They see what is there.

Children, and some brave adults, don't always believe certain things about the world simply because someone has told them they should. They are interested in the truth. And—this is important—they sometimes want to know the truth more than they want to be comfortable or safe. When the grandfather clock in *Tom's Midnight Garden* strikes thirteen, adding that mysterious hour to the night, Tom confronts his fears in order to seek the truth. He gets out of bed and sneaks downstairs— and thus begins his adventure.

Whether we are young or old our lives are full of magic—even if we don't fall down rabbit holes, find psammeads, meet wizards or walk into a new world through the back of an old wardrobe. As we grow up, people and things may try to force us to give up our ability to make and experience magic. They may tell us to stop believing in it. When that happens it's good to remember that magic is part of real life. You can find it in all kinds of places. The stories in this book show us that magic comes from things like truth, love and imagination.

The stories also tell us that to experience magic you must be open to change. If you want to go somewhere wonderful, you must be willing to believe in the unbelievable. You must believe you are brave enough to fight a dragon. You must believe you are smart enough to outwit a witch or demon. You must believe you can love something enough to make it real.

I still open dusty old wardrobes with a mix of fear and excitement.

I'm not a child anymore, but I still want to know the truth about people and things. I dig in the sand with care so I won't hurt whatever may
be buried there. And if one day, as Alice did at the beginning of her
adventures in Wonderland, I find a wafer with the words "Eat Me"
inscribed upon its sugary surface, I'll take a bite.

—*Jennifer Schwamm Willis*

from

The Once and Future King

by T.H. White

T. H. White (1906–1964) was born in Bombay, India and went to school in England. He loved the story of King Arthur and the Knights of the Round Table. In his book *The Once and Future King* he imagines Arthur's life as a boy. In this episode, Arthur (nicknamed Wart) meets the great wizard Merlyn for the first time.

The boy slept well in the woodland nest where he had laid himself down, in that kind of thin but refreshing sleep which people have when they begin to lie out of doors. At first he only dipped below the surface of sleep, and skimmed along like a salmon in shallow water, so close to the surface that he fancied himself in air. He thought himself awake when he was already asleep. He saw the stars above his face, whirling on their silent and sleepless axis, and the leaves of the trees rustling against them, and he heard small changes in the grass. These little noises of footsteps and soft-fringed wing-beats and stealthy bellies drawn over the grass blades or rattling against the bracken at first frightened or interested him, so that he moved to see what they were (but never saw), then soothed him, so that he no longer cared to see what they were but trusted them to be themselves, and finally left him altogether as he swam down deeper and deeper, nuzzling into the scented turf, into the warm ground, into the unending waters under the earth.

It had been difficult to go to sleep in the bright summer moonlight, but once he was there it was not difficult to stay. The sun came early, causing him to turn over in protest, but in going to sleep he had learned to vanquish light, and now the light could not rewake him. It was nine o'clock, five hours after daylight, before he rolled over, opened his eyes, and was awake at once. He was hungry.

The Wart had heard about people who lived on berries, but this did not seem practical at the moment, because it was July, and there were none. He found two wild strawberries and ate them greedily. They tasted nicer than anything, so that he wished there were more. Then he wished it was April, so that he could find some birds' eggs and eat those, or that he had not lost his goshawk Cully, so that the hawk could catch him a rabbit which he would cook by rubbing two sticks together like the base Indian. But he had lost Cully, or he would not have lost himself, and probably the sticks would not have lighted in any case. He decided that he could not have gone more than three or four miles from home, and that the best thing he could do would be to sit still and listen. Then he might hear the noise of the haymakers, if he were lucky with the wind, and he could hearken his way to the castle by that.

What he did hear was a faint clanking noise, which made him think that King Pellinore must be after the Questing Beast again, close by. Only the noise was so regular and single in intention that it made him think of King Pellinore doing some special action, with great patience and concentration—trying to scratch his back without taking off his armour, for instance. He went toward the noise.

There was a clearing in the forest, and in this clearing there was a snug cottage built of stone. It was a cottage, although the Wart could not notice this at the time, which was divided into two bits. The main bit was the hall or every-purpose room, which was high because it extended from floor to roof, and this room had a fire on the floor whose smoke came out eventually from a hole in the thatch of the roof. The other half of the cottage was divided into two rooms by a horizontal floor which made the top half into a bedroom and study, while the bottom half served for a larder, storeroom, stable and barn.

A white donkey lived in this downstairs room, and a ladder led to the one upstairs.

There was a well in front of the cottage, and the metallic noise which the Wart had heard was caused by a very old gentleman who was drawing water out of it by means of a handle and chain.

Clank, clank, clank, went the chain, until the bucket hit the lip of the well, and "Drat the whole thing!" said the old gentleman. "You would think that after all these years of study you could do better for yourself than a by-our-lady well with a by-our-lady bucket, whatever the by-our-lady cost."

"By this and by that," added the old gentleman, heaving his bucket out of the well with a malevolent glance, "why can't they get us the electric light and company's water?"

He was dressed in a flowing gown with fur tippets which had the signs of the zodiac embroidered over it, with various cabalistic signs, such as triangles with eyes in them, queer crosses, leaves of trees, bones of birds and animals, and a planetarium whose stars shone like bits of looking-glass with the sun on them. He had a pointed hat like a dunce's cap, or like the headgear worn by ladies of that time, except that the ladies were accustomed to have a bit of veil floating from the top of it. He also had a wand of lignum vitae, which he had laid down in the grass beside him, and a pair of horn-rimmed spectacles like those of King Pellinore. They were unusual spectacles, being without ear pieces, but shaped rather like scissors or like the antennae of the tarantula wasp.

"Excuse me, sir," said the Wart, "but can you tell me the way to Sir Ector's castle, if you don't mind?"

The aged gentleman put down his bucket and looked at him.

"Your name would be the Wart."

"Yes, sir, please, sir."

"My name," said the old man, "is Merlyn."

"How do you do?"

"How do."

When these formalities had been concluded, the Wart had leisure to look at him more closely. The magician was staring at him with a kind of unwinking and benevolent curiosity which made him feel that it would not be at all rude to stare back, no ruder than it would be to stare at one of his guardian's cows who happened to be thinking about his personality as she leaned her head over a gate.

Merlyn had a long white beard and long white moustaches which hung down on either side of it. Close inspection showed that he was far from clean. It was not that he had dirty fingernails, or anything like that, but some large bird seemed to have been nesting in his hair. The Wart was familiar with the nests of Spar-hark and Gos, the crazy conglomerations of sticks and oddments which had been taken over from squirrels or crows, and he knew how the twigs and the tree foot were splashed with white mutes, old bones, muddy feathers and castings. This was the impression which he got from Merlyn. The old man was streaked with droppings over his shoulders, among the stars and triangles of his gown, and a large spider was slowly lowering itself from the tip of his hat, as he gazed and slowly blinked at the little boy in front of him. He had a worried expression, as though he were trying to remember some name which began with Chol but which was pronounced in quite a different way, possibly Menzies or was it Dalziel? His mild blue eyes, very big and round under the tarantula spectacles, gradually filmed and clouded over as he gazed at the boy, and then he turned his head away with a resigned expression, as though it was all too much for him after all.

"Do you like peaches?"

"Very much indeed," said the Wart, and his mouth began to water so that it was full of sweet, soft liquid.

"They are scarcely in season," said the old man reprovingly, and he walked off in the direction of the cottage.

The Wart followed after, since this was the simplest thing to do, and offered to carry the bucket (which seemed to please Merlyn, who gave it to him) and waited while he counted the keys—while he muttered and mislaid them and dropped them in the grass. Finally, when they had got their way into the black and white home with as much trouble as if they were burgling it, he climbed up the ladder after his host and found himself in the upstairs room.

It was the most marvellous room that he had ever been in.

There was a real corkindrill hanging from the rafters, very life-like and horrible with glass eyes and scaly tail stretched out behind it. When its master came into the room it winked one eye in salutation, although it was stuffed. There were thousands of brown books in leather bindings, some chained to the book-shelves and others propped against each other as if they had had too much to drink and did not really trust themselves. These gave out a smell of must and solid brownness which was most secure. Then there were stuffed birds, popinjays, and maggotpies and kingfishers, and peacocks with all their feathers but two, and tiny birds like beetles, and a reputed phoenix which smelt of incense and cinnamon. It could not have been a real phoenix, because there is only one of these at a time. Over by the mantelpiece there was a fox's mask, with GRAFTON, BUCKINGHAM TO DAVENTRY, 2 HRS 20 MINS written under it, and also a forty-pound salmon with AWE, 43 MIN., BULLDOG written under it, and a very life-like basilisk with CROWHURST OTTER HOUNDS in Roman print. There were several boars' tusks and the claws of tigers and libbards mounted in symmetrical patterns, and a big head of Ovis Poli, six live grass snakes in a kind of aquarium, some nests of the solitary wasp nicely set up in a glass cylinder, an ordinary beehive whose inhabitants went in and out of the window unmolested, two young hedgehogs in cotton wool, a pair of badgers which immediately began to cry Yik-Yik-Yik-Yik in loud voices as soon as the magician appeared, twenty boxes which contained stick caterpillars and sixths of the puss-moth, and even an oleander that was worth sixpence—all feeding on the appropriate leaves—a guncase with all sorts of weapons which would not be invented for half a thousand years, a rod-box ditto, a chest of drawers full of salmon flies which had been tied by Merlyn himself, another chest whose drawers were labelled Mandragora, Mandrake, and Old Man's Beard, etc., a bunch of turkey feathers and goose-quills for making pens, an astrolabe, twelve pairs of boots, a dozen purse-nets, three dozen rabbit wires, twelve corkscrews, some ants' nests between two glass plates, ink-bottles of every possible colour from red to violet, darning-needles, a gold medal for being the best scholar at Winchester, four or five recorders, a nest of field mice all alive-o, two skulls, plenty of cut glass, Venetian glass, Bristol glass and a bottle of Mastic varnish, some satsuma china and some cloisonné, the fourteenth edition of the *Encyclopaedia Britannica* (marred as it was by the sensationalism of the popular plates), two paint-boxes (one oil, one water-colour), three globes of the known geographical world, a few fossils, the stuffed head of a cameleopard, six pismires, some glass retorts with cauldrons, bunsen burners, etc., and a complete set of cigarette cards depicting wild fowl by Peter Scott.

Merlyn took off his pointed hat when he came into this chamber, because it was too high for the roof, and immediately there was a scamper in one of the dark corners and a flap of soft wings, and a tawny owl was sitting on the black skull-cap which protected the top of his head.

"Oh, what a lovely owl!" cried the Wart.

But when he went up to it and held out his hand, the owl grew half as tall again, stood up as stiff as a poker, closed its eyes so that there was only the smallest slit to peep through—as you are in the habit of doing when told to shut your eyes at hide-and-seek—and said in a doubtful voice:

"There is no owl."

Then it shut its eyes entirely and looked the other way.

"It is only a boy," said Merlyn.

"There is no boy," said the owl hopefully, without turning round.

The Wart was so startled by finding that the owl could talk that he forgot his manners and came closer still. At this the bird became so nervous that it made a mess on Merlyn's head—the whole room was quite white with droppings—and flew off to perch on the farthest tip of the corkindrill's tail, out of reach.

"We see so little company," explained the magician, wiping his head with half a worn-out pair of pyjamas which he kept for that purpose, "that Archimedes is a little shy of strangers. Come, Archimedes, I want you to meet a friend of mine called Wart."

Here he held out his hand to the owl, who came waddling like a goose along the corkindrill's back—he waddled with this rolling gait so as to keep his tail from being damaged—and hopped down to Merlyn's finger with every sign of reluctance.

"Hold out your finger and put it behind his legs. No, lift it up under his train."

When the Wart had done this, Merlyn moved the owl gently backward, so that the boy's finger pressed against its legs from behind, and it either had to step back on the finger or get pushed off its balance altogether. It stepped back. The Wart stood there delighted, while the furry feet held tight on his finger and the sharp claws prickled his skin.

"Say how d'you do properly," said Merlyn.

"I will not," said Archimedes, looking the other way and holding tight.

"Oh, he *is* lovely," said the Wart again. "Have you had him long?"

"Archimedes has stayed with me since he was small, indeed since he had a tiny head like a chicken's."

"I wish he would talk to me."

"Perhaps if you were to give him this mouse here, politely, he might learn to know you better."

Merlyn took a dead mouse out of his skull-cap—"I always keep them there, and worms too, for fishing. I find it most convenient"—and handed it to the Wart, who held it out rather gingerly toward Archimedes. The nutty curved beak looked as it if were capable of doing damage, but Archimedes looked closely at the mouse, blinked at the Wart, moved nearer on the finger, closed his eyes and leaned forward. He stood there with closed eyes and an expression of rapture on his face, as if he were saying Grace, and then, with the absurdest sideways nibble, took the morsel so gently that he would not have broken a soap bubble. He remained leaning forward with closed eyes, with the mouse suspended from his beak, as if he were not sure what to do with it. Then he lifted his right foot—he was right-handed, though people say only men are—and took hold of the mouse. He held it up like a boy holding a stick of rock or a constable with his truncheon, looked at it, nibbled its tail. He turned it round so that it was head first, for the Wart had offered it the wrong way round, and gave one gulp. He looked round at the company with the tail hanging out of the corner of his mouth—as much as to say, "I wish you would not all stare at me so"—turned his head away, politely swallowed the tail, scratched his sailor's beard with his left toe, and began to ruffle out his feathers.

"Let him alone," said Merlyn. "Perhaps he does not want to be friends with you until he knows what you are like. With owls, it is never easy-come and easy-go."

"Perhaps he will sit on my shoulder," said the Wart, and with that he instinctively lowered his hand, so that the owl, who liked to be as high as possible, ran up the slope and stood shyly beside his ear.

"Now breakfast," said Merlyn.

The Wart saw that the most perfect breakfast was laid out neatly for two, on a table before the window. There were peaches. There were also melons, strawberries and cream, rusks, brown trout piping hot, grilled perch which were much nicer, chicken devilled enough to burn one's mouth out, kidneys and mushrooms on toast, fricassee, curry, and a choice of boiling coffee or best chocolate made with cream in large cups.

"Have some mustard," said the magician, when they had got to the kidneys.

The mustard-pot got up and walked over to his plate on thin silver legs that waddled like the owl's. Then it uncurled its handles and one handle lifted its lid with exaggerated courtesy while the other helped him to a generous spoonful.

"Oh, I love the mustard-pot!" cried the Wart. "Wherever did you get it?"

At this the pot beamed all over its face and began to strut a bit, but Merlyn rapped it on the head with a teaspoon, so that it sat down and shut up at once.

"It is not a bad pot," he said grudgingly. "Only it is inclined to give itself airs."

The Wart was so much impressed by the kindness of the old man, and particularly by the lovely things which he possessed, that he hardly liked to ask him personal questions. It seemed politer to sit still and to speak when he was spoken to. But Merlyn did not speak much, and when he did speak it was never in questions, so that the Wart had little opportunity for conversation. At last his curiosity got the better of him, and he asked something which had been puzzling him for some time.

"Would you mind if I ask you a question?"

"It is what I am for."

"How did you know to set breakfast for two?"

The old gentleman leaned back in his chair and lighted an enormous meerschaum pipe—Good gracious, he breathes fire, thought the Wart, who had never heard of tobacco—before he was ready to reply. Then he looked puzzled, took off his skull-cap—three mice fell out—and scratched in the middle of his bald head.

"Have you ever tried to draw in a looking-glass?" he asked.

"I don't think I have."

"Looking-glass," said Merlyn, holding out his hand. Immediately there was a tiny lady's vanity-glass in his hand.

"Not that kind, you fool," he said angrily. "I want one big enough to shave in."

The vanity-glass vanished, and in its place there was a shaving mirror about a foot square. He then demanded pencil and paper in quick succession; got an unsharpened pencil and the *Morning Post*; sent them back; got a fountain pen with no ink in it and six reams of brown paper suitable for parcels; sent them back; flew into a passion in which he said by-our-lady quite often, and ended up with a carbon pencil and some cigarette papers which he said would have to do.

He put one of the papers in front of the glass and made five dots.

"Now," he said, "I want you to join those five dots up to make a W, looking only in the glass."

The Wart took the pen and tried to do as he was bid.

"Well, it is not bad," said the magician doubtfully, "and in a way it does look a bit like an M."

Then he fell into a reverie, stroking his beard, breathing fire, and staring at the paper.

"About the breakfast?"

"Ah, yes. How did I know to set breakfast for two? That was why I showed you the looking-glass. Now ordinary people are born forwards in Time, if you understand what I mean, and nearly everything in the world goes forward too. This makes it quite easy for the ordinary people to live, just as it would be easy to join those five dots into a W if you were allowed to look at them forwards, instead of backwards and inside out. But I unfortunately was born at the wrong end of time, and I have to live backwards from in front, while surrounded by a lot of people living forwards from behind. Some people call it having second sight."

He stopped talking and looked at the Wart in an anxious way.

"Have I told you this before?"

"No, we only met about half an hour ago."

"So little time to pass?" said Merlyn, and a big tear ran down to the end of his nose. He wiped it off with his pyjamas and added anxiously, "Am I going to tell it you again?"

"I do not know," said the Wart, "unless you have not finished telling me yet."

"You see, one gets confused with Time, when it is like that. All one's tenses get muddled, for one thing. If you know what is going to happen to people, and not what *has* happened to them, it makes it difficult to prevent it happening, if you don't want it to have happened, if you see what I mean? Like drawing in a mirror."

The Wart did not quite see, but was just going to say that he was sorry for Merlyn if these things made him unhappy, when he felt a curious sensation at his ear. "Don't jump," said the old man, just as he was going to do so, and the Wart sat still. Archimedes, who had been standing forgotten on his shoulder all this time, was gently touching himself against him. His beak was right against the lobe of the ear, which its bristles made to tickle, and suddenly a soft hoarse voice whispered, "How d'you do," so that it sounded right inside his head.

"Oh, owl!" cried the Wart, forgetting about Merlyn's troubles instantly. "Look, he has decided to talk to me!"

The Wart gently leaned his head against the smooth feathers, and the tawny owl, taking the rim of his ear in its beak, quickly nibbled right round it with the smallest nibbles.

"I shall call him Archie!"

"I trust you will do nothing of the sort," exclaimed Merlyn instantly, in a stern and angry voice, and the owl withdrew to the farthest corner of his shoulder.

"Is it wrong?"

"You might, as well call me Wol, or Olly," said the owl sourly, "and have done with it.

"Or Bubbles," it added in a bitter voice.

Merlyn took the Wart's hand and said kindly, "You are young, and do not understand these things. But you will learn that owls are the most courteous, single-hearted and faithful creatures living. You must never be familiar, rude or vulgar with them, or make them look ridiculous. Their mother is Athene, the goddess of wisdom, and, although they are often ready to play the buffoon to amuse you, such conduct is the prerogative of the truly wise. No owl can possibly be called Archie."

"I am sorry, owl," said the Wart.

"And I am sorry, boy," said the owl. "I can see that you spoke in ignorance, and I bitterly regret that I should have been so petty as to take offence where none was intended."

The owl really did regret it, and looked so remorseful that Merlyn had to put on a cheerful manner and change the conversation.

"Well," said he, "now that we have finished breakfast, I think it is high time that we should all three find our way back to Sir Ector.

"Excuse me a moment," he added as an afterthought, and, turning round to the breakfast things, he pointed a knobbly finger at them and said in a stern voice, "Wash up."

At this all the china and cutlery scrambled down off the table, the cloth emptied the crumbs out of the window, and the napkins folded themselves up. All ran off down the ladder, to where Merlyn had left the bucket, and there was such a noise and yelling as if a lot of children had been let out of school. Merlyn went to the door and shouted,

"Mind, nobody is to get broken." But his voice was entirely drowned in shrill squeals, splashes, and cries of "My, it is cold," "I shan't stay in long," "Look out, you'll break me," or "Come on, let's duck the teapot."

"Are you really coming all the way home with me?" asked the Wart, who could hardly believe the good news.

"Why not? How else can I be your tutor?"

At this the Wart's eyes grew rounder and rounder, until they were about as big as the owl's who was sitting on his shoulder, and his face got redder and redder, and a breath seemed to gather itself beneath his heart.

"My!" exclaimed the Wart, while his eyes sparkled with excitement at the discovery. "I must have been on a Quest!"

from

The Witches

by Roald Dahl

Roald Dahl (1916–1990) was born in Wales to Norwegian immigrants and educated at English boarding schools. He served as a fighter pilot in the Royal Air Force before becoming a writer. "I know what children like," he once said, and he was right. A cigar-smoking grandmother who has had many dealings with witches here explains to her grandson exactly how to recognize one.

My grandmother was Norwegian. The Norwegians know all about witches, for Norway, with its black forests and icy mountains, is where the first witches came from. My father and my mother were also Norwegian, but because my father had a business in England, I had been born there and had lived there and had started going to an English school. Twice a year, at Christmas and in the summer, we went back to Norway to visit my grandmother. This old lady, as far as I could gather, was just about the only surviving relative we had on either side of our family. She was my mother's mother and I absolutely adored her. When she and I were together we spoke in either Norwegian or in English. It didn't matter which. We were equally fluent in both languages, and I have to admit that I felt closer to her than to my mother.

Soon after my seventh birthday, my parents took me as usual to spend Christmas with my grandmother in Norway. And it was over there, while my father and mother and I were driving in icy weather just north of Oslo, that our car skidded off the road and went tumbling-down into a rocky ravine. My parents were killed. I was firmly strapped into the back seat and received only a cut on the forehead.

I won't go into the horrors of that terrible afternoon. I still get the shivers when I think about it. I finished up, of course, back in my grand-mother's house with her arms around me tight and both of us crying the whole night long.

"What are we going to do now?" I asked her through the tears.

"You will stay here with me," she said, "and I will look after you."

"Aren't I going back to England?"

"No," she said. "I could never do that. Heaven shall take my soul, but Norway shall keep my bones."

The very next day, in order that we might both try to forget our great sadness, my grandmother started telling me stories. She was a wonderful story-teller and I was enthralled by everything she told me. But I didn't become really excited until she got on to the subject of witches. She was apparently a great expert on these creatures and she made it very clear to me that her witch stories, unlike most of the others, were not imaginary tales. They were all true. They were the *gospel* truth. They were history. Everything she was telling me about witches had actually happened and I had better believe it. What was worse, what was far, far worse, was that witches were still with us. They were all around us and I had better believe that, too.

"Are you *really* being truthful, Grandmamma? *Really* and *truly* truthful?"

"My darling," she said, "you won't last long in this world if you don't know how to spot a witch when you see one."

"But you told me that witches look like ordinary women, Grandmamma. So how can I spot them?"

"You must listen to me," my grandmother said. "You must remember everything I tell you. After that, all you can do is cross your heart and pray to heaven and hope for the best."

We were in the big living-room of her house in Oslo and I was ready for bed. The curtains were never drawn in that house, and through the windows I could see huge snowflakes falling slowly on to an outside world that was as black as tar. My grandmother was tremendously old and wrinkled, with a massive wide body which was smothered in grey lace. She sat there majestic in her armchair, filling every inch of it. Not even a mouse could have squeezed in to sit beside her. I myself, just seven years old, was crouched on the floor at her feet, wearing pyjamas, dressing-gown and slippers.

"You swear you aren't pulling my leg?" I kept saying to her. "You swear you aren't just pretending?"

"Listen," she said, "I have known no less than five children who have simply vanished off the face of this earth, never to be seen again. The witches took them."

"I still think you're just trying to frighten me," I said.

"I am trying to make sure you don't go the same way," she said. "I love you and I want you to stay with me."

"Tell me about the children who disappeared," I said.

My grandmother was the only grandmother I ever met who smoked cigars. She lit one now, a long black cigar that smelt of burning rubber. "The first child I knew who disappeared," she said, "was called Ranghild Hansen. Ranghild was about eight at the time, and she was playing with her little sister on the lawn. Their mother, who was baking bread in the kitchen, came outside for a breath of air. 'Where's Ranghild?' she asked.

"'She went away with the tall lady,' the little sister said.

"'What tall lady?' the mother said.

"'The tall lady in white gloves,' the little sister said. 'She took Ranghild by the hand and led her away.' No one," my grandmother said, "ever saw Ranghild again."

"Didn't they search for her?" I asked.

"They searched for miles around. Everyone in the town helped, but they never found her."

"What happened to the other four children?" I asked.

"They vanished just as Ranghild did."

"How, Grandmamma? How did they vanish?"

"In every case a strange lady was seen outside the house, just before it happened."

"But how did they vanish?" I asked.

"The second one was very peculiar," my grandmother said. "There was a family called Christiansen. They lived up on Holmenkollen, and they had an old oil-painting in the living-room which they were very proud of. The painting showed some ducks in the yard outside a farm-house. There were no people in the painting, just a flock of ducks on a grassy farmyard and the farmhouse in the background. It was a large painting and rather pretty. Well, one day their daughter Solveg came home from school eating an apple. She said a nice lady had given it to her on the street. The next morning little Solveg was not in her bed. The parents searched everywhere but they couldn't find her. Then all of a sudden her father shouted, 'There she is! That's Solveg feeding the ducks!' He was pointing at the oil-painting, and sure enough Solveg was in it. She was standing in the farmyard in the act of throwing bread to the ducks out of a basket. The father rushed up to the painting and touched her. But that didn't help. She was simply a part of the painting, just a picture painted on the canvas."

"Did you ever see that painting, Grandmamma, with the little girl in it?"

"Many times," my grandmother said. "And the peculiar thing was that little Solveg kept changing her position in the picture. One day she would actually be inside the farmhouse and you could see her face looking out of the window. Another day she would be far over to the left with a duck in her arms."

"Did you see her moving in the picture, Grandmamma?"

"Nobody did. Wherever she was, whether outside feeding the ducks or inside looking out of the window, she was always motionless, just a figure painted in oils. It was all very odd," my grandmother said. "Very odd indeed. And what was most odd of all was that as the years went by, she kept growing older in the picture. In ten years, the small girl had become a young woman. In thirty years, she was middle-aged. Then all at once, fifty-four years after it all happened, she disappeared from the picture altogether."

"You mean she died?" I said.

"Who knows?" my grandmother said. "Some very mysterious things go on in the world of witches."

"That's two you've told me about," I said. "What happened to the third one?"

"The third one was little Birgit Svenson," my grandmother said. "She lived just across the road from us. One day she started growing feathers all over her body. Within a month, she had turned into a large white chicken. Her parents kept her for years in a pen in the garden. She even laid eggs."

"What colour eggs?" I said.

"Brown ones," my grandmother said. "Biggest eggs I've ever seen in my life. Her mother made omelettes out of them. Delicious they were."

I gazed up at my grandmother who sat there like some ancient queen on her throne. Her eyes were misty-grey and they seemed to be looking at something many miles away. The cigar was the only real thing about her at that moment, and the smoke it made billowed round her head in blue clouds.

"But the little girl who became a chicken didn't disappear?" I said.

"No, not Birgit. She lived on for many years laying her brown eggs."

"You said all of them disappeared."

"I made a mistake," my grandmother said. "I am getting old. I can't remember everything."

"What happened to the fourth child?" I asked.

"The fourth was a boy called Harald," my grandmother said. "One morning his skin went all greyish-yellow. Then it became hard and crackly, like the shell of a nut. By evening, the boy had turned to stone."

"Stone?" I said. "You mean real stone?"

"Granite," she said. "I'll take you to see him if you like. They still keep him in the house. He stands in the hall, a little stone statue. Visitors lean their umbrellas up against him."

Although I was very young, I was not prepared to believe everything my grandmother told me. And yet she spoke with such conviction, with such utter seriousness, and with never a smile on her face or a twinkle in her eye, that I found myself beginning to wonder.

"Go on, Grandmamma," I said. "You told me there were five altogether. What happened to the last one?"

"Would you like a puff of my cigar?" she said.

"I'm only seven, Grandmamma."

"I don't care what age you are," she said. "You'll never catch a cold if you smoke cigars."

"What about number five, Grandmamma?"

"Number five," she said, chewing the end of her cigar as though it were a delicious asparagus, "was rather an interesting case. A nine-year-old boy called Leif was summer-holidaying with his family on the fjord, and the whole family was picnicking and swimming off some rocks on one of those little islands. Young Leif dived into the water and his father, who was watching him, noticed that he stayed under for an unusually long time. When he came to the surface at last, he wasn't Leif any more."

"What was he, Grandmamma?"

"He was a porpoise."

"He wasn't! He couldn't have been!"

"He was a lovely young porpoise," she said. "And as friendly as could be."

"Grandmamma," I said.

"Yes, my darling?"

"Did he really and truly turn into a porpoise?"

"Absolutely," she said. "I knew his mother well. She told me all about it. She told me how Leif the Porpoise stayed with them all that afternoon giving his brothers and sisters rides on his back. They had a wonderful time. Then he waved a flipper at them and swam away, never to be seen again."

"But Grandmamma," I said, "how did they know that the porpoise was actually Leif?"

"He talked to them," my grandmother said. "He laughed and joked with them all the time he was giving them rides."

"But wasn't there a most tremendous fuss when this happened?"
I asked.

"Not much," my grandmother said. "You must remember that here
in Norway we are used to that sort of thing. There are witches everywhere. There's probably one living in our street this very moment. It's
time you went to bed."

"A witch wouldn't come in through my window in the night, would
she?" I asked, quaking a little.

"No," my grandmother said. "A witch will never do silly things like
climbing up drainpipes or breaking into people's houses. You'll be
quite safe in your bed. Come along. I'll tuck you in."

The next evening, after my grandmother had given me my bath, she
took me once again into the living-room for another story.

"Tonight," the old woman said, "I am going to tell you how to
recognise a witch when you see one."

"Can you always be sure?" I asked.

"No," she said, "you can't. And that's the trouble. But you can make
a pretty good guess."

She was dropping cigar ash all over her lap, and I hoped she wasn't
going to catch on fire before she'd told me how to recognise a witch.

"In the first place," she said, "a REAL WITCH is certain always to be
wearing gloves when you meet her."

"Surely not *always*," I said. "What about in the summer when it's hot?"

"Even in the summer," my grandmother said. "She has to. Do you
want to know why?"

"Why?" I said.

"Because she doesn't have *finger-nails*. Instead of finger-nails, she
has thin curvy claws, like a cat, and she wears the gloves to hide them.
Mind you, lots of very respectable women wear gloves, especially in
winter, so this doesn't help you very much."

"Mamma used to wear gloves," I said.

"Not in the house," my grandmother said. "Witches wear gloves even in the house. They only take them off when they go to bed."

"How do you know all this, Grandmamma?"

"Don't interrupt," she said. "Just take it all in. The second thing to remember is that a real witch is always bald."

"Bald?" I said.

"Bald as a boiled egg," my grandmother said.

I was shocked. There was something indecent about a bald woman. "Why are they bald, Grandmamma?"

"Don't ask me why," she snapped. "But you can take it from me that not a single hair grows on a witch's head."

"How horrid!"

"Disgusting," my grandmother said.

"If she's bald, she'll be easy to spot," I said.

"Not at all," my grandmother said. "A REAL WITCH always wears a wig to hide her baldness. She wears a first-class wig. And it is almost impossible to tell a really first-class wig from ordinary hair unless you give it a pull to see if it comes off."

"Then that's what I'll have to do," I said.

"Don't be foolish," my grandmother said. "You can't go round pulling at the hair of every lady you meet, even if she is wearing gloves. Just you try it and see what happens."

"So that doesn't help much either," I said.

"None of these things is any good on its own," my grandmother said. "It's only when you put them all together that they begin to make a little sense. Mind you," my grandmother went on, "these wigs do cause a rather serious problem for witches."

"What problem, Grandmamma?"

"They make the scalp itch most terribly," she said. "You see, when an actress wears a wig, or if you or I were to wear a wig, we would be putting it on over our own hair, but a witch has to put it straight on to her naked scalp. And the underneath of a wig is always very rough and scratchy. It sets up a frightful itch on the bald skin. It causes nasty sores on the head. Wig-rash, the witches call it. And it doesn't half itch."

"What other things must I look for to recognise a witch?" I asked.

"Look for the nose-holes," my grandmother said. "Witches have slightly larger nose-holes than ordinary people. The rim of each nose-hole is pink and curvy, like the rim of a certain kind of seashell."

"Why do they have such big nose-holes?" I asked.

"For smelling with," my grandmother said. "A REAL WITCH has the most amazing powers of smell. She can actually smell out a child who is standing on the other side of the street on a pitch-black night."

"She couldn't smell me," I said. "I've just had a bath."

"Oh yes she could," my grandmother said. "The cleaner you happen to be, the more smelly you are to a witch."

"That can't be true," I said.

"An absolutely clean child gives off the most ghastly stench to a witch," my grandmother said. "The dirtier you are, the less you smell."

"But that doesn't make sense, Grandmamma."

"Oh yes it does," any grandmother said. "It isn't the *dirt* that the witch is smelling. It is *you*. The smell that drives a witch mad actually comes right out of your own skin. It comes oozing out of your skin in waves, and these waves, stink-waves the witches call them, go floating through the air and hit the witch right smack in her nostrils. They send her reeling."

"Now wait a minute, Grandmamma . . ."

"Don't interrupt," she said. "The point is this. When you haven't washed for a week and your skin is all covered over with dirt, then quite obviously the stink-waves cannot come oozing out nearly so strongly."

"I shall never have a bath again," I said.

"Just don't have one too often," my grandmother said. "Once a month is quite enough for a sensible child."

It was at moments like these that I loved my grandmother more than ever.

"Grandmamma," I said, "if it's a dark night, how can a witch tell the difference between a child and a grown-up?"

"Because grown-ups don't give out stink-waves," she said. "Only children do that."

"But I don't *really* give out stink-waves, do I?" I said. "I'm not giving them out at this very moment, am I?"

"Not to me you aren't," my grandmother said. "To me you are smelling like raspberries and cream. But to a witch you would be smelling absolutely disgusting."

"What would I be smelling of?" I asked.

"Dogs' droppings," my grandmother said.

I reeled. I was stunned. "*Dogs' droppings!*" I cried. "I am *not* smelling of dogs' droppings! I don't believe it! I *won't* believe it!"

"What's more," my grandmother said, speaking with a touch of relish, "to a witch you'd be smelling of *fresh* dogs' droppings."

"That simply is not true!" I cried. "I know I am not smelling of dogs' droppings, stale or fresh!"

"There's no point in arguing about it," my grandmother said. "It's a fact of life."

I was outraged. I simply couldn't bring myself to believe what my grandmother was telling me.

"So if you see a woman holding her nose as she passes you in the street," she went on, "that woman could easily be a witch."

I decided to change the subject. "Tell me what else to look for in a witch," I said.

"The eyes," my grandmother said. "Look carefully at the eyes, because the eyes of a REAL WITCH are different from yours and mine. Look in the middle of each eye where there is normally a little black dot. If she is a witch, the black dot will keep changing colour, and you will see fire and you will see ice dancing right in the very centre of the coloured dot. It will send shivers running all over your skin."

My grandmother leant back in her chair and sucked away contentedly at her foul black cigar. I squatted on the floor, staring up at her, fascinated. She was not smiling. She looked deadly serious.

"Are there other things?" I asked her.

"Of course there are other things," my grandmother said. "You don't seem to understand that witches are not actually women at all. They *look* like women. They talk like women. And they are able to act like women. But in actual fact, they are totally different animals. They are demons in human shape. That is why they have claws and bald heads and queer noses and peculiar eyes, all of which they have to conceal as best they can from the rest of the world."

"What else is different about them, Grandmamma?"

"The feet," she said. "Witches never have toes."

"No toes!" I cried. "Then what do they have?"

"They just have feet," my grandmother said. "The feet have square ends with no toes on them at all."

"Does that make it difficult to walk?" I asked.

"Not at all," my grandmother said. "But it does give them a problem with their shoes. All ladies like to wear small rather pointed shoes, but a witch, whose feet are very wide and square at the ends, has the most awful job squeezing her feet into those neat little pointed shoes."

"Why doesn't she wear wide comfy shoes with square ends?" I asked.

"She dare not," my grandmother said. "Just as she hides her baldness with a wig, she must also hide her ugly witch's feet by squeezing them into pretty shoes."

"Isn't that terribly uncomfortable?" I said.

"Extremely uncomfortable," my grandmother said. "But she has to put up with it."

"If she's wearing ordinary shoes, it won't help me to recognise her, will it, Grandmamma?"

"I'm afraid it won't," my grandmother said. "You might possibly see her limping very slightly, but only if you were watching closely."

"Are those the only differences then, Grandmamma?"

"There's one more," my grandmother said. "Just one more."

"What is it, Grandmamma?"

"Their spit is blue."

"Blue!" I cried. "Not blue! Their spit can't be *blue!*"

"Blue as a bilberry," she said.

"You don't mean it, Grandmamma! Nobody can have blue spit!"

"Witches can," she said.

"Is it like ink?" I asked.

"Exactly," she said. "They even use it to write with. They use those old-fashioned pens that have nibs and they simply lick the nib."

"Can you *notice* the blue spit, Grandmamma? If a witch was talking to me, would I be able to notice it?"

"Only if you looked carefully," my grandmother said. "If you looked very carefully you would probably see a slight blueish tinge on her teeth. But it doesn't show much."

"It would if she spat," I said.

"Witches never spit," my grandmother said. "They daren't."

I couldn't believe my grandmother would be lying to me. She went to church every morning of the week and she said grace before every meal, and somebody who did that would never tell lies. I was beginning to believe every word she spoke.

"So there you are," my grandmother said. "That's about all I can tell you. None of it is very helpful. You can still never be absolutely sure whether a woman is a witch or not just by looking at her. But if she is wearing the gloves, if she has the large nose-holes, the queer eyes and the hair that looks as though it might be a wig, and if she has a blueish tinge on her teeth—if she has all of these things, then you run like mad."

"Grandmamma," I said, "when you were a little girl, did *you* ever meet a witch?"

"Once," my grandmother said. "Only once."

"What happened?"

"I'm not going to tell you," she said. "It would frighten you out of your skin and give you bad dreams."

"Please tell me," I begged.

"No," she said. "Certain things are too horrible to talk about."

"Does it have something to do with your missing thumb?" I asked.

Suddenly, her old wrinkled lips shut tight as a pair of tongs and the hand that held the cigar (which had no thumb on it) began to quiver very slightly.

I waited. She didn't look at me. She didn't speak. All of a sudden she had shut herself off completely. The conversation was finished.

"Goodnight, Grandmamma," I said, rising from the floor and kissing her on the cheek.

She didn't move. I crept out of the room and went to my bedroom.

The next day, a man in a black suit arrived at the house carrying a briefcase, and he held a long conversation with my grandmother in the living-room. I was not allowed in while he was there, but when at last he went away, my grandmother came in to me, walking very slowly and looking very sad.

"That man was reading me your father's will," she said.

"What is a will?" I asked her.

"It is something you write before you die," she said. "And in it you say who is going to have your money and your property. But most important of all, it says who is going to look after your child if both the mother and father are dead."

A fearful panic took hold of me. "It did say you, Grandmamma?" I cried. "I don't have to go to somebody else, do I?"

"No," she said. "Your father would never have done that. He has asked me to take care of you for as long as I live, but he has also asked that I take you back to your own house in England. He wants us to stay there."

"But why?" I said. "Why can't we stay here in Norway? You would hate to live anywhere else! You told me you would!"

"I know," she said. "But there are a lot of complications with money and with the house that you wouldn't understand. Also, it said in the will that although all your family is Norwegian, you were born in England and you have started your education there and he wants you to continue going to English schools."

"Oh Grandmamma!" I cried. "*You* don't want to go and live in our English house, I know you don't!"

"Of course I don't," she said. "But I am afraid I must. The will said that your mother felt the same way about it, and it is important to respect the wishes of the parents."

There was no way out of it. We had to go to England, and my grand-mother started making arrangements at once. "Your next school term begins in a few days," she said, "so we don't have any time to waste."

On the evening before we left for England, my grandmother got on to her favourite subject once again. "There are not as many witches in England as there are in Norway," she said.

"I'm sure I won't meet one," I said.

"I sincerely hope you won't," she said, "because those English witches are probably the most vicious in the whole world."

As she sat there smoking her foul cigar and talking away, I kept looking at the hand with the missing thumb. I couldn't help it. I was fascinated by it and I kept wondering what awful thing had happened that time when she had met a witch. It must have been something absolutely appalling and gruesome otherwise she would have told me about it. Maybe the thumb had been twisted off. Or perhaps she had been forced to jam her thumb down the spout of a boiling kettle until it was steamed away. Or did someone pull it out of her hand like a tooth? I couldn't help trying to guess.

"Tell me what those English witches do, Grandmamma," I said.

"Well," she said, sucking away at her stinking cigar, "their favourite ruse is to mix up a powder that will turn a child into some creature or other that all grown-ups hate."

"What sort of a creature, Grandmamma?"

"Often it's a slug," she said. "A slug is one of their favourites. Then the grown-ups step on the slug and squish it without knowing it's a child."

"That's perfectly beastly!" I cried.

"Or it might be a flea," my grandmother said. "They might turn you into a flea, and without realising what she was doing your own mother would get out the flea-powder and then it's goodbye you."

"You're making me nervous, Grandmamma. I don't think I want to go back to England."

"I've known English witches," she went on, "who have turned chil-dren into pheasants and then sneaked the pheasants up into the woods the very day before the pheasant-shooting season opened."

"Owch," I said. "So they get shot?"

"Of course they get shot," she said. "And then they get plucked and roasted and eaten for supper."

I pictured myself as a pheasant flying frantically over the men with the guns, swerving and dipping as the guns exploded below me.

"Yes," my grandmother said, "it gives the English witches great pleasure to stand back and watch the grown-ups doing away with their own children."

"I really don't want to go to England, Grandmamma."

"Of course you don't," she said. "Nor do I. But I'm afraid we've got to."

"Are witches different in every country?" I asked.

"Completely different," my grandmother said. "But I don't know much about the other countries."

"Don't you even know about America?" I asked.

"Not really," she answered. "Although I have heard it said that over there the witches are able to make the grown-ups eat their own children."

"Never!" I cried. "Oh no, Grandmamma! That couldn't be true!"

"I don't know whether it's true or not," she said. "It's only a rumour I've heard."

"But how could they possibly make them eat their own children?" I asked.

"By turning them into hot-dogs," she said. "That wouldn't be too difficult for a clever witch."

"Does every single country in the world have its witches?" I asked.

"Wherever you find people, you find witches," my grandmother said. "There is a Secret Society of Witches in every country."

"And do they all know one another, Grandmamma?"

"They do not," she said. "A witch only knows the witches in her own country. She is strictly forbidden to communicate with any foreign witches. But an English witch, for example, will know all the other witches in England. They are all friends. They ring each other up. They swop deadly recipes. Goodness knows what else they talk about. I hate to think."

I sat on the floor, watching my grandmother. She put her cigar stub in the ashtray and folded her hands across her stomach. "Once a year," she went on, "the witches of each separate country hold their own secret meeting. They all get together in one place to receive a lecture from The Grand High Witch Of All The World."

"From *who*?" I cried.

"She is the ruler of them all," my grandmother said. "She is all-powerful. She is without mercy. All other witches are petrified of her. They see her only once a year at their Annual Meeting. She goes there to whip up excitement and enthusiasm, and to give orders. The Grand High Witch travels from country to country attending these Annual Meetings."

"Where do they have these meetings, Grandmamma?"

"There are all sorts of rumours," my grandmother answered. "I have heard it said that they just book into an hotel like any other group of women who are holding a meeting. I have also heard it said that some very peculiar things go on in the hotels they stay in. It is rumoured that the beds are never slept in, that there are burn marks on the bedroom carpets, that toads are discovered in the bathtubs, and that down in the kitchen the cook once found a baby crocodile swimming in his saucepan of soup."

My grandmother picked up her cigar and took another puff, inhaling the foul smoke deeply into her lungs.

"Where does The Grand High Witch live when she's at home?" I asked.

"Nobody knows," my grandmother said. "If we knew that, then she could be rooted out and destroyed. Witchophiles all over the world have spent their lives trying to discover the secret Headquarters of The Grand High Witch."

"What is a witchophile, Grandmamma?"

"A person who studies witches and knows a lot about them," my grandmother said.

"Are you a witchophile, Grandmamma?"

"I am a retired witchophile," she said. "I am too old to be active any longer. But when I was younger, I travelled all over the globe trying to track down The Grand High Witch. I never came even close to succeeding."

"Is she rich?" I asked.

"She's rolling," my grandmother said. "Simply rolling in money. Rumour has it that there is a machine in her headquarters which is exactly like the machine the government uses to print the bank-notes you and I use. After all, bank-notes are only bits of paper with special designs and pictures on them. Anyone can make them who has the right machine and the right paper. My guess is that The Grand High Witch makes all the money she wants and she dishes it out to witches everywhere."

"What about foreign money?" I asked.

"Those machines can make *Chinese* money if you want them to," my grandmother said. "It's only a question of pressing the right button."

"But Grandmamma," I said, "if nobody has ever seen The Grand High Witch, how can you be so sure she exists?"

My grandmother gave me a long and very severe look. "Nobody has ever seen the Devil," she said, "but we know he exists."

The next morning, we sailed for England and soon I was back in the old family house in Kent, but this time with only my grandmother to look after me. Then the Easter Term began and every weekday I went to school and everything seemed to have come back to normal again.

Now at the bottom of our garden there was an enormous conker tree, and high up in its branches Timmy (my best friend) and I had started to build a magnificent tree-house. We were able to work on it only at the weekends, but we were getting along fine. We had begun with the floor, which we built by laying wide planks between two quite far-apart branches and nailing them down. Within a month, we had finished the floor. Then we constructed a wooden railing around the floor and that left only the roof to be built. The roof was the difficult bit.

One Saturday afternoon when Timmy was in bed with flu, I decided to make a start on the roof all by myself. It was lovely being high up there in that conker tree, all alone with the pale young leaves coming out everywhere around me. It was like being in a big green cave. And the height made it extra exciting. My grandmother had told me that if I fell I would break a leg, and every time I looked down, I got a tingle along my spine.

I worked away, nailing the first plank on the roof. Then suddenly, out of the corner of my eye, I caught sight of a woman standing immediately below me. She was looking up at me and smiling in the most peculiar way. When most people smile, their lips go out sideways. This woman's lips went upwards and downwards, showing all her front teeth and gums. The gums were like raw meat.

It is always a shock to discover that you are being watched when you think you are alone.

And what was this strange woman doing in our garden anyway?

I noticed that she was wearing a small black hat and she had black gloves on her hands and the gloves came nearly up to her elbows.

Gloves! She was wearing *gloves!*

I froze all over.

"I have a present for you," she said, still staring at me, still smiling, still showing her teeth and gums.

I didn't answer.

"Come down out of that tree, little boy," she said, "and I shall give you the most exciting present you've ever had." Her voice had a curious rasping quality. It made a sort of metallic sound, as though her throat was full of drawing-pins.

Without taking her eyes from my face, she very slowly put one of those gloved hands into her purse and drew out a small green snake. She held it up for me to see.

"It's tame," she said.

The snake began to coil itself around her forearm. It was brilliant green.

"If you come down here, I shall give him to you," she said.

Oh Grandmamma, I thought, come and help me!

Then I panicked. I dropped the hammer and shot up that enormous tree like a monkey. I didn't stop until I was as high as I could possibly go, and there I stayed, quivering with fear. I couldn't see the woman now. There were layers and layers of leaves between her and me.

I stayed up there for hours and I kept very still. It began to grow dark. At last, I heard my grandmother calling my name.

"I'm up here," I shouted back.

"Come down at once!" she called out. "It's past your suppertime."

"Grandmamma!" I shouted. "Has that woman gone?"

"What woman?" my grandmother called back.

"The woman in the black gloves!"

There was silence from below. It was the silence of somebody who was too stunned to speak.

"Grandmamma!" I shouted again. "*Has she gone?*"

"Yes," my grandmother answered at last. "She's gone. I'm here, my darling. I'll look after you. You can come down now."

I climbed down. I was trembling. My grandmother enfolded me in her arms. "I've seen a witch," I said.

"Come inside," she said. "You'll be all right with me."

She led me into the house and gave me a cup of hot cocoa with lots of sugar in it. "Tell me everything," she said.

I told her.

By the time I had finished, it was my grandmother who was trembling. Her face was ashy grey and I saw her glance down at that hand of hers that didn't have a thumb. "You know what this means," she said. "It means that there is one of them in our district. From now on I'm not letting you walk alone to school."

"Do you think she could be after me specially?" I asked.

"No," she said. "I doubt that. One child is as good as any other to those creatures."

It is hardly surprising that after that I became a very witch-conscious little boy. If I happened to be alone on the road and saw a woman approaching who was wearing gloves, I would quickly skip across to the other side. And as the weather remained pretty cold during the whole of that month, nearly *everybody* was wearing gloves. Curiously enough though, I never saw the woman with the green snake again.

That was my first witch. But it wasn't my last.

from

Wizard's Hall

by Jane Yolen

Jane Yolen (born 1939) has written more than 170 books. *Wizard's Hall,* first published in 1991, is the story of Henry, an earnest young boy whose mother sends him away to a school for magicians. If you like the Harry Potter books, you will have fun comparing Henry to the more celebrated Harry.

Thornmallow was a wizard, only the most minor of wizards. He had learned some elementary Spelling and a smattering of Names. He had not yet learned his Changes thoroughly, nor his Transformations. And his Curses tended to splatter or dribble around the edges. He was rarely Punctual or Practical and his nose tended toward smudginess.

But he meant well. And he tried.

Magister Greybane of the long, thin beard was often heard to mutter when Thornmallow came for lessons in Prestonomics. Magister Beechvale had sick headaches when it was Thornmallow's turn to chant. And even Magister Briar Rose was known to feel a bit queasy upon the occasion of Thornmallow's exams.

But the fact remains that Thornmallow meant well. And he tried. He came to Wizard's Hall at the time of its greatest peril, the 113th student, the very last to be admitted in that horrible year. And it turned out the inhabitants of Wizard's Hall were glad indeed that Thornmallow studied there.

Not because he was the world's greatest wizard.
But because he meant well.
And he tried.

Thornmallow's real name was Henry. He was a small fellow, thin as a reed, with fair, unmanageable hair the color and shape of dandelion fluff. His eyes were a gooseberry green and hard to read. There was always a smudge or two on his nose as if the nose led him into trouble. But actually he was a quiet boy, shy and obedient to a fault.

He had never wanted to be a wizard.

As a youngster he'd fancied being a linewalker or a tree warden or a juggler, mostly outside work. But he'd outgrown each fancy in turn, as children often do, moving on to the next with hardly a backward glance.

One day, when he was eleven, he mentioned wizardry to his dear ma. He didn't mean it. Not really. It was just a passing thought.

She looked up from her butter churn and smiled.

"That's the job for you (Whomp!)," she said. "Steady work and (Whomp!) a good place in the world. That's the one." She gave one last Whomp! to the churn, got up from her stool, and with her kerchief wiped a smudge off Henry's nose. Then, stretching to get the knots out of her spine, she walked into the house to help him pack. She was never one for delay. She stuffed the bag with a change of shirts, a pair of woollies for the cold, a packet of rose petals for the sweetening, and hard journeycake for the road.

"That's the one!" she repeated with even more enthusiasm. "You had a great-uncle on your father's side—bless his soul—who took to wizardry." She hesitated, then shook her head. "Or was it card playing? Whatever."

"But what if I have no talent for it, Ma?" Henry had asked, somewhat sensibly and not a little nervous that she was packing him off so quickly.

"Talent don't matter," she'd answered, closing the bag. "I didn't know I had any talent for mothering until you came along. And look!" She gestured to him as if he were proof enough. "It only matters that you try."

Then she kissed him three times, once on each cheek for love and once on the forehead for wisdom, wiped his smudgy nose one last time, and closed the door behind him saying, "Don't forget to write."

Henry stared at his house for a long minute and bit his lower lip until tears came to his eyes. But he was a good boy and used to doing what he was told. So, wiping his eyes and leaving a brand-new smudge on the right side of his nose, he waved goodbye to his ma. Her smile shone out of the window at him like an off-center crescent moon. Then he turned. He could feel her smile warming his back and her kisses protecting his cheeks and face as he started on the road. Indeed, he didn't know if he had any talent for wizardry. Or for card playing. Whatever.

But he certainly knew he could try.

The way to Wizard's Hall was no secret. It was just over the Far-Rise Hills, turn left until morning. Every child in Hallowdale knew that. There was even a jump-rope rhyme about it:

> Tell me the place where wizards dwell,
> Tell me each step and turning,
> Over the mountains, under the hill,
> Turn left and walk till morning.

That certainly didn't rhyme as well as it might, but it fit the *tip-taps* of a jump rope perfectly. And of course, there ahead of him were the Far-Rise Hills, a day's journey away.

Henry needed no map.

It was late fall, and the last of autumn's colors had faded to a steady rust carpet beneath bare trees. Short bursts of wind hissed and hooted and whistled down the valley, pushing Henry onward from Hallowdale as surely as his dear ma had pushed him out the door.

The walk to the foothills was easy—a smooth and gently turning path lined with trees. Henry dodged a scallywag and two highwaymen along the way, but that was just in case. He doubted they had any interest in his poor goods. The journeycake was crumbled, and the woollies were well worn. But still he hid behind the trees, for his dear ma had always cautioned, *Better take care than need care.*

He also spent an hour up one of the taller beeches when a family of wild boar rooted by. Henry was no hero. Being small and thin had practically guaranteed that. Besides, he'd no practice in the art of being brave. To make up the time lost shivering amongst the leaves, he forwent both lunch and dinner until he was within sight of the hills.

"And isn't it a marvel," he whispered to himself as he chewed the crumbly cake, "just how good a dry meal can be. No wonder my dear ma always says, *Hunger is a great seasoner.*"

At the mountain's foot was a sign to make the passage simpler still:

THIS WAY TO WIZARD'S HALL

it announced in bold lettering. There was also a gold-leafed arrow, picked a bit raw by passing villains, pointing to the left. And sure enough, the path continued right up the mountain's face, with little yellow ribands marking every fifth tree, just as a reminder.

Clearly no one could get lost along the way.

Henry walked all night long. His only companions were the owls who swooped silently above him, for the crickets and frogs were long gone to their early winterings. Henry was actually glad of the quiet.

In the morning both sun and moon shone together, and right below them Henry could make out the towers of Wizard's Hall, standing tall and jagged against the sky. He knew there would be gardens, rosebushes, and trees. Everyone knew magic made things grow. Like manure. But the towers reminded Henry of the teeth of a great beast, and suddenly he was quite sure he didn't want to study wizardry at all. He knew with certainty that he'd make a better farmer or fisherman or even a cook.

He tried to turn and go home.

But as if the road itself knew it was Henry's fate to go to Wizard's Hall, it wouldn't let him turn. No sooner did he lift one foot to go home than the other was stuck fast. He could only move forward toward the Hall, not back.

It was magic for sure—and he was part of it.

He ran his tired fingers through his hair and remembered his ma's smile at the window. He remembered some of her last words.

"It only matters that you try."

Shrugging the pack higher on his shoulders, he sighed once out loud and thought he heard an answering sigh in the wind.

"To Wizard's Hall, then," he whispered.

The road loosed both his feet at once and tumbled him forward at a run toward his new home.

Wizard's Hall was a solidly built place of jagged stone towers and long arching windows. High gray stone walls curved around it, set with iron-work gates. There was not a tree or plant growing within the boundaries of those walls; it was as if magic had shattered the natural world.

Henry shivered when he looked through the gates and saw how barren the yard was, for he had been expecting much green. But he knew he could not fight his fate. So he walked steadily till he reached the main gate. There the iron was twisted into intricate symbols of power, laid out in a grid that looked like a quilt or like a beast—depending upon which eye he squinted with. It made his stomach queasy just looking.

Taking a deep breath, Henry knocked upon the gate and called out, "Hallooo?"

The gate made a rude sound, remarkably like a spit kazoo, and a small door just Henry's size opened in it.

Henry let out the breath he'd been holding. Red-faced, he trudged in.

Suddenly he found himself not in the barren yard nor yet in a hallway, but in a wood-paneled room hung with gray-blue tapestries fraying a bit at the sides. A large table, littered with parchment, stood in the center of the room. Some pieces of parchment were rolled up tightly with scarlet ribands, some were creased and folded, some were scrunched and discarded, some were held flat by dark inkwells or brass doorknobs or apple cores.

Behind the table sat an old man with skin the color of the parchment, eyes like blue marbles, and a white halo of hair.

"Good evening," the old man said gently.

As it was not evening at all but midday, and sunlight streamed in through the many-paned windows, quilting the floor with light, Henry was stuck for an answer.

"Or good morning," the old man added. "Whichever. I am Register Oakbend. Glad to meet you at last."

"At last?" Henry said. "But nobody knew I was coming. Not even me. Till yesterday."

The old man did not reply to this but merely held out his hand.

Only then did Henry realize that the wizard was quite blind, for his marble-blue eyes stared straight ahead and his hand was reaching slightly to the left of the table, though Henry was slightly to the right.

"Actually, sir," Henry said, gathering his courage, "it's coming on to noon."

Register Oakbend turned at Henry's voice so that now he was facing Henry directly, and lowered his hand. "I *said* whichever," he answered peevishly. "And that includes noon, young man. What did you say your name was?"

"Henry," said Henry, "though I didn't actually say it—yet."

"Said it now," said Register Oakbend. "The Book says *Better now than not*. But isn't Henry a silly name? H-E-N-R-Y, don't you know. Or H-E-N-R-I-E. Nothing to it. Simply a series of sounds without meaning. HEN-ER-REE. Now *Couchwillow*, there's a good one. Or *Stickybun*. Or *Daffy-down-dilly*, though that's really for a girl. How about *Broadleaf*? Do you like it? Does it fit?"

"Please, sir," said Henry in a quiet little voice, "my name is Henry."

"Listen carefully, boy. Words mean something, not just sounds thrown down willy-nilly. *Willy-nilly*—that's not a bad one. But I didn't ask what your name *is*. We haven't decided that yet. And you're going to need a good one. I asked what your name *was*." He cocked his head to one side.

"But, sir, my name has always been Henry. Always will be. My dear ma gave it to me." Henry's voice quavered a little bit at the mention of her.

"Despite popular opinion," Register Oakbend said, "mothers do not always know best. Especially about names. That is why children get called so many other things by their friends. I, for example, was called Niddy-Noddy by my companions, though my name at the time was Ned." He smiled, remembering.

"But my dear ma—" Henry began.

"Prickly sort of fellow, isn't he," murmured Register Oakbend. "But just what we desperately need."

Henry thought the old man was talking to himself until he heard an answering sound.

"*Squark!*" It came from a little white animal in a cage that was almost obscured by the mounds of parchment. Henry caught just a glimpse of it.

"Absolutely," replied Register Oakbend, nodding his head vigorously. "Right idea. That's the ticket."

"Squark?" Henry asked.

"Your name," the old man said. "Your name for *is*; for *now*; for Wizard's Hall."

"Squark," Henry repeated dismally, thinking for a moment about running away. Only for a moment. He was, after all, a good boy. And he *had* promised he would try. "Squark."

"Means Thornmallow: prickly on the outside, squishy within. Though I'll have to take that *squishy* on faith. But Dr. Mo is always right."

"Thornmallow," Henry whispered to himself, trying it out. Oddly he felt relieved. Thornmallow was certainly a great deal better than Squark for a name. And it was only his name for *is*, for *now*, for Wizard's Hall. When he went home for holidays, he could still be

Henry to his dear ma. Closing his eyes for a moment, he tried to feel like Thornmallow the Wizard. He only felt like Henry, thin as a reed with a nose that was often smudgy. Suddenly he remembered something and opened his eyes.

"Who is Dr. Mo?" he asked.

But Register Oakbend, cage, desk, and all had unaccountably disappeared.

Henry—now Thornmallow—croggled, swallowed hard, and looked around. He was no longer inside the Hall but outside it, this time in the treeless, shrubless, flowerless yard, standing on hard cobbles. Not sure what it all meant, he walked up to the front door. It, like the gate, was covered with a grid, but this grid looked entirely like a quilt and not at all like a beast. That made him feel a bit better. He knocked on it.

The door made a sighing noise and opened. Thornmallow walked in.

He was quite surprised that now it was cozy and snug inside, not unlike a larger version of his cottage. Unaccountably, he felt at home. Small gold-framed portraits of wizards hung along one wall, each of them looking old and wise. Beneath each frame was a name.

"Magister Greybane," he read silently. "Magister Bledwort. Magister Hyssop. Magister Briar Rose." Something about the last wizard reminded Henry of his dear ma. Perhaps it was because she was the only one smiling. He said her name aloud: "Magister Briar Rose."

The picture winked at him.

"I must be tired," Henry told himself and suddenly recalled he'd been walking all night. But when the picture winked a second time, mouthing his name, he felt his knees give way, and he sat down quite suddenly on the polished floor.

"Now, now, none of that, child," came a small voice from the picture. "It won't do. You are the last, and what we desperately need, and therefore most important to us. Be strong and stand. You must try, dear child. You *must* try."

The voice was remarkably like his dear ma's, only older. Henry stood at once, not even bothering to wonder what being *the last* meant or how desperate they were at Wizard's Hall.

Addressing the picture, he said, "Pardon me, Madame Magister, but my name is Hen—er—Thornmallow. I'm not quite sure what's happening, but I've come to try and be a wizard."

"Well, of course you have, Thornmallow," the picture answered. "Otherwise Door wouldn't have let you in, and Dr. Mo wouldn't have given you a name. You'd still be outside and called Hen-er. Now you are inside and called Thornmallow. Hmmmmmm, Thornmallow. Prickly on the outside, squishy within. I'll have to take that *prickly* on faith. But prickly is just what we need. Let's get you settled, shall we? And wipe that smudge off your nose."

Suddenly a small, compact woman in a musty, wine-colored robe with something that could have been egg stains on the front, stood by his side. The picture frame was empty. She plucked a handkerchief from the air and scrubbed at his face with it. Then, apparently satisfied, she guided him with two fingers on his elbow into a small room immediately to the right.

"This will be yours," she said. "See?" She made a quick gesture with her hand, and the handkerchief disappeared. At the same time, a portrait of his dear ma with her butter churn appeared on a small wooden stand. His clothes, clean-smelling and ironed, winkled out of his pack and hung themselves on pegs by the door. A little quilt covered with sunbursts tucked itself tidily over the bed.

"Do you like it?" asked Magister Briar Rose.

Thornmallow picked up the picture from the stand and collapsed onto the bed. He was about to thank Magister Briar Rose when he saw that in the picture his dear ma seemed quite sad.

Bursting into sobs, Thornmallow put his face into his hands and was quite a long time at it. When he was quiet at last, he looked up, but the wizard was gone.

"All this appearing and disappearing," Thornmallow told himself between sniffles, wishing the handkerchief hadn't vanished as well, "can be awfully hard on a body." At his words a handkerchief dropped out of the air, landing beside him on the bed.

NOW BLOW, in little flaming letters, flashed above the handkerchief.

He blew until his nose was quite clear. Then he lay down on the bed with the picture of his dear ma pressed next to his heart. He was asleep at once.

When Thornmallow awoke, he felt refreshed. Opening his eyes, he blinked twice, not quite believing what he saw. On the ceiling of his room was a star map with little lights that winked off and on, reciting their own names.

"The Ram," one group of stars said. "The Hunter," whispered another. He sat up.

Someone had taken off his boots and tucked them side by side under his bed. He reached over, picked them up, and drew them back on. They were freshly polished. He could almost see his face in them. Sitting on his bed, he began to wonder if all the magicks he had seen were tricks—or real.

Real! he decided at last and stood.

"The Bear," answered the stars.

When he opened the door of his room, he saw a long hall. Out of many similar doors poured boys his own age. Some were tall, some short, some weighty, and some as slim as he. None of them seemed to have combed their hair, though one—a boy with a bright yellow cock's comb—was intent on slicking his hair back with hasty fingers. All the boys were wearing long black scholastic gowns and carrying books.

"New boy?" called one as he raced by, going right to left. He was tall, with flaming red hair and a network of freckles like a map over his nose and cheeks.

Before Thornmallow could answer, the boy and his companion were gone. Not disappeared this time, but gone around a corner of the building. Thornmallow hurried after them and found himself in another long hall, this one filled with rushing girls in black scholar's robes running toward the right.

"Last bell!" one girl cried. She had a face the color of old wood, and her black hair was caught up in three plaits of equal weight: one on each side of her head and one standing straight up from it. She was short, with the eager look of certain small dogs.

"What bell?" Thornmallow ventured, but his words were immediately drowned out by three enormous and quite unmelodious *bongs*.

Even as the third *bong* sounded, the girls disappeared, funneling into separate rooms.

Standing in the middle of the now-empty hall, Thornmallow stared about him. His gooseberry eyes were wide, and his heart skiproped in his chest.

"What next?" he whispered. Being a wizard had so far been full of rushings about, of comings and goings, appearances and disappearances, not at all what he'd expected. But—as his dear ma was fond of saying—*Expectations always disappoint.*

Something touched his elbow. He jumped and turned to see Magister Briar Rose. There was something rather like strawberry jam on her right sleeve.

"About your classes," she said. "Close your eyes."

He obeyed. When she told him to open his eyes again, they were in another room, this one filled floor-to-ceiling with books. Or at least he and Magister Briar Rose were in the room. His stomach, he was sure, had been left behind.

"Don't worry," the old woman said. "You'll soon get used to it. Sit!"

He did as she commanded, collapsing onto the floor.

"Wherever did you learn your manners?" Magister Briar Rose asked. "Sit in the chair." She pointed. "Over there." She sat herself behind a book-littered table and poured herself a cup of black tea. Then she snatched a cracker from a nearby basket.

Red-faced, Thornmallow stood and walked over to the perfectly respectable high-backed wooden chair she had pointed at and lowered himself carefully onto its plump purple cushion.

There was a long silence while she seemed to be examining Thornmallow and the cracker alternately and with equal attention.

"Please, ma'am," he said at last, "may I ask a question?"

"Of course," she said. "But just the one. We have a great deal of business to get on with, now that you are finally here." As she spoke, she dipped the cracker into the tea.

"Then, ma'am, what is a *magister*?"

"Why—a teacher," she said and took a small bite of the now soggy cracker.

"Then . . ." He paused a minute, screwing up his courage, as he wasn't sure if this was a second question he was asking or part of the first.

"Then what, child? We haven't got all day." She brushed cracker crumbs off her chest.

"Then . . . why not just say *teacher*?"

"Ah." She leaned back and smiled at him, and he knew it was all right. "There's nothing magical about the word *teacher*, is there? Everyone knows it, and therefore it's common—and not fraught with magic. And we are about the business of magic here. There is this to remember: magic is tough and sometimes dangerous, and the words you use are always important."

Thornmallow was not sure he understood it all, but as she did not seem to want to elaborate, he had to be content. He was sure she would not tolerate another question.

"Now next time," Briar Rose said, "you must wear a scholar's robe."

He nodded, not even daring to ask where such a robe might be found.

"Why, in the wardrobe of course," she answered as if he had spoken aloud. "And now to your studies." She put the half-eaten cracker down. It jumped back into the basket.

Thornmallow gulped.

"Can you spell?"

Catching his breath, Thornmallow said in a voice that sounded rather as if it had suddenly ripped on a nail, "C-A-T spells *cat*?"

Magister Briar Rose chuckled, but it was not meant meanly at all. In fact it sounded as if she were laughing at herself instead of at Thornmallow. "No, child, not that kind of spelling. This kind. C-A-T . . ." She waved her hand in a decidedly odd manner and pointed at the floor.

A calico cat, hardly more than a kitten, materialized. It looked up wide but a moment's surprise in its green eyes, then settled at once into cleaning its back leg, ignoring them both.

"No," Thornmallow whispered. "Not at all like that."

The cat stopped cleaning itself, stood, and stalked out of the room.

"Elementary Spelling, then," Magister Briar Rose said, nodding her head and making a note of it on a piece of parchment. "What about Names?"

"Thornmallow," Thornmallow whispered. "Or Henry."

"Andrew John-Bruce-David-Bob," intoned Magister Briar Rose, staring at him.

Thornmallow felt himself growing smaller and smaller and smaller still—until he sat at the edge of a vast purple meadow that seemed to stretch behind him forever.

"No names," he said, his voice as tiny as he.

"Bob-Divad-Ecurb-Nhoj-Werdna," came a booming from above him. Magister Briar Rose was reciting the names backward.

Slowly Thornmallow expanded, as if he were steadily being pumped full of air. When the names stopped, he was his right size again.

"First Year Names, then," Magister Briar Rose added to her list, "though I thought that your arrival heralded something more exacting than that. How you can possibly help as a First Year is beyond me." She shrugged and cocked her head to one side. "Any Transformations?"

"None—none at all," Thornmallow squeaked quickly.

"Ah. Ah," she agreed. "I didn't expect so. Though I did hope . . ." A third line was added to the growing list. "Curses?"

He shook his head, afraid to make a sound.

She scratched the last of it onto the parchment and signed her name on the bottom with a flourish that, especially upside-down, looked nothing like Briar Rose. Then she dropped a bit of red wax onto the parchment from a burning taper and took a great seal shaped rather like the handle of a butter churn. With it she set her mark into the wax.

Just then, the room went dark, the light blinking off and leaving

Thornmallow with an awful feeling, as if pins and needles were sticking all over his body. A moment later the lights went on again.

"Was that a Curse, ma'am?" he asked. "Or a Transformation?"

Magister Briar Rose had an odd look on her face, and there were white spots on her cheek. "*That*," she said finally, "is a failure of power. You do not need to know more." She took a deep breath. "And *this* is for you." She handed him the list. "Now you are ready. And I hope—I truly hope—that you will do."

"Do what?" he began to ask, but the moment his hand touched the parchment, he found himself in a classroom. An elderly gentleman with thick drooping mustaches tied over his chest in a gray bow was sitting at the front on a high stool. He looked like some kind of long-legged bird on a nest. Before him, at small, compact desks, twenty boys and girls were chanting a rhyme.

Thornmallow no longer marveled at how he had gotten there. He only wondered if his stomach would ever catch up.

"Thornmallow, is it?" asked the gentleman with the mustaches. His voice was harsh and storklike. "Here at last to answer our need. Are you prickly on the outside?"

"Not really, sir," Thornmallow answered.

The man looked at him very sternly for a moment more, then checked something off on a paper that had suddenly materialized in his hand. "Yes, definitely prickly, I'd say, though I shall have to take that inside *squishy* on faith." He crumpled the paper, and it flared with a blue light and disappeared. "I am Magister Beechvale. Fifth row, fourth seat, if you please."

Thornmallow looked at the fifth row, fourth seat. It was occupied.

"Sir—" he began.

"Between Tansy and Willoweed. They will keep an eye on you these first days. First days are always difficult." He lifted his hand in a languid manner, as if pointing to the row, but his fingers wiggled mysteriously.

Thornmallow looked again. An empty school desk now stood ahead of the final desk. It was the fourth seat in the fifth row.

"Well—go ahead, boy," Magister Beechvale said in his stork voice.

Thornmallow walked to the desk and stared at it for a minute.

"Sit!" came the teacher's command.

He sat.

"Told you it was last bell," whispered the girl in the desk just ahead of his. She turned as she spoke and smiled at him. Her three black plaits seemed to wave a greeting.

Tansy, Thornmallow thought. *How odd. Tansy is a bright yellow flower, and she is a dark brown girl. If names are supposed to mean something, why isn't she called Bark or Earth.*

Someone tapped him on the shoulder. When he looked, he saw it was the redheaded boy with the freckle map on his face.

"Well come to Wizard's Hall, Thornmallow," he said, "and welcome as well. I'm Willoweed. Your expert guide. *Guardians,* we call them."

Thornmallow nodded. "Hello, Willoweed."

"We just call him Will," Tansy said. "And I am your other guardian. Everyone gets two guardians the first days. That's because first days are—"

"Always difficult," Will cut in.

Thornmallow was about to explain that his real name was not Thornmallow at all, and they could call him Henry, when the sharp clearing of a throat made him look up. Standing on his long bird legs, Magister Beechvale was pointing to the blackboard with a thin wand. Three words glowed at the tip:

PUNCTUALITY!

PUNCTUALITY!

PUNCTUALITY!

The wand tapped three times, and all the students recited as one. "Punctuality! Practicality! Personality!" Their voices were bell-like.

Thornmallow thought he'd better join in, and by the second round he'd added his voice to theirs, but somehow he was a whole tone off.

Someone in a nearby seat giggled. Thornmallow closed his mouth.

"Clear, round, perfect tones if you please," called out Magister Beechvale, "on these three important beginning words of wizardly wisdom." He hummed a note, and the class hummed after him. They began again on the first word.

Thornmallow tried once more. This time he was off by a tone and a half.

A blond girl in the front row raised her hand.

Magister Beechvale lifted the wand from the board. "Yes, Gorse?"

"Please, sir, but the new boy is tone-deaf."

"Nonsense!" Magister Beechvale replied. "No one admitted to Wizard's Hall is tone-deaf. Dr. Mo would sense it right away and send him packing. A wizard cannot be tone-deaf. And why is that, class?"

Together they sang, "A spell must be chanted on the dominant, or it will fail."

Thornmallow rose reluctantly to his feet. He had no idea what a dominant was, but he did know something else. "Please, sir, if you mean by tone-deaf that I cannot sing on key, well I am afraid that Mistress—er—Gorse is right. My dear ma always said, *Can't carry a tune in a brass bucket!* And on holidays old Master Robyn, the choirmaster, always cautioned me to just mouth the words when we sang the hymns. Tone-deaf—that's me!"

"Nonsense!" Magister Beechvale said again, only this time he sounded more like a screech owl than a stork. His mustaches waggled furiously. "You are just not trying hard enough. Sit down, young Thornapple."

"Thorn*mallow*, sir," Thornmallow whispered.

"Prickly indeed," muttered the magister, raising his stick to the board once more. "And we don't encourage *prickly* in my class. See to it you do not answer back again."

Thornmallow sat down and mouthed the rest of the recitation without a sound while the others sang joyfully around him. Hearing no rough edges on the notes, Magister Beechvale actually smiled.

Eventually they moved on from the wizard's wisdoms to a spell about roses in the snow, then one about dresses made of paper, and finally one about letting milk down from a dry cow. Thornmallow thought that the last might be something his dear ma could use. But this time, when he tried to join the chanting, he was at least two full tones wrong, and everyone in row four turned round to stare at him.

"To the front!" Magister Beechvale called three times.

At first Thornmallow didn't think the call was meant for him. Next he tried to *pretend* it wasn't for him. But the third time Magister Beechvale summoned, he added a couple of finger waggles, and without meaning to, Thornmallow leaped from his seat and trotted up to the front of the room. When, at Magister Beechvale's request, he turned and faced the other boys and girls, twenty pairs of eyes were staring at him, coldly waiting.

"You will sing each note with me," Magister Beechvale said, putting his hands over Thornmallow's ears. "And this time, you must really try." He hummed a note.

Thornmallow closed his eyes and thought for a moment about his dear ma. He *would*, he really *would* try. When he opened them again, though he couldn't actually *hear* the note Magister Beechvale was humming, the teacher's hands being clean over his ears, something else was happening. It was as if a quiet heat were radiating from those hands, spreading around and then into his ears, like some sort of little animal finding its wintering in a cave. The heat sought out the twisting tunnels of his ears and burrowed right down into his brain. And when it hit his brain, a tone sprang into it. He opened his mouth, and the heat—and the tone—came out.

The first note was not nearly close enough, but the second warm note was closer. By the third, he was right smack on pitch, and all the students applauded.

"I can feel it!" he cried out. "I can feel the note." It seemed to be going directly from Magister Beechvale's hands into his ears and out his mouth.

He was so excited, he called out the first spell they'd tried, surprised that he remembered it:

Red against white,
Day into night,
Let the winds blow,
Roses in snow.

It was so wonderful to sing in tune and to remember without trying that Thornmallow waved his hand in time to the chant. Only when Magister Beechvale's hands suddenly slipped off his ears, and he heard the sharp intake of breath from the class, did Thornmallow realize that something had gone wrong.

"Oooooh, the new boy's gonna get it!" cried blond Gorse, staring at the window.

Everyone followed her gaze, and then Thornmallow heard the *thud-thud-thud* as twenty bodies hit the floor and hid under their desks.

That sound was quickly swallowed up by another, louder noise as the windows all snapped open. The sky turned black. And an avalanche of snow bore down on the classroom, caving in the wall and covering Magister Beechvale and his stool.

On top of the snowdrift, which was almost as high as the ceiling, and right above the spot where the stool had been buried, sat a rose bush in full bloom, its petals drifting down like bloodspots against the white snow.

"Perhaps," Magister Beechvale said as he emerged from the drift, "perhaps . . ." His voice was suddenly soft and not at all storklike. He hesitated, dusting off great gobs of snow from his black robe. "Perhaps you needn't try *quite* so hard, Thornmarrow."

"*Mallow*, sir," Thornmallow whispered, swallowing hard. There were tears in his eyes, and he wanted to explain that he hadn't actually meant an avalanche, hadn't meant to ruin the classroom wall, hadn't meant to scare anyone, certainly hadn't meant to get Magister Beechvale wet. But no words came out, only a weak and embarrassing moan.

With a wave of his hand, Magister Beechvale muttered something under his breath. Immediately the snow disappeared inch by inch, until all that was left was a large damp stain on the floor. The wall rebuilt itself. And the rosebush became potted in a green stone urn with bright pink flamingos painted on the side.

Magister Beechvale gave Thornmallow a careful, quick pat on the head. This time there was no heat emanating from his hand. "Squishy indeed, Thornmallow," he said. "Squishy indeed."

from

Five Children and It

by E. Nesbit

Edith Nesbit (1858–1924) wrote some of the world's best stories about bored children looking for something to do and finding it. *Five Children and It*, the first book of a trilogy, includes this first encounter between five young children and a talented, odd, rather prickly creature called a psammead.

The house was three miles from the station, but before the dusty hired fly had rattled along for five minutes the children began to put their heads out of the carriage window and to say, 'Aren't we nearly there?' And every time they passed a house, which was not very often, they all said, 'Oh, *is* this it?' But it never was, till they reached the very top of the hill, just past the chalk-quarry and before you come to the gravel-pit. And then there was a white house with a green garden and an orchard beyond, and mother said, 'Here we are!'

'How white the house is,' said Robert.

'And look at the roses,' said Anthea.

'And the plums,' said Jane.

'It is rather decent,' Cyril admitted.

The Baby said, 'Wanty go walky'; and the fly stopped with a last rattle and jolt.

Everyone got its legs kicked or its feet trodden on in the scramble to get out of the carriage that very minute, but no one seemed to mind.

Mother, curiously enough, was in no hurry to get out; and even when she had come down slowly and by the step, and with no jump at all, she seemed to wish to see the boxes carried in, and even to pay the driver, instead of joining in that first glorious rush round the garden and the orchard and the thorny, thistly, briery, brambly wilderness beyond the broken gate and the dry fountain at the side of the house. But the children were wiser, for once. It was not really a pretty house at all; it was quite ordinary, and mother thought it was rather inconvenient, and was quite annoyed at there being no shelves, to speak of, and hardly a cupboard in the place. Father used to say that the ironwork on the roof and coping was like an architect's nightmare. But the house was deep in the country, with no other house in sight, and the children had been in London for two years, without so much as once going to the seaside even for a day by an excursion train, and so the White House seemed to them a sort of Fairy Palace set down in an Earthly Paradise: For London is like prison for children, especially if their relations are not rich.

Of course there are the shops and the theatres, and Maskelyne and Cook's, and things, but if your people are rather poor you don't get taken to the theatres, and you can't buy things out of the shops; and London has none of those nice things that children may play with without hurting the things or themselves—such as trees and sand and woods and waters. And nearly everything in London is the wrong sort of shape—all straight lines and flat streets, instead of being all sorts of odd shapes, like things are in the country. Trees are all different, as you know, and I am sure some tiresome person must have told you that there are no two blades of grass exactly alike. But in streets, where the blades of grass don't grow, everything is like everything else. This is why so many children who live in towns are so extremely naughty. They do not know what is the matter with them, and no more do their fathers and mothers, aunts, uncles, cousins, tutors, governesses, and nurses; but I know. And so do you now. Children in the country are naughty sometimes, too, but that is for quite different reasons.

The children had explored the gardens and the outhouses thoroughly before they were caught and cleaned for tea, and they saw quite well that they were certain to be happy at the White House. They thought so from the first moment, but when they found the back of the house covered with jasmine, all in white flower, and smelling like a bottle of the most expensive scent that is ever given for a birthday present; and when they had seen the lawn, all green and smooth, and quite different from the brown grass in the gardens at Camden Town; and when they had found the stable with a loft over it and some old hay still left, they were almost certain; and when Robert had found the broken swing and tumbled out of it and got a lump on his head the size of an egg, and Cyril had nipped his finger in the door of a hutch that seemed made to keep rabbits in, if you ever had any, they had no longer any doubts whatever.

The best part of it all was that there were no rules about not going to places and not doing things. In London almost everything is labelled 'You mustn't touch,' and though the label is invisible, it's just as bad, because you know it's there, or if you don't you jolly soon get told.

The White House was on the edge of a hill, with a wood behind it— and the chalk-quarry on one side and the gravel-pit on the other. Down at the bottom of the hill was a level plain, with queer-shaped white buildings where people burnt lime, and a big red brewery and other houses; and when the big chimneys were smoking and the sun was setting, the valley looked as if it was filled with golden mist, and the limekilns and oasthouses glimmered and glittered till they were like an enchanted city out of the *Arabian Nights*.

Now that I have begun to tell you about the place, I feel that I could go on and make this into a most interesting story about all the ordinary things that the children did—just the kind of things you do yourself, you know—and you would believe every word of it; and when I told about the children's being tiresome, as you are sometimes, your aunts would perhaps write in the margin of the story with a pencil, 'How true!' or 'How like life!' and you would see it and very likely be annoyed. So I will only tell you the really astonishing things that happened, and you may leave the book about quite safely, for no aunts and uncles either are likely to write 'How true!' on the edge of the story. Grown-up people find it very difficult to believe really wonderful things, unless they have what they call proof. But children will believe almost anything, and grown-ups know this. That is why they tell you that the earth is round like an orange, when you can see perfectly well that it is flat and lumpy; and why they say that the earth goes round the sun, when you can see for yourself any day that the sun gets up in the morning and goes to bed at night like a good sun as it is, and the earth knows its place, and lies as still as a mouse. Yet I daresay you believe all that about the earth and the sun, and if so you will find it quite easy to believe that before Anthea and Cyril and the others had been a week in the country they had found a fairy. At least they called it that, because that was what it called itself; and of course it knew best, but it was not at all like any fairy you ever saw or heard of or read about.

It was at the gravel-pits. Father had to go away suddenly on business, and mother had gone away to stay with Granny, who was not very well. They both went in a great hurry, and when they were gone the house seemed dreadfully quiet and empty, and the children wandered from one room to another and looked at the bits of paper and string on the floors left over from the packing, and not yet cleared up, and wished they had something to do. It was Cyril who said:

'I say, let's take our Margate spades and go and dig in the gravel-pits. We can pretend it's seaside.'

'Father said it was once,' Anthea said; 'he says there are shells there thousands of years old.'

So they went. Of course they had been to the edge of the gravel-pit and looked over, but they had not gone down into it for fear father should say they mustn't play there, and the same with the chalk-quarry. The gravel-pit is not really dangerous if you don't try to climb down the edges, but go the slow safe way round by the road, as if you were a cart.

Each of the children carried its own spade, and took it in turns to carry the Lamb. He was the baby, and they called him that because 'Baa' was the first thing he ever said. They called Anthea 'Panther', which seems silly when you read it, but when you say it it sounds a little like her name.

The gravel-pit is very large and wide, with grass growing round the edges at the top, and dry stringy wildflowers, purple and yellow. It is like a giant's washhand basin. And there are mounds of gravel, and holes in the sides of the basin where gravel has been taken out, and high up in the steep sides there are the little holes that are the little front doors of the little sand-martins' little houses.

The children built a castle, of course, but castle-building is rather poor fun when you have no hope of the swishing tide ever coming in to fill up the moat and wash away the drawbridge, and, at the happy last, to wet everybody up to the waist at least.

Cyril wanted to dig out a cave to play smugglers in, but the others thought it might bury them alive, so it ended in all spades going to work to dig a hole through the castle to Australia. These children, you see, believed that the world was round, and that on the other side the little Australian boys and girls were really walking wrong way up, like flies on the ceiling, with their heads hanging down into the air.

The children dug and they dug and they dug, and their hands got sandy and hot and red, and their faces got damp and shiny. The Lamb had tried to eat the sand, and had cried so hard when he found that it was not, as he had supposed, brown sugar, that he was now tired out, and was lying asleep in a warm fat bunch in the middle of the half-finished castle. This left his brothers and sisters free to work really hard, and the hole that was to come out in Australia soon grew so deep that Jane, who was called Pussy for short, begged the others to stop.

'Suppose the bottom of the hole gave way suddenly,' she said, 'and you tumbled out among the little Australians, all the sand would get in their eyes.'

'Yes,' said Robert; 'and they would hate us, and throw stones at us, and not let us see the kangaroos, or opossums, or blue-gums, or Emu Brand birds, or anything.'

Cyril and Anthea knew that Australia was not quite so near as all that, but they agreed to stop using the spades and go on with their hands. This was quite easy, because the sand at the bottom of the hole was very soft and fine and dry, like sea-sand. And there were little shells in it.

'Fancy it having been wet sea here once, all sloppy and shiny,' said Jane, 'with fishes and conger-eels and coral and mermaids.'

'And masts of ships and wrecked Spanish treasure. I wish we could find a gold doubloon, or something,' Cyril said.

'How did the sea get carried away?' Robert asked.

'Not in a pail, silly,' said his brother. 'Father says the earth got too hot underneath, like you do in bed sometimes, so it just hunched up its shoulders, and the sea had to slip off, like the blankets do off us, and the shoulder was left sticking out, and turned into dry land. Let's go and look for shells; I think that little cave looks likely, and I see something sticking out there like a bit of wrecked ship's anchor, and it's beastly hot in the Australian hole.'

The others agreed, but Anthea went on digging. She always liked to finish a thing when she had once begun it. She felt it would be a disgrace to leave that hole without getting through to Australia.

The cave was disappointing, because there were no shells, and the wrecked ship's anchor turned out to be only the broken end of a pick-axe handle, and the cave party were just making up their minds that the sand makes you thirstier when it is not by the seaside, and someone had suggested going home for lemonade, when Anthea suddenly screamed:

'Cyril! Come here! Oh, come quick! It's alive! It'll get away! Quick!'

They all hurried back.

'It's a rat, I shouldn't wonder,' said Robert. 'Father says they infest old places—and this must be pretty old if the sea was here thousands of years ago.'

'Perhaps it is a snake,' said Jane, shuddering.

'Let's look,' said Cyril, jumping into the hole. 'I'm not afraid of snakes. I like them. If it is a snake I'll tame it, and it will follow me everywhere, and I'll let it sleep round my neck at night.'

'No, you won't,' said Robert firmly. He shared Cyril's bedroom. 'But you may if it's a rat.'

'Oh, don't be silly!' said Anthea; 'it's not a rat, it's *much* bigger. And it's not a snake. It's got feet; I saw them; and fur! No—not the spade. You'll hurt it! Dig with your hands.'

'And let *it* hurt *me* instead! That's so likely, isn't it?' said Cyril, seizing a spade.

'Oh, don't!' said Anthea. 'Squirrel, *don't*. I—it sounds silly, but it said something. It really and truly did.'

'What?'

'It said, "You let me alone."'

But Cyril merely observed that his sister must have gone off her nut, and he and Robert dug with spades while Anthea sat on the edge of the hole, jumping up and down with hotness and anxiety. They dug carefully, and presently everyone could see that there really was something moving in the bottom of the Australian hole.

Then Anthea cried out, '*I'm* not afraid. Let me dig,' and fell on her knees and began to scratch like a dog does when he has suddenly remembered where it was that he buried his bone.

'Oh, I felt fur,' she cried, half laughing and half crying. 'I did indeed! I did!' when suddenly a dry husky voice in the sand made them all jump back, and their hearts jumped nearly as fast as they did.

'Let me alone,' it said. And now everyone heard the voice and looked at the others to see if they had too.

'But we want to see you,' said Robert bravely.

'I wish you'd come out,' said Anthea, also taking courage.

'Oh, well—if that's your wish;' the voice said, and the sand stirred and spun and scattered, and something brown and furry and fat came rolling out into the hole and the sand fell off it, and it sat there yawning and rubbing the ends of its eyes with its hands.

'I believe I must have dropped asleep,' it said, stretching itself.

The children stood round the hole in a ring, looking at the creature they had found. It was worth looking at. Its eyes were on long horns like a snail's eyes, and it could move them in and out like telescopes; it had ears like a bat's ears, and its tubby body was shaped like a spider's and covered with thick soft fur; its legs and arms were furry too, and it had hands and feet like a monkey's.

'What on earth is it?' Jane said. 'Shall we take it home?'

The thing turned its long eyes to look at her, and said: 'Does she always talk nonsense, or is it only the rubbish on her head that makes her silly?'

It looked scornfully at Jane's hat as it spoke.

'She doesn't mean to be silly,' Anthea said gently; 'we none of us do, whatever you may think! Don't be frightened; we don't want to hurt you, you know.'

'Hurt *me*!' it said. '*Me* frightened? Upon my word! Why, you talk as if I were nobody in particular.' All its fur stood out like a cat's when it is going to fight.

'Well,' said Anthea, still kindly; 'perhaps if we knew who you are in particular we could think of something to say that wouldn't make you cross. Everything we've said so far seems to have. Who are you? And don't get angry! Because really we don't know.'

'You don't know?' it said. ' Well, I knew the world had changed— but—well, really—do you mean to tell me seriously you don't know a Psammead when you see one?'

'A Sammyadd? That's Greek to me.'

'So it is to everyone,' said the creature sharply. 'Well, in plain English, then, a *Sand-fairy*. Don't you know a Sand-fairy when you see one?'

It looked so grieved and hurt that Jane hastened to say, 'Of course I see you are, *now*. It's quite plain now one comes to look at you.'

'You came to look at me, several sentences ago,' it said crossly, beginning to curl up again in the sand.

'Oh—don't go away again! Do talk some more,' Robert cried. 'I didn't know you were a Sand-fairy, but I knew directly I saw you that you were much the wonderfullest thing I'd ever seen.'

The Sand-fairy seemed a shade less disagreeable after this.

'It isn't talking I mind,' it said, 'as long as you're reasonably civil. But I'm not going to make polite conversation for you. If you talk nicely to me, perhaps I'll answer you, and perhaps I won't. Now say something.'

Of course no one could think of anything to say, but at last Robert thought of 'How long have you lived here?' and he said it at once.

'Oh, ages—several thousand years,' replied the Psammead.

'Tell us all about it. Do.'

'It's all in books.'

'*You* aren't!' Jane said. 'Oh, tell us everything you can about your-self! We don't know anything about you, and you *are* so nice.'

The Sand-fairy smoothed his long rat-like whiskers and smiled between them.

'Do please tell!' said the children all together.

It is wonderful how quickly you get used to things, even the most astonishing. Five minutes before, the children had had no more idea than you that there was such a thing as a sand-fairy in the world, and now they were talking to it as though they had known it all their lives.

It drew its eyes in and said:

'How very sunny it is—quite like old times. Where do you get your Megatheriums from now?'

'What?' said the children all at once. It is very difficult always to remember that 'what' is not polite, especially in moments of surprise or agitation.

'Are Pterodactyls plentiful now?' the Sand-fairy went on.

The children were unable to reply.

'What do you have for breakfast?' the Fairy said impatiently, 'and who gives it you?'

'Eggs and bacon, and bread-and-milk, and porridge and things. Mother gives it us. What are Mega-what's-its-names and Ptero-what-do-you-call-thems? And does anyone have them for breakfast?'

'Why, almost everyone had Pterodactyl for breakfast in my time! Pterodactyls were something like crocodiles and something like birds—I believe they were very good grilled. You see it was like this: of course there were heaps of sand-fairies then, and in the morning early you went out and hunted for them, and when you'd found one it gave you your wish. People used to send their little boys down to the seashore early in the morning before breakfast to get the day's wishes, and very often the eldest boy in the family would be told to wish for a Megatherium, ready jointed for cooking. It was as big as an elephant, you see, so there was a good deal of meat on it. And if they wanted fish, the Ichthyosaurus was asked for—he was twenty to forty feet long, so there was plenty of him. And for poultry there was the Plesiosaurus; there were nice pickings on that too. Then the other children could wish for other things. But when people had dinner-parties it was nearly always Megatheriums; and Ichthyosaurus, because his fins were a great delicacy and his tail made soup.'

'There must have been heaps and heaps of cold meat left over,' said Anthea, who meant to be a good housekeeper some day.

'Oh no,' said the Psammead, 'that would never have done. Why, of course at sunset what was left over turned into stone. You find the stone bones of the Megatherium and things all over the place even now, they tell me.'

'Who tell you?' asked Cyril; but the Sand-fairy frowned and began to dig very fast with its furry hands.

'Oh, don't go!' they all cried; 'tell us more about it when it was Megatheriums for breakfast! Was the world like this then?'

It stopped digging.

'Not a bit,' it said; 'it was nearly all sand where I lived, and coal grew on trees, and the periwinkles were as big as tea-trays—you find them now; they're turned into stone. We sand-fairies used to live on the seashore, and the children used to come with their little flint-spades and flint-pails and make castles for us to live in. That's thousands of years ago, but I hear that children still build castles on the sand. It's difficult to break yourself of a habit.'

'But why did you stop living in the castles?' asked Robert.

'It's a sad story,' said the Psammead gloomily. 'It was because they would build moats to the castles, and the nasty wet bubbling sea used to come in; and of course as soon as a sand-fairy got wet it caught cold, and generally died. And so there got to be fewer and fewer, and, whenever you found a fairy and had a wish, you used to wish for a Megatherium, and eat twice as much as you wanted, because it might be weeks before you got another wish.'

'And did *you* get wet?' Robert inquired.

The Sand-fairy shuddered. 'Only once,' it said; 'the end of the twelfth hair of my top left whisker—I feel the place still in damp weather. It was only once, but it was quite enough for me. I went away as soon as the sun had dried my poor dear whisker. I scurried away to the back of the beach, and dug myself a house deep in warm dry sand, and there I've been ever since. And the sea changed its lodgings after-wards. And now I'm not going to tell you another thing.'

'Just one more, please,' said the children. 'Can you give wishes now?'

'Of course,' said it; 'didn't I give you yours a few minutes ago? You said, "I wish you'd come out," and I did.'

'Oh, please, mayn't we have another?'

'Yes, but be quick about it. I'm tired of you.'

I daresay you have often thought what you would do if you had three wishes given you, and have despised the old man and his wife in the black-pudding story, and felt certain that if you had the chance you could think of three really useful wishes without a moment's hesita-tion. These children had often talked this matter over, but, now the chance had suddenly come to them, they could not make up their minds.

'Quick,' said the Sand-fairy crossly. No one could think of anything, only Anthea did manage to remember a private wish of her own and Jane's which they had never told the boys. She knew the boys would not care about it—but still it was better than nothing.

'I wish we were all as beautiful as the day,' she said in a great hurry.

The children looked at each other, but each could see that the others were not any better-looking than usual. The Psammead pushed out its long eyes, and seemed to be holding its breath and swelling itself out till it was twice as fat and furry as before. Suddenly it let its breath go in a long sigh.

'I'm really afraid I can't manage it,' it said apologetically; 'I must be out of practice.'

The children were horribly disappointed.

'Oh, *do* try again!' they said.

'Well,' said the Sand-fairy, 'the fact is, I was keeping back a little strength to give the rest of you your wishes with. If you'll be contented with one wish a day amongst the lot of you I daresay I can screw myself up to it. Do you agree to that?'

'Yes, oh yes!' said Jane and Anthea. The boys nodded. They did not believe the Sand-fairy could do it. You can always make girls believe things much easier than you can boys.

It stretched out its eyes farther than ever, and swelled and swelled and swelled.

'I do hope it won't hurt itself,' said Anthea.

'Or crack its skin,' Robert said anxiously.

Everyone was very much relieved when the Sand-fairy, after getting so big that it almost filled up the hole in the sand, suddenly let out its breath and went back to its proper size.

'That's all right,' it said, panting heavily. 'It'll come easier to-morrow.'

'Did it hurt much?' asked Anthea.

'Only my poor whisker, thank you,' said he, 'but you're a kind and thoughtful child. Good day.'

It scratched suddenly and fiercely with its hands and feet, and disappeared in the sand. Then the children looked at each other, and each child suddenly found itself alone with three perfect strangers, all radiantly beautiful.

They stood for some moments in perfect silence. Each thought that its brothers and sisters had wandered off, and that these strange children had stolen up unnoticed while it was watching the swelling form of the Sand-fairy. Anthea spoke first—

'Excuse me,' she said very politely to Jane, who now had enormous blue eyes and a cloud of russet hair, 'but have you seen two little boys and a little girl anywhere about?'

'I was just going to ask you that,' said Jane. And then Cyril cried: 'Why, it's *you*! I know the hole in your pinafore! You *are* Jane, aren't you? And you're the Panther; I can see your dirty handkerchief that you forgot to change after you'd cut your thumb! Crikey! The wish has come off, after all. I say, am I as handsome as you are?'

'If you're Cyril, I liked you much better as you were before,' said

Anthea decidedly. 'You look like the picture of the young chorister, with your golden hair; you'll die young, I shouldn't wonder. And if that's Robert, he's like an Italian organ-grinder. His hair's all black.'

'You two girls are like Christmas cards, then—that's all—silly Christmas cards,' said Robert angrily. 'And Jane's hair is simply carrots.'

It was indeed of that Venetian tint so much admired by artists.

'Well, it's no use finding fault with each other,' said Anthea; 'let's get the Lamb and lug it home to dinner. The servants will admire us most awfully, you'll see.'

Baby was just waking when they got to him, and not one of the children but was relieved to find that he at least was not as beautiful as the day, but just the same as usual.

'I suppose he's too young to have wishes naturally,' said Jane. 'We shall have to mention him specially next time.'

Anthea ran forward and held out her arms.

'Come to own Panther, ducky,' she said.

The Baby looked at her disapprovingly, and put a sandy pink thumb in his mouth. Anthea was his favourite sister.

'Come then,' she said.

'G'way long!' said the Baby.

'Come to own Pussy,' said Jane.

'Wants my Panty,' said the Lamb dismally, and his lip trembled.

'Here, come on, Veteran,' said Robert, 'come and have a yidey on Yobby's back.'

'Yah, narky narky boy,' howled the Baby, giving way altogether. Then the children knew the worst. *The Baby did not know them!*

They looked at each other in despair, and it was terrible to each, in this dire emergency, to meet only the beautiful eyes of perfect strangers, instead of the merry, friendly, commonplace, twinkling, jolly little eyes of its own brothers and sisters.

'This is most truly awful,' said Cyril when he had tried to lift up the Lamb, and the Lamb had scratched like a cat and bellowed like a bull. 'We've got to *make friends* with him! I can't carry him home screaming like that. Fancy having to make friends with our own baby!—it's too silly.'

That, however, was exactly what they had to do. It took over an hour, and the task was not rendered any easier by the fact that the Lamb was by this time as hungry as a lion and as thirsty as a desert.

At last he consented to allow these strangers to carry him home by turns, but as he refused to hold on to such new acquaintances he was a dead weight and most exhausting.

'Thank goodness, we're home!' said Jane, staggering through the iron gate to where Martha, the nursemaid, stood at the front door shading her eyes with her hand and looking out anxiously. 'Here! Do take Baby!'

Martha snatched the Baby from her arms.

'Thanks be, *he's* safe back,' she said. 'Where are the others, and who-ever to goodness gracious are all of you?'

'We're *us*, of course,' said Robert.

'And who's *us*, when you're at home?' asked Martha scornfully.

'I tell you it's *us*, only we're beautiful as the day,' said Cyril. 'I'm Cyril, and these are the others, and we're jolly hungry. Let us in, and don't be a silly idiot.'

Martha merely dratted Cyril's impudence and tried to shut the door in his face.

'I know we *look* different, but I'm Anthea, and we're so tired, and it's long past dinner-time.'

'Then go home to your dinners, whoever you are; and if our chil-dren put you up to this play-acting you can tell them from me they'll catch it, so they know what to expect!' With that she did bang the door. Cyril rang the bell violently. No answer. Presently cook put her head out of a bedroom window and said:

'If you don't take yourselves off, and that precious sharp, I'll go and fetch the police.' And she slammed down the window.

'It's no good,' said Anthea. 'Oh, do, do come away before we get sent to prison!'

The boys said it was nonsense, and the law of England couldn't put you in prison for just being as beautiful as the day, but all the same they followed the others out into the lane.

'We shall be our proper selves after sunset, I suppose,' said Jane.

'I don't know,' Cyril said sadly; 'it mayn't be like that now—things have changed a good deal since Megatherium times.'

'Oh,' cried Anthea suddenly, 'perhaps we shall turn into stone at sunset, like the Megatheriums did, so that there mayn't be any of us left over for the next day.'

She began to cry, so did Jane. Even the boys turned pale. No one had the heart to say anything.

It was a horrible afternoon. There was no house near where the children could beg a crust of bread or even a glass of water. They were afraid to go to the village, because they had seen Martha go down there with a basket, and there was a local constable. True, they were all as beautiful as the day, but that is a poor comfort when you are as hungry as a hunter and as thirsty as a sponge.

Three times they tried in vain to get the servants in the White House to let them in and listen to their tale. And then Robert went alone, hoping to be able to climb in at one of the back windows and so open the door to the others. But all the windows were out of reach, and Martha emptied a toilet jug of cold water over him from a top window, and said:

'Go along with you, you nasty little Eyetalian monkey.'

It came at last to their sitting down in a row under the hedge, with their feet in a dry ditch, waiting for sunset, and wondering whether, when the sun *did* set, they would turn into stone, or only into their own old natural selves; and each of them still felt lonely and among strangers, and tried not to look at the others, for, though their voices were their own, their faces were so radiantly beautiful as to be quite irritating to look at.

'I don't believe we *shall* turn to stone,' said Robert, breaking a long miserable silence, 'because the Sand-fairy said he'd give us another wish to-morrow, and he couldn't if we were stone, could he?'

The others said 'No,' but they weren't at all comforted.

Another silence, longer and more miserable, was broken by Cyril's suddenly saying, 'I don't want to frighten you girls, but I believe it's beginning with me already. My foot's quite dead. I'm turning to stone, I know I am, and so will you in a minute.'

'Never mind,' said Robert kindly, 'perhaps you'll be the only stone one, and the rest of us will be all right, and we'll cherish your statue and hang garlands on it.'

But when it turned out that Cyril's foot had only gone to sleep through his sitting too long with it under him, and when it came to life in an agony of pins and needles, the others were quite cross.

'Giving us such a fright for nothing!' said Anthea.

The third and miserablest silence of all was broken by Jane. She said: 'If we *do* come out of this all right, we'll ask the Sammyadd to make it so that the servants don't notice anything different, no matter what wishes we have.'

The others only grunted. They were too wretched even to make good resolutions.

At last hunger and fright and crossness and tiredness—four very nasty things—all joined together to bring one nice thing, and that was sleep. The children lay asleep in a row, with their beautiful eyes shut and their beautiful mouths open. Anthea woke first. The sun had set, and the twilight was coming on.

Anthea pinched herself very hard, to make sure, and when she found she could still feel pinching she decided that she was not stone, and then she pinched the others. They, also, were soft.

'Wake up,' she said, almost in tears of joy; 'it's all right, we're not stone. And oh, Cyril, how nice and ugly you do look, with your old freckles and your brown hair and your little eyes. And so do you all!' she added, so that they might not feel jealous.

When they got home they were very much scolded by Martha, who told them about the strange children.

'A good-looking lot, I must say, but that impudent.'

'I know,' said Robert, who knew by experience how hopeless it would be to try to explain things to Martha.

'And where on earth have you been all this time, you naughty little things, you?'

'In the lane.'

'Why didn't you come home hours ago?'

'We couldn't because of *them*,' said Anthea.

'Who?'

'The children who were as beautiful as the day. They kept us there till after sunset. We couldn't come back till they'd gone. You don't know how we hated them! Oh, do, do give us some supper—we are so hungry.'

'Hungry! I should think so,' said Martha angrily; 'out all day like this. Well, I hope it'll be a lesson to you not to go picking up with strange children—down here after measles, as likely as not! Now mind, if you see them again, don't you speak to them—not one word nor so much as a look—but come straight away and tell me. I'll spoil their beauty for them!'

'If ever we *do* see them again we'll tell you,' Anthea said; and Robert, fixing his eyes fondly on the cold beef that was being brought in on a tray by cook, added in heartfelt undertones—

'And we'll take jolly good care we never *do* see them again.'

And they never have.

The Troll

by T.H. White

In this strange tale by T. H. White (1906–1964), a son describes his father's terrifying encounter with a troll. The story offers some hints on how to behave when something seemingly ordinary turns out to be horrible.

M y father," said Mr. Marx, "used to say that an experience like the one I am about to relate was apt to shake one's interest in mundane matters. Naturally he did not expect to be believed, and he did not mind whether he was or not. He did not himself believe in the supernatural, but the thing happened, and he proposed to tell it as simply as possible. It was stupid of him to say that it shook his faith in mundane matters, for it was just as mundane as anything else. Indeed, the really frightening part about it was the horribly tangible atmosphere in which it took place. None of the outlines wavered in the least. The creature would have been less remarkable if it had been less natural. It seemed to overcome the usual laws without being immune to them.

"My father was a keen fisherman, and used to go to all sorts of places for his fish. On one occasion he made Abisko his Lapland base, a comfortable railway hotel, one hundred and fifty miles within the Arctic Circle. He traveled the prodigious length of Sweden (I believe it is as far from the south of Sweden to the north, as it is from the south of Sweden to the south of Italy) in the electric railway, and arrived tired out. He went to bed early, sleeping almost immediately, although it was bright daylight outside, as it is in those parts throughout the night at that time of the year. Not the least shaking part of his experience was that it should all have happened under the sun.

"He went to bed early, and slept, and dreamed. I may as well make it clear at once, as clear as the outlines of that creature in the northern sun, that his story did not turn out to be a dream in the last paragraph. The division between sleeping and waking was abrupt, although the feeling of both was the same. They were both in the same sphere of horrible absurdity, though in the former he was asleep and in the latter almost terribly awake. He tried to be asleep several times.

"My father always used to tell one of his dreams, because it somehow seemed of a piece with what was to follow. He believed that it was a consequence of the thing's presence in the next room. My father dreamed of blood.

"It was the vividness of the dreams that was impressive, their minute detail and horrible reality. The blood came through the keyhole of a locked door which communicated with the next room. I suppose the two rooms had originally been designed en suite. It ran down the door panel with a viscous ripple, like the artificial one created in the conduit of Trumpington Street. But it was heavy, and smelled. The slow welling of it sopped the carpet and reached the bed. It was warm and sticky. My father woke up with the impression that it was all over his hands. He was rubbing his first two fingers together, trying to rid them of the greasy adhesion where the fingers joined.

"My father knew what he had got to do. Let me make it clear that he was now perfectly wide awake, but he knew what he had got to do. He got out of bed, under this irresistible knowledge, and looked through the keyhole into the next room.

"I suppose the best way to tell the story is simply to narrate it, without an effort to carry belief. The thing did not require belief. It was not a feeling of horror in one's bones, or a misty outline, or anything that needed to be given actuality by an act of faith. It was as solid as a wardrobe. You don't have to believe in wardrobes. They are there, with corners.

"What my father saw through the keyhole in the next room was a Troll. It was eminently solid, about eight feet high, and dressed in brightly ornamented skins. It had a blue face, with yellow eyes, and on its head there was a woolly sort of nightcap with a red bobble on top. The features were Mongolian. Its body was long and sturdy, like the trunk of a tree. Its legs were short and thick, like the elephant's feet that used to be cut off for umbrella stands, and its arms were wasted: little rudimentary members like the forelegs of a kangaroo. Its head and neck were very thick and massive. On the whole, it looked like a grotesque doll.

"That was the horror of it. Imagine a perfectly normal golliwog (but without the association of a Christie minstrel) standing in the corner of a room, eight feet high. The creature was as ordinary as that, as tangible, as stuffed, and as ungainly at the joints: but it could move itself about.

"The Troll was eating a lady. Poor girl, she was tightly clutched to its breast by those rudimentary arms, with her head on a level with its mouth. She was dressed in a nightdress which had crumpled up under her armpits, so that she was a pitiful naked offering, like a classical picture of Andromeda. Mercifully, she appeared to have fainted.

"Just as my father applied his eye to the keyhole, the Troll opened its mouth and bit off her head. Then, holding the neck between the bright blue lips, he sucked the bare meat dry. She shriveled, like a squeezed orange, and her heels kicked. The creature had a look of thoughtful ecstasy. When the girl seemed to have lost succulence as an orange she was lifted into the air. She vanished in two bites. The Troll remained leaning against the wall, munching patiently and casting its eyes about it with a vague benevolence. Then it leaned forward from the low hips, like a jackknife folding in half, and opened its mouth to lick the blood up from the carpet. The mouth was incandescent inside, like a gas fire, and the blood evaporated before its tongue, like dust before a vacuum cleaner. It straightened itself, the arms dangling before it in patient uselessness, and fixed its eyes upon the keyhole.

"My father crawled back to bed, like a hunted fox after fifteen miles. At first it was because he was afraid that the creature had seen him through the hole, but afterward it was because of his reason. A man can attribute many nighttime appearances to the imagination, and can ultimately persuade himself that creatures of the dark did not exist. But this was an appearance in a sunlit room, with all the solidity of a wardrobe and unfortunately almost none of its possibility. He spent the first ten minutes making sure that he was awake, and the rest of the night trying to hope that he was asleep. It was either that, or else he was mad.

"It is not pleasant to doubt one's sanity. There are no satisfactory tests. One can pinch oneself to see if one is asleep, but there are no means of determining the other problem. He spent some time opening and shutting his eyes, but the room seemed normal and remained unaltered. He also soused his head in a basin of cold water, without result. Then he lay on his back, for hours, watching the mosquitoes on the ceiling.

"He was tired when he was called. A bright Scandinavian maid admitted the full sunlight for him and told him that it was a fine day. He spoke to her several times, and watched her carefully, but she seemed to have no doubts about his behavior. Evidently, then, he was not badly mad: and by now he had been thinking about the matter for so many hours that it had begun to get obscure. The outlines were blurring again, and he determined that the whole thing must have been a dream or a temporary delusion, something temporary, anyway, and finished with; so that there was no good in thinking about it longer. He got up, dressed himself fairly cheerfully, and went down to breakfast.

"These hotels used to be run extraordinarily well. There was a hostess always handy in a little office off the hall, who was delighted to answer any questions, spoke every conceivable language, and generally made it her business to make the guests feel at home. The particular hostess at Abisko was a lovely creature into the bargain. My father used to speak to her a good deal. He had an idea that when you had a bath in Sweden one of the maids was sent to wash you. As a matter of fact this sometimes used to be the case, but it was always an old maid and highly trusted. You had to keep yourself underwater and this was supposed to confer a cloak of invisibility. If you popped your knee out she was shocked. My father had a dim sort of hope that the hostess would be sent to bathe him one day: and I dare say he would have shocked her a good deal. However, this is beside the point. As he passed through the hall something prompted him to ask about the room next to his. Had anybody, he inquired, taken number 23?

"'But, yes,' said the lady manager with a bright smile, 'twenty-three is taken by a doctor professor from Uppsala and his wife, such a charming couple!'

"My father wondered what the charming couple had been doing, whilst the Troll was eating the lady in the nightdress. However, he decided to think no more about it. He pulled himself together, and went in to breakfast. The professor was sitting in an opposite corner (the manageress had kindly pointed him out), looking mild and short-sighted, by himself. My father thought he would go out for a long climb on the mountains, since exercise was evidently what his constitution needed.

"He had a lovely day. Lake Torne blazed a deep blue below him, for all its thirty miles, and the melting snow made a lacework of filigree around the tops of the surrounding mountain basin. He got away from the stunted birch trees, and the mossy bogs with the reindeer in them, and the mosquitoes, too. He forded something that might have been a temporary tributary of the Abiskojokk, having to take off his trousers to do so and tucking his shirt up around his neck. He wanted to shout, bracing himself against the glorious tug of the snow water, with his legs crossing each other involuntarily as they passed, and the boulders turning under his feet. His body made a bow wave in the water, which climbed and feathered on his stomach, on the upstream side. When he was under the opposite bank a stone turned in earnest, and he went in. He came up, shouting with laughter, and made out loud a remark which has since become a classic in my family, 'Thank God,' he said, 'I rolled up my sleeves.' He wrung out everything as best he could, and dressed again in the wet clothes, and set off up the shoulder of Niakatjavelk. He was dry and warm again in half a mile. Less than a thousand feet took him over the snow line, and there, crawling on hands and knees, he came face to face with what seemed to be the summit of ambition. He met an ermine. They were both on all fours, so that there was a sort of equality about the encounter, especially as the ermine was higher up than he was. They looked at each other for a fifth of a second, without saying anything, and then the ermine vanished. He searched for it everywhere in vain, for the snow was only patchy. My father sat down on a dry rock, to eat his well-soaked luncheon of chocolate and rye bread.

"Life is such unutterable hell, solely because it is sometimes beautiful. If we could only be miserable all the time, if there could be no such things as love or beauty or faith or hope, if I could be absolutely certain that my love would never be returned: how much more simple life would be. One could plod through the Siberian salt-mines of existence without being bothered about happiness. Unfortunately the happiness is there. There is always the chance (about eight hundred and fifty to one) that another heart will come to mine. I can't help hoping, and keeping faith, and loving beauty. Quite frequently I am not so miserable as it would be wise to be. And there, for my poor father sitting on his boulder above the snow, was stark happiness beating at the gates.

"The boulder on which he was sitting had probably never been sat upon before. It was a hundred and fifty miles within the Arctic Circle, on a mountain five thousand feet high, looking down on a blue lake. The lake was so long that he could have sworn it sloped away at the ends, proving to the naked eye that the sweet earth was round. The railway line and the half-dozen houses of Abisko were hidden in the trees. The sun was warm on the boulder, blue on the snow, and his body tingled smooth from the spate water. His mouth watered for the chocolate, just behind the tip of his tongue.

"And yet, when he had eaten the chocolate—perhaps it was heavy on his stomach—there was the memory of the Troll. My father fell suddenly into a black mood, and began to think about the supernatural. Lapland was beautiful in the summer, with the sun sweeping around the horizon day and night, and the small tree leaves twinkling. It was not the sort of place for wicked things. But what about the winter? A picture of the Arctic night came before him, with the silence and the snow. Then the legendary wolves and bears snuffled at the far encampments, and the nameless winter spirits moved on their darkling courses. Lapland had always been associated with sorcery, even by Shakespeare. It was at the outskirts of the world that the Old Things accumulated, like driftwood around the edges of the sea. If one wanted to find a wise woman, one went to the rims of the Hebrides; on the coast of Brittany one sought the mass of St. Secaire. And what an outskirt Lapland was! It was an outskirt not only of Europe, but of civilization. It had no boundaries. The Lapps went with the reindeer, and where the reindeer were, was Lapland. Curiously indefinite region, suitable to the indefinite things. The Lapps were not Christians. What a fund of power they must have had behind them, to resist the march of mind. All through the missionary centuries they had held to something: something had stood behind them, a power against Christ. My father realized with a shock that he was living in the age of the reindeer, a period contiguous to the mammoth and the fossil.

"Well, this was not what he had come out to do. He dismissed the nightmares with an effort, got up from his boulder, and began the scramble back to his hotel. It was impossible that a professor from Abisko could become a troll.

"As my father was going in to dinner that evening the manageress stopped him in the hall.

"'We have had a day so sad,' she said. 'The poor Dr. Professor has disappeared his wife. She has been missing since last night. The Dr. Professor is inconsolable.'

"My father then knew for certain that he had lost his reason.

"He went blindly to dinner, without making any answer, and began to eat a thick sour-cream soup that was taken cold with pepper and

sugar. The professor was still sitting in his corner, a sandy-headed man
with thick spectacles and a desolate expression. He was looking at my
father, and my father, with a soup spoon halfway to his mouth, looked
at him. You know that eye-to-eye recognition, when two people look
deeply into each other's pupils, and burrow to the soul? It usually
comes before love. I mean the clear, deep, milk-eyed recognition
expressed by the poet Donne. Their eyebeams twisted and did thread
their eyes upon a double string. My father recognized that the professor was a troll, and the professor recognized my father's recognition.
Both of them knew that the professor had eaten his wife.

"My father put down his soup spoon, and the professor began to
grow. The top of his head lifted and expanded, like a great loaf rising
in an oven; his face went red and purple, and finally blue; the whole
ungainly upperworks began to sway and topple toward the ceiling.
My father looked about him. The other diners were eating uncon-
cernedly. Nobody else could see it, and he was definitely mad at last.
When he looked at the Troll again, the creature bowed. The enormous superstructure inclined itself toward him from the hips, and
grinned seductively.

"My father got up from his table experimentally, and advanced
toward the Troll, arranging his feet on the carpet with excessive care. He
did not find it easy to walk, or to approach the monster, but it was a
question of his reason. If he was mad, he was mad; and it was essential
that he should come to grips with the thing, in order to make certain.

"He stood before it like a small boy, and held out his hand, saying,
'Good evening.'

"'Ho! Ho!' said the Troll, 'little mannikin. And what shall I have for
my supper tonight?'

"Then it held out its wizened furry paw and took my father by the
hand.

"My father went straight out of the dining-room, walking on air. He
found the manageress in the passage and held out his hand to her.

"'I am afraid I have burned my hand,' he said. 'Do you think you
could tie it up?'

"The manageress said, 'But it is a very bad burn. There are blisters all over the back. Of course, I will bind it up at once.'

He explained that he had burned it on one of the spirit lamps at the sideboard. He could scarcely conceal his delight. One cannot burn oneself by being insane.

"'I saw you talking to the Dr. Professor,' said the manageress, as she was putting on the bandage. 'He is a sympathetic gentleman, is he not?'

"The relief about his sanity soon gave place to other troubles. The Troll had eaten its wife and given him a blister, but it had also made an unpleasant remark about its supper that evening. It proposed to eat my father. Now very few people can have been in a position to decide what to do when a troll earmarks them for its next meal. To begin with, although it was a tangible troll in two ways, it had been invisible to the other diners. This put my father in a difficult position. He could not, for instance, ask for protection. He could scarcely go to the manageress and say, 'Professor Skal is an odd kind of werewolf, ate his wife last night, and proposes to eat me this evening.' He would have found himself in a loony-bin at once. Besides, he was too proud to do this, and still too confused. Whatever the proofs and blisters, he did not find it easy to believe in professors that turned into trolls. He had lived in the normal world all his life, and, at his age, it was difficult to start learning afresh. It would have been quite easy for a baby, who was still coordinating the world, to cope with the troll situation: for my father, not. He kept trying to fit it in somewhere, without disturbing the universe. He kept telling himself that it was nonsense: one did not get eaten by professors. It was like having a fever, and telling oneself that it was all right, really, only a delirium, only something that would pass.

"There was that feeling on the one side, the desperate assertion of all the truths that he had learned so far, the tussle to keep the world from drifting, the brave but intimidated refusal to give in or to make a fool of himself.

"On the other side there was stark terror. However much one struggled to be merely deluded, or hitched up momentarily in an odd pocket of space-time, there was panic. There was the urge to go away as quickly as possible, to flee the dreadful Troll. Unfortunately the last train had left Abisko, and there was nowhere else to go.

"My father was not able to distinguish these trends of thought. For him they were at the time intricately muddled together. He was in a whirl. A proud man, and an agnostic, he stuck to his muddled guns alone. He was terribly afraid of the Troll, but he could not afford to admit its existence. All his mental processes remained hung up, whilst he talked on the terrace, in a state of suspended animation, with an American tourist who had come to Abisko to photograph the Midnight Sun.

"The American told my father that the Abisko railway was the northernmost electric railway in the world, that twelve trains passed through it every day traveling between Uppsala and Narvik, that the population of Abo was 12,000 in 1862, and that Gustavus Adolphus ascended the throne of Sweden in 1611. He also gave some facts about Greta Garbo.

"My father told the American that a dead baby was required for the mass of St. Secaire, that an elemental was a kind of mouth in space that sucked at you and tried to gulp you down, that homeopathic magic was practiced by the aborigines of Australia, and that a Lapland woman was careful at her confinement to have no knots or loops about her person, lest these should make the delivery difficult.

"The American, who had been looking at my father in a strange way for some time, took offense at this and walked away; so that there was nothing for it but to go to bed.

"My father walked upstairs on will-power alone. His faculties seemed to have shrunk and confused themselves. He had to help himself with the banister. He seemed to be navigating himself by wireless, from a spot about a foot above his forehead. The issues that were involved had ceased to have any meaning, but he went on doggedly up the stairs, moved forward by pride and contrariety. It was physical fear that alienated him from his body, the same fear that he had felt as a boy, walking down long corridors to be beaten. He walked firmly up the stairs.

"Oddly enough, he went to sleep at once. He had climbed all day and been awake all night and suffered emotional extremes. Like a condemned man, who was to be hanged in the morning, my father gave the whole business up and went to sleep.

"He was woken at midnight exactly. He heard the American on the terrace below his window, explaining excitedly that there had been a cloud on the last two nights at 11:58, thus making it impossible to photograph the Midnight Sun. He heard the camera click.

"There seemed to be a sudden storm of hail and wind. It roared at his windowsill, and the window curtains lifted themselves taut, pointing horizontally into the room. The shriek and rattle of the tempest framed the window in a crescendo of growing sound, an increasing blizzard directed toward himself. A blue paw came over the sill.

"My father turned over and hid his head in the pillow. He could feel the doomed head dawning at the window and the eyes fixing themselves upon the small of his back. He could feel the places physically, about four inches apart. They itched. Or else the rest of his body itched, except those places. He could feel the creature growing into the room, glowing like ice, and giving off a storm. His mosquito curtains rose in its afflatus, uncovering him, leaving him defenseless. He was in such an ecstasy of terror that he almost enjoyed it. He was like a bather plunging for the first time into freezing water and unable to articulate. He was trying to yell, but all he could do was to throw a series of hooting noises from his paralyzed lungs. He became a part of the blizzard. The bedclothes were gone. He felt the Troll put out its hands.

"My father was an agnostic, but, like most idle men, he was not above having a bee in his bonnet. His favorite bee was the psychology of the Catholic Church. He was ready to talk for hours about psychoanalysis and the confession. His greatest discovery had been the rosary.

"The rosary, my father used to say, was intended solely as a factual occupation which calmed the lower centers of the mind. The automatic telling of the beads liberated the higher centers to meditate upon the mysteries. They were a sedative, like knitting or counting sheep. There was no better cure for insomnia than a rosary. For several years he had given up deep breathing or regular counting. When he was sleepless he lay on his back and told his beads, and there was a small rosary in the pocket of his pyjama coat.

"The Troll put out its hands, to take him around the waist. He became completely paralyzed, as if he had been winded. The Troll put its hands upon the beads.

"They met, the occult forces, in a clash above my father's heart. There was an explosion, he said, a quick creation of power. Positive and negative. A flash, a beam. Something like the splutter with which the antenna of a tram meets its overhead wires again, when it is being changed about.

"The Troll made a high squealing noise, like a crab being boiled, and began rapidly to dwindle in size. It dropped my father and turned about, and ran wailing, as if it had been terribly burned, for one window. Its color waned as its size decreased. It was one of those air-toys now, that expire with a piercing whistle. It scrambled over the windowsill, scarcely larger than a little child, and sagging visibly.

"My father leaped out of bed and followed it to the window. He saw it drop on the terrace like a toad, gather itself together, stumble off, staggering and whistling like a bat, down the valley of the Abiskojokk.

"My father fainted.

"In the morning the manageress said, 'There has been such a terrible tragedy. The poor Dr. Professor was found this morning in the lake. The worry about his wife had certainly unhinged his mind.'

"A subscription for the wreath was started by the American, to which my father subscribed five shillings; and the body was shipped off next morning, on one of the twelve trains that travel between Uppsala and Narvik every day."

The Snow Queen

by Hans Christian Andersen
adapted by Amy Ehrlich

Hans Christian Andersen (1805–1875) was 11
years old when his father died. At 14, Hans left
his home in Odense, Denmark for Copenhagen
to find a profession. He eventually discovered
writing, and in 1835 published his first fairy tales.
This story is one of his best.

Long, long ago, when trolls still lived upon the earth,
there was one more evil than all the others. He was called the devil. He
loved to mock human beings, and so he invented a mirror that made
everything that was beautiful and good appear strange and horrid.

At first the trolls only played with the mirror, holding it to the world
and laughing at the reflections. But one day they flew up into the sky
with it, and the mirror spun out of their hands. Down, down, down it
fell, shattering into a million pieces. Some were as tiny as grains of
sand, and when the wind came, it blew the pieces everywhere.

If one of these ever entered a person's eye, nothing looked right
again. But far worse was the fate of someone whose heart was pierced
by a sliver of the mirror. The person would soon forget the pain. He
would go on as before, never knowing that the heart inside him had
frozen into ice.

At a time when the tiniest fragments of the devil's mirror were still
swirling through the air, a boy and a girl lived very near each other in a

big city. The boy's name was Kai, and the girl's name was Gerda. They were good friends and loved nothing better than to play in the window gardens that leaned from the gables of their houses. In the summer they could sit under the rose trees and walk easily from one house to the other.

In the winter, when the windows were tightly closed and covered with ice, Gerda would run down the stairs and through the snowy yard to Kai's house. The two children heated copper coins upon the stove and pressed them to the windows. A perfect small peephole was made in this way, and they could see across the wintry sky.

"The white bees are swarming," said the old grandmother.

"Do they have a queen too?" asked Kai.

The grandmother nodded. "She always stays in the center of the swarm. On snowy nights she flies through the streets of the town and looks in at the windows. Perhaps you have seen the ice patterns she leaves behind."

"Yes, I've seen them!" exclaimed Kai, and then he knew that what the grandmother said was true.

Late that night, as Kai was getting ready for bed, he went to the window and looked out through his peephole. It was snowing softly. As Kai watched, the snowflakes piled one on the other until they took the shape of a woman. She was made of glittering ice. Her eyes shone like two stars, yet neither rest nor peace was in them. She nodded and beckoned to Kai. He jumped back in terror, and in that moment a shadow passed the window as if a great bird had flown by.

It was the last storm of winter. Soon the thaws came and the earth grew green. Once again roses bloomed in the window gardens, and the children were able to sit outside.

Late one afternoon, as the church bells struck the hour, Kai suddenly cried out.

"What is it?" asked Gerda.

"Something pricked my heart," Kai said, and then he gasped again. "Something sharp is in my eye."

Gerda looked into Kai's eyes. There was nothing to be seen, but she cried because she felt sorry for him.

"I think it is gone now," said Kai. But he was wrong. For one splinter of the devil's mirror had entered his eye, and the other had pierced his heart. Instantly he turned on Gerda and began to mock her. "Why are you crying? You look ugly when you cry. There is nothing the matter with me.

"Look!" he shouted. "That rose up there is growing all crooked, and that one has been eaten by a worm. How horrid they are!" Then he tore off the roses and stamped on them.

"What are you doing, Kai?" cried Gerda. And when he saw how frightened she was, he pulled off another flower and climbed through the window into his own house, leaving Gerda to sit outside all alone.

No longer would he consent to play with her. Now his games were more grownup. One winter day when snow was falling, he came by with his sled upon his back and wearing his woolen hat. He screamed into Gerda's ear as loudly as he could. "I have been allowed to go down to the square and play with the older boys!" And away he went without ever looking back.

Now it was the custom in that town for the bigger boys to tie their sleds to the farmers' carts. They would travel fast over the hard, packed snow and get a wonderful ride. While they were playing in this way, a big white sled came into the square and circled it twice. Quickly Kai tied his little sled to the big one. He wanted to show the older boys how daring he was.

Faster and faster they rode. Soon the town was far behind them. Kai wanted to untie his sled, but each time he was about to do it, the driver smiled at him so kindly that he didn't. It was as if they were already friends. The snow fell more thickly. Snowflakes swirled around them, and the sled moved like the wind. Kai was very frightened. He tried to say his prayers, but he could remember only his multiplication tables.

The snowflakes grew and grew until they looked like white hens running near them. At last the big sled stopped and the driver stood up. Kai knew her at once. She was the Snow Queen!

"How cold you look," she said. "Come closer and let me warm you." She put her cloak around Kai and kissed his forehead. Her kiss was like an icy wound, yet at once Kai felt stronger, and he did not notice how cold the air was. As he stared into the Snow Queen's face, he thought he had never seen anyone wiser or more beautiful. The longer he looked, the less he knew, and soon all memory of Gerda and the grandmother vanished.

They set out again, and now they left the earth and were flying in the air. They circled back over his town, but Kai did not even see it. Above oceans, lakes, and mountains they flew, spurred by the wind. He could hear the cry of the wolves and the cawing of the crows. The white moon came out and traveled with them across the sky. When daytime came, Kai slept at the feet of the Snow Queen.

It was a sad, gray winter. As time passed, people in the town began to say that Kai must have drowned in the icy river that ran close to the square where the boys played with sleds. But Gerda could not believe this.

One clear morning in early spring she put on her new red shoes and crept out of the house. Down to the river she went and threw her shoes into the water. "Is it true that you have taken Kai?" she asked the river. "Here are my new red shoes if you will give him back to me."

The shoes struck the water far from shore, but the river carried them back to her as if to say it had not taken Kai. Gerda did not understand. She thought she had not thrown the shoes far enough, so she climbed into a rowboat that was in the reeds and threw the shoes over the water again. Just then the boat drifted with the current, and Gerda found herself floating down the river.

"Perhaps it will carry me to where Kai is," thought Gerda, and she sat perfectly still in her stocking feet. The land along the shores was green and beautiful, and sparrows flew near the boat, chirping as if to comfort her. At last the boat drifted near a cherry orchard and came to rest upon the shore.

An old lady came out of a strange little house nearby and caught hold of the boat with her shepherd's crook. "You poor little thing," she said to Gerda. "Tell me who you are and how you have come to be here."

"I am searching for my playmate," said Gerda, and she told the old woman everything.

"You must not be sad. Your friend will probably pass this way soon. Come and eat my cherries and I will show you all the flowers in my garden." The old woman took Gerda by the hand and led her into the house. The windows were made of colored glass and a strange light shone in the room. On a table stood a silver bowl full of ripe cherries. As Gerda ate them and stayed with the woman, she thought of Kai less and less.

The old woman knew witchcraft, but she was not evil, and she had always wanted a little girl. That evening, when Gerda had fallen asleep, the woman went into the garden and pointed her shepherd's crook at the rose trees. At once they sank into the ground and disappeared. She was afraid that if Gerda saw the roses, she would think of Kai and run away.

In the morning she took the girl outside and showed her the garden. Gerda played in the golden sunshine with the flowers and came to know every one. But always something seemed to be missing, and she could not think what it was.

Many weeks passed and Gerda might have stayed forever, lulled by the old woman's kindness and the beauty of the place. But one day she noticed the painting of a rose on a broad-brimmed hat the woman often wore. At once she leaped up and ran outside. Why were there no roses among all the flowers in the garden? Gerda was so sad that she wept, and where her tears fell, a rose tree suddenly grew up. She breathed in the fragrance of the flowers and thought of the roses at home and of Kai.

"I have stayed here far too long!" she cried. "I must find Kai. Do you know where he is?" she asked the roses.

"He is not dead," they answered. "We have been down under the earth where the dead people are, and Kai was not there."

Gerda ran among the flowers, asking all of them if they had seen Kai. But though the flowers sang to her, they knew only the words to their own songs.

In despair Gerda ran from the garden and unlatched the door in the garden wall. Outside, the earth was cold and gray. Suddenly Gerda realized that it was late autumn. Back in the old woman's garden she had not seen the seasons change. There, it was always summer, and the flowers of every season bloomed at once.

"I have wasted so much time," thought Gerda. "I must not wait here any longer." She walked through fields and forests, though there was frost on the ground and her bare feet stung. The leaves on the trees had turned to yellow, and a cold autumn mist dripped down through their branches. How harsh and sad the world seemed!

Finally Gerda found herself in a dark forest. In the evening it began to snow. Then there was a whoosh of dark wings, and a large crow landed near her. "Caw, caw," he cried.

By this Gerda knew he was greeting her in a friendly way. "Do you know where my friend Kai is?" she asked him.

"Perhaps," said the crow slowly. "There is a castle not far from here and in it lives a princess. Recently she has taken a husband, a young man who is a stranger and is rumored to be afraid of nothing."

Gerda cried out in excitement. "That must be Kai!"

"Well, perhaps," the crow answered. "He is said to have long hair and bright, shining eyes. Many before him had tried to win the princess. But it was the stranger she wanted, because he was far cleverer than all the rest."

"Now I know it is Kai," said Gerda. "He is so clever that he can figure in fractions. Won't you take me to the castle, dear crow? I must see him at once."

The crow looked thoughtfully at Gerda, and then he nodded. "This way," he said. And he rose up into the air and flew ahead of her out of the forest.

As they entered the castle Gerda was nearly faint with longing. She was certain the bridegroom must be Kai. Soon she would see his face. He would smile at her and tell her how happy he was that she had found him at last.

Gerda followed the crow up the back stairs to the bridal chamber.

The castle was dim and quiet. But suddenly there was a whirling, rushing sound, and shadows of horses and hunters of dogs and falcons, moved upon the walls. Gerda drew back fearfully.

"Do not be afraid," said the crow. "They are only dreams come to fetch the princess and her bridegroom. They will be fast asleep, and you will learn if he is the one you seek."

At last they arrived in the royal bedchamber. Gerda peeked at the bridegroom where he lay and saw his long brown hair upon the pillow. "It is Kai!" she shouted with joy. Then the dreams rushed in again, and the young man awoke and looked her in the face.

But it was not Kai, not Kai at all!

With no thought for where she was, Gerda began to weep. "You poor thing," said the prince. "Tell us what is the matter."

As Gerda told them all that had happened, the princess held her close. They said she must spend the night, and in the morning when she awoke, they gave her a silk dress and a pair of boots and a golden coach drawn by four horses. For a time the crow rode with her. But when they came to the edge of the forest, he had to fly away. Gerda waved and waved until she could no longer see his wings shining in the distance. Now she was alone and felt sadder and more desolate than ever.

At length they came to a stand of trees along the roadside. Hidden among them was a band of robbers and the golden coach dazzled their eyes like a flame. "Gold! Gold!" they screamed, flinging themselves upon it. They grabbed hold of the horses and killed the coachman, and then they dragged Gerda out upon the road.

"She is lovely and plump," said an old robber woman. "I think I will have her for supper." She took a long knife from her belt, and her eyes sparkled with greed.

But just as the robber woman was about to slit poor Gerda's throat, her daughter, whom she was carrying upon her back, bit her hard. "No, she is mine. I want to play with her," said the little robber girl. She was a spoiled and willful child, and so the robbers had to give in.

Late that night, when they arrived at the robbers' castle, the girl asked Gerda if she was a princess.

"No, I am not," answered Gerda, and then she told her how she was looking for Kai and had come to be riding in such a fine carriage.

The robber girl looked very seriously at her then and nodded. "I won't allow them to kill you even if I do get angry at you. I will do it myself."

Gerda was very frightened. The walls of the robbers' castle were black with smoke, and ravens flew in and out of the tower. Dogs roamed freely through the halls. They jumped up in the air but they did not bark; that was not permitted.

In the corner where the robber girl slept were all her pet animals. Two wood pigeons were kept in a cage high up in the rafters, and a reindeer stood tied near her bed. "I like to keep them imprisoned," she told Gerda. "It amuses me to see their sorrow."

The little robber girl went to sleep with her knife clutched in her hand, but Gerda was afraid to close her eyes. She did not know if she was going to live or die. In the middle of the night, suddenly one of the wood pigeons cooed. "We have seen Kai. He sat in the Snow Queen's sled and white hens ran near them. She has carried him to a land far to the north. You must ask the reindeer where it is. He will know."

"Oh, yes. Ice and snow are always there. It is a wonderful place," the reindeer said. "There an animal can roam freely in the shining valleys. That is where I was born." Then he grew silent, remembering all he had lost.

In the morning Gerda told the robber girl what she had heard from the animals. The girl listened quite solemnly and then jumped out of bed and hugged Gerda. "I will help you. Leave me your pretty dress and your boots. You shall take the reindeer. He will carry you to your friend."

She tied Gerda onto the reindeer's back and gave her some meat and two loaves of bread. Away they went, as fast as they could, farther and farther north. They heard the wolves howl and the ravens call, and suddenly the sky was filled with great arcs of color. They were the northern lights.

At last they came to a little cottage at the border of Lapland. An old woman came out, and they told her where they were bound. "You must find my friend, the Finnish woman. She will be able to help you," the old woman said. She wrote a note on a piece of dried codfish, and they set out once more.

When they reached the Finnish woman's house, they had to knock on the chimney, for the door was nearly buried under the snow. But inside the house it was as hot as an oven. The Finnish woman gave the reindeer a piece of ice to cool his head and read three times what was written on the codfish.

Poor Gerda was so tired that she fell asleep in the corner. Then the reindeer and the Finnish woman talked together quietly. "You are very wise," the reindeer said. "Can't you make a magic drink so that Gerda will be able to defeat the Snow Queen?"

The woman smiled at him and patted his nose. "I can give her no more power than she has already. Don't you see how people and animals must serve her? Don't you see how she has been able to journey so far, though her feet are bare? No, my friend, Gerda's power is in her heart. Her goodness and innocence are the only weapons against the Snow Queen." She woke Gerda up then and lifted her onto the reindeer's back.

He ran a short way over the snowy earth and set her down beside a bush with red berries. It was at the edge of the Snow Queen's gardens. Gerda looked back at him only once and saw that his face was streaked with tears. Then she followed the path and ran toward the Snow Queen's palace as fast as she could.

Suddenly she saw hundreds of snowflakes. They whirled along just above the earth, growing larger as they came near. Some looked like huge porcupines, others like snakes writhing together; still others were like bears with cruel, grinning faces. All the snowflakes were blindingly white and horribly alive. They were the Snow Queen's army on the march.

Gerda stopped short. Her breath came fast, forming vapor in the frozen air. As she stood there it became more solid and shaped itself into a band of angels armed with shields and spears. They threw their spears at the snow creatures, shattering them into thousands of pieces. There were no more barriers after that, and Gerda was able to walk into the Snow Queen's palace.

The palace walls were glittering ice, and the windows and doors were made of wind. In the glare of the northern lights Gerda could see the gates opening before her. Echoing, vast, and cold was the Snow Queen's palace. Yet Gerda had come so far already and she was not afraid.

She ran through halls of drifted snow that turned and twisted for miles. At last she saw a tiny figure, blue with cold, seated on a frozen lake. As Gerda drew closer she saw that it was Kai. He was playing with pieces of ice, arranging them into patterns. The game was very important because the Snow Queen had promised that if he could form the right word she would give him the world and a new pair of skates. The word was "eternity," but Kai could not remember it no matter how hard he tried.

He did not even look up when Gerda rushed at him and threw her arms around his poor, stiff body. She began to cry, and her hot tears fell upon his heart and melted the ice away. Only then could he see her.

"Gerda, oh, Gerda. Is it really you? Where have you been for so long? What place is this, Gerda? Why is it so cold and empty here?" As he looked around him Kai burst into tears. He wept and wept until the grain of glass in his eye was washed away. Then he held on to Gerda as if he would never let her go.

So glad were they to be together that they never even noticed that the pieces of ice had formed themselves into the word Kai had been trying to make. Now the Snow Queen could return, and it would not matter, for Kai's right to freedom was written upon the frozen lake.

Then Gerda took his hand and they walked out of the Snow Queen's palace. They spoke of the grandmother and of the roses that bloomed in the window gardens. The wind had died down and the sun shone through the clouds. At last they reached the bush where the reindeer was waiting. Now there was a younger one, too, whose udder was full of warm milk for them to drink. Kai and Gerda climbed upon the reindeers' backs and the animals carried them along until blades of grass started to break through the snow.

"Good-bye, good-bye," the children called to the reindeer when they had come to a place where it was early spring. Here they heard birds singing and saw that the trees were all in bud. The towers of their own city were shining in the distance.

Soon they were walking up the stairs to the grandmother's house. Nothing had changed. The clock on the wall was ticking and the wheels inside it moved. But when Kai and Gerda stepped through the doorway, they knew that they had grown up. They were no longer children.

In the window gardens they saw the roses blooming. There were the little stools they used to sit upon. As they went out into the sunshine all memory of the Snow Queen's palace and its empty splendor vanished. There they sat, the two of them, and it was summer, a beautiful summer day.

from

Tom's Midnight Garden

by Philippa Pearce

Philippa Pearce (born 1920) grew up in the English countryside and worked in British television and publishing. Young Tom in this story has been sent to live at his uncle's house while his brother Peter recovers from the measles. When the grandfather clock downstairs strikes 13, Tom is absolutely determined to discover an explanation.

The striking of the grandfather clock became a familiar sound to Tom, especially in the silence of those nights when everyone else was asleep. He did not sleep. He would go to bed at the usual time, and then lie awake or half-awake for hour after hour. He had never suffered from sleeplessness before in his life, and wondered at it now; but a certain tightness and unease in his stomach should have given him an answer. Sometimes he would doze, and then, in his half-dreaming, he became two persons, and one of him would not go to sleep but selfishly insisted on keeping the other awake with a little muttering monologue on whipped cream and shrimp sauce and rum butter and real mayonnaise and all the other rich variety of his diet nowadays. From that Tom was positively relieved to wake up again.

Aunt Gwen's cooking was the cause of Tom's sleeplessness—that and lack of exercise. Tom had to stay indoors and do crossword puzzles and jigsaw puzzles, and never even answered the door when the milkman came, in case he gave the poor man measles. The only exercise he took was in the kitchen when he was helping his aunt to cook those large, rich meals—larger and richer than Tom had ever known before.

Tom had few ideas on the causes and cures of sleeplessness, and it never occurred to him to complain. At first he tried to read himself to sleep with Aunt Gwen's schoolgirl stories. They did not even bore him enough for that; but he persevered with them. Then Uncle Alan had found him still reading at half-past eleven at night. There had been an outcry. After that Tom was rationed to ten minutes reading in bed; and he had to promise not to switch the bedroom light on again after it had been switched off and his aunt had bidden him good night. He did not regret the reading, but the dragging hours seemed even longer in the dark.

One night he had been lying awake as usual, fretting against the dark and against the knowledge that his uncle and aunt would be sitting reading—talking—doing whatever they pleased—by the excellent electric lights of the sitting-room. Here *he* was, wide awake in the dark with nothing to do. He had borne it for what seemed many nights, but suddenly, tonight, he could bear it no more. He sat up, threw his bedclothes back with a masterful gesture, and stepped out of bed, though as yet with no clear purpose. He felt his way over to the bedroom door, opened it quietly and passed out into the tiny hall of the flat.

Tom could hear the sound of the ordered speaking of Uncle Alan, from behind the sitting-room door: he would be reading aloud from his favourite, clever weekly newspaper; Aunt Gwen would be devotedly listening, or asleep.

A moment's thought, and Tom had glided into the kitchen and thence into the larder. This would have been a routine move at home; he and Peter had often done it.

In Aunt Gwen's larder there were two cold pork chops, half a trifle, some bananas and some buns and cakes. Tom tried to persuade himself that he hesitated only because he didn't know which to choose, but he knew that he was not hungry. As a matter of form, he laid hold of a very plain, stale bun. Then, a great weariness of all food overcame him, and he put the bun down, leaving it to another day of existence.

He had been moving all this time in perfect silence—he would have been ashamed for his skill in such an expedition to have done otherwise. But he had ill-luck: as he went out from the kitchen and larder, he came face to face with his uncle coming from the sitting-room. His uncle's exclamation of surprise and disapproval brought his aunt out after him.

Tom knew that he was in the wrong, of course, but they need not have made such a fuss. Aunt Gwen was most upset because, if Tom slipped into the larder at night, that meant he was hungry. She was not feeding him properly. He was suffering from light starvation.

Uncle Alan, on the other hand, had not been unobservant of Tom at mealtimes, and he could not credit his being hungry. Besides, Tom had admitted he took nothing from the larder. Why had he been there, then? Was it a blind? What *was* it?

Tom never really convinced them of the simple truth: that a boy would naturally go into the larder, even if he were not hungry. Anyway, they pointed out, he was out of bed far too late. He was hustled back again, and his uncle stood over him to make a speech.

'Tom, there must be no more of this. You are not to put the light on again once it has been put out; nor, equally, are you to get out of bed. You must see the reasonableness—'

'Not even to get up in the morning?' Tom interrupted.

'Of course, that's different. Don't be silly, Tom. But you are not to get up otherwise. The reason is—'

'Can't I get up, even if I need to, badly?'

'Of course you must go to the lavatory, if you need to; but you will go straight back to bed afterwards. You go to bed at nine in the evening and get up at seven in the morning. That is ten hours. You need those ten hours' sleep because—'

'But, Uncle Alan, I don't sleep!'

'Will you be quiet, Tom!' shouted his uncle, suddenly losing his temper. 'I'm trying to reason with you! Now, where was I?'

'Ten hours' sleep,' said Tom subduedly.

'Yes, a child of your age needs ten hours of sleep. You must realize that, Tom. For that reason, you must be in bed for ten hours, as I have said. I am making clear to you, Tom, that Gwen and I wish you, entirely for your own good, to be in bed and, if possible, asleep for ten hours, as near as maybe, from nine o'clock at night. You understand, Tom?'

'Yes.'

'Now I want you to promise to observe our wishes. Will you promise, Tom?'

Why could a boy never refuse to promise these large demands? 'I suppose so,' said Tom. 'Yes.'

'There!' said Aunt Gwen; and Uncle Alan said: 'Good. I knew I could reason with you.'

'But, all the same, I don't sleep!'

Uncle Alan said sharply, 'All children sleep;' and Aunt Gwen added more gently: 'It's just your imagination, Tom.'

Poor Tom had no answer except contradiction, and he felt that would be unwise.

They left him.

He lay in the dark, planning a letter to his mother. 'Take me away. At once.' But no, that was perhaps cowardly, and would worry his mother dreadfully. He would unburden himself to Peter instead, although Peter, because of his measles, could not reply. He would tell Peter how miserably dull it was here, even at night: nothing to do, nowhere to go, nobody—to speak of—to do things with. 'It's the worst hole I've ever been in,' he wrote, in imagination. 'I'd do anything to get out of it, Peter—to be somewhere else—anywhere.' It seemed to him that his longing to be free swelled up in him and in the room, until it should surely be large enough to burst the walls and set him free indeed.

They had left him, and now they were going to bed. Uncle Alan took a bath, and Tom lay listening to him and hating him. For some reason, Tom could always hear what went on in the bathroom next door to his bedroom as clearly as if he were there himself: tonight he was almost in the bath with Uncle Alan. Later he heard other movements and conversation from elsewhere in the flat. Finally, the line of light under his door disappeared: that meant that the hall-light of the flat had been switched off for the night.

Slow silence, and then the grandfather clock struck for twelve. By midnight his uncle and aunt were always in bed, and asleep too, usually. Only Tom lay still open-eyed and sullen, imprisoned in wakefulness.

And at last—One! The clock struck the present hour; but, as if to show its independence of mind, went on striking—Two! For once Tom was not amused by its striking the wrong hour: Three! Four! 'It's one o'clock,' Tom whispered angrily over the edge of the bedclothes. 'Why don't you strike one o'clock, then, as the clocks would do at home?' Instead: Five! Six! Even in his irritation, Tom could not stop counting; it had become a habit with him at night. Seven! Eight! After all, the clock was the only thing that would speak to him at all in these hours of darkness. Nine! Ten! 'You are going it,' thought Tom, but yawning in the midst of his unwilling admiration. Yes, and it hadn't finished yet: Eleven! Twelve! 'Fancy striking midnight twice in one night!' jeered Tom, sleepily. Thirteen! proclaimed the clock, and then stopped striking.

Thirteen? Tom's mind gave a jerk: had it really struck thirteen? Even mad old clocks never struck that. He must have imagined it. Had he not been falling asleep, or already sleeping? But no, awake or dozing, he had counted up to thirteen. He was sure of it.

He was uneasy in the knowledge that this happening made some difference to him: he could feel that in his bones. The stillness had become an expectant one; the house seemed to hold its breath; the darkness pressed up to him, pressing him with a question: Come on, Tom, the clock has struck thirteen—what are you going to do about it?

'Nothing,' said Tom aloud. And then, as an afterthought: 'Don't be silly!'

What *could* he do, anyway? He had to stay in bed, sleeping or trying to sleep, for ten whole hours, as near as might be, from nine o'clock at night to seven o'clock the next morning. That was what he had promised when his uncle had reasoned with him.

Uncle Alan had been so sure of his reasoning; and yet Tom now began to feel that there had been some flaw in it . . . Uncle Alan, without discussing the idea, had taken for granted that there were twenty-four hours in a day—twice twelve hours. But suppose, instead, there were twice thirteen? Then, from nine at night to seven in the morning— with the thirteenth hour somewhere between—was more than ten hours: it was eleven. He could be in bed for ten hours, and still have an hour to spare—an hour of freedom.

But steady, steady! This was ridiculous: there simply were not thirteen hours in a half day, everyone knew that. But why had the clock said there were, then? You couldn't get round that. Yes, but everyone knew the grandfather clock struck the hours at the wrong times of day—one o'clock when it was really five, and so on. Admittedly, argued the other Tom—the one that would never let the sleepy Tom go to sleep— admittedly the clock struck the hours at the wrong time; but, all the same, they *were* hours—real hours—hours that really existed. Now the clock had struck thirteen, affirming that—for this once at least— there was an extra, thirteenth hour.

'But it just can't be true,' said Tom aloud. The house, which appeared to have been following the argument, sighed impatiently. 'At least, I think it isn't true; and anyway it's muddling.' Meanwhile you're missing your chance, whispered the house. 'I can't honourably take it,' said Tom, 'because I don't believe the grandfather clock was telling the truth when it struck thirteen.' Oh, said the house coldly, so it's a liar, is it?

Tom sat up in bed, a little angry in his turn. 'Now,' he said, 'I'm going to prove this, one way or the other. I'm going to see what the clock fingers say. I'm going down to the hall.'

This was a real expedition. Tom put on his bedroom slippers, but decided against his dressing-gown: after all, it was summer. He closed his bedroom door carefully behind him, so that it should not bang in his absence. Outside the front door of the flat he took off one of his slippers; he laid it on the floor against the doorjamb and then closed the door on to it, as on to a wedge. That would keep the door open for his return.

The lights on the first-floor landing and in the hall were turned out, for the tenants were all in bed and asleep, and Mrs Bartholomew was asleep and dreaming. The only illumination was a sideways shaft of moonlight through the long window part way up the stairs. Tom felt his way downstairs and into the hall.

Here he was checked. He could find the grandfather clock—a tall and ancient figure of black in the lesser blackness—but he was unable to read its face. If he opened its dial-door and felt until he found the position of the clock-hands, then his sense of touch would tell him the time. He fumbled first at one side of the door, then at the other; but there seemed no catch—no way in. He remembered how the pendulum-case door had not yielded to him either, on that first day. Both must be kept locked.

Hurry! hurry! the house seemed to whisper round him. The hour is passing . . . passing . . .

Tom turned from the clock to feel for the electric-light switch. Where had it been? His fingers swept the walls in vain: nowhere.

Light—light: that was what he needed! And the only light was the moonbeam that glanced sideways through the stairway window and spent itself at once and uselessly on the wall by the window-sill.

Tom studied the moonbeam, with an idea growing in his mind. From the direction in which the beam came, he saw that the moon must be shining at the back of the house. Very well, then, if he opened the door at the far end of the hall—at the back of the house, that is— he would let that moonlight in. With luck there might be enough light for him to read the clock-face.

He moved down the hall to the door at its far end. It was a door he had never seen opened—the Kitsons used the door at the front. They said that the door at the back was only a less convenient way to the street, through a backyard—a strip of paving where dustbins were kept and where the tenants of the ground-floor back flat garaged their car under a tarpaulin.

Never having had occasion to use the door, Tom had no idea how it might be secured at night. If it were locked, and the key kept elsewhere . . . But it was not locked, he found; only bolted. He drew the bolt and, very slowly, to make no sound, turned the door-knob.

Hurry! whispered the house; and the grandfather clock at the heart of it beat an anxious tick, tick.

Tom opened the door wide and let in the moonlight. It flooded in, as bright as daylight—the white daylight that comes before the full rising of the sun. The illumination was perfect, but Tom did not at once turn to see what it showed him of the clock-face. Instead he took a step forward on to the doorstep. He was staring, at first in surprise, then with indignation, at what he saw outside. That they should have deceived him—lied to him—like this! They had said, 'It's not worth your while going out at the back, Tom.' So carelessly they had described it: 'A sort of back-yard, very poky, with rubbish bins. Really, there's nothing to see.'

Nothing . . . Only this: a great lawn where flowerbeds bloomed; a towering fir-tree, and thick, beetle-browed yews that humped their shapes down two sides of the lawn; on the third side, to the right, a greenhouse almost the size of a real house; from each corner of the lawn, a path that twisted away to some other depths of garden, with other trees.

Tom had stepped forward instinctively, catching his breath in surprise; now he let his breath out in a deep sigh. He would steal out here tomorrow, by daylight. They had tried to keep this from him, but they could not stop him now—not his aunt, nor his uncle, nor the back flat tenants, nor even particular Mrs Bartholomew. He would run full tilt over the grass, leaping the flower-beds; he would peer through the glittering panes of the greenhouse—perhaps open the door and go in; he would visit each alcove and archway clipped in the yew-trees—he would climb the trees and make his way from one to another through thickly interlacing branches. When they came calling him, he would hide, silent and safe as a bird, among this richness of leaf and bough and tree-trunk.

The scene tempted him even now: it lay so inviting and clear before him—clear-cut from the stubby leaf-pins of the nearer yew-trees to the curled-back petals of the hyacinths in the crescent-shaped corner beds.

Yet Tom remembered his ten hours and his honour. Regretfully he turned from the garden, back indoors to read the grandfather clock.

He re-crossed the threshold, still absorbed in the thought of what he had seen outside. For that reason, perhaps, he could not at once make out how the hall had become different: his eyes informed him of some shadowy change; his bare foot was trying to tell him something . . .

The grandfather clock was still there, anyway, and must tell him the true time. It must be either twelve or one: there was no hour between. There is no thirteenth hour.

Tom never reached the clock with his inquiry, and may be excused for forgetting, on this occasion, to check its truthfulness. His attention was distracted by the opening of a door down the hall—the door of the ground-floor front flat. A maid trotted out.

Tom had seen housemaids only in pictures, but he recognized the white apron, cap and cuffs, and the black stockings. (He was not expert in fashions, but the dress seemed to him to be rather long for her.) She was carrying paper, kindling wood and a box of matches.

He had only a second in which to observe these things. Then he realized that he ought to take cover at once; and there was no cover to take. Since he must be seen, Tom determined to be the first to speak—to explain himself.

He did not feel afraid of the maid: as she came nearer, he saw that she was only a girl. To warn her of his presence without startling her, Tom gave a cough; but she did not seem to hear it. She came on. Tom moved forward into her line of vision; she looked at him, but looked through him, too, as though he were not there. Tom's heart jumped in a way he did not understand. She was passing him.

'I say!' he protested loudly; but she paid not the slightest attention. She passed him, reached the front door of the ground-floor back flat, turned the door-handle and went in. There was no bell-ringing or unlocking of the door.

Tom was left gaping; and, meanwhile, his senses began to insist upon telling him of experiences even stranger than this encounter. His one bare foot was on cold flagstone, he knew; yet there was a contradictory softness and warmth to this flagstone. He looked down and saw that he was standing on a rug—a tiger-skin rug. There were other rugs down the hall. His eyes now took in the whole of the hall—a hall that was different. No laundry box, no milk bottles, no travel posters on the walls. The walls were decorated with a rich variety of other objects instead: a tall Gothic barometer, a fan of peacock feathers, a huge engraving of a battle (hussars and horses and shot-riddled banners) and many other pictures. There was a big dinner gong, with its wash-leathered gong-stick hanging beside it. There was a large umbrella stand holding umbrellas and walking-sticks and a parasol and an air-gun and what looked like the parts of a fishing-rod. Along the wall projected a series of bracket-shelves, each table-high. They were of oak, except for one towards the middle of the hall, by the grandfather clock. That was of white marble, and it was piled high with glass cases of stuffed birds and animals. Enacted on its chilly surface were scenes of hot bloodshed: an owl clutched a mouse in its claws; a ferret looked up from the killing of its rabbit; in a case in the middle a red fox slunk along with a gamefowl hanging from its jaws.

In all that crowded hall, the only object that Tom recognized was the grandfather clock. He moved towards it, not to read its face, but simply to touch it—to reassure himself that this at least was as he knew it.

His hand was nearly upon it, when he heard a little breath behind him that was the maid passing back the way she had come. For some reason, she did not seem to make as much sound as before. He heard her call only faintly: 'I've lit the fire in the parlour.'

She was making for the door through which she had first come, and, as Tom followed her with his eyes, he received a curious impression: she reached the door, her hand was upon the knob, and then she seemed to go. That was it exactly: she went, but not through the door. She simply thinned out, and went.

Even as he stared at where she had been, Tom became aware of something going on furtively and silently about him. He looked round sharply, and caught the hall in the act of emptying itself of furniture and rugs and pictures. They were not positively going, perhaps, but rather beginning to fail to be there. The Gothic barometer, for instance, was there, before he turned to look at the red fox; when he turned back, the barometer was still there, but it had the appearance of something only sketched against the wall, and the wall was visible through it; meanwhile the fox had slunk into nothingness, and all the other creatures were going with him; and, turning back again swiftly to the barometer, Tom found that gone already.

In a matter of seconds the whole hall was as he had seen it on his first arrival. He stood dumbfounded. He was roused from his stupefaction by the chill of a draught at his back: it reminded him that the garden door was left open. Whatever else had happened, he had really opened that door; and he must shut it. He must go back to bed.

He closed the door after a long look: 'I shall come back,' he promised silently to the trees and the lawn and the greenhouse.

Upstairs, again, in bed, he pondered more calmly on what he had seen in the hall. Had it been a dream? Another possible explanation occurred to him: ghosts. That was what they could all have been: ghosts. The hall was haunted by the ghost of a housemaid and a barometer and a stuffed fox and a stuffed owl and by the ghosts of dozens of other things. Indeed, if it were haunted at all, the hall was overhaunted.

Ghosts . . . Tom doubtfully put his hand up out of the bedclothes to see if his hair were standing on end. It was not. Nor, he remembered, had he felt any icy chill when the maid had looked at him and through him.

He was dissatisfied with his own explanation, and suddenly sick of needing to explain at all. It was not as if the hall were of great interest, with or without a maid and all the rest; the garden was the thing. That was real. Tomorrow he would go into it: he almost had the feel of treetrunks between his hands as he climbed; he could almost smell the heavy blooming of the hyacinths in the corner beds. He remembered that smell from home: indoors, from his mother's bulb pots, at Christmas and the New Year; outside, in their flower-bed, in the late spring. He fell asleep thinking of home.

from

The Secret Garden

by Frances Hodgson Burnett

Frances Hodgson Burnett (1849–1924) wrote many books for both children and adults. *The Secret Garden* tells what a young boy named Colin Craven—an invalid since his mother's death—and an orphaned girl named Mary discover in a long-abandoned garden. They are helped by a curmudgeonly gardener named Ben and an unusual boy named Dickon.

One of the strange things about living in the world is that it is only now and then one is quite sure one is going to live for ever and ever and ever. One knows it sometimes when one gets up at the tender, solemn dawn-time and goes out and stands alone and throws one's head far back and looks up and up and watches the pale sky slowly changing and flushing and marvellous unknown things happening until the East almost makes one cry out and one's heart stands still at the strange, unchanging majesty of the rising of the sun—which has been happening every morning for thousands and thousands and thousands of years. One knows it then for a moment or so. And one knows it sometimes when one stands by oneself in a wood at sunset and the mysterious deep gold stillness slanting through and under the branches seems to be saying slowly again and again something one cannot quite hear, however much one tries. Then sometimes the immense quiet of the dark-blue at night with millions of stars waiting and watching makes one sure; and sometimes a sound of far-off music makes it true; and sometimes a look in someone's eyes.

And it was like that with Colin when he first saw and heard and felt the springtime inside the four high walls of a hidden garden. That afternoon the whole world seemed to devote itself to being perfect and radiantly beautiful and kind to one boy. Perhaps out of pure heavenly goodness the spring came and crowded everything it possibly could into that one place. More than once Dickon paused in what he was doing and stood still with a sort of growing wonder in his eyes, shaking his head softly.

'Eh! It is graidely,' he said. 'I'm twelve goin' on thirteen an' there's a lot o' afternoons in thirteen years, but seems to me like I never seed one as graidely as this 'ere.'

'Aye, it is a graidely one,' said Mary, and she sighed for mere joy. 'I'll warrant it's th' graideliest one as ever was in this world.'

'Does tha' think,' said Colin, with dreamy carefulness, 'as happen it was made loike this 'ere all o' purpose for me?'

'My word!' cried Mary admiringly, 'that there is a bit o' good Yorkshire. Tha'rt shapin' first rate—that—tha' art.'

And delight reigned.

They drew the chair under the plum-tree, which was snow-white with blossoms and musical with bees. It was like a king's canopy, a fairy king's. There were flowering cherry-trees near and apple-trees whose buds were pink and white, and here and there one had burst open wide. Between the blossoming branches of the canopy, bits of blue sky looked down like wonderful eyes.

Mary and Dickon worked a little here and there and Colin watched them. They brought him things to look at—buds which were opening, buds which were tight closed, bits of twig whose leaves were just showing green, the feather of a woodpecker which had dropped on the grass, the empty shell of some bird early hatched. Dickon pushed the chair slowly round and round the garden, stopping every other moment to let him look at wonders springing out of the earth or trailing down from trees. It was like being taken in state round the country of a magic king and queen and down all the mysterious riches it contained.

'I wonder if we shall see the robin?' said Colin.

'Tha'll see him often enow after a bit,' answered Dickon. 'When th' eggs hatches out th' little chap he'll be kep' so busy it'll make his head swim. Tha'll see him flyin' backward an' for'ard carryin' worms nigh as big as himsel' an' that much noise goin' on in th' nest when he gets there as fair flusters him so as he scarce knows which big mouth to drop th' first piece in. An' gapin' beaks an' squawks on every side. Mother says as when she sees th' work a robin has to keep them gapin' beaks filled, she feels like she was a lady with nothin' to do. She says she's seen th' little chaps when it seemed like th' sweat must be droppin' off 'em, though folk can't see it.'

This made them giggle so delightedly that they were obliged to cover their mouths with their hands, remembering that they must not be heard. Colin had been instructed as to the law of whispers and low voices several days before. He liked the mysteriousness of it and did his best, but in the midst of excited enjoyment it is rather difficult never to laugh above a whisper.

Every moment of the afternoon was full of new things and every hour the sunshine grew more golden. The wheeled-chair had been drawn back under the canopy and Dickon had sat down on the grass and had just drawn out his pipe when Colin saw something he had not had time to notice before.

'That's a very old tree over there, isn't it?' he said.

Dickon looked across the grass at the tree and Mary looked and there was a brief moment of stillness.

'Yes,' answered Dickon, after it, and his low voice had a very gentle sound.

Mary gazed at the tree and thought.

'The branches are quite grey and there's not a single leaf anywhere,' Colin went on. 'It's quite dead, isn't it?'

'Aye,' admitted Dickon. 'But them roses as has climbed all over it will near hide every bit o' th' dead wood when they're full o' leaves an' flowers. It won't look dead then. It'll be th' prettiest of all.'

Mary still gazed at the tree and thought.

'It looks as if a big branch had been broken off,' said Colin. 'I wonder how it was done.'

'It's been done many a year,' answered Dickon. 'Eh!' with a sudden relieved start and laying his hand on Colin, 'Look at that robin! There he is! He's been foragin' for his mate.'

Colin was almost too late, but he just caught sight of him, the flash of red-breasted bird with something in his beak. He darted through the greenness and into the close-grown corner and out of sight. Colin leaned back on his cushion again, laughing a little.

'He's taking her tea to her. Perhaps it's five o'clock. I think I'd like some tea myself.'

And so they were safe.

'It was Magic which sent the robin,' said Mary secretly to Dickon afterwards. 'I know it was Magic.' For both she and Dickon had been afraid Colin might ask something about the tree whose branch had broken off ten years ago, and they had talked it over together and Dickon had stood and rubbed his head in a troubled way.

'We mun look as if it wasn't no different from th' other trees,' he had said. 'We couldn't never tell him how it broke, poor lad. If he says anything about it we mun—we mun try to look cheerful.'

'Aye, that we mun,' had answered Mary.

But she had not felt as if she looked cheerful when she gazed at the tree. She wondered and wondered in those few moments if there was any reality in that other thing Dickon had said. He had gone on rubbing his rust-red hair in a puzzled way, but a nice comforted look had begun to grow in his blue eyes.

'Mrs Craven was a very lovely young lady,' he had gone on rather hesitatingly. 'An' Mother she thinks maybe she's about Misselthwaite many a time lookin' after Mester Colin, same as all mothers do when they're took out o' th' world. They have to come back, tha' sees. Happen she's been in the garden an' happen it was her set us to work, an' told us to bring him here.'

Mary had thought he meant something about Magic. She was a great believer in Magic. Secretly she quite believed that Dickon worked Magic, of course, good Magic, on everything near him and that was why people liked him so much and wild creatures knew he was their friend. She wondered, indeed, if it were not possible that his gift had brought the robin just at the right moment when Colin asked that dangerous question. She felt that his Magic was working all the afternoon and making Colin look an entirely different boy. It did not seem possible that he could be the crazy creature who had screamed and beaten and bitten his pillow. Even his ivory whiteness seemed to change. The faint glow of colour which had shown on his face and neck and hands when he first got inside the garden really never quite died away. He looked as if he were made of flesh instead of ivory or wax.

They saw the robin carry food to his mate two or three times, and it was so suggestive of afternoon tea that Colin felt they must have some.

'Go and make one of the menservants bring some in a basket to the rhododendron walk,' he said. 'And then you and Dickon can bring it here.'

It was an agreeable idea; easily carried out, and when the white cloth was spread upon the grass, with hot tea and buttered toast and crumpets, a delightfully hungry meal was eaten, and several birds on domestic errands paused to inquire what was going on and were led into investigating crumbs with great activity. Nut and Shell whisked up trees with pieces of cake, and Soot took the entire half of a buttered crumpet into a corner and pecked at and examined and turned it over and made hoarse remarks about it until he decided to swallow it all joyfully in one gulp.

The afternoon was dragging towards its mellow hour. The sun was deepening the gold of its lances, the bees were going home and the birds were flying past less often. Dickon and Mary were sitting on the grass, the tea-basket was repacked ready to be taken back to the house, and Colin was lying against his cushions with his heavy locks pushed back from his forehead and his face looking quite a natural colour.

'I don't want this afternoon to go,' he said; 'but I shall come back tomorrow, and the day after, and the day after, and the day after.'

'You'll get plenty of fresh air, won't you?' said Mary.

'I'm going to get nothing else,' he answered. 'I've seen the spring now and I'm going to see the summer. I'm going to see everything grow here. I'm going to grow here myself.'

'That tha' will,' said Dickon. 'Us'll have thee walkin' about here an' diggin' same as other folk afore long.'

Colin flushed tremendously.

'Walk!' he said. 'Dig! Shall I?'

Dickon's glance at him was delicately cautious. Neither he nor Mary had ever asked if anything was the matter with his legs.

'For sure tha' will,' he said stoutly. 'Tha'—tha's got legs o' thine own, same as other folks!'

Mary was rather frightened until she heard Colin's answer.

'Nothing really ails them,' he said, 'but they are so thin and weak. They shake so that I'm afraid to try to stand on them.'

Both Mary and Dickon drew a relieved breath.

'When tha'stops bein' afraid tha'lt stand on'em,' Dickon said with renewed cheer. 'An' tha'lt stop bein' afraid in a bit.'

'I shall?' said Colin, and he lay still, as if he were wondering about things.

They were really very quiet for a little while. The sun was dropping lower. It was that hour when everything stills itself, and they really had had a busy and exciting afternoon. Colin looked as if he were resting luxuriously. Even the creatures had ceased moving about and had drawn together and were resting near them. Soot had perched on a low branch and drawn up one leg and dropped the grey film drowsily over his eyes. Mary privately thought he looked as if he might snore in a minute.

In the midst of this stillness it was rather startling when Colin half lifted his head and exclaimed in a loud, suddenly alarmed whisper:

'Who is that man?'

Dickon and Mary scrambled to their feet.

'Man?' they both cried in low, quick voices.

Colin pointed to the high wall.

'Look!' he whispered excitedly. 'Just look!'

Mary and Dickon wheeled about and looked. There was Ben Weatherstaff's indignant face glaring at them over the wall from the top of a ladder! He actually shook his fist at Mary.

'If I wasn't a bachelder, an' tha' was a wench o' mine,' he cried, 'I'd give thee a hidin'!'

He mounted another step threateningly, as if it were his energetic intention to jump down and deal with her; but as she came towards him he evidently thought better of it and stood on the top step of his ladder shaking his fist down at her.

'I never thowt much o' thee!' he harangued, 'I couldna' abide thee th' first time I set eyes on thee. A scrawny, buttermilk-faced young besom allus askin' questions an' pokin' tha' nose where it wasna' wanted. I never knowed how tha' got so thick wi' me. If it hadna' been for th' robin—drat him—'

'Ben Weatherstaff,' called out Mary, finding her breath. She stood below him and called up to him with a sort of gasp. 'Ben Weatherstaff, it was the robin who showed me the way!'

Then it did seem as if Ben really would scramble down on her side of the wall, he was so outraged.

'Tha' young bad 'un!' he called down to her. 'Layin' tha' badness on a robin—not but what he's impidint enow for anythin'. Him showin' thee th' way! Him! Eh! tha' young nowt'—she could see his next words burst out because he was overpowered by curiosity—'however i' this world did tha' get in?'

'It was the robin who showed me the way,' she protested obstinately. 'He didn't know he was doing it, but he did. And I can't tell you from here, while you're shaking your fist at me.'

He stopped shaking his fist very suddenly at that very moment and his jaw actually dropped as he stared over her head at something he saw coming over the grass towards him.

At the first sound of his torrent of words Colin had been so surprised that he had only sat up and listened as if he were spellbound. But in the midst of it he had recovered himself and beckoned imperiously to Dickon.

'Wheel me over there!' he commanded. 'Wheel me quite close and stop right in front of him!'

And this, if you please, this is what Ben Weatherstaff beheld and which made his jaw drop. A wheeled-chair with luxurious cushions and robes which came towards him looking rather like some sort of state coach because a young rajah leaned back in it with royal command in his great, black-rimmed eyes and a thin white hand extended haughtily towards him. And it stopped right under Ben Weatherstaff's nose. It was really no wonder his mouth dropped open.

'Do you know who I am?' demanded the rajah.

How Ben Weatherstaff stared! His red old eyes fixed themselves on what was before him as if he were seeing a ghost. He gasped and gazed and gulped a lump down his throat and did not say a word.

'Do you know who I am?' demanded Colin still more imperiously. 'Answer!'

Ben Weatherstaff put his gnarled hand up and passed it over his eyes and over his forehead and then he did answer in a queer, shaky voice.

'Who tha' art?' he said. 'Aye, that I do—wi' tha' mother's eyes starin' at me out o' tha' face. Lord knows how tha' come here. But tha'rt th' poor cripple.'

Colin forgot that he had ever had a back. His face flushed scarlet and he sat bolt upright.

'I'm not a cripple!' he cried out furiously. 'I'm not!'

'He's not!' cried Mary, almost shouting up the wall in her fierce indignation. 'He's not got a lump as big as a pin! I looked and there was none there—not one!'

Ben Weatherstaff passed his hand over his forehead again and gazed as if he could never gaze enough. His hand shook and his mouth shook and his voice shook. He was an ignorant old man and a tactless old man and he could only remember the things he had heard.

'Tha'—tha' hasn't got a crooked back?' he said hoarsely.

'No!' shouted Colin.

'Tha'—tha' hasn't got crooked legs?' quavered Ben more hoarsely yet.

It was too much. The strength which Colin usually threw into his tantrums rushed through him now in a new way. Never yet had he been accused of crooked legs—even in whispers—and the perfectly simple belief in their existence which was revealed by Ben Weatherstaff's voice was more then rajah flesh and blood could endure. His anger and insulted pride made him forget everything but this one moment, and filled him with power he had never known before, an almost unnatural strength.

'Come here!' he shouted to Dickon, and he actually began to tear the coverings off his lower limbs and disentangle himself. 'Come here! Come here! This minute!'

Dickon was by his side in a second. Mary caught her breath in a short gasp and felt herself turn pale.

'He can do it! He can do it! He can do it! He can!' she gabbled over to herself under her breath as fast as she could.

There was a brief, fierce scramble, the rugs were tossed on to the ground, Dickon held Colin's arm, the thin legs were out, the thin feet were on the grass. Colin was standing upright—upright—as straight as an arrow and looking strangely tall—his head thrown back and his strange eyes flashing lightning.

'Look at me!' he flung up at Ben Weatherstaff. 'Just look at me— you! Just look at me!'

'He's as straight as I am,' cried Dickon. 'He's as straight as any lad i' Yorkshire!'

What Ben Weatherstaff did Mary thought queer beyond measure. He choked and gulped and suddenly tears ran down his weather-wrinkled cheeks as he struck his old hands together.

'Eh!' he burst forth, 'th' lies folk tells! Tha'rt as thin as a lath an' as white as a wraith, but there's not a knob on thee. Tha'lt make a mon yet. God bless thee!'

Dickon held Colin's arms strongly, but the boy had not begun to falter. He stood straighter and straighter and looked Ben Weatherstaff in the face.

'I'm your master,' he said, 'when my father is away. And you are to obey me. This is my garden. Don't dare to say a word about it! You get down from that ladder and go out to the Long Walk and Miss Mary will meet you and bring you here. I want to talk to you. We did not want you, but now you will have to be in the secret. Be quick!'

Ben Weatherstaff's crabbed old face was still wet with that one queer rush of tears. It seemed as if he could not take his eyes from thin, straight Colin standing on his feet with his head thrown back.

'Eh! lad,' he almost whispered. 'Eh! my lad!' And then remembering himself he suddenly touched his hat gardener fashion and said, 'Yes, sir! Yes, sir!' and obediently disappeared as he descended the ladder.

★ ★ ★

When his head was out of sight, Colin turned to Mary.

'Go and meet him,' he said, and Mary flew across the grass to the door under the ivy.

Dickon was watching him with sharp eyes. There were scarlet spots on his cheeks and he looked amazing, but he showed no signs of falling.

'I can stand,' he said, and his head was still held up and he said it quite grandly.

'I told thee tha' could as soon as tha' stopped bein' afraid,' answered Dickon. 'An' tha's stopped.'

'Yes, I've stopped,' said Colin.

Then suddenly he remembered something Mary had said.

'Are you making Magic?' he asked sharply.

Dickon's curly mouth spread in a cheerful grin.

'Tha's doin' Magic thysel',' he said. 'It's same Magic as made these 'ere work out o' th' earth,' and he touched with his thick boot a clump of crocuses in the grass.

Colin looked down at them.

'Aye,' he said slowly, 'there couldna' be bigger Magic than that there—there couldna' be.'

He drew himself up straighter than ever.

'I'm going to walk to that tree,' he said, pointing to one a few feet away from him. 'I'm going to be standing when Weatherstaff comes here. I can rest against the tree if I like. When I want to sit down I will sit down, but not before. Bring a rug from the chair.'

He walked to the tree, and though Dickon held his arm he was wonderfully steady. When he stood against the tree trunk it was not too plain that he supported himself against it, and he still held himself so straight that he looked tall.

When Ben Weatherstaff came through the door in the wall he saw him standing there and he heard Mary muttering something under her breath.

'What art sayin'?' he asked rather testily, because he did not want his attention distracted from the long, thin, straight boy figure and proud face.

But she did not tell him. What she was saying was this:

'You can do it! You can do it! I told you you could! You can do it! You can do it! You *can*!'

She was saying it to Colin because she wanted to make Magic and keep him on his feet looking like that. She could not bear that he should give in before Ben Weatherstaff. He did not give in. She was uplifted by a sudden feeling that he looked quite beautiful in spite of this thinness. He fixed his eyes on Ben Weatherstaff in his funny, imperious way.

'Look at me!' he commanded. 'Look at me all over! Am I a hunchback? Have I got crooked legs?'

Ben Weatherstaff had not quite got over his emotion, but he had recovered a little and answered almost in his usual way.

'Not tha'; he said. 'Nowt o' th' sort. What's tha' been doin' with hysel'—hidin' out o' sight an' lettin' folk think tha' was cripple an' half-witted?'

'Half-witted!' said Colin angrily. 'Who thought that?'

'Lots o' fools,' said Ben. 'Th' world's full o' jackasses brayin' an' they never bray nowt but lies. What did tha' shut thysel' up for?'

'Everyone thought I was going to die,' said Colin shortly. 'I'm not!'

And he said it with such decision Ben Weatherstaff looked him over, up and down, down and up.

'Tha' die!' he said with dry exultation. 'Nowt o' th' sort. Tha's got too much pluck in thee. When I seed thee put tha' legs on th' ground in such a hurry I knowed tha' was all right. Sit thee down on th' rug a bit, young Mester, an' give me thy orders.'

There was a queer mixture of crabbed tenderness and shrewd understanding in his manner. Mary had poured out speech as rapidly as she could as they had come down the Long Walk. The chief thing to be remembered, she had told him, was that Colin was getting well—getting well. The garden was doing it. No one must let him remember about having humps and dying.

The rajah condescended to seat himself on a rug under the tree.

'What work do you do in the gardens, Weatherstaff?' he inquired.

'Anythin' I'm told to do,' answered old Ben. 'I'm kep' on by favour—because she liked me.'

'She?' said Colin.

'Tha' mother,' answered Ben Weatherstaff.

'My mother?' said Colin, and he looked about him quietly. 'This was her garden, wasn't it?'

'Aye, it was that!' and Ben Weatherstaff looked about him too. 'She were main fond of it.'

'It is my garden now. I am fond of it. I shall come here every day,' announced Colin. 'But it is to be a secret. My orders are that no one is to know that we come here. Dickon and my cousin have worked and made it come alive. I shall send for you sometimes to help—but you must come when no one can see you.'

Ben Weatherstaff's face twisted itself in a dry old smile.

'I've come here before when no one saw me,' he said.

'What!' exclaimed Colin. 'When?'

'Th' last time I was here,' rubbing his chin and looking round, 'was about two year' ago.'

'But no one has been in it for ten years!' cried Colin. 'There was no door!'

'I'm no one,' said old Ben dryly. 'An' I didn't come through th' door, I come over th' wall. Th' rheumatics held me back th' last two year'.'

'Tha' come an' did a bit o' prunin'!' cried Dickon. 'I couldn't make out how it had been done.'

'She was so fond of it—she was!' said Ben Weatherstaff slowly. 'An' she was such a pretty young thing. She says to me once, "Ben," says she laughin', "if ever I'm ill or if I go away you must take care of my roses." When she did go away th' orders was no one was ever to come nigh. But I come,' with grumpy obstinacy. 'Over th' wall I come—until th' rheumatics stopped me—an' I did a bit of work once a year. She'd gave her order first.'

'It wouldn't have been as wick as it is if tha' hadn't done it,' said Dickon. 'I did wonder.'

'I'm glad you did it, Weatherstaff,' said Colin. 'You'll know how to keep the secret.'

'Aye, I'll know, sir,' answered Ben. 'An' it'll be easier for a man wi' rheumatics to come in at th' door.'

On the grass near the tree Mary had dropped her trowel. Colin stretched out his hand and took it up. An odd expression came into his face and he began to scratch at the earth. His thin hand was weak enough, but presently as they watched him—Mary with quite breathless interest—he drove the end of the trowel into the soil and turned some over.

'You can do it! You can do it!' said Mary to herself. 'I tell you, you can!'

Dickon's round eyes were full of eager curiousness, but he said not a word. Ben Weatherstaff looked on with interested face.

Colin persevered. After he had turned a few trowelfuls of soil he spoke exultantly to Dickon in his best Yorkshire.

'Tha' said as tha'd have me walkin' about here same as other folk— an' tha' said tha'd have me diggin'. I thowt tha' was just leein' to please me. This is only th' first day an' I've walked—an' here I am diggin''

Ben Weatherstaff's mouth fell open again when he heard him, but he ended by chuckling.

'Eh!' he said, 'that sounds as if tha'd got wits enow. Tha'rt a Yorkshire lad for sure. An' tha'rt diggin', too. How'd tha' like to plant a bit o' somethin? I can get thee a rose in a pot.'

'Go and get it!' said Colin, digging excitedly. 'Quick! Quick!'

It was done quickly enough indeed. Ben Weatherstaff went his way forgetting rheumatics. Dickon took his spade and dug the hole deeper and wider than a new digger with thin hands could make it. Mary slipped out to run and bring back a watering-can. When Dickon had deepened the hole, Colin went on turning the soft earth over and over. He looked up at the sky, flushed and glowing with the strangely new exercise, slight as it was.

'I want to do it before the sun goes quite—quite down,' he said.

Mary thought that perhaps the sun held back a few minutes just on purpose. Ben Weatherstaff brought the rose in its pot from the greenhouse. He hobbled over the grass as fast as he could. He had begun to be excited, too. He knelt down by the hole and broke the pot from the mould.

'Here, lad,' he said, handing the plant to Colin. 'Set it in the earth thysel' same as th' king does when he goes to a new place.'

The thin white hands shook a little and Colin's flush grew deeper as he set the rose in the mould and held it while old Ben made firm the earth. It was filled in and pressed down and made steady. Mary was leaning forward on her hands and knees. Soot had flown down and marched forward to see what was being done. Nut and Shell chattered about it from the cherry-tree.

'It's planted!' said Colin at last. 'And the sun is only slipping over the edge. Help me up, Dickon. I want to be standing when it goes. That's part of the Magic.'

And Dickon helped him, and the Magic—or whatever it was—so gave him strength that when the sun did slip over the edge and end the strange, lovely afternoon for them, there he actually stood on his own two feet—laughing.

Dr Craven had been waiting some time at the house when they returned to it. He had indeed begun to wonder if it might not be wise to send someone out to explore the garden paths. When Colin was brought back to his room, the poor man looked him over seriously.

'You should not have stayed so long,' he said. 'You must not over-exert yourself.'

'I am not tired at all,' said Colin. 'It has made me well. Tomorrow I am going out in the morning as well as in the afternoon.'

'I am not sure that I can allow it,' answered Dr Craven. 'I am afraid it would not be wise.'

'It would not be wise to try to stop me,' said Colin quite seriously. 'I am going.'

Even Mary had found out that one of Colin's chief peculiarities was that he did not know in the least what a rude little brute he was with his way of ordering people about. He had lived on a sort of desert island all his life and as he had been the king of it he had made his own manners and had had no one to compare himself with. Mary had indeed been rather like him herself, and since she had been at Misselthwaite had gradually discovered that her own manners had not been of the kind which is usual or popular. Having made this discovery, she naturally thought it of enough interest to communicate to Colin. So she sat and looked at him curiously for a few minutes after Dr Craven had gone. She wanted to make him ask her why she was doing it, and of course she did.

'What are you looking at me for?' he said.

'I'm thinking that I am rather sorry for Dr Craven.'

'So am I,' said Colin calmly, but not without an air of some satisfaction. 'He won't get Misselthwaite at all now I'm not going to die.'

'I'm sorry for him because of that, of course,' said Mary, 'but I was thinking just then that it must have been very horrid to have had to be polite for ten years to a boy who was always rude. I would never have done it.'

'Am I rude?' Colin inquired undisturbedly.

'If you had been his own boy and he had been a slapping sort of man,' said Mary, 'he would have slapped you.'

'But he daren't,' said Colin.

'No, he daren't,' answered Mistress Mary, thinking the thing out quite without prejudice. 'Nobody ever dared to do anything you didn't like—because you were going to die and things like that. You were such a poor thing.'

'But,' announced Colin stubbornly, 'I am not going to be a poor thing. I won't let people think I'm one. I stood on my feet this afternoon.'

'It is always having your own way that has made you so queer,' Mary went on, thinking aloud.

Colin turned his head, frowning.

'Am I queer?' he demanded.

'Yes,' answered Mary, 'very. But you needn't be cross,' she added impartially, 'because so am I queer—and so is Ben Weatherstaff. But I am not as queer as I was before I began to like people and before I found the garden.'

'I don't want to be queer,' said Colin. 'I am not going to be,' and he frowned again with determination.

He was a very proud boy. He lay thinking for a while and then Mary saw his beautiful smile begin and gradually change his whole face.

'I shall stop being queer,' he said, 'if I go every day to the garden. There is Magic in there—good Magic, you know, Mary, I am sure there is.'

'So am I,' said Mary.

'Even if it isn't real Magic,' Colin said, 'we can pretend it is. *Something* is there—*something!*'

'It's Magic,' said Mary, 'but not black. It's as white as snow.'

They always called it Magic, and indeed it seemed like it in the months that followed—the wonderful months—the radiant months—the amazing ones. Oh! the things which happened in that garden! If you have never had a garden, you cannot understand, and if you have had a garden, you will know that it would take a whole book to describe all that came to pass there. At first it seemed that green things would never cease pushing their way through the earth, in the grass, in the beds, even in the crevices of the walls. Then the green things began to show buds, and the buds began to unfurl and show colour, every shade of blue, every shade of purple, every tint and hue of crimson. In its happy days flowers had been tucked away into every inch and bole and corner. Ben Weatherstaff had seen it done and had himself scraped out mortar from between the bricks of the wall and made pockets of earth for lovely clinging things to grow on. Iris and white lilies rose out of the grass in sheaves, and the green alcoves filled themselves with amazing armies of the blue and white flower lances of tall delphiniums or columbines or campanulas.

'She was main fond o' them—she was,' Ben Weatherstaff said. 'She liked them things as was allus pointin' up to th' blue sky, she used to tell. Not as she was one o' them as looked down on th' earth—not her. She just loved it, but she said as th' blue sky allus looked so joyful.'

The seeds Dickon and Mary had planted grew as if fairies had tended them. Satiny poppies of all tints danced in the breeze by the score, gaily defying flowers which had lived in the garden for years, and which it might be confessed seemed rather to wonder how such new people had got there. And the roses—the roses! Rising out of the grass, tangled round the sun-dial, wreathing the tree-trunks, and hanging from their branches, climbing up the walls and spreading over them with long garlands falling in cascades—they came alive day by day, hour by hour. Fair, fresh leaves, and buds—and buds—tiny at first, but swelling and working Magic until they burst and uncurled into cups of scent delicately spilling themselves over their brims and filling the garden air.

Colin saw it all, watching each change as it took place. Every morning he was brought out and every hour of each day, when it didn't rain, he spent in the garden. Even grey days pleased him. He would lie on the grass 'watching things growing,' he said. If you watched long enough, he declared, you could see buds unsheathe themselves. Also you could make the acquaintance of strange, busy insect things running about on various unknown but evidently serious errands, sometimes carrying tiny scraps of straw or feather or food, or climbing blades of grass as if they were trees from whose tops one could look out to explore the country. A mole throwing up its mound at the end of its burrow and making its way out at last with the long-nailed paws, which looked so like elfish hands, had absorbed him one whole morning. Ants' ways, beetles' ways, bees' ways, frogs' ways, birds' ways, plants' ways, gave him a new world to explore, and when Dickon revealed them all and added foxes' ways, otters' ways, ferrets' ways, squirrels' ways, and trouts' and water-rats' and badgers' ways, there was no end to the things to talk about and think over.

And this was not the half of the Magic. The fact that he had really once stood on his feet had set Colin thinking tremendously, and when Mary told him of the spell she had worked, he was excited and approved of it greatly. He talked of it constantly.

'Of course, there must be lots of Magic in the world,' he said wisely one day, 'but people don't know what it is like or how to make it. Perhaps the beginning is just to say nice things are going to happen until you make them happen. I am going to try an experiment.'

The next morning when they went to the secret garden, he sent at once for Ben Weatherstaff. Ben came as quickly as he could, and found the rajah standing on his feet under a tree and looking very grand, but also very beautifully smiling.

'Good morning, Ben Weatherstaff,' he said. 'I want you and Dickon and Miss Mary to stand in a row and listen to me because I am going to tell you something very important.'

'Aye, aye, sir!' answered Ben Weatherstaff, touching his forehead. (One of the long-concealed charms of Ben Weatherstaff was that in his boyhood he had once run away to sea and had made voyages. So he could reply like a sailor.)

'I am going to try a scientific experiment,' explained the rajah. 'When I grow up I am going to make great scientific discoveries and I am going to begin now with this experiment.'

'Aye, aye, sir!' said Ben Weatherstaff promptly, though this was the first time he had heard of great scientific discoveries.

It was the first time Mary had heard of them, either, but even at this stage she had begun to realize that, queer as he was, Colin had read about a great many singular things and was somehow a very convincing sort of boy. When he held up his head and fixed his strange eyes on you, it seemed as if you believed him almost in spite of yourself, though he was only ten years old—going on eleven. At this moment he was especially convincing because he suddenly felt the fascination of actually making a sort of speech like a grown-up person.

'The great scientific discoveries I am going to make,' he went on, 'will be about Magic. Magic is a great thing, and scarcely anyone knows anything about it except a few people in old books—and Mary a little, because she was born in India, where there are fakirs. I believe Dickon knows some Magic, but perhaps he doesn't know he knows it. He charms animals and people. I would never have let him come to see me if he had not been an animal-charmer—which is a boy-charmer, too, because a boy is an animal. I am sure there is Magic in everything, only we have not sense enough to get hold of it and make it do things for us—like electricity and horses and steam.'

This sounded so imposing that Ben Weatherstaff became quite excited and really could not keep still.

'Aye, aye, sir,' he said, and he began to stand up quite straight.

'When Mary found this garden it looked quite dead,' the orator proceeded. 'Then something began pushing things up out of the soil and making things out of nothing. One day things weren't there and another they were. I had never watched things before, and it made me feel very curious. Scientific people are always curious, and I am going to be scientific. I keep saying to myself: "What is it? What is it?" It's something. It can't be nothing! I don't know its name, so I call it Magic. I have never seen the sun rise, but Mary and Dickon have, and from what they tell me I am sure that is Magic, too. Something pushes it up and draws it. Sometimes since I've been in the garden I've looked up through the trees at the sky and I have had a strange feeling of being happy as if something were pushing and drawing in my chest and making me breathe fast. Magic is always pushing and drawing and making things out of nothing. Everything is made out of Magic, leaves and trees, flowers and birds, badgers and foxes and squirrels and people. So it must be all around us. In this garden—in all the places. The Magic in this garden has made me stand up and know I am going to live to be a man. I am going to make the scientific experiment of trying to get some and put it in myself and make it push and draw me and make me strong. I don't know how to do it, but I think that if you keep thinking about it and calling it, perhaps it will come. Perhaps that is the first baby way to get it. When I was going to try to stand that first time, Mary kept saying to herself as fast as she could, "You can do it! You can do it!" and I did. I had to try myself at the same time, of course, but her Magic helped me—and so did Dickon's. Every morning and evening and as often in the day-time as I can remember I am going to say, "Magic is in me! Magic is making me well! I am going to be as strong as Dickon, as strong as Dickon!" And you must all do it, too. That is my experiment. Will you help, Ben Weatherstaff?'

'Aye, aye, sir!' said Ben Weatherstaff. 'Aye, aye!'

'If you keep doing it every day as regularly as soldiers go through drill, we shall see what will happen and find out if the experiment succeeds. You learn things by saying them over and over and thinking about them until they stay in your mind for ever, and I think it will be the same with Magic. If you keep calling it to come to you and help you, it will get to be part of you and it will stay and do things.'

'I once heard an officer in India tell my mother that there were fakirs who said words over and over thousands of times,' said Mary.

'I've heard Jem Fettleworth's wife say th' same thing over thousands o' times—callin' Jem a drunken brute,' said Ben Weatherstaff dryly. 'Summat allus comes o' that, sure enough. He gave her a good hidin' an' went to th' Blue Lion an' got as drunk as a lord.'

Colin drew his brows together and thought a few minutes. Then he cheered up.

'Well,' he said, 'you see something did come of it. She used the wrong Magic until she made him beat her. If she'd used the right Magic and had said something nice, perhaps he wouldn't have got as drunk as a lord and perhaps—perhaps he might have brought her a new bonnet.'

Ben Weatherstaff chuckled and there was shrewd admiration in his little old eyes.

'Tha'rt a clever lad as well as a straight-legged one, Mester Colin,' he said. 'Next time I see Bess Fettleworth I'll give her a bit of a hint o' what Magic will do for her. She'd be rare an' pleased if tli' sinetifik 'speriment worked—an' so 'ud Jem.'

Dickon had stood listening to the lecture, his round eyes shining with curious delight. Nut and Shell were on his shoulders, and he held a long-eared, white rabbit in his arm and stroked and stroked it softly while it laid its ears along its back and enjoyed itself.

'Do you think the experiment will work?' Colin asked him, wondering what he was thinking. He so often wondered what Dickon was thinking when he saw him looking at him or at one of his 'creatures' with his happy, wide smile.

He smiled now, and his smile was wider than usual.

'Aye,' he answered, 'that I do. It'll work same as th' seeds do when th' sun shines on 'em. It'll work for sure. Shall us begin it now?'

Colin was delighted and so was Mary. Fired by recollections of fakirs and devotees in illustrations, Colin suggested that they should all sit cross-legged under the tree, which made a canopy.

'It will be like sitting in a sort of temple,' said Colin. 'I'm rather tired and I want to sit down.'

'Eh!' said Dickon, 'tha' mustn't begin by sayin' tha'rt tired. Tha' might spoil th' Magic.'

Colin turned and looked at him—into his innocent, round eyes.

'That's true,' he said slowly. 'I must only think of the Magic.'

It all seemed most majestic and mysterious when they sat down in their circle. Ben Weatherstaff felt as if he had somehow been led into appearing at a prayer-meeting. Ordinarily he was very fixed in being what he called 'agen' prayer-meetin's', but this being the rajah's affair, he did not resent it, and was, indeed, inclined to be gratified at being called upon to assist. Mistress Mary felt solemnly enraptured. Dickon held his rabbit in his arm, and perhaps he made some charmer's signal no one heard, for when he sat down, cross-legged like the rest, the crow, the fox, the squirrels, and the lamb slowly drew near and made part of the circle, settling each into a place of rest as if of their own desire.

'The "creatures" have come,' said Colin gravely. 'They want to help us.'

Colin really looked quite beautiful, Mary thought. He held his head high as if he felt like a sort of priest, and his strange eyes had a wonderful look in them. The light shone on him through the tree canopy.

'Now we will begin,' he said. 'Shall we sway backwards and forwards, Mary, as if we were dervishes?'

'I canna' do no swayin' back'ard and for'ard,' said Ben Weatherstaff. 'I've got th' rheumatics.'

'The Magic will take them away,' said Colin in a High Priest tone, 'but we won't stay until it has done it. We will only chant.'

'I canna' do no chantin',' said Ben Weathstaff, a trifle testily. 'They turned me out o' th' church choir th' only time I ever tried it.'

No one smiled. They were all too much in earnest. Colin's face was not even crossed by a shadow. He was thinking only of the Magic.

'Then I will chant,' he said. And he began, looking like a strange boy spirit. 'The sun is shining—the sun is shining. That is the Magic. The flowers are growing—the roots are stirring. That is the Magic. Being alive is the Magic—being strong is the Magic. The Magic is in me—the Magic is in me. It is in me—it is in me. It's in every one of us. It's in Ben Weatherstaff's back. Magic! Magic! Come and help!' He said it a great many times—not a thousand times, but quite a goodly number. Mary listened entranced. She felt as if it were at once queer and beautiful and she wanted him to go on and on. Ben Weatherstaff began to feel soothed into a sort of dream which was quite agreeable. The humming of the bees in the blossoms mingled with the chanting voice and drowsily melted into a doze. Dickon sat cross-legged with his rabbit asleep on his arm and a hand resting on the lamb's back. Soot had pushed away a squirrel and huddled close to him on his shoulder; the grey film dropped over his eyes. At last Colin stopped.

'Now I am going to walk round the garden,' he announced.

Ben Weatherstaff's head had just dropped forward and he lifted it with a jerk.

'You have been asleep,' said Colin.

'Nowt o' th' sort,' mumbled Ben. 'Th' sermon was good enow—but I'm bound to get out afore th' collection.'

He was not quite awake yet.

'You're not in church,' said Colin.

'Not me,' said Ben, straightening himself. 'Who said I were? I heard every bit of it. You said th' Magic was in in my back. Th' doctor calls it rheumatics.'

The rajah waved his hand.

'That was the wrong Magic,' he said. 'You will get better. You have my permission to go to your work. But come back tomorrow.'

'I'd like to see thee walk round the garden,' grunted Ben.

It was not an unfriendly grunt, but it was a grunt. In fact, being a stubborn old party and not having entire faith in Magic, he made up his mind that if he were sent away he would climb his ladder and look over the wall so that he might be ready to hobble back if there were any stumbling.

The rajah did not object to his staying, and so the procession was formed. It really did look like a procession. Colin was at its head with Dickon on one side and Mary on the other. Ben Weatherstaff walked behind, and the 'creatures' trailed after them, the lamb and the fox cub keeping close to Dickon, the white rabbit hopping along or stopping to nibble and Soot following with the solemnity of a person who felt himself in charge.

It was a procession which moved slowly, but with dignity. Every few yards it stopped to rest. Colin leaned on Dickon's arm and privately Ben Weatherstaff kept a sharp look-out but now and then Colin took his hand from its support and walked a few steps alone. His head was held up all the time and he looked very grand.

'The Magic is in me!' he kept saying. 'The Magic is making me strong! I can feel it! I can feel it!'

It seemed very certain that something was upholding and uplifting him. He sat on the seats in the alcoves and once or twice he sat down on the grass and several times he paused in the path and leaned on Dickon, but he would not give up until he had gone all round the garden. When he returned to the canopy tree his cheeks were flushed and he looked triumphant.

'I did it! The Magic worked!' he cried. 'That is my first scientific discovery.'

'What will Dr Craven say?' broke out Mary.

'He won't say anything,' Colin answered, 'because he will not be told. This is to be the biggest secret of all. No one is to know anything about it until I have grown so strong that I can walk and run like any other boy. I shall come here every day in my chair and I shall be taken back in it. I won't have people whispering and asking questions and I won't let my father hear about it until the experiment has quite succeeded. Then some time when he comes back to Misselthwaite I shall just walk into his study and say: "Here I am. I am like any other boy. I am quite well and I shall live to be a man. It has been done by a scientific experiment".'

'He will think he is in a dream,' cried Mary. 'He won't believe his eyes.'

Colin flushed triumphantly. He had made himself believe that he was going to get well, which was really more than half the battle, if he had been aware of it. And the thought which stimulated him more than any other was this imagining what his father would look like when he saw that he had a son who was as straight and strong as other fathers' sons. One of his darkest miseries in the unhealthy, morbid past days had been his hatred of being a sickly, weak-backed boy, whose father was afraid to look at him.

'He'll be obliged to believe them,' he said. 'One of the things I am going to do, after the Magic works and before I begin to make scientific discoveries, is to be an athlete.'

'We shall have thee takin' to boxin' in a week or so,' said Ben Weatherstaff. 'Tha'lt end wi' winnin' th' Belt an' bein' champion prize-fighter of all England.'

Colin fixed his eyes on him sternly.

'Weatherstaff,' he said, 'that is disrespectful. You must not take liberties because you are in the secret. However much the Magic works, I shall not be a prize-fighter. I shall be a Scientific Discoverer.'

from

Beowulf

translated by Seamus Heaney

Someone (no one knows who) composed this epic poem in England a very long time ago— around the 8th century A.D. *Beowulf* tells the story of a Scandinavian hero who saves the Danes from the fearsome monster Grendel and later fights a terrible dragon. It just may be that the mysterious author of this great poem was describing something that really happened. These verses tell us about Beowulf's confrontation with the dragon.

Beowulf spoke, made a formal boast
for the last time. "I risked my life
often when I was young. Now I am old,
but as king of the people I shall pursue this fight
for the glory of winning, if the evil one will only
abandon his earth-fort and face me in the open."

Then he addressed each dear companion
one final time, those fighters in their helmets,
resolute and high-born: "I would rather not
use a weapon if I knew another way
to grapple with the dragon and make good my boast
as I did against Grendel in days gone by.
But I shall be meeting molten venom
in the fire he breathes, so I go forth
in mail-shirt and shield. I won't shift a foot
when I meet the cave-guard: what occurs on the wall

between the two of us will turn out as fate,
overseer of men, decides. I am resolved.
I scorn further words against this sky-borne foe.

"Men at arms, remain here on the barrow,
safe in your armour, to see which one of us
is better in the end at bearing wounds
in a deadly fray. This fight is not yours,
nor is it up to any man except me
to measure his strength against the monster
or to prove his worth. I shall win the gold
by my courage, or else mortal combat,
doom of battle, will bear your lord away."

Then he drew himself up beside his shield.
The fabled warrior in his warshirt and helmet
trusted in his own strength entirely
and went under the crag. No coward path.
Hard by the rock-face that hale veteran,
a good man who had gone repeatedly
into combat and danger and come through,
saw a stone arch and a gushing stream
that burst from the barrow, blazing and wafting
a deadly heat. It would be hard to survive
unscathed near the hoard, to hold firm
against the dragon in those flaming depths.
Then he gave a shout. The lord of the Geats
unburdened his breast and broke out
in a storm of anger. Under grey stone
his voice challenged and resounded clearly.
Hate was ignited. The hoard-guard recognized
a human voice, the time was over
for peace and parleying. Pouring forth
in a hot battle-fume, the breath of the monster

burst from the rock. There was a rumble under ground.
Down there in the barrow, Beowulf the warrior
lifted his shield: the outlandish thing
writhed and convulsed and viciously
turned on the king, whose keen-edged sword,
an heirloom inherited by ancient right,
was already in his hand. Roused to a fury,
each antagonist struck terror in the other.
Unyielding, the lord of his people loomed
by his tall shield, sure of his ground,
while the serpent looped and unleashed itself.
Swaddled in flames, it came gliding and flexing
and racing towards its fate. Yet his shield defended
the renowned leader's life and limb
for a shorter time than he meant it to:
that final day was the first time
when Beowulf fought and fate denied him
glory in battle. So the king of the Geats
raised his hand and struck hard
at the enamelled scales, but scarcely cut through:
the blade flashed and slashed yet the blow
was far less powerful than the hard-pressed king
had need of at that moment. The mound-keeper
went into a spasm and spouted deadly flames:
when he felt the stroke, battle-fire
billowed and spewed. Beowulf was foiled
of a glorious victory. The glittering sword,
infallible before that day,
failed when he unsheathed it, as it never should have.
For the son of Ecgtheow, it was no easy thing
to have to give ground like that and go
unwillingly to inhabit another home
in a place beyond; so every man must yield
the leasehold of his days.

                              Before long
the fierce contenders clashed again.
The hoard-guard took heart, inhaled and swelled up
and got a new wind; he who had once ruled
was furled in fire and had to face the worst.
No help or backing was to be had then
from his high-born comrades; that hand-picked troop
broke ranks and ran for their lives
to the safety of the wood. But within one heart
sorrow welled up: in a man of worth
the claims of kinship cannot be denied.

His name was Wiglaf, a son of Weohstan's,
a well-regarded Shylfing warrior
related to Aelfhere. When he saw his lord
tormented by the heat of his scalding helmet,
he remembered the bountiful gifts bestowed on him,
how well he lived among the Waegmundings,
the freehold he inherited from his father before him.
He could not hold back: one hand brandished
the yellow-timbered shield, the other drew his sword—
an ancient blade that was said to have belonged
to Eanmund, the son of Ohthere, the one
Weohstan had slain when he was an exile without friends.
He carried the arms to the victim's kinfolk,
the burnished helmet, the webbed chain-mail
and that relic of the giants. But Onela returned
the weapons to him, rewarded Weohstan
with Eanmund's war-gear. He ignored the blood-feud,
the fact that Eanmund was his brother's son.

Weohstan kept that war-gear for a lifetime,
the sword and the mail-shirt, until it was the son's turn
to follow his father and perform his part.

Then, in old age, at the end of his days
among the Weather-Geats, he bequeathed to Wiglaf
innumerable weapons.

                        And now the youth
was to enter the line of battle with his lord,
his first time to be tested as a fighter.
His spirit did not break and the ancestral blade
would keep its edge, as the dragon discovered
as soon as they came together in the combat.

Sad at heart, addressing his companions,
Wiglaf spoke wise and fluent words:
"I remember that time when mead was flowing,
how we pledged loyalty to our lord in the hall,
promised our ring-giver we would be worth our price,
make good the gift of the war-gear,
those swords and helmets, as and when
his need required it. He picked us out
from the army deliberately, honoured us and judged us
fit for this action, made me these lavish gifts—
and all because he considered us the best
of his arms-bearing thanes. And now, although
he wanted this challenge to be one he'd face
by himself alone—the shepherd of our land,
a man unequalled in the quest for glory
and a name for daring—now the day has come
when this lord we serve needs sound men
to give him their support. Let us go to him,
help our leader through the hot flame
and dread of the fire. As God is my witness,
I would rather my body were robed in the same
burning blaze as my gold-giver's body
than go back home bearing arms.
That is unthinkable, unless we have first
slain the foe and defended the life

of the prince of the Weather-Geats. I well know
the things he has done for us deserve better.
Should he alone be left exposed
to fall in battle? We must bond together,
shield and helmet, mail-shirt and sword."
Then he waded the dangerous reek and went
under arms to his lord, saying only:
"Go on, dear Beowulf, do everything
you said you would when you were still young
and vowed you would never let your name and fame
be dimmed while you lived. Your deeds are famous,
so stay resolute, my lord, defend your life now
with the whole of your strength. I shall stand by you."

After those words, a wildness rose
in the dragon again and drove it to attack,
heaving up fire, hunting for enemies,
the humans it loathed. Flames lapped the shield,
charred it to the boss, and the body armour
on the young warrior was useless to him.
But Wiglaf did well under the wide rim
Beowulf shared with him once his own had shattered
in sparks and ashes.
                                    Inspired again
by the thought of glory, the war-king threw
his whole strength behind a sword-stroke
and connected with the skull. And Naegling snapped.
Beowulf's ancient iron-grey sword
let him down in the fight. It was never his fortune
to be helped in combat by the cutting edge
of weapons made of iron. When he wielded a sword,
no matter how blooded and hard-edged the blade
his hand was too strong, the stroke he dealt
(I have heard) would ruin it. He could reap no advantage.

★ ★ ★

Then the bane of that people, the fire-breathing dragon,
was mad to attack for a third time.
When a chance came, he caught the hero
in a rush of flame and clamped sharp fangs
into his neck. Beowulf's body
ran wet with his life-blood: it came welling out.

Next thing, they say, the noble son of Weohstan
saw the king in danger at his side
and displayed his inborn bravery and strength.
He left the head alone, but his fighting hand
was burned when he came to his kinsman's aid.
He lunged at the enemy lower down
so that his decorated sword sank into its belly
and the flames grew weaker.
                              Once again the king
gathered his strength and drew a stabbing knife
he carried on his belt, sharpened for battle.
He stuck it deep into the dragon's flank.
Beowulf dealt it a deadly wound.
They had killed the enemy, courage quelled his life;
that pair of kinsmen, partners in nobility,
had destroyed the foe. So every man should act,
be at hand when needed; but now, for the king,
this would be the last of his many labours
and triumphs in the world.
                              Then the wound
dealt by the ground-burner earlier began
to scald and swell; Beowulf discovered
deadly poison suppurating inside him,
surges of nausea, and so, in his wisdom,
the prince realized his state and struggled
towards a seat on the rampart. He steadied his gaze
on those gigantic stones, saw how the earthwork
was braced with arches built over columns.

And now that thane unequalled for goodness
with his own hands washed his lord's wounds,
swabbed the weary prince with water,
bathed him clean, unbuckled his helmet.

Beowulf spoke: in spite of his wounds,
mortal wounds, he still spoke
for he well knew his days in the world
had been lived out to the end: his allotted time
was drawing to a close, death was very near.

"Now is the time when I would have wanted
to bestow this armour on my own son,
had it been my fortune to have fathered an heir
and live on in his flesh. For fifty years
I ruled this nation. No king
of any neighbouring clan would dare
face me with troops, none had the power
to intimidate me. I took what came,
cared for and stood by things in my keeping,
never fomented quarrels, never
swore to a lie. All this consoles me,
doomed as I am and sickening for death;
because of my right ways, the Ruler of mankind
need never blame me when the breath leaves my body
for murder of kinsmen. Go now quickly,
dearest Wiglaf, under the grey stone
where the dragon is laid out, lost to his treasure;
hurry to feast your eyes on the hoard.
Away you go: I want to examine
that ancient gold, gaze my fill
on those garnered jewels; my going will be easier
for having seen the treasure, a less troubled letting-go
of the life and lordship I have long maintained."

★ ★ ★

And so, I have heard, the son of Weohstan
quickly obeyed the command of his languishing
war-weary lord; he went in his chain-mail
under the rock-piled roof of the barrow,
exulting in his triumph, and saw beyond the seat
a treasure-trove of astonishing richness,
wall-hangings that were a wonder to behold,
glittering gold spread across the ground,
the old dawn-scorching serpent's den
packed with goblets and vessels from the past,
tarnished and corroding. Rusty helmets
all eaten away. Armbands everywhere,
artfully wrought. How easily treasure
buried in the ground, gold hidden
however skilfully, can escape from any man!

And he saw too a standard, entirely of gold,
hanging high over the hoard,
a masterpiece of filigree; it glowed with light
so he could make out the ground at his feet
and inspect the valuables. Of the dragon there was no
remaining sign: the sword had despatched him.
Then, the story goes, a certain man
plundered the hoard in that immemorial howe,
filled his arms with flagons and plates,
anything he wanted; and took the standard also,
most brilliant of banners.
                                    Already the blade
of the old king's sharp killing-sword
had done its worst: the one who had for long
minded the hoard, hovering over gold,
unleashing fire, surging forth
midnight after midnight, had been mown down.

Wiglaf went quickly, keen to get back,

excited by the treasure. Anxiety weighed
on his brave heart—he was hoping he would find
the leader of the Geats alive where he had left him
helpless, earlier, on the open ground.
So he came to the place, carrying the treasure,
and found his lord bleeding profusely,
his life at an end; again he began
to swab his body. The beginnings of an utterance
broke out from the king's breast-cage.
The old lord gazed sadly at the gold.

"To the everlasting Lord of All,
to the King of Glory, I give thanks
that I behold this treasure here in front of me,
that I have been allowed to leave my people
so well endowed on the day I die.
Now that I have bartered my last breath
to own this fortune, it is up to you
to look after their needs. I can hold out no longer.
Order my troop to construct a barrow
on a headland on the coast, after my pyre has cooled.
It will loom on the horizon at Hronesness
and be a reminder among my people—
so that in coming times crews under sail
will call it Beowulf's Barrow, as they steer
ships across the wide and shrouded waters."

Then the king in his great-heartedness unclasped
the collar of gold from his neck and gave it
to the young thane, telling him to use
it and the warshirt and the gilded helmet well.

"You are the last of us, the only one left
of the Waegmundings. Fate swept us away,
sent my whole brave high-born clan

to their final doom. Now I must follow them."
That was the warrior's last word.
He had no more to confide. The furious heat
of the pyre would assail him. His soul fled from his breast
to its destined place among the steadfast ones.

It was hard then on the young hero,
having to watch the one he held so dear
there on the ground, going through
his death agony. The dragon from underearth,
his nightmarish destroyer, lay destroyed as well,
utterly without life. No longer would his snakefolds
ply themselves to safeguard hidden gold.
Hard-edged blades, hammered out
and keenly filed, had finished him
so that the sky-roamer lay there rigid,
brought low beside the treasure-lodge.

Never again would he glitter and glide
and show himself off in midnight air,
exulting in his riches: he fell to earth
through the battle-strength in Beowulf's arm.
There were few, indeed, as far as I have heard,
big and brave as they may have been,
few who would have held out if they had had to face
the outpourings of that poison-breather
or gone foraging on the ring-hall floor
and found the deep barrow-dweller
on guard and awake.
                          The treasure had been won,
bought and paid for by Beowulf's death.
Both had reached the end of the road
through the life they had been lent.

                          ★ ★ ★

                        Before long
the battle-dodgers abandoned the wood,
the ones who had let down their lord earlier,
the tail-turners, ten of them together.
When he needed them most, they had made off.
Now they were ashamed and came behind shields,
in their battle-outfits, to where the old man lay.
They watched Wiglaf, sitting worn out,
a comrade shoulder to shoulder with his lord,
trying in vain to bring him round with water.
Much as he wanted to, there was no way
he could preserve his lord's life on earth
or alter in the least the Almighty's will.
What God judged right would rule what happened
to every man, as it does to this day.

from

The Lion, the Witch and
the Wardrobe

by C.S. Lewis

Once there were four children whose names
were Peter, Susan, Edmund and Lucy. This story is about something
that happened to them when they were sent away from London during
the war because of the air-raids. They were sent to the house of an old
Professor who lived in the heart of the country, ten miles from the
nearest railway station and two miles from the nearest post office. He
had no wife and he lived in a very large house with a housekeeper
called Mrs. Macready and three servants. (Their names were Ivy,
Margaret and Betty, but they do not come into the story much.) He
himself was a very old man with shaggy white hair, which grew over
most of his face as well as on his head, and they liked him almost at
once; but on the first evening when he came out to meet them at the
front door he was so odd-looking that Lucy (who was the youngest)
was a little afraid of him, and Edmund (who was the next youngest)
wanted to laugh and had to keep on pretending he was blowing his
nose to hide it.

As soon as they had said good night to the Professor and gone upstairs on the first night, the boys came into the girls' room and they all talked it over.

"We've fallen on our feet and no mistake," said Peter. "This is going to be perfectly splendid. That old chap will let us do anything we like."

"I think he's an old dear," said Susan.

"Oh, come off it!" said Edmund, who was tired and pretending not to be tired, which always made him bad-tempered. "Don't go on talking like that."

"Like what?" said Susan; "and anyway, it's time you were in bed."

"Trying to talk like Mother," said Edmund. "And who are you to say when I'm to go to bed? Go to bed yourself."

"Hadn't we all better go to bed?" said Lucy. "There's sure to be a row if we're heard talking here."

"No there won't," said Peter. "I tell you this is the sort of house where no one's going to mind what we do. Anyway, they won't hear us. It's about ten minutes' walk from here down to that dining room, and any amount of stairs and passages in between."

"What's that noise?" said Lucy suddenly. It was a far larger house than she had ever been in before and the thought of all those long passages and rows of doors leading into empty rooms was beginning to make her feel a little creepy.

"It's only a bird, silly," said Edmund.

"It's an owl," said Peter. "This is going to be a wonderful place for birds. I shall go to bed now. I say, let's go and explore to-morrow. You might find anything in a place like this. Did you see those mountains as we came along? And the woods? There might be eagles. There might be stags. There'll be hawks."

"Badgers!" said Lucy.

"Snakes!" said Edmund.

"Foxes!" said Susan.

But when next morning came, there was a steady rain falling, so thick that when you looked out of the window you could see neither the mountains nor the woods nor even the stream in the garden.

"Of course it *would* be raining!" said Edmund. They had just finished breakfast with the Professor and were upstairs in the room he had set apart for them—a long, low room with two windows looking out in one direction and two in another.

"Do stop grumbling, Ed," said Susan. "Ten to one it'll clear up in an hour or so. And in the meantime we're pretty well off. There's a wireless and lots of books."

"Not for me," said Peter, "I'm going to explore in the house."

Everyone agreed to this and that was how the adventures began. It was the sort of house that you never seem to come to the end of, and it was full of unexpected places. The first few doors they tried led only into spare bedrooms, as everyone had expected that they would; but soon they came to a very long room full of pictures and there they found a suit of armour; and after that was a room all hung with green, with a harp in one corner; and then came three steps down and five steps up, and then a kind of little upstairs hall and a door that led out onto a balcony, and then a whole series of rooms that led into each other and were lined with books—most of them very old books and some bigger than a Bible in a church. And shortly after that they looked into a room that was quite empty except for one big wardrobe; the sort that has a looking-glass in the door. There was nothing else in the room at all except a dead blue-bottle on the window-sill.

"Nothing there!" said Peter, and they all trooped out again—all except Lucy. She stayed behind because she thought it would be worth while trying the door of the wardrobe, even though she felt almost sure that it would be locked. To her surprise it opened quite easily, and two moth-balls dropped out.

Looking into the inside, she saw several coats hanging up—mostly long fur coats. There was nothing Lucy liked so much as the smell and feel of fur. She immediately stepped into the wardrobe and got in among the coats and rubbed her face against them, leaving the door open, of course, because she knew that it is very foolish to shut oneself into any wardrobe. Soon she went further in and found that there was a second row of coats hanging up behind the first one. It was almost quite dark in there and she kept her arms stretched out in front of her so as not to bump her face into the back of the wardrobe. She took a step further in—then two or three steps—always expecting to feel woodwork against the tips of her fingers. But she could not feel it.

"This must be a simply enormous wardrobe!" thought Lucy, going still further in and pushing the soft folds of the coats aside to make room for her. Then she noticed that there was something crunching under her feet. "I wonder is that more moth-balls?" she thought, stooping down to feel it with her hands. But instead of feeling the hard, smooth wood of the floor of the wardrobe, she felt something soft and powdery and extremely cold. "This is very queer," she said, and went on a step or two further.

Next moment she found that what was rubbing against her face and hands was no longer soft fur but something hard and rough and even prickly. "Why, it is just like branches of trees!" exclaimed Lucy. And then she saw that there was a light ahead of her; not a few inches away when the back of the wardrobe ought to have been, but a long way off. Something cold and soft was falling on her. A moment later she found that she was standing in the middle of a wood at night-time with snow under her feet and snowflakes falling through the air.

Lucy felt a little frightened, but she felt very inquisitive and excited as well. She looked back over her shoulder and there, between the dark tree-trunks, she could still see the open doorway of the wardrobe and even catch a glimpse of the empty room from which she had set out. (She had, of course, left the door open, for she knew that it is a very silly thing to shut oneself into a wardrobe.) It seemed to be still daylight there. "I can always get back if anything goes wrong," thought Lucy. She began to walk forward, *crunch-crunch*, over the snow and through the wood towards the other light.

In about ten minutes she reached it and found that it was a lamp-post. As she stood looking at it, wondering why there was a lamp-post in the middle of a wood and wondering what to do next, she heard a pitter patter of feet coming towards her. And soon after that a very strange person stepped out from among the trees into the light of the lamp-post.

He was only a little taller than Lucy herself and he carried over his head an umbrella, white with snow. From the waist upwards he was like a man, but his legs were shaped like a goat's (the hair on them was glossy black) and instead of feet he had goat's hoofs. He also had a tail, but Lucy did not notice this at first because it was neatly caught up over the arm that held the umbrella so as to keep it from trailing in the snow. He had a red woollen muffler round his neck and his skin was rather reddish too. He had a strange, but pleasant little face with a short pointed beard and curly hair, and out of the hair there stuck two horns, one on each side of his forehead. One of his hands, as I have said, held the umbrella: in the other arm he carried several brown paper parcels. What with the parcels and the snow it looked just as if he had been doing his Christmas shopping. He was a Faun. And when he saw Lucy he gave such a start of surprise that he dropped all his parcels.

"Goodness gracious me!" exclaimed the Faun.

"Good evening," said Lucy. But the Faun was so busy picking up his parcels that at first he did not reply. When he had finished he made her a little bow.

"Good evening, good evening," said the Faun. "Excuse me—I don't want to be inquisitive—but should I be right in thinking that you are a Daughter of Eve?"

"My name's Lucy," said she, not quite understanding him.

"But you are—forgive me—you are what they call a girl?" asked the Faun.

"Of course I'm a girl," said Lucy.

"You are in fact Human?"

"Of course I'm human," said Lucy, still a little puzzled.

"To be sure, to be sure," said the Faun. "How stupid of me! But I've never seen a Son of Adam or a Daughter of Eve before. I am delighted. That is to say—" and then he stopped as if he had been going to say something he had not intended but had remembered in time. "Delighted, delighted," he went on. "Allow me to introduce myself. My name is Tumnus."

"I am very pleased to meet you, Mr. Tumnus," said Lucy.

"And may I ask, O Lucy, Daughter of Eve," said Mr. Tumnus, "how you have come into Narnia?"

"Narnia? What's that?" said Lucy.

"This is the land of Narnia," said the Faun, "where we are now; all that lies between the lamp-post and the great castle of Cair Paravel on the eastern sea. And you—you have come from the wild woods of the west?"

"I—I got in through the wardrobe in the spare room," said Lucy.

"Ah!" said Mr. Tumnus in a rather melancholy voice, "if only I had worked harder at geography when I was a little Faun, I should no doubt know all about those strange countries. It is too late now."

"But they aren't countries at all," said Lucy, almost laughing. "It's only just back there—at least—I'm not sure. It is summer there."

"Meanwhile," said Mr. Tumnus, "it is winter in Narnia, and has been for ever so long, and we shall both catch cold if we stand here talking in the snow. Daughter of Eve from the far land of Spare Oom where eternal summer reigns around the bright city of War Drobe, how would it be if you came and had tea with me?"

"Thank you very much, Mr. Tumnus," said Lucy. "But I was wondcering whether I ought to be getting back."

"It's only just round the corncr," said the Faun, "and there'll be a roaring fire—and toast—and sardines—and cake."

"Well, it's very kind of you," said Lucy. "But I shan't be able to stay long."

"If you will take my arm, Daughter of Eve," said Mr. Tumnus, "I shall be able to hold the umbrella over both of us. That's the way. Now—off we go."

And so Lucy found herself walking through the wood arm in arm with this strange creature as if they had known one another all their lives.

They had not gone far before they came to a place where the ground became rough and there were rocks all about and little hills up and little hills down. At the bottom of one small valley Mr. Tumnus turned suddenly aside as if he were going to walk straight into an unusually large rock, but at the last moment Lucy found he was leading her into the entrance of a cave. As soon as they were inside she found herself blinking in the light of a wood fire. Then Mr. Tumnus stooped and took a flaming piece of wood out of the fire with a neat little pair of tongs, and lit a lamp. "Now we shan't be long," he said, and immediately put a kettle on.

Lucy thought she had never been in a nicer place. It was a little, dry, clean cave of reddish stone with a carpet on the floor and two little chairs ("one for me and one for a friend," said Mr. Tumnus) and a table and a dresser and a mantelpiece over the fire and above that a picture of an old Faun with a grey beard. In one corner there was a door which Lucy thought must lead to Mr. Tumnus' bedroom, and on one wall was a shelf full of books. Lucy looked at these while he was setting out the tea things. They had titles like *The Life and Letters of Silenus* or *Nymphs and Their Ways* or *Men, Monks and Gamekeepers; a Study in Popular Legend* or *Is Man a Myth?*

"Now, Daughter of Eve!" said the Faun.

And really it was a wonderful tea. There was a nice brown egg, lightly boiled, for each of them, and then sardines on toast, and then buttered toast, and then toast with honey, and then a sugar-topped cake. And when Lucy was tired of eating the Faun began to talk. He had wonderful tales to tell of life in the forest. He told about the midnight dances and how the Nymphs who lived in the wells and the Dryads who lived in the trees came out to dance with the Fauns; about long hunting parties after the milk-white Stag who could give you wishes if you caught him; about feasting and treasure-seeking with the wild Red Dwarfs in deep mines and caverns far beneath the forest floor; and then about summer when the woods were green and old Silenus on his fat donkey would come to visit them, and sometimes Bacchus himself, and then the streams would run with wine instead of water and the whole forest would give itself up to jollification for weeks on end. "Not that it isn't always winter now," he added gloomily. Then to cheer himself up he took out from its cast on the dresser a strange little flute that looked as if it were made of straw and began to play. And the tune he played made Lucy want to cry and laugh and dance and go to sleep all at the same time. It must have been hours later when she shook herself and said,

"Oh Mr. Tumnus—I'm so sorry to stop you, and I do love that tune— but really, I must go home. I only meant to stay for a few minutes."

"It's no good *now*, you know," said the Faun, laying down his flute and shaking his head at her very sorrowfully.

"No good?" said Lucy, jumping up and feeling rather frightened. "What do you mean? I've got to go home at once. The others will be wondering what has happened to me." But a moment later she asked, "Mr. Tumnus! Whatever is the matter?" for the Faun's brown eyes had filled with tears and then the tears began trickling down his cheeks, and soon they were running off the end of his nose; and at last he covered his face with his hands and began to howl.

"Mr. Tumnus! Mr. Tumnus!" said Lucy in great distress. "Don't! Don't! What is the matter? Aren't you well? Dear Mr. Tumnus, do tell me what is wrong." But the Faun continued sobbing as if his heart would break. And even when Lucy went over and put her arms round him and lent him her handkerchief, he did not stop. He merely took the handkerchief and kept on using it, wringing it out with both hands whenever it got too wet to be any more use, so that presently Lucy was standing in a damp patch.

"Mr. Tumnus!" bawled Lucy in his ear, shaking him. "Do stop. Stop it at once! You ought to be ashamed of yourself, a great big Faun like you. What on earth are you crying about?"

"Oh—oh—oh!" sobbed Mr. Tumnus, "I'm crying because I'm such a bad Faun."

"I don't think you're a bad Faun at all," said Lucy. "I think you are a very good Faun. You are the nicest Faun I've ever met."

"Oh—oh—you wouldn't say that if you knew," replied Mr. Tuinnus between his sobs. "No, I'm a bad Faun. I don't suppose there ever was a worse Faun since the beginning of the world."

"But what have you done?" asked Lucy.

"My old father, now," said Mr. Tumnus, "that's his picture over the mantelpiece. He would never have done a thing like this."

"A thing like what?" said Lucy.

"Like what I've done," said the Faun. "Taken service under the White Witch. That's what I am. I'm in the pay of the White Witch."

"The White Witch? Who is she?"

"Why, it is she that has got all Narnia under her thumb. It's she that makes it always winter. Always winter and never Christmas; think of that!"

"How awful!" said Lucy. "But what does she pay *you* for?"

"That's the worst of it," said Mr. Tumnus with a deep groan. "I'm a kidnapper for her, that's what I am. Look at me, Daughter of Eve. Would you believe that I'm the sort of Faun to meet a poor innocent child in the wood, one that had never done me any harm, and pretend to be friendly with it, and invite it home to my cave, all for the sake of lulling it asleep and then handing it over to the White Witch?"

"No," said Lucy. "I'm sure you wouldn't do anything of the sort."

"But I have," said the Faun.

"Well," said Lucy rather slowly (for she wanted to be truthful and yet not to be too hard on him), "well, that was pretty bad. But you're so sorry for it that I'm sure you will never do it again."

"Daughter of Eve, don't you understand?" said the Faun. "It isn't something I *have* done. I'm doing it now, this very moment."

"What do you mean?" cried Lucy, turning very white.

"You are the child," said Mr. Tumnus. "I had orders from the White Witch that if ever I saw a Son of Adam or a Daughter of Eve in the wood, I was to catch them and hand them over to her. And you are the first I ever met. And I've pretended to be your friend and asked you to tea, and all the time I've been meaning to wait till you were asleep and then go and tell *her*."

"Oh but you won't, Mr. Tumnus," said Lucy. "You won't, will you? Indeed, indeed you really mustn't."

"And if I don't," said he, beginning to cry again, "she's sure to find out. And she'll have my tail cut off, and my horns sawn off, and my beard plucked out, and she'll wave her wand over my beautiful cloven hoofs and turn them into horrid solid hoofs like a wretched horse's. And if she is extra and specially angry she'll turn me into stone and I shall be only a statue of a Faun in her horrible house until the four thrones at Cair Paravel are filled—and goodness knows when that will happen, or whether it will ever happen at all."

"I'm very sorry, Mr. Tumnus," said Lucy. "But please let me go home."

"Of course I will," said the Faun. "Of course I've got to. I see that now. I hadn't known what Humans were like before I met you. Of course I can't give you up to the Witch; not now that I know you. But we must be off at once. I'll see you back to the lamp-post. I suppose you can find your own way from there back to Spare Oom and War Drobe?"

"I'm sure I can," said Lucy.

"We must go as quietly as we can," said Mr. Tumnus. "The whole wood is full of *her* spies. Even some of the trees are on her side."

They both got up and left the tea things on the table, and Mr. Tumnus once more put up his umbrella and gave Lucy his arm, and they went out into the snow. The journey back was not at all like the journey to the Faun's cave; they stole along as quickly as they could, without speaking a word, and Mr. Tumnus kept to the darkest places. Lucy was relieved when they reached the lamp post again.

"Do you know your way from here, Daughter of Eve?" said Tumnus.

Lucy looked very hard between the trees and could just see in the distance a patch of light that looked like daylight. "Yes," she said, "I can see the wardrobe door."

"Then be off home as quick as you can," said the Faun, "and—c-can you ever forgive me for what I meant to do?"

"Why, of course I can," said Lucy, shaking him heartily by the hand. "And I do hope you won't get into dreadful trouble on my account."

"Farewell, Daughter of Eve," said he. "Perhaps I may keep the handkerchief?"

"Rather!" said Lucy, and then ran towards the far-off patch of daylight as quickly as her legs would carry her. And presently instead of rough branches brushing past her she felt coats, and instead of crunch-

ing snow under her feet she felt wooden boards, and all at once she
found herself jumping out of the wardrobe into the same empty room
from which the whole adventure had started. She shut the wardrobe
door tightly behind her and looked around, panting for breath. It was
still raining and she could hear the voices of the others in the passage.

"I'm here," she shouted. "I'm here. I've come back, I'm all right."

from

At the Back of the North Wind

by George Macdonald

Scottish clergyman George Macdonald (1824–1905) wrote poems, novels and children's books. He was friends with many famous Victorian writers and scholars. Macdonald was an amiable man, but poor health led him to spend most of each year in a house in Italy—where he hosted lots of parties. There, his friends would read from their books and perform plays. In this story a young boy makes friends with the mysterious North Wind.

I have been asked to tell you about the back of the north wind. An old Greek writer mentions a people who lived there, and were so comfortable that they could not bear it any longer, and drowned themselves. My story is not the same as his. I do not think Herodotus had got the right account of the place. I am going to tell you how it fared with a boy who went there.

He lived in a low room over a coach-house; and that was not by any means at the back of the north wind, as his mother very well knew. For one side of the room was built only of boards, and the boards were so old that you might run a penknife through into the north wind. And then let them settle between them which was the sharper! I know that when you pulled it out again the wind would be after it like a cat after a mouse, and you would know soon enough you were *not* at the back of the north wind. Still, this room was not very cold, except when the north wind blew stronger than usual: the room I have to do with now was always cold, except in summer, when the sun took the matter into his own hands. Indeed, I am not sure whether I ought to call it a room at all; for it was just a loft where they kept hay and straw and oats for the horses. And when little Diamond—but stop: I must tell you that his father, who was a coachman, had named him after a favourite horse, and his mother had had no objection—when little Diamond, then, lay there in bed, he could hear the horses under him munching away in the dark, or moving sleepily in their dreams. For Diamond's father had built him a bed in the loft with boards all round it, because they had so little room in their own end over the coach-house; and Diamond's father put old Diamond in the stall under the bed, because he was a quiet horse, and did not go to sleep standing, but lay down like a reasonable creature. But, although he was a surprisingly reasonable creature, yet, when young Diamond woke in the middle of the night, and felt the bed shaking in the blasts of the north wind, he could not help wondering whether, if the wind should blow the house down, and he were to fall through into the manger, old Diamond mightn't eat him up before he knew him in his night-gown. And although old Diamond was very quiet all night long, yet when he woke he got up like an earthquake, and then young Diamond knew what o'clock it was, or at least what was to be done next, which was—to go to sleep again as fast as he could.

There was hay at his feet and hay at his head, piled up in great trusses to the very roof. Indeed it was sometimes only through a little lane with several turnings, which looked as if it had been sawn out for him, that he could reach his bed at all. For the stock of hay was, of course, always in a state either of slow ebb or of sudden flow. Sometimes the whole space of the loft, with the little panes in the roof for the stars to look in, would lie open before his open eyes as he lay in bed; sometimes a yellow wall of sweet-smelling fibres closed up his view at the distance of half a yard. Sometimes, when his mother had undressed him in her room and told him to trot to bed by himself, he would creep into the heart of the hay and lie there thinking how cold it was outside in the wind, and how warm it was inside there in his bed, and how he could go to it when he pleased, only he wouldn't just yet; he would get a little colder first. And ever as he grew colder, his bed would grow warmer, till at last he would scramble out of the hay, shoot like an arrow into his bed, cover himself up, and snuggle down, thinking what a happy boy he was. He had not the least idea that the wind got in at a chink in the wall, and blew about him all night. For the back of his bed was only of boards an inch thick, and on the other side of them was the north wind.

Now, as I have already said, these boards were soft and crumbly. To be sure, they were tarred on the outside, yet in many places they were more like tinder than timber. Hence it happened that the soft part having worn away from about it, little Diamond found one night, after he lay down, that a knot had come out of one of them, and that the wind was blowing in upon him in a cold and rather imperious fashion. Now he had no fancy for leaving things wrong that might be set right; so he jumped out of bed again, got a little strike of hay, twisted it up, folded it in the middle, and having thus made it into a cork, stuck it into the hole in the wall. But the wind began to blow loud and angrily, and as Diamond was falling asleep, out blew his cork and hit him on the nose, just hard enough to wake him up quite and let him hear the wind whistling shrill in the hole. He searched for his haycork, found it, stuck it in harder, and was just dropping off once more, when, pop! with an angry whistle behind it, the cork struck him again, this time on the cheek. Up he rose once more, made a fresh stopple of hay, and corked the hole severely. But he was hardly down again before—pop! it came on his forehead. He gave it up, drew the clothes above his head, and was soon fast asleep.

Although the next day was very stormy, Diamond forgot all about the hole, for he was busy making a cave by the side of his mother's fire with a broken chair, a three-legged stool, and a blanket, and then sitting in it. His mother, however, discovered it, and pasted a bit of brown paper over it, so that, when Diamond had snuggled down the next night, he had no occasion to think of it.

Presently, however, he lifted his head and listened. Who could that be talking to him? The wind was rising again and getting very loud and full of rushes and whistles. He was sure someone was talking—and very near him, too, it was. But he was not frightened, for he had not yet learned how to be; so he sat up and hearkened. At last the voice, which, though quite gentle, sounded a little angry, appeared to come from the back of the bed. He crept nearer to it, and laid his ear against the wall. Then he heard nothing but the wind, which sounded very loud indeed. The moment, however, that he moved his head from the wall, he heard the voice again, close to his ear. He felt about with his hand, and came upon the piece of paper his mother had pasted over the hole. Against this he laid his ear, and then he heard the voice quite distinctly. There was, in fact, a little corner of the paper loose, and through that, as from a mouth in the wall, the voice came.

"What do you mean, little boy—closing up my window?"

"What window?" asked Diamond.

"You stuffed hay into it three times last night. I had to blow it out again three times."

"You can't mean this little hole! It isn't a window; it's a hole in my bed."

"I did not say it was *a* window: I said it was *my* window."

"But it can't be a window, because windows are holes to see out of."

"Well, that's just what I made this window for."

"But you are outside: you can't want a window."

"You are quite mistaken. Windows are to see out of, you say. Well, I'm in my house, and I want windows to see out of it."

"But you've made a window into my bed."

"Well, your mother has got three windows into my dancing room, and you have three into my garret."

"But I heard Father say, when my mother wanted him to make a window through the wall, that it was against the law, for it would look into Mr. Dyves's garden."

The voice laughed.

"The law would have some trouble to catch me!" it said.

"But if it's not right, you know," said Diamond, "that's no matter. You shouldn't do it."

"I am so tall I am above *that* law," said the voice.

"You must have a tall house, then," said Diamond.

"Yes, a tall house: the clouds are inside it."

"Dear me!" said Diamond, and thought a minute. "I think, then, you can hardly expect me to keep a window in my bed for you. Why don't you make a window into Mr. Dyves's bed?"

"Nobody makes a window into an ash-pit," said the voice, rather sadly. "I like to see nice things out of my windows."

"But he must have a nicer bed than I have, though mine is *very* nice—so nice that I couldn't wish a better."

"It's not the bed I care about: it's what is in it.—But you just open that window."

"Well, Mother says I shouldn't be disobliging; but it's rather hard. You see, the north wind will blow right in my face if I do."

"I am the north wind."

"Oh-o-oh!" said Diamond, thoughtfully. "Then will you promise not to blow on my face if I open your window?"

"I can't promise that."

"But you'll give me the toothache. Mother's got it already."

"But what's to become of me without a window?"

"I'm sure I don't know. All I say is, it will be worse for me than for you."

"No, it will not. You shall not be the worse for it—I promise you that. You will be much the better for it. Just you believe what I say, and do as I tell you."

"Well, I *can* pull the clothes over my head," said Diamond, and feeling with his little sharp nails, he got hold of the open edge of the paper and tore it off at once.

In came a long whistling spear of cold, and struck his little naked chest. He scrambled and tumbled in under the bedclothes, and covered himself up; there was no paper now between him and the voice, and he felt a little—not frightened exactly—I told you he had not learned that yet—but rather queer; for what a strange person this North Wind must be that lived in the great house—"called Out-of-Doors, I suppose," thought Diamond—and made windows into people's beds! But the voice began again; and he could hear it quite plainly, even with his head under the bedclothes. It was a still more gentle voice now, although six times as large and loud as it had been, and he thought it sounded a little like his mother's.

"What is your name, little boy?" it asked.

"Diamond," answered Diamond, under the bedclothes.

"What a funny name!"

"It's a very nice name," returned its owner.

"I don't know that," said the voice.

"Well, I do," retorted Diamond, a little rudely.

"Do you know to whom you are speaking!"

"No," said Diamond.

And indeed he did not. For to know a person's name is not always to know the person's self.

"Then I must not be angry with you. You had better look and see, though."

"Diamond is a very pretty name," persisted the boy, vexed that it should not give satisfaction.

"Diamond is a useless thing rather," said the voice.

"That's not true. Diamond is very nice—as big as two—and so quiet all night! And doesn't he make a jolly row in the morning, getting upon his four great legs! It's like thunder."

"You don't seem to know what a diamond is."

"Oh, don't I just! Diamond is a great and good horse; and he sleeps right under me. He is old Diamond, and I am young Diamond; or, if you like it better, for you're very particular, Mr. North Wind, he's big Diamond, and I'm little Diamond; and I don't know which of us my father likes best."

A beautiful laugh, large but very soft and musical, sounded somewhere beside him, but Diamond kept his head under the clothes.

"I'm not Mr. North Wind," said the voice.

"You told me that you were the north wind," insisted Diamond.

"I did not say *Mister* North Wind," said the voice.

"Well, then, I do; for Mother tells me I ought to be polite."

"Then let me tell you I don't think it at all polite of you to say *Mister* to me."

"Well, I didn't know better. I'm very sorry."

"But you ought to know better."

"I don't know that."

"I do. You can't say it's polite to lie there talking—with your head under the bedclothes, and never look up to see what kind of person you are talking to.—I want you to come out with me."

"I want to go to sleep," said Diamond, very nearly crying, for he did not like to be scolded, even when he deserved it.

"You shall sleep all the better to-morrow night."

"Besides," said Diamond, "you are out in Mr. Dyves's garden, and I can't get there. I can only get into our own yard."

"Will you take your head out of the bedclothes?" said the voice, just a little angrily.

"No!" answered Diamond, half peevish, half frightened.

The instant he said the word, a tremendous blast of wind crashed in a board of the wall, and swept the clothes off Diamond. He started up in terror. Leaning over him was the large, beautiful, pale face of a woman. Her dark eyes looked a little angry, for they had just begun to flash; but a quivering in her sweet upper lip made her look as if she were going to cry. What was the most strange was that away from her head streamed out her black hair in every direction, so that the darkness in the hay-loft looked as if it were made of her hair; but as Diamond gazed at her in speechless amazement, mingled with confidence—for the boy was entranced with her mighty beauty—her hair began to gather itself out of the darkness, and fell down all about her again, till her face looked out of the midst of it like a moon out of a cloud. From her eyes came all the light by which Diamond saw her face and her hair; and that was all he did see of her yet. The wind was over and gone.

"Will you go with me now, you little Diamond? I am sorry I was forced to be so rough with you," said the lady.

"I will; yes, I will," answered Diamond, holding out both his arms.

"But," he added, dropping them, "how shall I get my clothes? They are in Mother's room, and the door is locked."

"Oh, never mind your clothes. You will not be cold. I shall take care of that. Nobody is cold with the north wind."

"I thought everybody was," said Diamond.

"That is a great mistake. Most people make it, however. They are cold because they are not with the north wind, but without it."

If Diamond had been a little older, and had supposed himself a good deal wiser, he would have thought the lady was joking. But he was not older, and did not fancy himself wiser, and therefore understood her well enough. Again he stretched out his arms. The lady's face drew back a little.

"Follow me, Diamond," she said.

"Yes," said Diamond, only a little ruefully.

"You're not afraid?" said the north wind.

"No, ma'am; but Mother never would let me go without shoes: she never said anything about clothes, so I daresay she wouldn't mind that."

"I know your mother very well," said the lady. "She is a good woman. I have visited her often. I was with her when you were born. I saw her laugh and cry both at once. I love your mother, Diamond."

"How was it you did not know my name, then, ma'am? Please, am I to say *ma'am* to you, ma'am?"

"One question at a time, dear boy. I knew your name quite well, but I wanted to hear what you would say for it. Don't you remember that day when the man was finding fault with your name—how I blew the window in?"

"Yes, yes," answered Diamond, eagerly. "Our window opens like a door, right over the coach-house door. And the wind—you, ma'am—came in, and blew the Bible out of the man's hands, and the leaves went all flutter, flutter on the floor, and my mother picked it up and gave it back to him open, and there—"

"Was your name in the Bible—the sixth stone in the high priest's breastplate."

"Oh!—a stone, was it?" said Diamond. "I thought it had been a horse—I did."

"Never mind. A horse is better than a stone any day. Well, you see. I know all about you and your mother."

"Yes. I will go with you."

"Now for the next question: you're not to call me *ma'am*. You must call me just my own name—respectfully, you know—just North Wind."

"Well, please, North Wind, you are so beautiful, I am quite ready to go with you."

"You must not be ready to go with everything beautiful all at once, Diamond."

"But what's beautiful can't be bad. You're not bad, North Wind?"

"No; I'm not bad. But sometimes beautiful things grow bad by doing bad, and it takes some time for their badness to spoil their beauty. So little boys may be mistaken if they go after things because they are beautiful."

"Well, I will go with you because you are beautiful and good, too."

"Ah, but there's another thing, Diamond. What If I should look ugly without being bad—look ugly myself because I am making ugly things beautiful? What then?"

"I don't quite understand you, North Wind. You tell me what then."

"Well, I will tell you. If you see me with my face all black, don't be frightened. If you see me flapping wings like a bat's, as big as the whole sky, don't be frightened. If you hear me raging ten times worse than Mrs. Bill, the blacksmith's wife—even if you see me looking in at people's windows like Mrs. Eve Dropper, the gardener's wife—you must believe that I am doing my work. Nay, Diamond, if I change into a serpent or a tiger, you must not let go your hold of me, for my hand will never change in yours if you keep a good hold. If you keep a hold, you will know who I am all the time, even when you look at me and can't see me the least like the north wind. I may look something very awful. Do you understand?"

"Quite well," said little Diamond.

"Come along, then," said North Wind, and disappeared behind the mountain of hay.

Diamond crept out of bed and followed her.

When Diamond got round the corner of the hay, for a moment he hesitated. The stair by which he would naturally have gone down to the door was at the other side of the loft, and looked very black indeed, for it was full of North Wind's hair as she descended before him. And just beside him was the ladder going straight down into the stable, up which his father always came to fetch the hay for Diamond's dinner. Through the opening in the floor the faint gleam of the stable lantern was enticing, and Diamond thought he would run down that way.

The stair went close past the loose-box in which Diamond the horse lived. When Diamond the boy was half-way down, he remembered that it was of no use to go this way, for the stable door was locked. But at the same moment there was horse Diamond's great head poked out of his box onto the ladder, for he knew boy Diamond although he was in his night-gown, and wanted him to pull his ears for him. This Diamond did very gently for a minute or so, and patted and stroked his neck too, and kissed the big horse, and had begun to take the bits of straw and hay out of his mane, when all at once he recollected that the Lady North Wind was waiting for him in the yard.

"Good night, Diamond," he said, and darted up the ladder, across the loft, and down the stair to the door. But when he got out into the yard, there was no lady.

Now it is always a dreadful thing to think there is somebody and find nobody. Children in particular have not made up their minds to it; they generally cry at nobody, especially when they wake up at night. But it was an especial disappointment to Diamond, for his little heart had been beating with joy: the face of North Wind was so grand! To have a lady like that for a friend—with such long hair, too! Why, it was longer than twenty Diamonds' tails! She was gone. And there he stood, with his bare feet on the stones of the paved yard.

It was a clear night overhead, and the stars were shining. Orion in particular was making the most of his bright belt and golden sword. But the moon was only a poor thin crescent. There was just one great, jagged, black and grey cloud in the sky, with a steep side to it like a precipice; and the moon was against this side, and looked as if she had rambled off the top of the cloud-hill, and broken herself in rolling down the precipice. She did not seem comfortable, for she was looking down into the deep pit waiting for her. At least that was what Diamond thought as he stood for a moment staring at her. But he was quite wrong, for the moon was not afraid, and there was no pit she was going down into, for there were no sides to it, and a pit without sides to it is not a pit at all. Diamond, however, had not been out so late before in all his life, and things looked so strange about him!—just as if he had got into Fairyland, of which he knew quite as much as anybody; for his mother had no money to buy books to set him wrong on the subject. I have seen this world—only sometimes, just now and then, you know—look as strange as ever I saw Fairyland. But I confess that I have not yet seen Fairyland at its best. I am always *going* to see it so some time. But if you had been out in the face and not at the back of the north wind, on a cold *rather* frosty night, and in your night-gown, you would have felt it all quite as strange as Diamond did. He cried a little, just a little, he was so disappointed to lose the lady—of course, you, little man, wouldn't have done that! But for my part, I don't mind people crying so much as I mind what they cry about, and how they cry—whether they cry quietly like ladies and gentlemen, or go shrieking like vulgar emperors, or ill-natured cooks; for all emperors are not gentlemen, and all cooks are not ladies—nor all queens and princesses for that matter, either.

But it can't be denied that a little gentle crying does one good. It did Diamond good; for as soon as it was over he was a brave boy again.

"She shan't say it was my fault, anyhow!" said Diamond. "I daresay she is hiding somewhere to see what I will do. I will look for her."

So he went round the end of the stable towards the kitchen-garden. But the moment he was clear of the shelter of the stable, sharp as a knife came the wind against his little chest and his bare legs. Still he would look in the kitchen-garden, and went on. But when he got round the weeping-ash that stood in the corner, the wind blew much stronger, and it grew stronger and stronger till he could hardly fight against it. And it was so cold! All the flashy spikes of the stars seemed to have got somehow into the wind. Then he thought of what the lady had said about people being cold because they were not *with* the north wind. How it was that he should have guessed what she meant at that very moment I cannot tell, but I have observed that the most wonderful thing in the world is how people come to understand anything. He turned his back to the wind and trotted again towards the yard; whereupon, strange to say, it blew so much more gently against his calves than it had blown against his shins that he began to feel almost warm by contrast.

You must not think it was cowardly of Diamond to turn his back to the wind: he did so only because he thought Lady North Wind had said something like telling him to do so. If she had said to him that he must hold his face to it, Diamond would have held his face to it. But the most foolish thing is to fight for no good, and to please nobody.

Well, it was just as if the wind was pushing Diamond along. If he turned round, it grew very sharp on his legs especially, and so he thought the wind might really be Lady North Wind, though he could not see her, and he had better let her blow him wherever she pleased. So she blew and blew, and he went and went, until he found himself standing at a door in a wall, which door led from the yard into a little belt of shrubbery, flanking Mr. Coleman's house. Mr. Coleman was his father's master, and the owner of Diamond. He opened the door, and went through the shrubbery, and out into the middle of the lawn, still hoping to find North Wind. The soft grass was very pleasant to his bare feet, and felt warm after the stones of the yard; but the lady was nowhere to be seen. Then he began to think that after all he must have done wrong, and she was offended with him for not following close after her, but staying to talk to the horse, which certainly was neither wise nor polite.

There he stood in the middle of the lawn, the wind blowing his night-gown till it flapped like a loose sail. The stars were very shiny over his head; but they did not give light enough to show that the grass was green; and Diamond stood alone in the strange night, which looked half solid all about him. He began to wonder whether he was in a dream or not. It was important to determine this; "For," thought Diamond, "if I am in a dream, I am safe in my bed, and I needn't cry. But if I'm not in a dream, I'm out here, and perhaps I had better cry, or, at least, I'm not sure whether I can help it." He came to the conclusion, however, that, whether he was in a dream or not, there could be no harm in not crying for a little while longer: he could begin whenever he liked.

The back of Mr. Coleman's house was to the lawn, and one of the drawing-room windows looked out upon it. The ladies had not gone to bed, for the light was still shining in that window. But they had no idea that a little boy was standing on the lawn in his night-gown, or they would have run out in a moment. And as long as he saw that light, Diamond could not feel quite lonely. He stood staring, not at the great warrior Orion in the sky, nor yet at the disconsolate, neglected moon going down in the west, but at the drawingroom window with the light shining through its green curtains. He had been in that room once or twice that he could remember at Christmas times; for the Colemans were kind people, though they did not care much about children.

All at once the light went nearly out: he could only see a glimmer of the shape of the window. Then, indeed, he felt that he was left alone. It was so dreadful to be out in the night after *everybody* was gone to bed! That was more than he *could* bear. He burst out crying in good earnest, beginning with a wail like that of the wind when it is waking up.

Perhaps you think this was very foolish; for could he not go home to his own bed again when he liked? Yes; but it looked dreadful to him to creep up that stair again and lie down in his bed again, and know that North Wind's window was open beside him, and she gone, and he might never see her again. He would be just as lonely there as here. Nay, it would be much worse if he had to think that the window was nothing but a hole in the wall.

At the very moment when he burst out crying, the old nurse who had grown to be one of the family, for she had not gone away when Miss Coleman did not want any more nursing, came to the back door, which was of glass, to close the shutters. She thought she heard a cry, and peering out with a hand on each side of her eyes like Diamond's blinkers, she saw something white on the lawn. Too old and too wise to be frightened, she opened the door and went straight towards the white thing to see what it was. And when Diamond saw her coming he was not frightened either, though Mrs. Crump was a little cross sometimes; for there is a good kind of crossness that is only disagreeable, and there is a bad kind of crossness that is very nasty indeed. So she came up with her neck stretched out, and her head at the end of it, and her eyes foremost of all, like a snail's, peering into the night to see what it could be that went on glimmering white before her. When she did see, she made a great exclamation and threw up her hands. Then without a word, for she thought Diamond was walking in his sleep, she caught hold of him, and led him towards the house. He made no objection, for he was just in the mood to be grateful for notice of any sort, and Mrs. Crump led him straight into the drawing-room.

Now, from the neglect of the new housemaid, the fire in Miss Coleman's bedroom had gone out, and her mother had told her to brush her hair by the drawing-room fire—a disorderly proceeding which a mother's wish could justify. The young lady was very lovely, though not nearly so beautiful as North Wind; and her hair was extremely long, for it came down to her knees—though that was nothing at all to North Wind's hair. Yet when she looked round, with her hair all about her, as Diamond entered, he thought for one moment that it was North Wind, and pulling his hand front Mrs. Crump's, he stretched out his arms and ran towards Miss Coleman. She was so pleased that she threw down her brush and almost knelt on the floor to receive him in her arms. He saw the next moment that she was not

Lady North Wind, but she looked so like her he could not help running into her arms and bursting into tears afresh. Mrs. Crump said the
poor child had walked out in his sleep, and Diamond thought she
ought to know, and did not contradict her: for anything he knew, it
might be so indeed. He let them talk on about him, and said nothing;
and when, after their astonishment was over, and Miss Coleman had
given him a sponge-cake, it was decreed that Mrs. Crump should take
him to his mother, he was quite satisfied.

His mother had to get out of bed to open the door when Mrs.
Crump knocked. She was indeed surprised to see her boy; and having
taken him in her arms and carried him to his bed, returned and had a
long confabulation with Mrs. Crump, for they were still talking when
Diamond fell fast asleep and could hear them no longer.

Diamond woke very early in the morning, and thought what a curious
dream he had had. But the memory grew brighter and brighter in his
head, until it did not look altogether like a dream, and he began to
doubt whether he had not really been abroad in the wind last night.
He came to the conclusion that, if he had really been brought home by
Mrs. Crump, she would say something to him about it, and that would
settle the matter. Then he got up and dressed himself, but finding that
his father and mother were not yet stirring, he went down the ladder to
the stable. There he found that even old Diamond was not awake yet,
for he, as well as young Diamond, always got up the moment he woke,
and now he was lying as flat as a horse could lie upon his nice trim bed
of straw.

"I'll give old Diamond a surprise," thought the boy; and creeping
up very softly, before the horse knew, he was astride of his back. Then
it was young Diamond's turn to have more of a surprise than he had
expected; for as with an earthquake, with a rumbling and a rocking
hither and thither, a sprawling of legs and heaving as of many backs,
young Diamond found himself hoisted up in the air, with both hands

twisted in the horse's mane. The next instant old Diamond lashed out with both his hind legs, and giving one cry of terror young Diamond found himself lying on his neck, with his arms as far round it as they would go. But then the horse stood as still as a stone, except that he lifted his head gently up to let the boy slip down to his back. For when he heard young Diamond's cry he knew that there was nothing to kick about; for young Diamond was a good boy, and old Diamond was a good horse, and the one was all right on the back of the other.

As soon as Diamond had got himself comfortable on the saddle place, the horse began pulling at the hay, and the boy began thinking. He had never mounted Diamond himself before, and he had never got off him without being lifted down. So he sat, while the horse ate, wondering how he was to reach the ground.

But while he meditated, his mother woke, and her first thought was to see her boy. She had visited him twice during the night, and found him sleeping quietly. Now his bed was empty, and she was frightened.

"Diamond! Diamond! Where are you, Diamond?" she called out.

Diamond turned his head where he sat like a knight on his steed in an an enchanted stall, and cried aloud—

"Here, Mother!"

"Where, Diamond?" she returned.

"Here, Mother, on Diamond's back."

She came running to the ladder, and peeping down, saw him aloft on the great horse.

"Come down, Diamond," she said.

"I can't," answered Diamond.

"How did you get up?" asked his mother.

"Quite easily," answered he; "but when I got up, Diamond would get up too, and so here I am."

His mother thought he had been walking in his sleep again, and hurried down the ladder. She did not much like going up to the horse, for she had not been used to horses; but she would have gone into a lion's den, not to say a horse's stall, to help her boy. So she went and lifted him off Diamond's back, and felt braver all her life after. She carried him in her arms up to her room; but, afraid of frightening him at his own sleep-walking, as she supposed it, said nothing about last night. Before the next day was over, Diamond had almost concluded the whole adventure a dream.

For a week his mother watched him very carefully, going into the loft several times a night—as often, in fact, as she woke. Every time she found him fast asleep.

All that week it was hard weather. The grass showed white in the morning with the hoar-frost which clung like tiny comfits to every blade. And as Diamond's shoes were not good, and his mother had not quite saved up enough money to get him the new pair she so much wanted for him, she would not let him run out. He played all his games over and over indoors, especially that of driving two chairs harnessed to the baby's cradle; and if they did not go very fast, they went as fast as could be expected of the best chairs in the world, although one of them had only three legs, and the other only half a back.

At length his mother brought home his new shoes, and no sooner did she find they fitted him than she told him he might run out in the yard and amuse himself for an hour.

The sun was going down when he flew from the door like a bird from its cage. All the world was new to him. A great fire of sunset burned on the top of the gate that led from the stables to the house; above the fire in the sky lay a large lake of green light, above that a golden cloud, and over that the blue of the wintry heavens. And Diamond thought that, next to his own home, he had never seen any place he would like so much to live in as that sky. For it is not fine things that make home a nice place, but your mother and your father.

As he was looking at the lovely colours, the gates were thrown open, and there was old Diamond and his friend in the carriage, dancing with impatience to get at their stalls and their oats. And in they came. Diamond was not in the least afraid of his father driving over him, but, careful not to spoil the grand show he made with his fine horses and his multitudinous cape with a red edge to every fold, he slipped out of the way and let him dash right on to the stables. To be quite safe he had to step into the recess of the door that led from the yard to the shrubbery.

As he stood there he remembered how the wind had driven him to this same spot on the night of his dream. And once more he was almost sure that it was no dream. At all events, he would go in and see whether things looked at all now as they did then. He opened the door, and passed through the little belt of shrubbery. Not a flower was to be seen in the beds on the lawn. Even the brave old chrysanthemums and Christmas roses had passed away before the frost. What? Yes! There was one! He ran and knelt down to look at it.

It was a primrose—a dwarfish thing, but perfect in shape—a baby-wonder. As he stooped his face to see it close, a little wind began to blow, and two or three long leaves that stood up behind the flower shook and waved and quivered, but the primrose lay still in the green hollow, looking up at the sky, and not seeming to know that the wind was blowing at all. It was just a one eye that the dull black wintry earth had opened to look at the sky with. All at once Diamond thought it was saying its prayers, and he ought not to be staring at it so. He ran to the stable to see his father make Diamond's bed. Then his father took him in his arms, carried him up the ladder, and set him down at the table where they were going to have their tea.

"Miss is very poorly," said Diamond's father; "Mis'ess has been to the doctor with her to-day, and she looked very glum when she came out again. I was a-watching of them to see what doctor had said."

"And didn't Miss look glum too?" asked his mother.

"Not half as glum as Mis'ess," returned the coachman. "You see—"

But he lowered his voice, and Diamond could not make out more than a word here and there. For Diamond's father was not only one of the finest of coachmen to look at, and one of the best of drivers, but one of the most discreet of servants as well. Therefore he did not talk about family affairs to anyone but his wife, whom he had proved better than himself long ago, and was careful that even Diamond should hear nothing he could repeat again concerning Master and his family.

It was bedtime soon, and Diamond went to bed and fell fast asleep.

He awoke all at once, in the dark.

"Open the window, Diamond," said a voice.

Now Diamond's mother had once more pasted up North Wind's window.

"Are you North Wind?" said Diamond. "I don't hear you blowing."

"No; but you hear me talking. Open the window, for I haven't over-much time."

"Yes," returned Diamond. "But, please, North Wind, where's the use? You left me all alone last time."

He had got up on his knees, and was busy with his nails once more at the paper over the hole in the wall. For now that North Wind spoke again, he remembered all that had taken place before as distinctly as if it had happened only last night.

"Yes, but that was your fault," returned North Wind. "I had work to do; and besides, a gentleman should never keep a lady waiting."

"But I'm not a gentleman," said Diamond, scratching away at the paper.

"I hope you won't say so ten years after this."

"I'm going to be a coachman, and a coachman is not a gentleman," persisted Diamond.

"We call your father a gentleman in our house," said North Wind.

"He doesn't call himself one," said Diamond.

"That's of no consequence: every man ought to be a gentleman, and your father is one."

Diamond was so pleased to hear this that he scratched at the paper like ten mice, and getting hold of the edge of it, tore it off. The next instant a young girl glided across the bed and stood upon the floor.

"Oh, dear!" said Diamond, quite dismayed. "I didn't know—who are you, please?"

"I'm North Wind."

"Are you really?"

"Yes. Make haste."

"But you're no bigger than me."

"Do you think I care about how big or how little I am? Didn't you see me this evening? I was less then."

"No. Where were you?"

"Behind the leaves of the primrose. Didn't you see them blowing?"

"Yes."

"Make haste, then, if you want to go with me."

"But you are not big enough to take care of me. I think you are only Miss North Wind."

"I am big enough to show you the way, anyhow. But if you won't come, why, you must stay."

"I must dress myself. I didn't mind with a grown lady, but I couldn't go with a little girl in my night-gown."

"Very well. I'm not in such a hurry as I was the other night. Dress as fast as you can, and I'll go and shake the primrose leaves till you come."

"Don't hurt it," said Diamond.

North Wind broke out in a little laugh like the breaking of silver bubbles, and was gone in a moment. Diamond saw—for it was a star-lit night, and the mass of hay was at a low ebb now—the gleam of something vanishing down the stair, and, springing out of bed, dressed himself as fast as ever he could. Then he crept out into the yard, through the door in the wall, and away to the primrose. Behind it stood North Wind, leaning over it and looking at the flower as if she had been its mother.

"Come along," she said, jumping up and holding out her hand.

Diamond took her hand. It was cold, but so pleasant and full of life, it was better than warm. She led him across the garden. With one bound she was on the top of the wall. Diamond was left at the foot.

"Stop, stop!" he cried. "Please, I can't jump like that."

"You don't try," said North Wind, who from the top looked down a foot taller than before.

"Give me your hand again, and I will try," said Diamond.

She reached down, Diamond laid hold of her hand, gave a great spring, and stood beside her.

"This *is* nice!" he said.

Another bound, and they stood in the road by the river. It was full tide, and the stars were shining clear in its depths, for it lay still, waiting for the turn to run down again to the sea. They walked along its side. But they had not walked far before its surface was covered with ripples, and the stars had vanished from its bosom.

And North Wind was now tall as a full-grown girl. Her hair was flying about her head, and the wind was blowing a breeze down the river. But she turned aside and went up a narrow lane, and as she went her hair fell down around her.

"I have some rather disagreeable work to do to-night," she said, "before I get out to sea, and I must set about it at once. The disagreeable work must be looked after first."

So saying, she laid hold of Diamond and began to run, gliding along faster and faster. Diamond kept up with her as well as he could. She made many turnings and windings, apparently because it was not quite easy to get him over walls and houses. Once they ran through a hall where they found back and front doors open. At the foot of the stair North Wind stood still, and Diamond, hearing a great growl, started in terror, and there, instead of North Wind, was a huge wolf by his side. He let go his hold in dismay, and the wolf bounded up the stair. The windows of the house rattled and shook as if guns were firing, and the sound of a great fall came from above. Diamond stood with white face staring up at the landing.

"Surely," he thought, "North Wind can't be eating one of the children!" Coming to himself all at once, he rushed after her with his little fist clenched. There were ladies in long trains going up and down the stairs, and gentlemen in white neckties attending on them, who stared at him, but none of them were of the people of the house, and they said nothing. Before he reached the head of the stair, however, North Wind met him, took him by the hand, and hurried down and out of the house.

"I hope you haven't eaten a baby, North Wind!" said Diamond, very solemnly.

North Wind laughed merrily, and went tripping on faster. Her grassy robe swept and swirled about her steps, and wherever it passed over withered leaves, they went fleeing and whirling in spirals, and running on their edges like wheels, all about her feet.

"No," she said at last, "I did not eat a baby. You would not have had to ask that foolish question if you had not let go your hold of me. You would have seen how I served a nurse that was calling a child bad names and telling her she was wicked. She had been drinking. I saw an ugly gin bottle in a cupboard."

"And you frightened her?" said Diamond.

"I believe so!" answered North Wind, laughing merrily. "I flew at her throat, and she tumbled over on the floor with such a crash that they ran in. She'll be turned away tomorrow—and quite time, if they knew as much as I do."

"But didn't you frighten the little one?"

"She never saw me. The woman would not have seen me either if she had not been wicked."

"Oh!" said Diamond, dubiously.

"Why should you see things," returned North Wind, "that you wouldn't understand or know what to do with? Good people see good things; bad people, bad things."

"Then are you a bad thing?"

"No. For *you* see me, Diamond, dear," said the girl, and she looked down at him, and Diamond saw the loving eyes of the great lady beaming from the depths of her falling hair.

"I had to make myself look like a bad thing before she could see me. If I had put on any other shape than a wolf's she would not have seen me, for that is what is growing to be her own shape inside of her."

"I don't know what you mean," said Diamond, "but I suppose it's all right."

They were now climbing the slope of a grassy ascent. It was Primrose Hill, in fact, although Diamond had never heard of it. The moment they reached the top, North Wind stood and turned her face towards London. The stars were still shining clear and cold overhead. There was not a cloud to be seen. The air was sharp, but Diamond did not find it cold.

"Now," said the lady, "whatever you do, do not let my hand go. I might have lost you the last time, only I was not in a hurry then; now I am in a hurry."

Yet she stood still for a moment.

★ ★ ★

And as she stood looking towards London, Diamond saw that she was trembling.

"Are you cold, North Wind?" he asked.

"No, Diamond," she answered, looking down upon him with a smile; "I am only getting ready to sweep one of my rooms. Those careless, greedy, untidy children make it in such a mess."

As she spoke he could have told by her voice, if he had not seen with his eyes, that she was growing larger and larger. Her head went up and up towards the stars; and as she grew, still trembling through all her body, her hair also grew—longer and longer, and lifted itself from her head, and went out in black waves. The next moment, however, it fell back around her, and she grew less and less till she was only a tall woman. Then she put her hands behind her head, and gathered some of her hair, and began weaving and knotting it together. When she had done, she bent down her beautiful face close to his, and said:

"Diamond, I am afraid you would not keep hold of me, and if I were to drop you, I don't know what might happen; so I have been making a place for you in my hair. Come."

Diamond held out his arms, for with that grand face looking at him, he believed like a baby. She took him in her hands, threw him over her shoulder, and said, "Get in, Diamond."

And Diamond parted her hair with his hands, crept between, and feeling about, soon found the woven nest. It was just like a pocket, or like the shawl in which gipsy women carry their children. North Wind put her hands to her back, felt all about the nest, and finding it safe, said:

"Arc you comfortable, Diamond?"

"Yes, indeed," answered Diamond.

The next moment he was rising in the air. North Wind grew towering up to the place of the clouds. Her hair went streaming out from her till it spread like a mist over the stars. She flung herself abroad in space.

Diamond held on by two of the twisted ropes which, parted and interwoven, formed his shelter, for he could not help being a little afraid. As soon as he had come to himself, he peeped through the woven meshes, for he did not dare to look over the top of the nest. The earth was rushing past like a river or a sea below him. Trees and water and green grass hurried away beneath. A great roar of wild animals rose as they rushed over the Zoological Gardens, mixed with a chattering of monkeys and a screaming of birds; but it died away in a moment behind them. And now there was nothing but the roofs of houses, sweeping along like a great torrent of stones and rocks. Chimney-pots fell, and tiles flew from the roofs; but it looked to him as if they were left behind by the roofs and the chimneys as they scudded away. There was a great roaring, for the wind was dashing against London like a sea; but at North Wind's back Diamond, of course, felt nothing of it all. He was in a perfect calm. He could hear the sound of it, that was all.

By and by he raised himself and looked over the edge of his nest. There were the houses rushing up and shooting away below him, like a fierce torrent of rocks instead of water. Then he looked up to the sky, but could see no stars; they were hidden by the blinding masses of the lady's hair which swept between. He began to wonder whether she would hear him if he spoke. He would try.

"Please, North Wind," he said, "what is that noise?"

From high over his head came the voice of North Wind, answering him gently:

"The noise of my besom. I am the old woman that sweeps the cobwebs from the sky; only I'm busy with the floor now."

"What makes the houses look as if they were running away?"

"I am sweeping so fast over them."

"But, please, North Wind, I knew London was very big, but I didn't know it was so big as this. It seems as if we should never get away from it."

"We are going round and round, else we should have left it long ago."

"Is this the way you sweep, North Wind?"

"Yes; I go round and round with my great besom."

"Please, would you mind going a little slower, for I want to see the streets?"

"You won't see much now."

"Why?"

"Because I have nearly swept all the people home."

"Oh! I forgot," said Diamond, and was quiet after that, for he did not want to be troublesome.

But she dropped a little towards the roofs of the houses, and Diamond could see down into the streets. There were very few people about, though. The lamps flickered and flared again, but nobody seemed to want them.

Suddenly Diamond espied a little girl coming along a street. She was dreadfully blown by the wind, and a broom she was trailing behind her was very troublesome. It seemed as if the wind had a spite at her—it kept worrying her like a wild beast, and tearing at her rags. She was so lonely there!

"Oh! please, North Wind," he cried, "won't you help that little girl?"

"No, Diamond; I mustn't leave my work."

"But why shouldn't you be kind to her?"

"I am kind to her: I am sweeping the wicked smells away."

"But you're kinder to me, dear North Wind. Why shouldn't you be as kind to her as you are to me?"

"There are reasons, Diamond. Everybody can't be done to all the same. Everybody is not ready for the same thing."

"But I don't see why I should be kinder used than she."

"Do you think nothing's to be done but what you can see, Diamond, you silly! It's all right. Of course you can help her if you like. You've got nothing particular to do at this moment; I have."

"Oh! do let us help her, then. But you won't be able to wait, perhaps?"

"No, I can't wait; you must do it yourself. And, mind, the wind will get a hold of you, too."

"Don't you want me to help her, North Wind?"

"Not without having some idea what will happen. If you break down and cry, that won't be much of a help to her, and it will make a goose of little Diamond."

"I want to go," said Diamond. "Only there's just one thing—how am I to get home?"

"If you're anxious about that, perhaps you had better go with me. I am bound to take you home again, if you do."

"There!" cried Diamond, who was still looking after the little girl. "I'm sure the wind will blow her over, and perhaps kill her. Do let me go."

They had been sweeping more slowly along the line of the street. There was a lull in the roaring.

"Well, though I cannot promise to take you home," said North Wind, as she sank nearer and nearer to the tops of the houses, "I can promise you it will be all right in the end. You will get home somehow. Have you made up your mind what to do?"

"Yes; to help the little girl," said Diamond firmly.

The same moment North Wind dropped into the street and stood, only a tall lady, but with her hair flying up over the housetops. She put her hands to her back, took Diamond, and set him down in the street. The same moment he was caught in the fierce coils of the blast, and all but blown away. North Wind stepped back a step, and at once towered in stature to the height of the houses. A chimney-pot crashed at Diamond's feet. He turned in terror, but it was to look for the little girl, and when he turned again the lady had vanished, and the wind was roaring along the street as if it had been the bed of an invisible torrent. The little girl was scudding before the blast, her hair flying too, and behind her she dragged her broom. Her little legs were going as fast as ever they could to keep her from falling. Diamond crept into the shelter of a doorway, thinking to stop her; but she passed him like a bird, crying gently and pitifully.

"Stop! stop! little girl," shouted Diamond, starting in pursuit.

"I can't," wailed the girl, "the wind won't leave go of me."

Diamond could run faster than she, and he had no broom. In a few moments he had caught her by the frock, but it tore in his hand, and away went the little girl. So he had to run again, and this time he ran so fast that he got before her, and turning round caught her in his arms, when down they went both together, which made the little girl laugh in the midst of her crying.

"Where are you going?" asked Diamond, rubbing the elbow that had stuck farthest out. The arm it belonged to was twined round a lamp-post as he stood between the little girl and the wind.

"Home," she said, gasping for breath.

"Then I will go with you," said Diamond.

And then they were silent for a while, for the wind blew worse than ever, and they had both to hold onto the lamppost.

"Where is your crossing?" asked the girl at length.

"I don't sweep," answered Diamond.

"What *do* you do, then?" asked she. "You ain't big enough for most things."

"I don't know what I do do," answered he, feeling rather ashamed. "Nothing, I suppose. My father's Mr. Coleman's coachman."

"Have you a father?" she said, staring at him as if a boy with a father was a natural curiosity.

"Yes. Haven't *you*?" returned Diamond.

"No; nor mother neither. Old Sal's all I've got." And she began to cry again.

"I wouldn't go to her if she wasn't good to me," said Diamond.

"But you must go somewheres."

"Move on," said the voice of a policeman behind them.

"I told you so," said the girl. "You must go somewheres. They're always at it."

"But old Sal doesn't beat you, does she?"

"I wish she would."

"What do you mean?" asked Diamond, quite bewildered.

"She would if she was my mother. But she wouldn't lie abed a-cuddlin' of her ugly old bones, and laugh to hear me crying at the door."

"You don't mean she won't let you in to-night?"

"It'll be a good chance if she does."

"Why are you out so late, then?" asked Diamond.

"My crossing's a long way off at the West End, and I had been indulgin' in doorsteps and mewses."

"We'd better have a try anyhow," said Diamond. "Come along."

As he spoke Diamond thought he caught a glimpse of North Wind turning a corner in front of them; and when they turned the corner too, they found it quiet there, but he saw nothing of the lady.

"Now you lead me," he said, taking her hand, "and I'll take care of you."

The girl withdrew her hand, but only to dry her eyes with her frock, for the other had enough to do with her broom. She put it in his again, and led him, turning after turning, until they stopped at a cellar-door in a very dirty lane. There she knocked.

"I shouldn't like to live here," said Diamond.

"Oh, yes, you would, if you had nowhere else to go to," answered the girl. "I only wish we may get in."

"I don't want to go in," said Diamond.

"Where do you mean to go, then?"

"Home to my home."

"Where's that?"

"I don't exactly know."

"Then you're worse off than I am."

"Oh, no, for North Wind—" began Diamond, and stopped, he hardly knew why.

"*What?*" said the girl, as she held her ear to the door listening.

But Diamond did not reply. Neither did old Sal.

"I told you so," said the girl. "She is wide awake, hearkening. But we don't get in."

"What will you do, then?" asked Diamond.

"Move on," she answered.

"Where?"

"Oh, anywheres. Bless you, I'm used to it."

"Hadn't you better come home with me, then?"

"That's a good joke, when you don't know where it is. Come on."

"But where?"

"Oh, nowheres in particular. Come on."

Diamond obeyed. The wind had now fallen considerably. They wandered on and on, turning in this direction and that, without any reason for one way more than another, until they had got out of the thick of the houses into a waste kind of place. By this time they were both very tired. Diamond felt a good deal inclined to cry, and thought he had been very silly to get down from the back of North Wind; not that he would have minded it if he had done the girl any good; but he thought he had been of no use to her. He was mistaken there, for she was far happier for having Diamond with her than if she had been wandering about alone. She did not seem so tired as he was.

"Do let us rest a bit," said Diamond.

"Let's see," she answered. "There's something like a railway there. Perhaps there's an open arch."

They went towards it and found one, and better still, there was an empty barrel lying under the arch.

"Hullo! here we are!" said the girl. "A barrel's the jolliest bed going— on the tramp, I mean. We'll have forty winks, and then go on again."

She crept in, and Diamond crept in beside her. They put their arms around each other, and when he began to grow warm, Diamond's courage began to come back.

"This *is* jolly!" he said. "I'm *so* glad!"

"I don't think so much of it," said the girl. "I'm used to it, I suppose. But I can't think how a kid like you comes to be out all alone this time o' night."

She called him a *kid*, but she was not really a month older than he was; only she had had to work for her bread, and that so soon makes people older.

"But I shouldn't have been out so late if I hadn't got down to help you," said Diamond. "North Wind is gone home long ago."

"I think you must ha' got out o' one o' them Hidget Asylms," said the girl. "You said something about the north wind afore that I couldn't get the rights of."

So now, for the sake of his character, Diamond had to tell her the whole story.

She did not believe a word of it. She said she wasn't such a flat as to believe all that bosh. But as she spoke there came a great blast of wind through the arch, and set the barrel rolling. So they made haste to get out of it, for they had no notion of being rolled over and over as if they had been packed tight and wouldn't hurt, like a barrel of herrings.

"I thought we should have had a sleep," said Diamond; "but I can't say I'm very sleepy after all. Come, let's go on again."

They wandered on and on, sometimes sitting on a doorstep, but always turning into lanes or fields when they had a chance.

They found themselves at last on a rising ground that sloped rather steeply on the other side. It was a waste kind of spot below, bounded by an irregular wall, with a few doors in it. Outside lay broken things in general, from garden rollers to flower-pots and wine-bottles. But the moment they reached the brow of the rising ground, a gust of wind seized them and blew them down hill as fast as they could run. Nor could Diamond stop before he went bang against one of the doors in the wall. To his dismay it burst open. When they came to themselves they peeped in. It was the back door of a garden.

"Ah, ah!" cried Diamond, after staring for a few moments, "I thought so! North Wind takes nobody in! Here I am in Master's garden! I tell you what, little girl, you just bore a hole in old Sal's wall, and put your mouth to it, and say, 'Please, North Wind, mayn't I go out with you?' and then you'll see what'll come."

"I daresay I shall. But I'm out in the wind too often already to want more of it."

"I said *with* the north wind, not *in* it."

"It's all one."

"It's *not* all one."

"It *is* all one."

"But I know best."

"And I know better. I'll box your ears," said the girl.

Diamond got very angry. But he remembered that even if she did box his ears, he mustn't box hers again, for she was a girl, and all that boys must do, if girls are rude, is to go away and leave them. So he went in at the door.

"Good-bye, mister," said the girl.

This brought Diamond to his senses.

"I'm sorry I was cross," he said. "Come in, and my mother will give you some breakfast."

"No, thank you. I must be off to my crossing."

"I'm very sorry for you," said Diamond.

"Well, it *is* a life to be tired of—what with old Sal, and so many holes in my shoes."

"I wonder you're so good. I should kill myself."

"Oh, no, you wouldn't! When I think of it, I always want to see what's coming next, and so I always wait till next is over. Well! I suppose there's somebody happy somewheres. But it ain't in them carriages. Oh, my, *how* they *do* look sometimes—fit to bite your head off! Good-bye!"

She ran up the hill and disappeared behind it. Then Diamond shut the door as he best could, and ran through the kitchen-garden to the stable. And wasn't he glad to get into his own blessed bed again!

from

Half Magic

by Edward Eager

Edward Eager (1911–1964) started writing
children's stories when he was looking for books
to read to his son, Fritz. Edward himself loved
the stories of E. Nesbit. He often made reference
to her books in his own—see if you can find one
here—hoping to encourage children to go back
and read her wonderful tales of magic.

It began one day in summer about thirty years ago,
and it happened to four children.

Jane was the oldest and Mark was the only boy, and between them
they ran everything.

Katharine was the middle girl, of docile disposition and a comfort
to her mother. She knew she was a comfort, and docile, because she'd
heard her mother say so. And the others knew she was, too, by now,
because ever since that day Katharine *would* keep boasting about what
a comfort she was, and how docile, until Jane declared she would utter
a piercing shriek and fall over dead if she heard another word about it.
This will give you some idea of what Jane and Katharine were like.

Martha was the youngest, and very difficult.

The children never went to the country or a lake in the summer, the
way their friends did, because their father was dead and their mother
worked very hard on the other newspaper, the one almost nobody on
the block took. A woman named Miss Bick came in every day to care for
the children, but she couldn't seem to care for them very much, nor they

for her. And she wouldn't take them to the country or a lake; she said it was too much to expect and the sound of waves affected her heart.

"Clear Lake isn't the ocean; you can hardly hear it," Jane told her.

"It would attract lightning," Miss Bick said, which Jane, thought cowardly, besides being unfair arguing. If you're going to argue, and Jane usually was, you want people to line up all their objections at a time; then you can knock them all down at once. But Miss Bick was always sly.

Still, even without the country or a lake, the summer was a fine thing, particularly when you were at the beginning of it, looking ahead into it. There would be months of beautifully long, empty days, and each other to play with, and the books from the library.

In the summer you could take out ten books at a time, instead of three, and keep them a month, instead of two weeks. Of course you could take only four of the fiction books, which were the best, but Jane liked plays and they were non-fiction, and Katharine liked poetry and that was non-fiction, and Martha was still the age for picture-books, and they) didn't count as fiction but were often nearly as good.

Mark hadn't found out yet what kind of non-fiction he liked, but he was still trying. Each month he would carry home his ten books and read the four good fiction ones in the first four days, and then read one page each from the other six, and then give up. Next month he would take them back and try again. The non-fiction books he tried were mostly called things like "When I was a Boy in Greece," or "Happy Days on the Prairie"—things that made them sound like stories, only they weren't. They made Mark furious.

"It's being made to learn things not on purpose. It's unfair," he said. "It's sly." Unfairness and slyness the four children hated above all.

The library was two miles away, and walking there with a lot of heavy already-read books was dull, but coming home was splendid—walking slowly, stopping from time to time on different strange front steps, dipping into the different books. One day Katharine, the poetry-lover, tried to read *Evangeline* out loud on the way home, and Martha sat right down on the sidewalk after seven blocks of it, and refused to go a step farther if she had to hear another word of it. That will tell you about Martha.

After that Jane and Mark made a rule that nobody could read bits out loud and bother the others. But this summer the rule was changed. This summer the children had found some books by a writer named E. Nesbit, surely the most wonderful books in the world. They read every one that the library had, right away, except a book called *The Enchanted Castle*, which had been out.

And now yesterday *The Enchanted Castle* had come in, and they took it out, and Jane, because she could read fastest and loudest, read it out loud all the way home, and when they got home she went on reading and when their mother came home they hardly said a word to her, and when dinner was served they didn't notice a thing they ate. Bedtime came at the moment when the magic ring in the book changed from a ring of invisibility to a wishing ring. It was a terrible place to stop, but their mother had one of her strict moments; so stop they did.

And so naturally they all woke up even earlier than usual this morning, and Jane started right in reading out loud and didn't stop till she got to the end of the last page.

There was a contented silence when she closed the book, and then, after a little, it began to get discontented.

Martha broke it, saying what they were all thinking.

"Why don't things like that ever happen to *us*?"

"Magic never happens, not really," said Mark, who was old enough to be sure about this.

"How do you know?" asked Katharine, who was nearly as old as Mark, but not nearly so sure about anything.

"Only in fairy stories."

"It *wasn't* a fairy story. There weren't any dragons or witches or poor woodcutters, just real children like us!"

They were all talking at once now.

"They *aren't* like us. We're never in the country for the summer, and walk down strange roads and find castles!"

"We never go to the seashore and meet mermaids and sand-fairies!"

"Or go to our uncle's, and there's a magic garden!"

"If the Nesbit children do stay in the city it's London, and *that's* interesting, and then they find phoenixes and magic carpets! Nothing like that ever happens here!"

"There's Mrs. Hudson's house," Jane said. "That's a *little* like a castle."

"There's the Miss Kings' garden."

"We could *pretend* . . ."

It was Martha who said this, and the others turned on her.

"Beast!"

"Spoilsport!"

Because of course the only way pretending is any good is if you never say right out that that's what you're doing. Martha knew this perfectly well, but. in her youth she sometimes forgot. So now Mark threw a pillow at her, and so did Jane and Katharine, and in the excitement that followed their mother woke up, and Miss Bick arrived and started giving orders, and "all was flotsam and jetsam," in the poetic words of Katharine.

Two hours later, with breakfast eaten, Mother gone to work and the dishes done, the four children escaped at last, and came out into the sun. It was fine weather, warm and blue-skied and full of possibilities, and the day began well, with a glint of something metal in a crack in the sidewalk.

"Dibs on the nickel," Jane said, and scooped it into her pocket with the rest of her allowance, still jingling there unspent. She would get round to thinking about spending it after the adventures of the morning.

The adventures of the morning began with promise. Mrs. Hudson's house looked *quite* like an Enchanted Castle, with its store wall around and iron dog on the lawn. But when Mark crawled into the peony bed and Jane stood on his shoulders and held Martha up to the kitchen window, all Martha saw was Mrs. Hudson mixing something in a bowl.

"Eye of newt and toe of frog, probably," Katharine thought, but Martha said it looked more like simple one-egg cake.

And then when one of the black ants that live in all peony beds bit Mark, and he dropped Jane and Martha with a crash, nothing happened except Mrs. Hudson's coming out and chasing them with a broom the way she always did, and saying she'd tell their mother. This didn't worry them much, because their mother always said it was Mrs.

Hudson's own fault, that people who had trouble with children brought it on themselves, but it was boring.

So then the children went farther down the street and looked at the Miss Kings' garden. Bees were humming pleasantly round the columbines, and there were Canterbury bells and purple foxgloves looking satisfactorily old-fashioned, and for a moment it seemed as though anything might happen.

But then Miss Mamie King came out and told them that a dear little fairy lived in the biggest purple foxglove, and this wasn't the kind of talk the children wanted to hear at all. They stayed only long enough to be polite, before trooping dispiritedly back to sit on their own front steps.

They sat there and couldn't think of anything exciting to do, and nothing went on happening, and it was then that Jane was so disgusted that she said right out loud she wished there'd be a fire!

The other three looked shocked at hearing such wickedness, and then they looked more shocked at what they heard next.

What they heard next was a fire-siren!

Fire trucks started tearing past—the engine, puffing out smoke the way it used to do in those days, the Chief's car, the hook-and-ladder, the Chemicals!

Mark and Katharine and Martha looked at Jane, and Jane looked back at them with wild wonder in her eyes. Then they started running.

The fire was eight blocks away, and it took them a long time to get there, because Martha wasn't allowed to cross streets by herself, and couldn't run fast yet, like the others; so they had to keep waiting for her to catch up, at all the corners.

And when they finally reached the house where the trucks had stopped, it wasn't the house that was on fire. It was a playhouse in the back yard, the fanciest playhouse the children had ever seen, two stories high and with dormer windows.

You all know what watching a fire is like, the glory of the flames streaming out through the windows, and the wonderful moment when the roof falls in, or even better if there's a tower and it falls through the roof. This playhouse *did* have a tower, and it fell through the roof most beautifully, with a crash and a shower of sparks.

And the fact that it *was* a playhouse, and small like the children, made it seem even more like a special fire that was planned just for them. And the little girl the playhouse belonged to turned out to be an unmistakably spoiled and unpleasant type named Genevieve, with long golden curls that had probably never been cut; so *that* was all right. And furthermore, the children overheard her father say he'd buy her a new playhouse with the insurance money.

So altogether there was no reason for any but feelings of the deepest satisfaction in the breasts of the four children, as they stood breathing heavily and watching the firemen deal with the flames, which they did with that heroic calm typical of fire departments the world over.

And it wasn't until the last flame was drowned, and the playhouse stood there a wet and smoking mess of ashes and charred boards that guilt rose up in Jane and turned her joy to ashes, too.

"Oh, what you did," Martha whispered at her.

"I don't want to talk about it," Jane said. But she went over to a woman who seemed to be the nurse of the golden-haired Genevieve, and asked her how it started.

"All of a piece it went up, like the Fourth of July as ever was," said the nurse. "And it's my opinion," she added, looking at Jane very suspiciously, "that it was *set!* What are *you* doing here, little girl?"

Jane turned right around and walked out of the yard, holding herself as straight as possible and trying to keep from running. The other three went after her.

"Is Jane magic?" Martha whispered to Katharine.

"I don't know. I think so," Katharine whispered back.

Jane glared at them. They went for two blocks in ,silence.

"Are we magic, too?"

"I don't know. I'm scared to find out."

Jane glared. Once more silence fell.

But this time Martha couldn't hold herself in for more than half a block.

"Will we be burnt as *witches?*"

Jane whirled on them furiously.

"I wish," she started to say.

"*Don't!*" Katharine almost screamed, and Jane turned white, shut her lips tight, and started walking faster.

Mark made the others run to catch up.

"This won't do any good. We've got to talk it over," he told Jane.

"Yes, talk it over," said Martha, looking less worried. She had great respect for Mark, who was a boy and knew everything.

"The thing is," Mark went on, "was it just an accident, or did we want so much to be magic we got that way, somehow? The thing is, each of us ought to make a wish. That'll prove it one way or the other."

But Martha balked at this. You could never tell with Martha. Sometimes she would act just as grown-up as the others, and then suddenly she would be a baby. Now she was a baby. Her lip trembled, and she said she didn't want to make a wish and she *wouldn't* make a wish and she wished they'd never started to play this game in the first place.

After consultation, Mark and Katharine decided this could count as Martha's wish, but it didn't seem to have come true, because if it had they wouldn't remember any of the morning, and yet they remembered it all too clearly. But just as a test Mark turned to Jane.

"What have we been doing?" he asked.

"Watching a fire," Jane said bitterly, and at that moment the fire trucks went by on their way home to the station, to prove it.

So then Mark rather depressedly wished his shoes were seven-league boots, but when the tried to jump seven leagues it turned out they weren't.

Katharine wished Shakespeare would come up and talk to her. She forgot to say exactly *when* she wanted this to happen, but after they waited a minute and he didn't appear, they decided he probably wasn't coming.

So it seemed that if there was any magic among them, Jane had it all.

But try as they might, they couldn't persuade Jane to make another wish, even a little safe one. She just kept shaking her head at all their arguments, and when argument descended to insult she didn't say a word, which was most unlike Jane.

When they got home she said she had a headache, and went out on the sleeping porch, and shut the door. She wouldn't even come downstairs for lunch, but stayed out there alone all the afternoon, moodily eating a whole box of Social Tea biscuits and talking to Carrie, the cat. Miss Bick despaired of her.

When their mother came home she knew something was wrong. But being an understanding parent she didn't ask questions.

At dinner she announced that she was going out for the evening. Jane didn't look up from her brooding silence, but the others were interested. The children always hoped their mother was going on exciting adventures, though she seldom was. Tonight she was going to see Aunt Grace and Uncle Edwin.

"Why?" Mark wanted to know.

"They were very kind to me after your father died. They have been very kind to *you*."

"Useful presents!" Mark was scornful.

"Will Aunt Grace say 'Just a little chocolate cake, best you ever tasted, I made it myself?'" Katharine wanted to know.

"You shouldn't laugh at your Aunt Grace. I don't know what your father would say."

"Father laughed at her, too."

"It isn't the same thing."

"Why?"

This kind of conversation was always very interesting to the children, and could have gone on forever so far as they were concerned, but somehow no grown ups ever seemed to feel that way about conversations. Their mother put a stop to this one by leaving for Aunt Grace's

When she had gone things got strange again. Jane kept hovering in and out of the room where the others were playing a half-hearted game of Flinch, until everyone was driven wild.

Finally Mark burst out.

"Why don't you tell us?"

Jane shook her head.

"I can't You wouldn't understand."

Naturally this made everyone furious. "Just because she's magic she thinks she's smarter!" Martha said.

"*I* don't think she's magic at all!" This was Katherine. "Only she's afraid to make a wish and find out!"

"I'm not! *I am!*" Jane cried not very clearly. "Only I don't know why, or how much! It's like having one foot almost asleep, but not quite— you can't use it and you can't enjoy it! I'm afraid to even *think* a wish! I'm afraid to think at *all!*"

If you have ever had magic powers descend on you suddenly out of the blue, you'll know how Jane felt.

When you have magic powers and know it, it can be a fine feeling, like a pleasant tingling inside. But in order to enjoy that tingling, you have to know just how much magic you have and what the rules are for using it. And Jane didn't have any idea how much she had or how to use it, and this made her unhappy and the others couldn't see why, and said so, and Jane answered back, and by the time they went to bed no one was speaking to anyone else.

What bothered Jane most was a feeling that she'd forgotten something, and that if she could remember it she'd know the reason for everything that had happened. It was as if the reason were there in her mind somewhere, if only she could reach it. She leaned into her mind, reaching, reaching . . .

The next thing she knew, she was sitting straight up in bed and the clock was striking eleven, and she had remembered. It was as though she'd gone on thinking in her sleep. Sometimes this happens.

She got up and felt her way to the dresser where she'd put her money, without looking at it, when she came home from the fire. First she felt the top of the dresser. Then she lit the lamp and looked.

The nickel she'd found in the crack in the sidewalk was gone.

And then Jane began thinking really hard.

Aunt Grace settled herself among the cushions of the davenport as though she expected to stay there a long time.

"I think you showed them to me last time, Aunt Grace."

"No, no, dear, that was *Glacier* Park. Edwin, move the floor lamp so Alison can see. This is the Old Faithful geyser. It comes up faithfully every hour, you see. That woman standing there isn't anyone we know.

It's some woman from Ohio who kept trying to get in the picture. Edwin had to speak to her. Turn over the page."

The next page of the snapshot album showed Old Faithful from a different angle. The woman from Ohio had got only half way into the picture; otherwise it looked just the same as the first one.

The children's mother patted back a yawn.

"I really must be going, Aunt Grace."

"Nonsense, dear. You must stay for cake and coffee. Just a little chocolate cake, best you ever tasted, I made it myself."

The children's mother suppressed a smile. Katharine had said Aunt Grace would say that—she always did.

The clock struck eleven.

"Oh, dear," their mother said to herself. "And that long bus ride home, too! I wish I were home right now!"

Next moment all the lights in the room seemed to have gone out, only there seemed to be a moon and some stars shining in through the roof.

Their mother looked for Aunt Grace's stuffy, kind face, but Aunt Grace wasn't there. Instead, a clump of rather gangling milkweeds stared back at her. The hot, stuffy chair seemed suddenly to have grown cold and prickly. She looked down and around.

She was sitting on a weedy hummock by the side of a road. There were no houses in sight, nor any light but the far-off moon and stars.

What had happened? Had she suddenly gone mad? Or could she have said good-by to Aunt Grace and Uncle Edwin, started to walk home instead of taking the bus, and then fainted?

But why couldn't she remember saying good-by? Such a thing had never happened to her before in her life!

She thought she recognized the stretch of road before her. Aunt Grace and Uncle Edwin lived in a suburb, with half a mile of open country between them and the town. Half a mile with only one bus stop, the children's mother remembered. She must be somewhere in that half-mile, but would the bus stop be ahead or behind her?

The sky ahead showed a glow from the lights of town, and she started walking toward it.

The moon was a thin new one and didn't shed much light, and the woodsy thickets on either side of the road were dark and spooky. Things moved in the branches of trees. The children's mother didn't like it at all.

What was she, a successful newspaperwoman and the mother of four children, doing, wandering the roads by night like this?

When she was set upon and murdered by highwaymen and her body was found next morning, what would the children think? What would anyone think? It must be a bad dream. Soon she would wake up. Now she would keep walking.

She kept walking.

Behind her an engine throbbed and lights shone. She turned, holding up her hand, hoping it was the bus.

It wasn't the bus, just someone's car. But the car stopped by her, and rather a small gentleman looked out.

"Would you like a ride?"

"Well, no, not really," the children's mother said, which was not true at all; she would like one very much. But she had always told the children particularly not to go riding with strangers.

"Did your car break down?"

"Well, no, not exactly."

"Just taking a walk?"

"Well, no."

The rather small gentleman had opened the door of the car now.

"Get in," he said.

To her surprise, the children's mother got in. They rode along for a bit in silence. The children's mother tried to study the gentleman's face out of the corner of her eye, and was displeased to see that he wore a beard. Beards always seemed to her rather sinister. Why would anyone wear one, unless he had something to hide?

But this beard was only a small, pointed one, and the rest of the gentleman's face, or as much of it as she could see in the dark car, seemed pleasant. She found herself wanting to tell him of her strange adventure. Of course she couldn't. It would sound too silly.

The gentleman broke the silence.

"Lonely out this way after dark," he said. "Rather dangerous for walking, I should say."

"I should say so, too," said the children's mother. "I can't think what can have happened. There I was, talking to Aunt Grace, and suddenly *there* I was, by the side of the road!"

And, in spite of having decided not to, she began telling the small gentleman all about it.

"There's only one explanation," she said, at the end of it. "I must have lost my memory, just for a minute."

"Oh, there's never only *one* explanation," said the rather small gentleman. "It depends on which one you want to believe! *I* believe in believing six impossible things before breakfast, myself. Not that I usually get the chance. The trouble with life is that not enough impossible things happen for us to believe in, don't you agree? Where did you say you live?"

"I didn't," said the children's mother. Really, this night was growing odder and odder. She wasn't used to meeting people who talked exactly like the White Queen, or to giving her address to perfect strangers, either—still, if she wanted to get home there didn't seem to be anything else to do.

She gave him her address, and a moment later they were driving up before the house.

She thanked the small gentleman for his trouble. He bowed, hesitated as though he meant to say something further, then seemed to think better of it, and drove away.

It wasn't until he was gone that the children's mother realized that she didn't even know his name, nor he hers. Still, they would probably never see each other again.

She turned and started up the walk, then stopped in horror.

All the lights in the living room were ablaze!

Thinking of every terrible thing that could possibly have happened, she ran up the walk, turned her key in the lock, and hurried inside.

Huddled on a corner of the sofa sat Jane, wrapped in a blanket and looking small and white and forlorn.

Her mother was by her side and had her arms round her in a second. All thoughts of her own strange evening, and of the rather small gentleman, vanished from her head.

"What is it, tummy-ache or bad dreams?" she cried. "You should have telephoned me!"

"It isn't either one," Jane said. "Mother, did you borrow a nickel that was on my dresser?"

"*What?*" cried her mother. "Did you wait up all this time to ask me *that?*"

And immediately she began to scold, as is the habit of parents when they've been worried about their children and find that they needn't have been.

"Really, Jane, you must *not* be so money-grubbing!" she said. "Yes, I borrowed a nickel for carfare. I only had one nickel and a five-dollar bill, and they're always so mean about making change . . ."

"Did you *spend* it?" Jane interrupted, her voice horrified.

"I spent a nickel, going. What does it matter? I'll pay you back tomorrow."

"Did you spend the other nickel, coming home?"

Her mother looked confused, for a moment.

"Well, no, as a matter of fact I didn't. Someone gave me a lift."

"Do you know which one you spent, the one you had or the one you borrowed?"

"Oh, for Heaven's sake! No, I don't!"

"Could I have the one you didn't spend? Now, please?"

"Jane, what *is* all this? Anyone would think you were a starving Little Match Girl, or something!" Then her mother relented. "Oh well, if it'll make you happy!"

She dug in her purse.

"Here. Now go to bed."

Jane took one quick look at the thing her mother had given her, then folded her hand tightly around it. She had guessed right. It wasn't a nickel.

She lingered in the doorway.

"Mother."

"What is it now?"

"Well, did you . . . did anything . . . anything sort of *unusual* happen tonight?"

"What do you mean? Of course not! Why?"

"Oh, nothing!"

Jane searched in her mind for an excuse. She couldn't tell her mother the truth; she'd never believe it. It would only upset her.

"It's just that I . . . I had this *dream* about you, and I got worried. I dreamed you *wished* for something!"

"You did? That's strange." Her mother looked interested suddenly. She went on, almost to herself, as though she were remembering. "As a matter of fact, I *did* wish something. I wished I were at home. And it was just then that . . ."

"That *what?*" Jane was excited.

Her mother put on her "drop the subject" expression.

"Nothing. I came home. Someone gave me a ride. A . . . a friend of Uncle Edwin's."

She didn't look at Jane. It was awful to be lying like this, to her own child. But she couldn't tell Jane the truth; she'd never believe it. It would only upset her.

"I see." But Jane didn't leave. She stood tracing a pattern in the hall carpet with one foot. She went on carefully, not looking at her mother.

"In my dream, when you wished you were home, I'm not sure what came next. I don't think you *were* home, exactly . . ."

"Ha! I certainly wasn't!"

"But you were *somewhere!*"

"Somewhere in a weed patch, half way out Bancroft Street, most likely!"

Now Jane looked up, and straight at her.

"We're just talking about my dream, aren't we? It didn't really happen?"

"Of course not."

It was her mother who was looking away now. But now Jane knew,

Clutching the thing in her hand tighter, she ran up the stairs and into her room.

Her mother stood thinking. How strange that Jane should have guessed!

No stranger, though, than everything else about this strange evening. Probably none of it had really happened at all. Probably she was ill and imagining things—coming down with flu or something, She had better get some rest. She turned out the living room lights and went upstairs.

Jane stood in her own room, looking at the thing in her hand. It was the size of a nickel and the shape of a nickel and the color of a nickel, but it wasn't a nickel.

It was worn thin—probably by centuries of time, Jane told herself And instead of a buffalo or a Liberty head, it bore strange signs. Jane held it closer to the light to study the signs.

There was a rap at the door.

"Lights out!" called her mother's voice.

Jane put out the light.

But she knew that she held in her hand the talisman that was going to turn this summer into a time of wild adventure and delight for all of them.

She must hide it in a safe place till morning.

Feeling her way across the room in the dark, she opened the closet door. There was a shoebag on the inside of the door, one of those flowered cotton affairs with many compartments for shoes, though Jane seldom remembered to put hers away in it.

She dropped the magic thing into one of the compartments in the shoebag. No one would disturb it there.

Then she got into bed.

Her last thought was that she must wake up early in the morning, by dawn at *least*, and call the others.

They must hold a Conference, and decide just how they were going to use this wonderful gift that had descended upon them out of the blue it was going to be an Enchanted Summer!

And Jane fell asleep.

The Nose

by Nikolai Gogol

Nikolai Gogol (1809–1852) was born in the Ukraine and grew up on his parents' estate. He worked in the government and then as a teacher before becoming a full-time writer. After the Tsar criticized one of his plays, Gogol left Russia and went to live in Europe. Late in his life he came under the influence of a fanatical priest and burned his last writings before they were published. There is a terrible rumor that Gogel was buried alive.

On March 25th there took place, in Petersburg, an extraordinarily strange occurrence. The barber Ivan Yakovlevich, who lives on Voznesensky Avenue (his family name has been lost and even on his signboard, where a gentleman is depicted with a lathered cheek and the inscription "Also bloodletting," there is nothing else)— the barber Ivan Yakovlevich woke up rather early and smelled fresh bread. Raising himself slightly in bed he saw his spouse, a rather respectable lady who was very fond of drinking coffee, take some newly baked loaves out of the oven.

"I won't have any coffee today, Praskovya Osipovna," said Ivan Yakovlevich. "Instead, I would like to eat a bit of hot bread with onion." (That is to say, Ivan Yakovlevich would have liked both the one and the other, but he knew that it was quite impossible to demand two things at once, for Praskovya Osipovna very much disliked such whims.) "Let the fool eat the bread; all the better for me," the wife thought to herself, "there will be an extra cup of coffee left." And she threw a loaf onto the table.

For the sake of propriety Ivan Yakovlevich put a tailcoat on over his shirt and, sitting down at the table, poured out some salt, got two onions ready, picked up a knife and, assuming a meaningful expression, began to slice the bread. Having cut the loaf in two halves, he looked inside and to his astonishment saw something white. Ivan Yakovlevich poked it carefully with the knife and felt it with his finger. "Solid!" he said to himself. "What could it be?"

He stuck in his finger and extracted—a nose! Ivan Yakovlevich was dumbfounded. He rubbed his eyes and felt the object: a nose, a nose indeed, and a familiar one at that. Ivan Yakovlevich's face expressed horror. But this horror was nothing compared to the indignation which seized his spouse.

"You beast, where did you cut off a nose?" she shouted angrily. "Scoundrel! drunkard! I'll report you to the police myself. What a ruffian! I have already heard from three people that you jerk their noses about so much when shaving that it's a wonder they stay in place."

But Ivan Yakovlevich was more dead than alive. He recognized the nose as that of none other than Collegiate Assessor Kovalyov, whom he shaved every Wednesday and Sunday.

"Hold on, Praskovya Osipovna! I shall put it in a corner, after I've wrapped it in a rag: let it lie there for a while, and later I'll take it away."

"I won't even hear of it. That I should allow a cut-off nose to lie about in my room? You dry stick! All he knows is how to strop his razor, but soon he'll be in no condition to carry out his duty, the rake, the villain! Am I to answer for you to the police? You piece of filth, you blockhead! Away with it! Away! Take it anywhere you like! Out of my sight with it!"

Ivan Yakovlevich stood there as though bereft of senses. He thought and thought—and really did not know what to think. "The devil knows how it happened," he said at last, scratching behind his ear with his hand. "Was I drunk or wasn't I when I came home yesterday, I really can't say. Whichever way you look at it, this is an impossible occurrence. After all, bread is something baked, and a nose is something altogether different. I can't make it out at all."

Ivan Yakovlevich fell silent. The idea that the police might find the nose in his possession and bring a charge against him drove him into a complete frenzy. He was already visualizing the scarlet collar, beautifully embroidered with silver, the saber—and he trembled all over. At last he got out his underwear and boots, pulled on all these tatters and, followed by rather weighty exhortations from Praskovya Osipovna, wrapped the nose in a rag and went out into the street.

He wanted to shove it under something somewhere, either into the hitching-post by the gate—or just drop it as if by accident and then turn off into a side street. But as bad luck would have it, he kept running into people he knew, who at once would ask him, "Where are you going?" or "Whom are you going to shave so early?" so that Ivan Yakovlevich couldn't find the right moment. Once he actually did drop it, but a policeman some distance away pointed to it with his halberd and said: "Pick it up—you've dropped something there," and Ivan Yakovlevich was obliged to pick up the nose and hide it in his pocket. He was seized with despair, all the more so as the number of people in the street constantly increased when the shops began to open.

He decided to go to St. Isaac's Bridge—might he not just manage to toss it into the Neva? But I am somewhat to blame for having so far said nothing about Ivan Yakovlevich, in many ways a respectable man.

Like any self-respecting Russian artisan, Ivan Yakovlevich was a terrible drunkard. And although every day he shaved other people's chins his own was ever unshaven. Ivan Yakovlevich's tailcoat (Ivan Yakovlevich never wore a frockcoat) was piebald, that is to say, it was all black but dappled with brownish-yellow and gray; the collar was shiny, and in place of three of the buttons hung just the ends of thread. Ivan Yakovlevich was a great cynic, and when Collegiate Assessor Kovalyov told him while being shaved, "Your hands, Ivan Yakovlevich, always stink," Ivan Yakovlevich would reply with the question, "Why should they stink?" "I don't know, my dear fellow," the Collegiate Assessor would say, "but they do," and Ivan Yakovlevich, after taking a pinch of snuff, would, in retaliation, lather all over his cheeks and under his nose, and behind his ear, and under his chin—in other words, wherever his fancy took him.

This worthy citizen now found himself on St. Isaac's Bridge. To begin with, he took a good look around, then leaned on the railings as though to look under the bridge to see whether or not there were many fish swimming about, and surreptitiously tossed down the rag containing the nose. He felt as though all of a sudden a ton had been lifted off him: Ivan Yakovlevich even smirked. Instead of going to shave some civil servants' chins he set off for an establishment bearing a sign "Snacks and Tea" to order a glass of punch when he suddenly noticed, at the end of the bridge, a police officer of distinguished appearance, with wide sideburns, wearing a three-cornered hat and with a sword. His heart sank: the officer was wagging his finger at him and saying, "Step this way, my friend."

Knowing the etiquette, Ivan Yakovlevich removed his cap while still some way off, and approaching with alacrity said, "I wish your honor good health."

"No, no, my good fellow, not 'your honor.' Just you tell me, what were you doing over there, standing on the bridge?"

"Honestly, sir, I've been to shave someone and only looked to see if the river were running fast."

"You're lying, you're lying. This won't do. Just be so good as to answer."

"I am ready to shave your worship twice a week, or even three times, and no complaints," replied Ivan Yakovlevich.

"No, my friend, all that's nonsense. I have three barbers who shave me and deem it a great honor, too. Just be so good as to tell me, what were you doing over there?"

Ivan Yakovlevich turned pale. . . . But here the whole episode becomes shrouded in mist, and of what happened subsequently absolutely nothing is known.

Collegiate Assessor Kovalyov woke up rather early and made a "b-rr-rr" sound with his lips as he was wont to do on awakening, although he could not have explained the reason for it. Kovalyov stretched and asked for the small mirror standing on the table. He wanted to have a look at the pimple which had, the evening before, appeared on his nose. But to his extreme amazement he saw that he had, in the place of his nose, a perfectly smooth surface. Frightened, Kovalyov called for some water and rubbed his eyes with a towel: indeed, no nose! He ran his hand over himself to see whether or not he was asleep. No, he didn't think so. The Collegiate Assessor jumped out of bed and shook himself—no nose! He at once ordered his clothes to be brought to him, and flew off straight to the chief of police.

In the meantime something must be said about Kovalyov, to let the reader see what sort of man this collegiate assessor was. Collegiate assessors who receive their rank on the strength of scholarly diplomas can by no means be equated with those who make the rank in the Caucasus. They are two entirely different breeds. Learned collegiate assessors . . . But Russia is such a wondrous land that if you say something about one collegiate assessor all the collegiate assessors from Riga to Kamchatka will not fail to take it as applying to them, too. The same is true of all our ranks and titles. Kovalyov belonged to the Caucasus variety of collegiate assessors. He had only held that rank for two years and therefore could not forget it for a moment; and in order to lend himself added dignity and weight he never referred to himself as collegiate assessor but always as major. "Listen, my dear woman," he would usually say on meeting in the street a woman selling shirt fronts, "come to my place, my apartment is on Sadovaya; just ask where Major Kovalyov lives, anyone will show you." And if the woman he met happened to be a pretty one, he would also give some confidential instructions, adding, "You just ask, lovely, for Major Kovalyov's apartment."—That is why we, too, will henceforth refer to this collegiate assessor as Major.

Major Kovalyov was in the habit of taking a daily stroll along Nevsky Avenue. The collar of his dress shirt was always exceedingly clean and starched. His sidewhiskers were of the kind you can still see on provincial and district surveyors, or architects (provided they are Russians), as well as on those individuals who perform various police duties, and in general on all those men who have full rosy cheeks and are very good at boston; these sidewhiskers run along the middle of the cheek straight up to the nose. Major Kovalyov wore a great many cornelian seals, some with crests and others with Wednesday, Thursday, Monday, etc., engraved on them. Major Kovalyov had come to Petersburg on business, to wit, to look for a post befitting his rank; if he could arrange it, that of a vice-governor; otherwise, that of a procurement officer in some important government department. Major Kovalyov was not averse to getting married, but only in the event that the bride had a fortune of two hundred thousand. And therefore the reader can now judge for himself what this major's state was when he saw, in the place of a fairly presentable and moderate-sized nose, a most ridiculous flat and smooth surface.

As bad luck would have it, not a single cab showed up in the street, and he was forced to walk, wrapped up in his cloak, his face covered with a handkerchief, pretending that his nose was bleeding. "But perhaps I just imagined all this—a nose cannot disappear in this idiotic way." He stepped into a coffeehouse just in order to look at himself in a mirror. Fortunately, there was no one there. Serving boys were sweeping the rooms and arranging the chairs; some of them, sleepy-eyed, were bringing out trays of hot turnovers; yesterday's papers, coffee-stained, lay about on tables and chairs. "Well, thank God, there is no one here," said the Major. "Now I can have a look." Timidly he approached the mirror and glanced at it. "Damnation! How disgusting!" he exclaimed after spitting. "If at least there were something in place of the nose, but there's nothing!"

Biting his lips with annoyance, he left the coffee-house and decided, contrary to his habit, not to look or to smile at anyone. Suddenly he stopped dead in his tracks before the door of a house. An inexplicable phenomenon took place before his very eyes: a carriage drew up to the entrance; the doors opened; a gentleman in uniform jumped out, slightly stooping, and ran up the stairs. Imagine the horror and at the same time the amazement of Kovalyov when he recognized that it was his own nose! At this extraordinary sight everything seemed to whirl before his eyes; he felt that he could hardly keep on his feet. Trembling all over as though with fever, he made up his mind, come what may, to await the gentleman's return to the carriage. Two minutes later the Nose indeed came out. He was wearing a gold-embroidered uniform with a big stand-up collar and doeskin breeches; there was a sword at his side. From his plumed hat one could infer that he held the rank of a state councillor. Everything pointed to his being on the way to pay a call. He looked right and left, shouted to his driver, "Bring the carriage round," got in and was driven off.

Poor Kovalyov almost went out of his mind. He did not even know what to think of this strange occurrence. Indeed, how could a nose which as recently as yesterday had been on his face and could neither ride nor walk—how could it be in uniform? He ran after the carriage, which fortunately had not gone far but had stopped before the Kazan Cathedral.

He hurried into the cathedral, made his way past the ranks of old beggarwomen with bandaged faces and two slits for their eyes, whom he used to make such fun of, and went inside. There were but few worshippers there: they all stood by the entrance. Kovalyov felt so upset that he was in no condition to pray and searched with his eyes for the gentleman in all the church corners. At last he saw him standing to one side. The Nose had completely hidden his face in his big stand-up collar and was praying in an attitude of utmost piety.

"How am I to approach him?" thought Kovalyov. "From everything, from his uniform, from his hat, one can see that he is a state councillor. I'll be damned if I know how to do it."

He started clearing his throat, but the Nose never changed his devout attitude and continued his genuflections.

"My dear sir," said Kovalyov, forcing himself to take courage, "my dear sir . . ."

"What is it you desire?" said the Nose turning round.

"It is strange, my dear sir . . . I think . . . you ought to know your place. And all of a sudden I find you—and where? In church. You'll admit . . . "

"Excuse me, I cannot understand what you are talking about. . . . Make yourself clear."

"How shall I explain to him?" thought Kovalyov and, emboldened, began: "Of course, I . . . however, I am a major. For me to go about

without my nose, you'll admit, is unbecoming. It's all right for a ped-
dler woman who sells peeled oranges on Voskresensky Bridge, to sit
without a nose. But since I'm expecting—and besides, having many
acquaintances among the ladies-Mrs. Chekhtaryova, a state councillor's
wife, and others . . . Judge for yourself . . . I don't know, my dear sir . . ."
(Here Major Kovalyov shrugged his shoulders.) "Forgive me, if one
were to look at this in accordance with rules of duty and honor . . . you
yourself can understand. . . ."

"I understand absolutely nothing," replied the Nose. "Make yourself more clear."

"My dear sir," said Kovalyov with a sense of his own dignity, "I don't
know how to interpret your words . . . The whole thing seems to me
quite obvious . . . Or do you wish . . . After all, you are my own nose!"

The Nose looked at the major and slightly knitted his brows.

"You are mistaken, my dear sir, I exist in my own right. Besides,
there can be no close relation between us. Judging by the buttons on
your uniform, you must be employed in the Senate or at least in the
Ministry of Justice. As for me, I am in the scholarly line."

Having said this, the Nose turned away and went back to his
prayers.

Kovalyov was utterly flabbergasted. He knew not what to do or even
what to think. Just then he heard the pleasant rustle of a lady's dress:
an elderly lady, all in lace, had come up near him and with her, a slim
one, in a white frock which agreeably outlined her slender figure, and
in a straw-colored hat, light as a cream-puff. Behind them, a tall footman with huge sidewhiskers and a whole dozen collars, stopped and
opened a snuff-box.

Kovalyov stepped closer, pulled out the cambric collar of his dress
shirt, adjusted his seals hanging on a golden chain and, smiling in all
directions, turned his attention to the ethereal young lady who, like a
spring flower, bowed her head slightly and put her little white hand
with its translucent fingers to her forehead. The smile on Kovalyov's
face grew even wider when from under her hat he caught a glimpse of
her little round dazzling-white chin and part of her cheek glowing with

the color of the first rose of spring. But suddenly he sprang back as though scalded. He remembered that there was absolutely nothing in the place of his nose, and tears came to his eyes. He turned round, intending without further ado to tell the gentleman in uniform that he was merely pretending to be a state councillor, that he was a rogue and a cad and nothing more than his, the major's, own nose. . . . But the Nose was no longer there; he had managed to dash off, probably to pay another call.

This plunged Kovalyov into despair. He went back, stopped for a moment under the colonnade and looked carefully, this way and that, for the Nose to turn up somewhere. He remembered quite well that the latter had a plumed hat and a gold-embroidered uniform, but he had not noticed his overcoat, or the color of his carriage or of his horses, not even whether he had a footman at the back, and if so in what livery. Moreover, there was such a multitude of carriages dashing back and forth and at such speed that it was difficult to tell them apart; but even if he did pick one of them out, he would have no means of stopping it. The day was fine and sunny. There were crowds of people on Nevsky Avenue. A whole flowery cascade of ladies poured over the sidewalk, all the way down from Police Bridge to Anichkin Bridge. Here came a court councillor he knew, and was used to addressing as lieutenant-colonel, especially in the presence of strangers. Here, too, was Yarygin, a head clerk in the Senate, a great friend of his, who invariably lost at boston when he went up eight. Here was another major who had won his assessorship in the Caucasus, waving to Kovalyov to join him. . . .

"O hell!" said Kovalyov. "Hey, cabby, take me straight to the chief of police!"

Kovalyov got into the cab and kept shouting to the cabman, "Get going as fast as you can."

"Is the chief of police at home?" he called out as he entered the hall.

"No, sir," answered the doorman, "he has just left."

"You don't say."

"Yes," added the doorman, "he has not been gone long, but he's gone. Had you come a minute sooner perhaps you might have found him in."

Without removing the handkerchief from his face, Kovalyov got back into the cab and in a voice of despair shouted, "Drive on!"

"Where to?" asked the cabman.

"Drive straight ahead!"

"What do you mean straight ahead? There is a turn here. Right or left?"

This question nonplussed Kovalyov and made him think again. In his plight the first thing for him to do was to apply to the Police Department, not because his cause had anything to do directly with the police, but because they could act much more quickly than any other institution; while to seek satisfaction from the superiors of the department by which the Nose claimed to be employed would be pointless because from the Nose's own replies it was obvious that this fellow held nothing sacred, and that he was capable of lying in this case, too, as he had done when he had assured Kovalyov that they had never met. Thus Kovalyov was on the point of telling the cabman to take him to the Police Department when the thought again occurred to him that this rogue and swindler, who had already treated him so shamelessly during their first encounter, might again seize his first chance to slip out of town somewhere, and then all search would be futile or might drag on, God forbid, a whole month. Finally, it seemed, heaven itself brought him to his senses. He decided to go straight to the newspaper office and, before it was too late, place an advertisement with a detailed description of the Nose's particulars, so that anyone coming across him could immediately deliver him or at least give information about his whereabouts. And so, his mind made up, he told the cabby to drive to the newspaper office, and all the way down to it kept whacking him in the back with his first, saying, "Faster, you villain! faster, you rogue!"—"Ugh, mister!" the cabman would say, shaking his head and flicking his reins at the horse whose coat was as long as a lapdog's. At last the cab drew up to a stop, and Kovalyov, panting, ran into a small reception room where a gray-haired clerk in an old tailcoat and glasses sat at a table and, pen in his teeth, counted newly brought in coppers.

"Who accepts advertisements here?" cried Kovalyov. "Ah, good morning!"

"How do you do," said the gray-haired clerk, raising his eyes for a moment and lowering them again to look at the neat stacks of money.

"I should like to insert—"

"Excuse me. Will you wait a moment," said the clerk as he wrote down a figure on a piece of paper with one hand and moved two beads on the abacus with the fingers of his left hand. A liveried footman, whose appearance suggested his sojourn in an aristocratic house, and who stood by the table with a note in his hand, deemed it appropriate to demonstrate his savoir-faire: "Would you believe it, sir, this little mutt is not worth eighty kopecks, that is, I wouldn't even give eight kopecks for it; but the countess loves it, honestly she does—and so whoever finds it will get one hundred rubles! To put it politely, just as you and I are talking, people's tastes differ: if you're a hunter, keep a pointer or a poodle; don't grudge five hundred, give a thousand, but then let it be a good dog."

The worthy clerk listened to this with a grave expression while at the same time trying to count the number of letters in the note brought to him. All around stood a great many old women, salespeople and house porters with notes. One of them offered for sale a coachman of sober conduct; another, a little-used carriage brought from Paris in 1814; still others, a nineteen-year-old serf girl experienced in laundering work and suitable for other kinds of work; a sound droshky with one spring missing; a young and fiery dappled-gray horse seventeen years old; turnip and radish seed newly received from London; a summer residence with all the appurtenances—to wit, two stalls for horses and a place for planting a grove of birches or firs; there was also an appeal to those wishing to buy old boot soles, inviting them to appear for final bidding every day between eight and three o'clock. The room in which this entire company was crowded was small, and the air in it was extremely thick; but Collegiate Assessor Kovalyov was not in a position to notice the smell, because he kept his handkerchief pressed to his face and because his nose itself was goodness knows where.

"My dear sir, may I ask you . . . It is very urgent," he said at last with impatience.

"Presently, presently! Two rubles forty-three kopecks! Just a moment! One ruble sixty-four kopecks," recited the gray-haired gentleman, tossing the notes into the faces of the old women and the house porters. "What can I do for you?" he said at last, turning to Kovalyov.

"I wish . . .," said Kovalyov. "There has been a swindle or a fraud . . . I still can't find out. I just wish to advertise that whoever hands this scoundrel over to me will receive an adequate reward."

"Allow me to inquire, what is your name?"

"What do you want my name for? I can't give it to you. I have many acquaintances: Mrs. Chekhtaryova, the wife of a state councillor; Pelageya Grigoryevna Podtochina, the wife of a field officer . . . What if they suddenly were to find out? Heaven forbid! You can simply write down: a collegiate assessor or, still better, a person holding the rank of major."

"And was the runaway your household serf?"

"What do you mean, household serf? That wouldn't be such a bad swindle! The runaway was . . . my nose. . . ."

"Hmm! what a strange name! And did this Mr. Nosov rob you of a big sum?"

"My nose, I mean to say—You've misunderstood me. My nose, my very own nose has disappeared goodness knows where. The devil must have wished to play a trick on me!"

"But how did it disappear? I don't quite understand it."

"Well, I can't tell you how; but the main thing is that it is now gallivanting about town and calling itself a state councillor. And that is why I am asking you to advertise that whoever apprehends it should deliver it to me immediately and without delay. Judge for yourself. How, indeed, can I do without such a conspicuous part of my body? It isn't like some little toe which I put into my boot, and no one can see whether it is there or not. On Thursdays I call at the house of Mrs. Chekhtaryova, a state councillor's wife. Mrs. Podtochina, Pelageya Grigoryevna, a field officer's wife, and her very pretty daughter, are also very good friends of mine, and you can judge for yourself how can I now . . . I can't appear at their house now."

The clerk thought hard, his lips pursed tightly in witness thereof.

"No, I can't insert such an advertisement in the papers," he said at last after a long silence.

"How so? Why?"

"Well, the paper might lose its reputation. If everyone were to write that his nose had run away, why . . . As it is, people say that too many absurd stories and false rumors are printed."

"But why is this business absurd? I don't think it is anything of the sort."

"That's what you think. But take last week, there was another such case. A civil servant came in, just as you have, bringing a note, was billed two rubles seventy-three kopecks, and all the advertisement consisted of was that a black-coated poodle had run away. Doesn't seem to amount to much, does it now? But it turned out to be a libel. This so-called poodle was the treasurer of I don't recall what institution."

"But I am not putting in an advertisement about a poodle—it's about my very own nose; that is, practically the same as about myself."

"No, I can't possibly insert such an advertisement."

"But when my nose actually has disappeared!"

"If it has disappeared, then it's a doctor's business. They say there are people who can fix you up with any nose you like. However, I observe that you must be a man of gay disposition and fond of kidding in company."

"I swear to you by all that is holy! Perhaps, if it comes to that, why I'll show you."

"Why trouble yourself?" continued the clerk, taking a pinch of snuff. "However, if it isn't too much trouble," he added, moved by curiosity, "I'd like to have a look."

The collegiate assessor removed the handkerchief from his face.

"Very strange indeed!" said the clerk. "It's absolutely flat, like a pancake fresh off the griddle. Yes, incredibly smooth."

"Well, will you go on arguing after this? You see yourself that you can't refuse to print my advertisement. I'll be particularly grateful and am very glad that this opportunity has given me the pleasure of making your acquaintance. . . ." The major, as we can see, decided this time to use a little flattery.

"To insert it would be easy enough, of course," said the clerk, "but I don't see any advantage to you in it. If you really must, give it to someone who wields a skillful pen and let him describe this as a rare phenomenon of nature and publish this little item in *The Northern Bee*" (here he took another pinch of snuff) "for the benefit of the young" (here he wiped his nose), "or just so, as a matter of general interest."

The collegiate assessor felt completely discouraged. He dropped his eyes to the lower part of the paper where theatrical performances were announced. His face was about to break out into a smile as he came across the name of a pretty actress, and his hand went to his pocket to check whether he had a blue note, because in his opinion field officers ought to sit in the stalls—but the thought of his nose spoiled it all.

The clerk himself seemed to be moved by Kovalyov's embarrassing situation. Wishing at least to ease his distress he deemed it appropriate to express his sympathy in a few words: "I really am grieved that such a thing happened to you. Wouldn't you care for a pinch of snuff? It dispels headaches and melancholy; it's even good for hemorrhoids." With those words the clerk offered Kovalyov his snuff-box, rather deftly snapping open the lid which pictured a lady in a hat.

This unpremeditated action made Kovalyov lose all patience. "I can't understand how you find this a time for jokes," he said angrily. "Can't you see that I lack the very thing one needs to take snuff? To hell with your snuff! I can't bear the sight of it now, even if you offered me some râpé itself, let alone your wretched Berezin's." After saying this he left the newspaper office, deeply vexed, and went to visit the district police inspector, a man with a passion for sugar. In his house the entire parlor, which served also as the dining room, was stacked with sugar loaves which local tradesmen brought to him out of friendship. At the moment his cook was pulling off the inspector's regulation topboots; his sword and all his military trappings were already hanging peacefully in the corners, and his three-year-old son was reaching for his redoubtable three-cornered hat, while the inspector himself was preparing to taste the fruits of peace after his day of warlike, martial pursuits.

Kovalyov came in at the moment when the inspector had just

stretched, grunted and said, "Oh, for a couple of hours' good snooze!"
It was therefore easy to see that the collegiate assessor had come at
quite the wrong time. And I wonder whether he would have been welcome even if he had brought several pounds of tea or a piece of cloth.
The police inspector was a great patron of all arts and manufactures,
but he preferred a bank note to everything else. "This is the thing," he
would usually say. "There can be nothing better than it—it doesn't ask
for food, it doesn't take much space, it'll always fit into a pocket, and
if you drop it it won't break."

The inspector received Kovalyov rather coolly and said that after
dinner was hardly the time to conduct investigations, that nature itself
intended that man should rest a little after a good meal (from this the
collegiate assessor could see that the aphorisms of the ancient sages
were not unknown to the police inspector), that no real gentleman
would allow his nose to be pulled off, and that there were many majors
in this world who hadn't even decent underwear and hung about in all
sorts of disreputable places.

This last was too close for comfort. It must be observed that
Kovalyov was extremely quick to take offense. He could forgive whatever was said about himself, but never anything that referred to rank or
title. He was even of the opinion that in plays one could allow refer-
ences to junior officers, but that there should be no criticism of field
officers. His reception by the inspector so disconcerted him that he
tossed his head and said with an air of dignity, spreading his arms
slightly: "I confess that after such offensive remarks on your part, I've
nothing more to add. . . ." and left the room.

He came home hardly able to stand on his feet. It was already dusk.
After all this fruitless search his apartment appeared to him melancholy or extraordinarily squalid. Coming into the entrance hall he
caught sight of his valet Ivan who, lying on his back on the soiled
leather sofa, was spitting at the ceiling and rather successfully hitting
one and the same spot. Such indifference on the man's part infuriated
him; he struck him on the forehead with his hat, saying, "You pig,
always doing something stupid!"

Ivan jumped up abruptly and rushed to take off his cloak.

Entering his room the major, tired and sad, sank into an armchair and at last, after several sighs, said:

"O Lord, O Lord! What have I done to deserve such misery? Had I lost an arm or a leg, it would not have been so bad; had I lost my ears, it would have been bad enough but nevertheless bearable; but without a nose a man is goodness knows what; he's not a bird, he's not a human being; in fact, just take him and throw him out the window! And if at least it had been chopped off in battle or in a duel, or if I myself had been to blame; but it disappeared just like that, with nothing, nothing at all to show for it. But no, it can't be," he added after some thought. "It's unbelievable that a nose should disappear; absolutely unbelievable. I must be either dreaming or just imagining it. Maybe, somehow, by mistake instead of water I drank the vodka which I rub on my chin after shaving. That fool Ivan didn't take it away and I probably gulped it down." To satisfy himself that he was not drunk the major pinched himself so hard that he cried out. The pain he felt fully convinced him that he was wide awake. He stealthily approached the mirror and at first half-closed his eyes, thinking that perhaps the nose would appear in its proper place; but the same moment he sprang back exclaiming, "What a caricature of a face!"

It was indeed incomprehensible. If a button, a silver spoon, a watch, or some such thing had disappeared—but to disappear, and for whom to disappear? and besides in his own apartment, too! . . . After considering all the circumstances, Major Kovalyov was inclined to think that most likely it was the fault of none other than the field officer's wife, Mrs. Podtochina, who wanted him to marry her daughter. He, too, liked to flirt with her but avoided a final showdown. And when the field officer's wife told him point-blank that she wanted to marry her daughter off to him, he eased off on his attentions, saying that he was still young, that he had to serve another five years when he would be exactly forty-two. And so the field officer's wife, presumably in revenge, had decided to put a curse on him and hired for this purpose some old witchwomen, because it was impossible even to suppose that the nose had been simply cut off: no one had entered his room; the barber, Ivan Yakovlevich, had shaved him as recently as Wednesday and throughout that whole day and even on Thursday his nose was all there—he remembered and knew it very well. Besides, he would have felt the pain and no doubt the wound could not have healed so soon and be as smooth as a pancake. Different plans of action occurred to him: should he formally summons Mrs. Podtochina to court or go to her himself and expose her in person? His reflections were interrupted by light breaking through all the cracks in the door, which told him that Ivan had lit the candle in the hall. Soon Ivan himself appeared, carrying it before him and brightly illuminating the whole room. Kovalyov's first gesture was to snatch his handkerchief and cover the place where his nose had been only the day before, so that indeed the silly fellow would not stand there gaping at such an oddity in his master's strange appearance.

Barely had Ivan gone into his cubbyhole when an unfamiliar voice was heard in the hall saying, "Does Collegiate Assessor Kovalyov live here?" "Come in. Major Kovalyov is here," said Kovalyov, jumping up quickly and opening the door.

In came a police officer of handsome appearance with sidewhiskers that were neither too light nor too dark, and rather full cheeks, the very same who at the beginning of this story was standing at the end of St. Isaac's Bridge.

"Did you happen to mislay your nose?"

"That's right."

"It has been recovered."

"What are you saying!" exclaimed Major Kovalyov. He was tonguetied with joy. He stared at the police officer standing in front of him, on whose full lips and cheeks the trembling light of the candle flickered. "How?"

"By an odd piece of luck—he was intercepted on the point of leaving town. He was about to board a stagecoach and leave for Riga. He even had a passport made out a long time ago in the name of a certain civil servant. Strangely enough, I also at first took him for a gentleman.

But fortunately I had my glasses with me and I saw at once that it was a nose. You see, I am nearsighted and when you stand before me all I can see is that you have a face, but I can't make out if you have a nose or a beard or anything. My mother-in-law, that is, my wife's mother, can't see anything, either."

Kovalyov was beside himself. "Where is it? Where? I'll run there at once."

"Don't trouble yourself. Knowing that you need it I have brought it with me. And the strange thing is that chief villain in this business is that rascally barber from Voznesensky Street who is now in a lockup. I have long suspected him of drunkenness and theft, and as recently as the day before yesterday he stole a dozen buttons from a certain shop. Your nose is quite in order." With these words the police officer reached into his pocket and pulled out a nose wrapped up in a piece of paper.

"That's it!" shouted Kovalyov. "That's it, all right! Do join me in a little cup of tea today."

"I would consider it a great pleasure, but I simply can't: I have to drop in at a mental asylum. . . . All food prices have gone up enormously. . . . I have my mother-in-law, that's my wife's mother, living with me, and my children; the eldest is particularly promising, a very clever lad, but we haven't the means to educate him."

Kovalyov grasped his meaning and, snatching up a red banknote from the table, thrust it into the hands of the inspector who, clicking his heels, went out the door. Almost the very same instant Kovalyov heard his voice out in the street where he was admonishing with his fist a stupid peasant who had driven his cart onto the boulevard.

After the police officer had left, the collegiate assessor remained for a few minutes in a sort of indefinable state and only after several minutes recovered the capacity to see and feel: his unexpected joy had made him lose his senses. He carefully took the newly found nose in both his cupped hands and once again examined it thoroughly.

"That's it, that's it, all right," said Major Kovalyov. "Here on the left side is the pimple which swelled up yesterday." The major very nearly laughed with joy.

But there is nothing enduring in this world, and that is why even joy is not as keen in the moment that follows the first; and a moment later it grows weaker still and finally merges imperceptibly into one's usual state of mind, just as a ring on the water, made by the fall of a pebble, merges finally into the smooth surface. Kovalyov began to reflect and realized that the whole business was not yet over: the nose was found but it still had to be affixed, put in its proper place.

"And what if it doesn't stick?"

At this question, addressed to himself, the major turned pale.

Seized by unaccountable fear, he rushed to the table and drew the looking-glass closer, to avoid affixing the nose crookedly. His hands trembled. Carefully and deliberately, he put it in its former place. O horror! the nose wouldn't stick. . . . He carried it to his mouth, warmed it slightly with his breath, and again brought it to the smooth place between his two cheeks; but the nose just wouldn't stay on.

"Well, come on, come on, you fool!" he kept saying to it. But the nose was as though made of wood and plopped back on the table with a strange corklike sound. The major's face was twisted in convulsion. "Won't it really grow on?" he said fearfully. But no matter how many times he tried to fit it in its proper place, his efforts were unsuccessful as before.

He called Ivan and sent him for the doctor who occupied the best apartment on the first floor of the same house. The doctor was a fine figure of a man; he had beautiful pitch-black sidewhiskers, a fresh, healthy wife, ate raw apples first thing in the morning, and kept his mouth extraordinarily clean, rinsing it every morning for nearly three quarters of an hour and polishing his teeth with five different kinds of little brushes. The doctor came at once. After asking him how long ago the mishap had occurred, he lifted Major Kovalyov's face by the chin and flicked him with his thumb on the very spot where the nose used to be, so that the major had to throw his head back with such force that he hit the back of it against the wall. The doctor said this didn't matter and, suggesting that he move a little away from the wall, told him first to bend his head to the right, and, after feeling the spot where the nose had been, said "Hmm!" Then he told him to bend his head to the left and said "Hmm!"; and in conclusion he again flicked him with his thumb so that Major Kovalyov jerked his head like a horse whose teeth are being examined. Having carried out this test, the doctor shook his head and said: "No, can't be done. You'd better stay like this, or we might make things even worse. Of course, it can be stuck on. I daresay, I could do it right now for you, but I assure you it'll be worse for you."

"I like that! How am I to remain without a nose?" said Kovalyov. "It couldn't possibly be worse than now. This is simply a hell of a thing! How can I show myself anywhere in such a scandalous state? I have acquaintances in good society; why, this evening, now, I am expected at parties in two houses. I know many people: Mrs. Chekhtaryova, a state councillor's wife, Mrs. Podtochina, a field officer's wife . . . although after what she's done now I'll have nothing more to do with her except through the police. I appeal to you," pleaded Kovalyov, "is there no way at all? Fix it on somehow, even if not very well, just so it stays on; in an emergency, I could even prop it up with my hand. And besides, I don't dance, so I can't do any harm by some careless movement. As regards my grateful acknowledgment of your visits, be assured that as far as my means allow. . . ."

"Would you believe it," said the doctor in a voice that was neither loud nor soft but extremely persuasive and magnetic, "I never treat people out of self-interest. This is against my principles and my calling. It is true that I charge for my visits, but solely in order not to offend by my refusal. Of course I could affix your nose; but I assure you on my honor, if you won't take my word for it, that it will be much worse. Rather, let nature take its course. Wash the place more often with cold water, and I assure you that without a nose you'll be as healthy as if you had one. As for the nose itself, I advise you to put the nose in a jar with alcohol, or, better still, pour into the jar two tablespoonfuls of aqua fortis and warmed-up vinegar—and then you can get good money for it. I'll buy it myself, if you don't ask too much."

"No, no! I won't sell it for anything!" exclaimed Major Kovalyov in desperation. "Let it rather go to blazes!"

"Excuse me!" said the doctor, bowing himself out, "I wanted to be of some use to you. . . . Never mind! At least you saw my good will." Having said this the doctor left the room with a dignified air. Kovalyov didn't even notice his face and in his benumbed state saw nothing but the cuffs of his snow-white shirt peeping out of the sleeves of his black tailcoat.

The very next day he decided, before lodging a complaint, to write to Mrs. Podtochina requesting her to restore him his due without a fight. The letter ran as follows:

Dear Madam Alexandra Grigoryevna,

I fail to understand your strange behavior. Be assured that, acting in this way, you gain nothing and certainly will not force me to marry your daughter. Believe me that the incident with my nose is fully known to me, just as is the fact that you—and no one else—are the principal person involved. Its sudden detachment from its place, its flight and its disguise, first as a certain civil servant, then at last in its own shape, is nothing other than the result of a spell cast by you or by those who engage like you in such noble pursuits. I for my part deem it my duty to forewarn you that if the abovementioned nose is not back in its place this very day I shall be forced to resort to the defense and protection of the law.
Whereupon I have the honor to remain, with my full respect,

Your obedient servant
Platon Kovalyov

★ ★ ★

Dear Sir
Platon Kuzmich,

Your letter came as a complete surprise to me. I frankly
confess that I never expected it, especially as regards
your unjust reproaches. I beg to inform you that I never
received in my house the civil servant you mention, neither in disguise nor in his actual shape. It is true that Fil-
ipp Ivanovich Potanchikov had been visiting me. And
though he did indeed seek my daughter's hand, being
himself of good sober conduct and great learning, I never
held out any hopes to him. You also mention your nose.
If by this you mean that I wanted to put your nose out
of joint, that is, to give you a formal refusal, then I am
surprised to hear you mention it, for I, as you know, was
of the exactly opposite opinion, and if you now seek my
daughter in marriage in the lawful way, I am ready to
give you immediate satisfaction, for this has always been
the object of my keenest desire, in the hope of which I
remain always at your service,

Alexandra Podtochina

"No," said Kovalyov, after he had read the letter. "She certainly isn't
guilty. Impossible! The letter is written in a way no person guilty of a
crime can write." The collegiate assessor was an expert in this matter,
having been sent several times to take part in a judicial investigation
while still serving in the Caucasus. "How then, how on earth could this
have happened? The devil alone can make it out," he said at last in
utter dejection.

In the meantime rumors about this extraordinary occurrence had
spread all over the capital and, as is usual in such cases, not without
some special accretions. In those days the minds of everybody were
particularly inclined toward things extraordinary: not long before, the

whole town had shown an interest in experiments with the effects of hypnotism. Moreover, the story of the dancing chairs in Konyushen-naya Street was still fresh in memory, and one should not be surprised therefore that soon people began saying that Collegiate Assessor Kovalyov's nose went strolling along Nevsky Avenue at precisely three o'clock. Throngs of curious people came there every day. Someone said that the Nose was in Junker's store: and such a crowd and jam was created outside Junker's that the police had to intervene. One profitseeker of respectable appearance, with sidewhiskers, who sold a variety of dry pastries at the entrance to a theater, had specially con-structed excellent, sturdy wooden benches, on which he invited the curious to mount for eighty kopecks apiece. One veteran colonel made a point of leaving his house earlier than usual and with much difficulty made his way through the crowd, but to his great indigna-tion saw in the window of the shop instead of the nose an ordinary woollen undershirt and a lithograph showing a young girl straighten-ing her stocking and a dandy, with a lapeled waistcoat and a small beard, peeping at her from behind a tree—a picture which had been hanging in the same place for more than ten years. Moving away he said with annoyance, "How can they confound the people by such silly and unlikely rumors?" Then a rumor went round that Major Kovalyov's nose was out for a stroll, not on Nevsky Avenue but in Tau-rida Gardens, that it had been there for ages; that when Khosrev-Mirza lived there he marveled greatly at this strange freak of nature. Some students from the Surgical Academy went there. One aristo-cratic, respectable lady, in a special letter to the Superintendent of the Gardens, asked him to show her children this rare phenomenon, accompanied, if possible, with an explanation edifying and instruc-tive for the young.

All the men about town, the habitués of society parties, who liked to amuse ladies and whose resources had by that time been exhausted, were extremely glad of all these goings-on. A small percentage of respectable and well-meaning people were extremely displeased. One gentleman said indignantly that he could not understand how in this enlightened age such senseless stories could spread and that he was surprised at the government's failure to take heed of it. This gentleman apparently was one of those gentlemen who would like to embroil the government in everything, even in their daily quarrels with their wives. After that . . . but here again the whole incident is shrouded in fog, and what happened afterwards is absolutely unknown.

Utterly nonsensical things happen in this world. Sometimes there is absolutely no rhyme or reason in them: suddenly the very nose which had been going around with the rank of a state councillor and created such a stir in the city, found itself again, as though nothing were the matter, in its proper place, that is to say, between the two cheeks of Major Kovalyov. This happened on April 7th. Waking up and chancing to look in the mirror, he sees—his nose! He grabbed it with his hand— his nose indeed! "Aha!" said Kovalyov, and in his joy he very nearly broke into a barefooted dance round the room, but Ivan's entry stopped him. He told Ivan to bring him some water to wash in and, while washing, glanced again at the mirror—his nose! Drying himself with his towel, he again glanced at the mirror—his nose!

"Take a look, Ivan, I think there's a pimple on my nose," he said, and in the meantime thought, "How awful if Ivan says: 'Why, no sir, not only there is no pimple but also the nose itself is gone!' "

But Ivan said: "Nothing, sir, no pimple—your nose is fine!"

"That's great, damn it!" the major said to himself, snapping his fingers. At that moment the barber Ivan Yakovlevich peeped in at the door but as timidly as a cat which had just been whipped for stealing lard.

"First you tell me—are your hands clean?" Kovalyov shouted to him before he had approached.

"They are."

"You're lying."

"I swear they are, sir."

"Well, we'll see."

Kovalyov sat down. Ivan Yakovlevich draped him with a napkin and instantly, with the help of a shaving brush, transformed his chin and part of his cheek into the whipped cream served at merchants' names-day parties. "Well, I never!" Ivan Yakovlevich said to himself, glancing at his nose, and then cocked his head on the other side and looked at it sideways: "Look at that! Just you try and figure that out," he continued and took a good look at his nose. At last, gently, with the greatest care imaginable, he raised two fingers to grasp it by the tip. Such was Ivan Yakovlevich's method.

"Now, now, now, look out there!" cried Kovalyov. Dumbfounded and confused as never before in his life, Ivan Yakovlevich let his hands drop. At last he began cautiously tickling him with the razor under the chin, and although it wasn't at all handy for him and difficult to shave without holding on to the olfactory portion of the face, nevertheless, somehow bracing his gnarled thumb against the cheek and the lower jaw, he finally overcame all obstacles and finished shaving him.

When everything was ready, Kovalyov hastened to dress, hired a cab and went straight to the coffeehouse. Before he was properly inside the door he shouted, "Boy, a cup of chocolate!" and immediately made for the mirror: the nose was there. He turned round cheerfully and looked ironically, slightly screwing up one eye, at two military gentlemen one of whom had a nose no bigger than a waistcoat button. After that he set off for the office of the department where he was trying to obtain the post of a vice-governor or, failing that, of a procurement officer. Passing through the reception room, he glanced in the mirror: the nose was there. Then he went to visit another collegiate assessor or major, a great wag, to whom he often said in reply to various derisive remarks: "Oh, come off it, I know you, you're a kidder." On the way there he thought: "If the major doesn't explode with laughter on seeing me, it's a sure sign that everything is in its proper place." The collegiate assessor did not explode. "That's great, that's great, damn it!" Kovalyov thought to himself. On the street he met Mrs. Podtochina, the field officer's wife, together with her daughter, bowed to them and was hailed with joyful exclamations, and so everything was all right, no part of him was missing. He talked with them a very long time and, deliberately taking out his snuff-box, right in front of them kept stuffing his nose with snuff at both entrances for a very long time, saying to himself: "So much for you, you women, you stupid hens! I won't marry the daughter all the same. Anything else, par amour—by all means." And from that time on, Major Kovalyov went strolling about as though nothing had happened, both on Nevsky Avenue, and in the theaters, and everywhere. And his nose too, as though nothing had happened, stayed on his face, betraying no sign of having played truant. And thereafter Major Kovalyov was always seen in good humor, smiling, running after absolutely all the pretty ladies, and once even stopping in front of a little shop in Gostinny Dvor and buying himself the ribbon of some order, goodness knows why, for he hadn't been decorated with any order.

That is the kind of affair that happened in the northern capital of our vast empire. Only now, on second thoughts, can we see that there is much that is improbable in it. Without speaking of the fact that the supernatural detachment of the nose and its appearance in various places in the guise of a state councillor is indeed strange, how is it that Kovalyov did not realize that one does not advertise for one's nose through the newspaper office? I do not mean to say that advertising rates appear to me too high: that's nonsense, and I am not at all one of those mercenary people. But it's improper, embarrassing, not nice! And then again—how did the nose come to be in a newly baked loaf, and how about Ivan Yakovlevich? . . . No, this is something I can't understand, positively can't understand. But the strangest, the most incomprehensible thing of all, is how authors can choose such subjects. I confess that this is quite inconceivable; it is indeed . . . no, no, I just can't understand it at all! In the first place, there is absolutely no benefit in it for the fatherland; in the second place . . . but in the second place, there is no benefit either. I simply don't know what to make of it. . . .

And yet, in spite of it all, though, of course, we may assume this and that and the other, perhaps even . . . And after all, where aren't there incongruities? But all the same, when you think about it, there really is something in all this. Whatever anyone says, such things happen in this world; rarely, but they do.

A Jew of Persia

by Mark Helprin

Mark Helprin (born 1947) as a young man served
in the British Merchant Navy, the Israeli infantry
and the Israeli Air Force. He knows a lot about
fighting, as you'll see when you read this story.

He had tried to explain for his sons the sense of
mountains so high, sharp, and bare that winds blew ice into waves and
silver crowns, of air so thin and cold it tattooed the skin and lungs with
the blue of heaven and the bronze of sunshining rock crevasse. He had
tried to tell them of the house in which he had lived, made of mountain rock, with terraces, and ten fires within—when shutters were
thrown open and hit the stone like the report of a shell in an echoing
valley he could see mountains of white ice two hundred miles distant.
The eggs there were milk-white, the milk like cloud. In winter it often
snowed in one day enough to trap and kill horses and bulls. He had
been a sawyer, guiding his saws through countless timbers all day long
in the open air, so that his body was as intensely powerful as (he would
say) gunpowder in a brass casing. Then, when he was younger and
worked at the timbers, he could by the pressure of his hands and arms
break a heavy iron chain. And there was not much else, at least as he
thought of it twenty and more years later. These things were so deep

and wonderful that they could bear telling a thousand times a thousand times. But he could not say them even once to his sons, for they did not know Persian, which he had almost forgotten, and his Hebrew was of the shacks and hot streets and blood-guttered markets.

This life of his came to be like the fall of an angel, and yet by the tenets of his belief he believed himself lucky. He had come alone from Persia's mountainous north, where the air was cross-currented and symphonically clear, to Tel Aviv where air was obsolete and the entire city heated like potters' kilns in Iran. When in late 1948 he had stepped off a small ship in Jaffa, he had said to himself, Najime, it will be profitable to find the large oven which heats up the city, for there they are undoubtedly drying vast amounts of wood, and may need me to saw. For several hours he had glided about the city in his boots of fur and leather asking passers-by in Persian, "Where is the great oven?" The passers-by, obviously ignorant of Persian, jaded by the sight of ambulant wolflike lunatic-looking Persians and Turcomans, would throw up their hands, shrug their shoulders, and say to themselves in Yiddish, He should only not kill me dear God. And Najime would continue on, still in search of the all-pervasive heat.

Instead of his crooked, ancient, and vast stone house with ether forcing its way shrieking through the cracks, and fires flickering, instead of sheepskins and earthenware pitchers of iced white wine, instead of the little synagogue where sawyers, sheepherders, and merchants watched the sun rise golden from a cradle of distant mountains and light gold chains coming triangularly from the ceiling, instead of tall candles, and contests of strength in the bitter cold, he found a tin shack almost melting, filthy sacks for a bed, no breeze, rationed food, a synagogue of brown Yemenites and Moroccans who were softer and soaking in Arabic and the desert and knowing a God who possessed another face than his rugged, whistling, clean, and mystic God of altitudes, hunters, and eagles' flight. That was the angel's fall, and he often inflated himself with longing, letting the remaining Persian words circle around by themselves in his head, reluctant to talk to others whose dialects were not the same.

But his balance on the scaffolded logs had long before taught him of polarities, and he was well aware of the blessings of his situation. To his eldest son Yacov he had often said, There is plenty of balance here for what was lost. Of course he knew that the boy, knowing no other country, brought up as it were in a sewing box, would never sense except in the airy sadness of dreams what Persia had been like, and that since he had become a sergeant in the army and had been in battles he had learned his own lessons and only tolerated his strange father, although he loved him, for his father was a rough peasant who had walked halfway across Asia from deep in the past, and the young man already had a small car and a telephone of his own. But Najime went on anyway, as he often did, saying, "There are two main things which balance out the loss, two main things. The first is that I have come to a Jewish country where I can live as a Jew (although you know I lived as a Jew there too), and have helped to build the third commonwealth, a new land for us. The soldiers I see are our soldiers, and that is good, and Hebrew is our language. That is good." He stopped, beaming, and poured himself a glass of grapefruit juice from an old bottle. His son looked at him with an habitual incredulousness.

"Nu?" said the stocky ex-sergeant. "And . . . ?"

"That's all," said Najime, "what else?"

"What is the second reason? You said there were two."

"I can't tell you."

"Why not?"

"I can't say."

"Nonsense," said Yacov, slamming the table with his fist. "You always say there are two reasons and then give only one."

"I know," said Najime, strangely upset, then retreating into his thoughts and memories like an old man.

"You are *not* such an old man, you know. You can't do this. What is the second reason? I know. You can't tell me."

They had had this exchange a hundred times a hundred times, and always with the same result. But once at a wedding Najime had consumed three bottles of wine. Then when his son had pressed him for the second reason he had blurted out, "Because I saw the Devil, and he had fur in his eyes." He had started to shake, and the boy in the new uniform had seen the hair on his father's arms and neck stand up. What did he mean? Certainly he had not seen the Devil. But from then on he would elaborate no further, and any inquiry about (directly) the Devil, or (indirectly in order, he thought, subtly to pry out the secret) the strange condition of having fur in the eyes, brought Yacov a hard slap in the face and a long stream of expletives in mountain Persian.

And so they had continued to live out their lives in the Ha Tikva Quarter, a place where all the functions of human existence combined ungraciously and people were struck like bells in no chorus, camel bells upset and sad but active in contrast to the still green palms, a tree with a lisp in the wind and infinite patience, variegated sun shadows, shelterer of doves, the green rafters of Tel Aviv. All this in the Ha Tikva was sometimes struck down by the Hamsin, and more significantly, sometimes blown onto another course by winds of war and death and change. And at these times the inhabitants paused in the struggle, and very like sailors on a coasting ship breaching a passage of high cliffs and tumultuous blue-green waters into an unknown gulf or sea, waited for the change, marking a point in their lives, aware of time and their part in it. And one day this violent wind was blowing through Ha Tikva, at least for Najime and his son.

Najime was sitting on his chair, listening to the BBC Arabic service (of which he understood nothing) and looking out onto the street. In the distance he saw the tops of a few skyscrapers, and closer, a row of palms which caught a sea breeze never to reach him. Closer still was a series of old concrete buildings which had been built with sea water a generation or more before and which like lepers had been losing bits and pieces ever since. Before him was a street of hard-packed dust lined with sterile date palms, tin shacks, dogs, and chickens. Yacov was sitting in the back of the room cleaning a submachine gun he had stolen from the army. He had its various parts and springs assembled unassembled before him ready to be oiled, and was about to begin work on the magazines when he was startled by the crash of his father's chair.

Najime had crouched like a hunter among the rocks, and was staring out the window, jaw hanging open. "What is it!" screamed Yacov,
as he like the trained soldier he was vaulted over the kitchen table to
his father's side, wincing in mid-air as he heard the several dozen
springs, nuts, and molded pieces of his gun jangle onto the floor.

"It's him."

"Who?" said Yacov, staring in terrified sympathy at the familiar
street.

"That man. The one with the flat chin and half-grown beard."

"That little guy?"

"Yes."

"Well what about him? What's with you? Are you crazy?"

The little old man on the street, in appearance a cross between a
beggar and a mushroom, turned into an alley and vanished. Yacov
glanced at the metal pieces on the floor and then at his father. He was
disgusted and perplexed. But his father's wells had been tapped. He
picked up his son and threw him across the room onto the bed, ran to
close the shutters, bolted the door, and stood there in chevrons of light.

"You dog-headed baby, you cackling jackass. What do you know?
Now listen, because the time has come. I was afraid of it for twenty-five
years, but it stares me in the face at last and I feel like dying, and that is
the only way to enter a fight. I will fight," he said, upraising a still very
strong arm, "and I will die, but I will use sword and dagger until they
heat from friction in the air. The dust will rise about me. I will be fierce."

"What are you talking about?" said Yacov, who was himself now
terrified like a child whose father is in danger. The older man sat
down, and after a short silence, began to speak in a determined vision
of the past.

"I was a young man, the strongest in the village, at least among the
Jews, because I sawed beams all day and had done so from the earliest
I could remember. Because of that I had great lungs, great balance, and
great muscular power. I was a skilled swordsman too, for there was no
sword in the world which was not to me as light as a feather compared
to my saws, sledgehammers, and axes. I could run for half a day at a

time up and down the valleys, and raise beams alone which five men together would not approach. Naturally, I won most of the contests.

"One day a messenger came from the Grand Rabbi in the capital. In the presence of our Rabbi and the elders he commanded us to collect our gold, our silver, our jewels, our coins, and bring them to him in the capital on an appointed day. He said that the Jews of the world were in the midst of returning, that the ingathering of the exiles was about to begin, that all the Jews of Iran, and India, the East, and the West, were giving their treasure. You can imagine how it struck us. Two thousand years, and at last we were leaving our beloved mountains for the land of our fathers.

"Although we were rich in many things and close to God, we were nevertheless a poor village. All of our gold and silver including every-thing from the synagogue itself filled only one sack on a donkey. On the other side, to balance the load, we placed a sack of dried and smoked meats, cheeses, and dried fruits. I was to go alone in order not to attract attention, but fully armed, as there were many bandits in those mountains at the time, and probably still are. I had the finest sword and dagger in the village. We attempted to borrow a rifle from the Muslims, but they would not hear of it. On top of the sacks we put false containers which made it seem as if we had a donkey loaded with dried dung. I was dressed poorly, my weapons hidden. After a good night's sleep and a meal, I set out.

"Three days from our village and any other I arrived at a great pass in the mountains, to which I had been only once before, as a child. This pass is essentially a vast gorge with paths cut into the rock walls on either side. Once you have chosen a side you must stay with it until the end, about an hour's travel, because a sane donkey would not walk backwards with no room to turn. The other path is completely inac-cessible although only a stone's throw distant, because the gorge in between is easily a kilometer deep. It was this pass which kept the rail-ways, armies, and telegraphs from our village. It was this barrier which allowed us to follow our own desires freely, and yet because of it the bandits were also free and they plagued us.

"But no bandit had ever struck there, simply because were he to have done so and encountered greater force he would have had no way to escape, and besides, the place was dangerous enough just to traverse. At the end of the pass was a government station full of troops. So if one reached the entrance he assumed himself safe from attack. Naturally the troops themselves exacted a small extra-legal tax, but that was looked upon as inevitable, as a sort of toll.

"I found myself at the entrance to the pass, thinking I was safe from bandits and even exempt from the soldiers' 'tax.' If the Grand Rabbi had treasure coming to him from all parts of the country, he had undoubtedly donated part of it to an official in the palace to make sure that it arrived intact. My donkey had a bad right eye, which was lucky for me. My natural inclination was to travel on the left, with the gorge on my right, and since the animal's left eye was best, that is what we were forced to do. I made sure the sacks were evenly balanced, put a blinder on his right eye so that he would look only at the path, and said a prayer. Then I led him out.

"We were doing well, and the animal's brown legs were steady and not shaking as they would have done had he been other than a donkey and smart enough to fear heights. Halfway through I saw two men, one on each path. They were bandits, and each one had a rifle. How clever they were! The one on the far side trained his rifle on me, while the other calmly awaited my approach. What have you got there, Jew, said the one closest to me. Just dung for fires, I said. (I must also have said sir.)

"He believed me, and was going to let me pass when the other one, on the far side, said, Look in his sacks, little brother, for I think there is gold there. It seemed very strange that he should know that, and he too was rather strange. Even from that distance I sensed something about him which frightened me, and the donkey was very agitated in his presence. Well, they thought they had the mastery of design in that matter, but they hadn't. Perhaps if I had been carrying just smoked meats or tools or my own money, I would not have been able to think out a way to beat them. There were after all two of them, each with a rifle and a knife. I had only a sword and dagger. And most important, I could do nothing to the older one across the gorge who in complete safety had his rifle aimed at my heart. Even were he not there I could not have gone in any but one direction, straight into his little brother, who was by no means little. But I was carrying the wealth of my father and my father's father, and of all my cousins, and of the synagogue in the village. And it was for a very special purpose, very special indeed, so I thought so hard my head began to boil and the veins in my hands stood out. (I was also quite frightened.)

"After I had thought of what to do it seemed so simple and obvious that I laughed out loud, and it echoed in the gorge. They looked at one another in confusion, but then the older one said, Little brother, we can also rob madmen. Then the little brother ordered me to spill out my sacks for him. No sir, I said, you cannot make me do that, even if you kill me. If I am to be robbed that is one thing, robbing myself is another.

"He thought for a while and then said, That makes sense, Jew, and then very casually went to the sack of dried fruits and meats and began to go through it. You see he was not afraid of me because I was a Jew. When you say 'I am a Jew,' they think you are weak. But of course we are as strong as anyone else, and because of that we often give them big surprises. Afterwards they hate us because they think we have tricked them. But usually it is they who have tricked themselves. Their eyes have done the tricking. As soon as little brother saw my clothing he lost all fear, because knowing that I was a Jew he did not think there was a man underneath.

"He has false sacks of dung, he yelled to his brother, and then began to lay out the meat and fruit against the wall of the path next to the donkey. I knew exactly what to do; it had come to me in a flash. I came close to him and said, Keep the meat and fruit, eat well, but in God's mercy let me pass. He looked up and said, I am going to eat well, but I am also going to kill you, for if I don't kill you I will have no appetite, and he laughed.

"At this I imagined as best I could that he was a branch on a long timber which awaited trimming before being sawed into logs. How many tens of thousands of times I had knocked off those thick branches with one stroke of my ax. But it was different with a man. I had never killed a man, and I found that I could not move. I was paralyzed. Then I realized that I could not fool myself into imagining that he was a branch to be severed, because he clearly was a man. So I thought, This is a man, not a tree, and I am going to kill him. I was afraid, and I knew that the minute I reached for my sword all hell would break out. I knew that if I hesitated they would kill me, and that if I did nothing they would kill me. This made me so angry that I pulled out my sword and with the most powerful stroke I had ever given (and the fastest), ten times as powerful as was necessary, I simply cut him in half.

"I dropped my sword immediately and grabbed the lower half of his body, throwing it with all my might over into the gorge. Meanwhile his brother had begun firing his rifle and had hit my donkey, who went down on one knee. I could not stand the idea of having the body of the man I had just killed next to me, so at further risk of losing all the gold and my life I picked it up and sent it flying in a wide arc into the gorge. It seemed to hang motionless at the top of the arc, and since the other had stopped firing in his horror at this I had time to grab the faltering donkey and pull him back onto the path. Then the big brother began to fire many bullets, quite accurately I must admit, but they all went into the poor dead animal in front of me. He was smart though, because he began firing into the rocks, which broke into shrapnel and bloodied me all up. I took a silver bowl and some trays from the sack and put it over my head and them over my body, remaining there quite comfortably for another half hour eating lamb and pears and wincing at each shot and ricochet. Then he stopped, thinking either that I was dead, or that if I were not he wasn't going to change the situation.

"I looked at him through a little space between the donkey's neck and the ground, and I cannot adequately describe what I saw. I was not afraid of him until that point, because I had planned to stay there until dark and then carry the treasure to the army station. Were he to move back to where I had begun he would have given me an hour's head start, during which I could easily get to the army base. Were he to wait until dark, the darkness would shield me from his fire. I knew he could not go forward for fear that the troops ahead would kill him, so you see I had turned what they believed to be their great advantage, the safety of the gorge, into *my* great advantage. And I was unafraid, until I looked under the curve of the donkey's neck and saw big brother.

"What had been a simple ordinary bandit was suddenly something most different. I could not believe my eyes, and rubbed them. *His* eyes were red circular coals, but made of fur, and they flashed and glowed. His chin had extended until it looked like the flat wooden pallet bakers use for taking bread out of the oven, and he was foaming at the mouth. Up and down the rock walls sparks flew, and as he gesticulated and mouthed the words of evil animals a hot wind came through the crevasse, and hot drops of rain, and then thunder. The wind, at least it seemed to me, was trying to blow the donkey's body off the path. The more big brother danced and fumed, the higher the wind became and the more the donkey moved bit by bit, almost imperceptibly. After a while big brother seemed to get tired, the wind died down, and darkness began to fall. Then he seemed to be like a bandit again, with the almost pitiful exaggerated half-bearded chin, and he called out to me: I am going to hunt you down and cut your throat with a razor. I will follow you anywhere on earth, in these mountains, on the seas, in cities, anywhere. I will strike when you think you are safe and comfortable. I can walk through walls—nothing can keep me out—and when I cut your throat I will be laughing and wild with pleasure, and you will be frozen like a board, unable to move as the razor glides. I can do that. You know me, and your life will be far worse than your death, which will be a well of terror.

"Well, I don't scare that easily, so when darkness fell I cut the treasure from the donkey and pushed him off the ledge, as if to bury him. I heard a hissing of air as he fell into the blue-black darkness. Then, even though it was dark, I almost ran over that path all the way to the army station. I dared not tell them what had happened for fear that they would go mad (those peasant soldiers living alone on mountain-tops were really crazy, believe me), but they took me in for a night.

"You don't believe that they were really crazy? They spent hours slapping each other's faces. They moaned and whimpered like dogs. They used to go around on stilts to scare away devils. This is not crazy?"

By this time it was dark: no more light came in through the louvres, and the old man had been talking into the night for longer than he thought. Yacov reached out to touch him as if to make sure he were really there, then got up to turn on the light, which blinded them both. Surely this was something his father had imagined long ago on a terrifying day and night in the mountains, and yet even if not entirely consistent, it was convincing. With the excitement of a fool who knows one small thing, Yacov asked his father, "If he were really the Devil, why could he not have flown across the gorge on the wind and killed you with his teeth, or have sent a snake from above to poison you?"

"He wasn't the Devil. He was only a half devil, perhaps the son of the Devil and a human woman. He had powers, but they were limited. That is why he has grown old, and why I was able to beat him. Very few men, at least not the likes of me, can beat the Devil. But one of his sons, well, that's different."

"How can you be sure he knows you are here?"

"Because *he* is here."

"Well, I think we should wait and see what happens. Maybe it's nothing at all. Maybe we are dreaming."

"Of course my son," said Najime, "of course we'll wait, that's part of it." He expected the weeks to pass, and they did.

Meanwhile, stories had been spreading about the newcomer. It seems he had arrived from nowhere with a large wagon full of the finest avocados. Since avocados were out of season, he sold them at a very high price and was almost immediately transformed from beggar to prosperous merchant. When people asked him, as they did, where he had gotten so many thousands of avocados he said that his brother had a farm in the desert, where it was so hot that he could grow anything he wanted year round, even at night. It was said that beggars were envious of him, a beggar become rich, and so spread stories such as the one asserting that he sold avocados from his wagon for two weeks day and night and never seemed to run out.

A hundred men threw themselves at his feet and begged to buy this wagon. He picked the richest of them all and told him to run and get his daughter. When the man returned with the beautiful young girl she went wild with desire for the hideous old man and asked for his wrinkled hand in marriage. With tears in his eyes, the father gave consent. They were married the next day. Twenty-five minutes after the wedding feast the father died suddenly of what an autopsy later revealed as starvation.

The stranger then moved into the family house, sold it that evening at a great profit even though everyone knew the city was about to tear it down to build a melon exchange, and pooled his considerable assets to buy up all the salt in Tel Aviv. This was considered a foolish move, until several days later when news came from the south that the country's salt mines had become filled with hot poisonous gas from fissures in the earth. The salt merchants got together and put all their capital into a large order of Turkish salt to be brought on a ship they purchased as a consortium. News came that the ship had been sunk by the Lebanese. The stranger bought what remained of their businesses for practically nothing, and went to the docks to meet the ship, which had not been sunk, but had doubled in size.

From this point, his dealings became unknown to the people of Ha Tikva, except that it was known that he had somehow gained control of the area's crime. Every robbery, every drug transaction, every prostitute, fell ultimately under his direction. He caused otherwise friendly murderers to fight among themselves, shoot, miss, and kill innocent bystanders. Dancers pulled their muscles. Hats would not fit on old men who had worn them for thirty years. Honest citizens would suddenly kick a police officer, and when brought to trial full of regret and shame, find themselves able to speak only Japanese.

Something was wrong in Ha Tikva. It became the topic of conversation at all the tables and in all the cafés. A man suggested to his friends that the strange things which happened were only a concealment and distraction in the case of the stranger who had arrived and done so well so suddenly. "You know, you may have a point there," said one of them just before the house collapsed, from termites said the newspaper, even though the house was made of stone.

The stranger was not to be seen, except on Friday nights, when a uniformed Cossack drove him through the streets in a lacquered red car. They invariably stopped in front of the house of Najime the Persian, the old sawyer, where the stranger sat from eight-thirty to nine-fifteen turning his feet to the front and then to the back again and again, and laughing a very ugly laugh that made children run to their mothers and rats race into their darkest tunnels—only to crash head-long against one another.

Najime stood slightly bent in back of the closed wood louvres, looking calmly at big brother from the mountain pass of a quarter of a century before. Yacov begged to be allowed to shoot him. "That is not the way," said Najime, "either the gun would explode, or you would miss and kill a friend. You see, he has undoubtedly grown in powers, but so have I. Like you, I probably would have wanted just to go and shoot him, and maybe then, when he and I were younger, I would have had a fair chance. But a young man is no match for him now. Look at all he has done and can do. He can kill effortlessly, but he must kill me as he said he would because I would not fear otherwise. And because he must kill me that way, he will not allow himself to be killed beforehand. So put your gun away. Either he will come here, or I will go to him. But I must think about this, because if I am right he has become so skillful in evil that we may even be dealing with the Devil himself. Anyway, this is beyond you, Yacov, because it calls for the strength of the past, the power of memory, the resolve of an old man's history, and because you are stupid.

"I have one advantage. I am not afraid. I must beat him down if only for the sake of the people of Ha Tikva. Even if I lose he may leave of his own will, but there is no guarantee. Now let me think about it, as if I were trying to find a way to move a large timber through a small door of a little house. Let me think for a while."

Najime walked every day to the seaside, and stayed there from noon to evening, smoking his pipe and staring at the white foam of the waves and their curling, like his smoke. He knew that an idea of victory could come either deliberately or on the air. But he knew also that ideas of victory which seem to travel on the air alight always on the shoulders of those who have been laboring in thought.

So for a week he left every day, descending the stairs and walking across crowded boulevards, past great white ruins in the old part of the city, which was being leveled and cleared. But one morning as he and Yacov both were shaving in front of a copper bowl filled with boiling water, he clenched his fist around the razor, lifted his eyes, and said, "Aha! I did it once, and now I'll do it again!" He began to dance around the room, singing, jumping, and prancing, because he had solved his problem.

"Wonderful!" said Yacov, "What are you going to do?"

"Shut up!"

"Why shut up? I'm your son. Tell me."

"Shut up. I'll tell you, assuming that I'm alive, by tomorrow night."

The next morning, Najime arose and put on his best clothes. It was the day before a holiday and many people were dressed for the occasion even then. He wore an old double-breasted pin stripe suit, the stripes hardly visible, the cloth rough, deep, and blue. On his head he carried a Greek straw hat with a chocolate brown band, and in his belt under the coat was the knife he had brought from Persia. The handle was of leather washers, unusual for such a good knife since it deserved an ornamental grip. But in commissioning it Najime had not wanted that. The finest quality leather had become smooth and black over the years from the oil of his hand. A heavy nickel guard, curved inward, made it seem like a small sword. The blade itself was about a foot long, double edged only a few inches back from the tip in a fluted curve. It was cast from the best Swedish steel, which the smith had purchased from a Russian. Najime had sharpened it over the years, and especially carefully the night before. He had spent a good deal of his life sharpening blades. The knife was so sharp that he feared for the scabbard.

"Goodbye Yacov my son. I am going to the synagogue, and then to the barber." He winked.

Najime left and crossed the street, nodding and greeting as was his custom; alert as a young man hunting in the mountains he stood and prayed by the side of the road, since they were cleaning the synagogue. "Dear God, help me to know evil and to fight it. Help me to resist it, not that I would be evil myself, but that one of its principal parts is to appear as right and proper. And that is something I have wanted to discuss for a long time, but later. I am going, I believe, to do what you would have me do. Although I have not heard from you about this it seems the right thing to do."

He came to the street of the barber shop and walked toward it, adjusting his knife. Once inside he went directly to one of the old chairs and sat down, asking for a shave. The barber, a little Moroccan, began to lather Najime's face, already as cleanly shaven as a man's face could be. Najime had taken pains to do that just an hour before. The barber's manner was casual but somehow very mechanical and automatic, as if he were teaching young barbers. He then went to the razor drawer, picked out a very large razor with a transparent ice-blue handle, and began to sharpen it.

Within the white cloth Najime drew his knife, and as the barber approached with a look of boredom and sleep, Najime jumped from the chair, teeth exposed, the two sides of his mustache raised, and with a tremendously loud cry (the kind that used to go from one mountaintop to another), he stabbed the barber deep in his heart, pushing the knife right up to the hilt.

The other barbers and customers froze while their coworker and barber of many years staggered in a half-circle, and then fell face down on the floor. Najime dropped back into the chair, feeling like a man who has just beaten the Devil. While the police were summoned, a soldier who had witnessed the incident through the window entered the shop and pompously trained his rifle on Najime, who had an angelic look.

The police came. They handcuffed Najime to the chair, and began to write in their books the statements of all concerned. The barbers stated that this man had come to their shop and killed Amzaleg, who was a third owner. They then described the killing in great detail, gesticulating, and glancing now and then at the body for fear of offending it with the color of their portraiture. Najime was silently shaking his head no. To everyone in the shop (by that time about 350 people, various animals, hawkers and vendors of every description, prostitutes plying their trade, entertainers, musicians, etc., etc.), he looked like a madman from an entirely different civilization.

A policeman turned to him and said, "What do you mean, shaking your head no like that?"

Najime replied, "That man is not their friend Amzaleg. Amzaleg is probably in bed with stomach trouble." The two remaining barbers looked at one another, confirming the presence of a madman. "He," continued Najime, "is an old enemy of mine from Persia who swore to kill me with a razor, and that was what he was about to do."

"Nonsense!" screamed the two remaining barbers like twins. "That is Amzaleg, our friend and partner."

"Turn him over," said Najime, hardly able to wait until it was done. And when it was done, the long, flat, half-bearded chin was not that of Amzaleg the Moroccan barber, but of the big brother on the mountain.

"Incredible," said the two barbers in unison.

Later, after he had been released by the police, Najime went home under what seemed to be lighter and cooler skies. Ha Tikva was awakening from a week of hard work and about to await the sunset and fine food of the holiday. It felt as though there were going to be a rainstorm, although there was not going to be one. Yacov was inside, having heard out the window of all the strange events in the barber shop. When his father came in and took off his coat, the son was reverentially silent. But seeing that the older man was in a good frame of mind, to say the least, he cautiously asked, "How did you know he was the barber?"

"Well," said Najime, "as a precautionary measure I shaved this morning as cleanly as I could, and that seemed to make no difference to this 'barber.' But that was just a precaution, for any barber might have been tired, and overlooked it."

"Then how did you know he would be there?"

"I didn't know for sure, but I took a chance. You see, he vowed to kill me with a razor, and I have never been to a barber in my life. Therefore, if I went to a barber, it would have to be him. That is Devil's conduct, and I have encountered it before. My suspicion was confirmed when I noticed that he had no wedding ring. Every barber in Israel wears a wedding ring. And then, I could feel his presence the way sheep in mountains can feel the approach of a hunter. I have spent a lifetime waiting. I have won."

And both father and son heard the bakers screaming, "It rises! It rises!" about their newly baked bread. For during the previous few weeks the bread in Ha Tikva Quarter had not risen. Najime was left to spend the rest of his life pondering on whether he had beaten the Devil or just the Devil's son, and thinking about the clear air of his mountains and the championships he had been born to take in sawing, chopping, and many village games.

The Book of Beasts
by E. Nesbit

Edith Nesbit's (1858–1924) best work includes fairy tales that narrate nonsensical events in a no-nonsense tone. People in her stories often behave foolishly, and outcomes are uncertain. You may not believe what happens when a young boy in this story opens a forbidden book.

He happened to be building a Palace when the news came, and he left all the bricks kicking about the floor for Nurse to clear up—but then the news was rather remarkable news. You see, there was a knock at the front door and voices talking downstairs, and Lionel thought it was the man come to see about the gas which had not been allowed to be lighted since the day when Lionel made a swing by tying his skipping-rope to the gas-bracket.

And then, quite suddenly, Nurse came in, and said, 'Master Lionel, dear, they've come to fetch you to go and be King.'

Then she made haste to change his smock and to wash his face and hands and brush his hair, and all the time she was doing it Lionel kept wriggling and fidgeting and saying, 'Oh, don't, Nurse,' and, 'I'm sure my ears are quite clean,' or, 'Never mind my hair, it's all right,' and, 'That'll do.'

'You're going on as if you was going to be an eel instead of a King,' said Nurse.

The minute Nurse let go for a moment Lionel bolted off without waiting for his clean handkerchief, and in the drawing-room there were two very grave-looking gentlemen in red robes with fur, and gold coronets with velvet sticking up out of the middle like the cream in the very expensive jam tarts.

They bowed low to Lionel, and the gravest one said:

'Sire, your great-great-great-great-great-grandfather, the King of this country, is dead, and now you have got to come and be King.'

'Yes, please, sir,' said Lionel; 'when does it begin?'

'You will be crowned this afternoon,' said the grave gentle man who was not quite so grave-looking as the other.

'Would you like me to bring Nurse, or what time would you like me to be fetched, and hadn't I better put on my velvet suit with the lace collar?' said Lionel, who had often been out to tea.

'Your Nurse will be removed to the Palace later. No, never mind about changing your suit; the Royal robes will cover all that up.'

The grave gentlemen led the way to a coach with eight white horses, which was drawn up in front of the house where Lionel lived. It was No. 7, on the left-hand side of the street as you go up.

Lionel ran upstairs at the last minute, and he kissed Nurse and said: "Thank you for washing me. I wish I'd let you do the other ear. No—there's no time now. Give me the hanky. Good-bye, Nurse.'

'Good-bye, ducky,' said Nurse; 'be a good little King now, and say "please" and "thank you", and remember to pass the cake to the little girls, and don't have more than two helps of anything.'

So off went Lionel to be made a King. He had never expected to be a King any more than you have, so it was all quite new to him—so new that he had never even thought of it. And as the coach went through the town he had to bite his tongue to be quite sure it was real, because if his tongue was real it showed he wasn't dreaming. Half an hour before he had been building with bricks in the nursery; and now—the streets were all fluttering with flags; every window was crowded with people waving handkerchiefs and scattering flowers; there were scarlet soldiers everywhere along the pavements, and all the bells of all the churches were ringing like mad, and like a great song to the music of their ringing he heard thousands of people shouting, 'Long live Lionel! Long live our little King!'

He was a little sorry at first that he had not put on his best clothes, but he soon forgot to think about that. If he had been a girl he would very likely have bothered about it the whole time.

As they went along, the grave gentlemen, who were the Chancellor and the Prime Minister, explained the things which Lionel did not understand.

'I thought we were a Republic,' said Lionel. 'I'm sure there hasn't keen a King for some time.'

'Sire, your great-great-great-great-great-grandfather's death happened when my grandfather was a little boy,' said the Prime Minister, 'and since then your loyal people have been saving up to buy you a crown—so much a week, you know, according to people's means— sixpence a week from those who have first-rate pocket-money, down to a halfpenny a week from those who haven't so much. You know it's the rule that the crown must be paid for by the people.'

'But hadn't my great-great-however-much-it-is-grandfather a crown?'

'Yes, but he sent it to be tinned over, for fear of vanity, and he had had all the jewels taken out, and sold them to buy books. He was a strange man; a very good King he was, but he had his faults—he was fond of books. Almost with his last breath he sent the crown to be tinned—and he never lived to pay the tinsmith's bill.'

Here the Prime Minister wiped away a tear, and just then the carriage stopped and Lionel was taken out of the carriage to be crowned. Being crowned is much more tiring work than you would suppose, and by the time it was over, and Lionel had worn the Royal robes for an hour or two and had had his hand kissed by everybody whose business it was to do it, he was quite worn out, and was very glad to get into the palace nursery.

Nurse was there, and tea was ready: seedy cake and plummy cake, and jam and hot buttered toast, and the prettiest china with red and gold and blue flowers on it, and real tea, and as many cups of it as you liked. After tea Lionel said:

'I think I should like a book. Will you get me one, Nurse?'

'Bless the child,' said Nurse, 'you don't suppose you've lost the use of your legs with just being a King? Run along, do, and get your books yourself.'

So Lionel went down into the library. The Prime Minister and the Chancellor were there, and when Lionel came in they bowed very low, and were beginning to ask Lionel most politely what on earth he was coming bothering for now—when Lionel cried out:

'Oh, what a worldful of books! Are they yours?'

'They are yours, your Majesty,' answered the Chancellor. 'They were the property of the late King, your great-great—'

'Yes, I know,' Lionel interrupted. 'Well, I shall read them all. I love to read. I am so glad I learned to read.'

'If I might venture to advise your Majesty,' said the Prime Minister, 'I should *not* read these books. Your great—'

'Yes?' said Lionel, quickly.

'He was a very good King—oh, yes, really a very superior King in his way, but he was a little—well, strange.'

'Mad?' asked Lionel, cheerfully.

'No, no'—both the gentlemen were sincerely shocked. 'Not mad; but if I may express it so, he was—er—too clever by half. And I should not like a little King of mine to have anything to do with his books.'

Lionel looked puzzled.

'The fact is,' the Chancellor went on, twisting his red beard in an agitated way, 'your great—'

'Go on,' said Lionel.

'Was *called* a wizard.'

'But he wasn't?'

'Of course not—a most worthy King was your great—'

'I see.'

'But I wouldn't touch his books.'

'Just this one,' cried Lionel, laying his hands on the cover of a great brown book that lay on the study table. It had gold patterns on the brown leather, and gold clasps with turquoises and rubies in the twists of them, and gold corners, so that the leather should not wear out too quickly.

'I *must* look at this one,' Lionel said, for on the back in big letters he read: 'The Book of Beasts.'

The Chancellor said, 'Don't be a silly little King.'

But Lionel had got the gold clasps undone, and he opened the first page, and there was a beautiful Butterfly all red, and brown, and yellow, and blue, so beautifully painted that it looked as if it were alive.

'There,' said Lionel, 'isn't that lovely? Why—'

But as he spoke the beautiful Butterfly fluttered its many coloured wings on the yellow old page of the book, and flew up and out of the window.

'Well!' said the Prime Minister, as soon as he could speak for the lump of wonder that had got into his throat and tried to choke him, 'that's magic, that is.'

But before he had spoken the King had turned the next page, and there was a shining bird complete and beautiful in every blue feather of him. Under him was written, 'Blue Bird of Paradise', and while the King gazed enchanted at the charming picture the Blue Bird fluttered his wings on the yellow page and spread them and flew out of the book.

Then the Prime Minister snatched the book away from the King and shut it up on the blank page where the bird had been, and put it on a very high shelf. And the Chancellor gave the King a good shaking, and said:

'You're a naughty, disobedient little King,' and was very angry indeed.

'I don't see that I've done any harm,' said Lionel. He hated being shaken, as all boys do; he would much rather have been slapped.

'No harm?' said the Chancellor. 'Ah—but what do you know about it? That's the question. How do you know what might have been on the next page—a snake or a worm, or a centipede or a revolutionist, or something like that.'

'Well, I'm sorry if I've vexed you,' said Lionel. 'Come, let's kiss and
be friends.' So he kissed the Prime Minister, and they settled down for
a nice quiet game of noughts and crosses, while the Chancellor went to
add up his accounts.

But when Lionel was in bed he could not sleep for thinking of the
book, and when the full moon was shining with all her might and light
he got up and crept down to the library and climbed up and got 'The
Book of Beasts'.

He took it outside on to the terrace, where the moonlight was as
bright as day, and he opened the book, and saw the empty pages with
'Butterfly' and 'Blue Bird of Paradise' underneath, and then he turned
the next page. There was some sort of red thing sitting under a palm tree,
and under it was written 'Dragon'. The Dragon did not move, and the
King shut up the book rather quickly and went back to bed.

But the next day he wanted another look, so he got the book out
into the garden, and when he undid the clasps with the rubies and
turquoises, the book opened all by itself at the picture with 'Dragon'
underneath, and the sun shone full on the page. And then, quite
suddenly, a great Red Dragon came out of the book, and spread vast
scarlet wings and flew away across the garden to the far hills, and
Lionel was left with the empty page before him, for the page was quite
empty except for the green palm tree and the yellow desert, and the little streaks of red where the paint brush had gone outside the pencil
outline of the Red Dragon.

And then Lionel felt that he had indeed done it. He had not been
king twenty-four hours, and already he had let loose a Red Dragon to
worry his faithful subjects' lives out. And they had been saving up so
long to buy him a crown, and everything!

Lionel began to cry.

Then the Chancellor and the Prime Minister and the Nurse all came
running to see what was the matter. And when they saw the book they
understood, and the Chancellor said:

'You naughty little King! Put him to bed, Nurse, and let him think
over what he's done.'

'Perhaps, my Lord,' said the Prime Minister, 'we'd better first find out just exactly what he *has* done.'

Then Lionel, in floods of tears, said:

'It's a Red Dragon, and it's gone flying away to the hills, and I am so sorry, and, oh, do forgive me!'

But the Prime Minister and the Chancellor had other things to think of than forgiving Lionel. They hurried off to consult the police and see what could be done. Everyone did what they could. They sat on committees and stood on guard, and lay in wait for the Dragon, but he stayed up in the hills, and there was nothing more to *be* done. The faithful Nurse, meanwhile, did not neglect her duty. Perhaps she did more than anyone else, for she slapped the King and put him to bed without his tea, and when it got dark she would not give him a candle to read by.

'You are a naughty little King,' she said, 'and nobody will love you.'

Next day the Dragon was still quiet, though the more poetic of Lionel's subjects could see the redness of the Dragon shining through the green trees quite plainly. So Lionel put on his crown and sat on his throne and said he wanted to make some laws.

And I need hardly say that though the Prime Minister and the Chancellor and the Nurse might have the very poorest opinion of Lionel's private judgement, and might even slap him and send him to bed, the minute he got on his throne and set his crown on his head, he became infallible—which means that everything he said was right, and that he couldn't possibly make a mistake. So when he said:

"There is to be a law forbidding people to open books in schools or elsewhere'—he had the support of at least half of his subjects, and the other half—the grown-up half—pretended to think he was quite right.

Then he made a law that everyone should always have enough to eat. And this pleased everyone except the ones who had always had too much.

And when several other nice new laws were made and written down he went home and made mud-houses and was very happy. And he said to his Nurse:

'People will love me now I've made such a lot of pretty new laws for them.'

But Nurse said: 'Don't count your chickens, my dear. You haven't seen the last of that Dragon yet.'

Now the next day was Saturday. And in the afternoon the Dragon suddenly swooped down upon the common in all his hideous redness, and carried off the Football Players, umpires, goal-posts, football, and all.

Then the people were very angry indeed, and they said:

'We might as well be a Republic. After saving up all these years to get his crown, and everything!'

And wise people shook their heads and foretold a decline in the National Love of Sport. And, indeed, football was not at all popular for some time afterwards.

Lionel did his best to be a good King during the week, and the people were beginning to forgive him for letting the Dragon out of the book. 'After all,' they said, 'football is dangerous game, and perhaps it is wise to discourage it.'

Popular opinion held that the Football Players, being tough and hard, had disagreed with the Dragon so much that he had gone away to some place where they only play cats' cradle and games that do not make you hard and tough.

All the same, Parliament met on the Saturday afternoon, a convenient time, when most of the Members would be free to attend, to consider the Dragon. But unfortunately the Dragon, who had only been asleep, woke up because it was Saturday, and he considered the Parliament, and afterwards there were not any Members left, so they tried to make a new Parliament, but being an M.P. had somehow grown as unpopular as football playing, and no one would consent to be elected, so they had to do without a Parliament. When the next Saturday came round everyone was a little nervous, but the Red Dragon was pretty quiet that day and only ate an Orphanage.

Lionel was very, very unhappy. He felt that it was his disobedience that had brought this trouble on the Parliament and the Orphanage and the Football Players, and he felt that it was his duty to try and do something. The question was, what?

The Blue Bird that had come out of the book used to sing very nicely in the Palace rose-garden, and the Butterfly was very tame, and would perch on his shoulder when he walked among the tall lilies: so Lionel saw that *all* the creatures in the Book of Beasts could not be wicked, like the Dragon, and he thought:

'Suppose I could get another beast out who would fight the Dragon?'

So he took the Book of Beasts out into the rose-garden and opened the page next to the one where the Dragon had been just a tiny bit to see what the name was. He could only see 'cora', but he felt the middle of the page swelling up thick with the creature that was trying to come out, and it was only by putting the book down and sitting on it suddenly very hard, that he managed to get it shut. Then he fastened the clasps with the rubies and turquoises in them and sent for the Chancellor, who had been ill on Saturday week, and so had not been eaten with the rest of the Parliament, and he said:

'What animal ends in "cora"?'

The Chancellor answered:

'The Manticora, of course.'

'What is he like?' asked the King.

'He is the sworn foe of Dragons,' said the Chancellor. 'He drinks their blood. He is yellow, with the body of a lion and the face of a man. I wish we had a few Manticoras here now. But the last died hundreds of years ago—worse luck!'

Then the King ran and opened the book at the page that had 'cora' on it, and there was the picture—Manticora, all yellow, with a lion's body and a man's face, just as the Chancellor had said. And under the picture was written, 'Manticora'.

And in a few minutes the Manticora came sleepily out of the book, rubbing its eyes with its hands and mewing piteously. It seemed very stupid, and when Lionel gave it a push and said, 'Go along and fight the Dragon, do,' it put its tail between its legs and fairly ran away. It went and hid behind the Town Hall, and at night when the people were asleep it went round and ate all the pussy-cats in the town. And then it mewed more than ever. And on the Saturday morning, when people were a little timid about going out, because the Dragon had no regular hour for calling, the Manticora went up and down the streets and drank all the milk that was left in the cans at the doors for people's teas, and it ate the cans as well.

And just when it had finished the very last little ha'porth, which was short measure, because the milkman's nerves were quite upset, the Red Dragon came down the street looking for the Manticora. It edged off when it saw him coming, for it was not at all the Dragon-fighting kind; and, seeing no other door open, the poor, hunted creature took refuge in the General Post Office, and there the Dragon found it, trying to conceal itself among the ten o'clock mail. The Dragon fell on the Manticora at once, and the mail was no defence. The mewings were heard all over the town. All the pussies and the milk the Manticora had had seemed to have strengthened its mew wonderfully. Then there was a sad silence, and presently the people whose windows looked that way saw the Dragon come walking down the steps of the General Post Office spitting fire and smoke, together with tufts of Manticora fur, and the fragments of the registered letters. Things were growing very serious. However popular the King might become during the week, the Dragon was sure to do something on Saturday to upset the people's loyalty.

The Dragon was a perfect nuisance for the whole of Saturday, except during the hour of noon, and then he had to rest under a tree or he would have caught fire from the heat of the sun. You see, he was very hot to begin with.

At last came a Saturday when the Dragon actually walked into the Royal nursery and carried off the King's own pet Rocking-Horse. Then the King cried for six days, and on the seventh he was so tired that he had to stop. Then he heard the Blue Bird singing among the roses and saw the Butterfly fluttering among the lilies, and he said:

'Nurse, wipe my face, please. I am not going to cry any more.'

Nurse washed his face, and told him not to be a silly little King. 'Crying,' said she, 'never did anyone any good yet.'

'I don't know,' said the little King, 'I seem to see better, and to hear better now that I've cried for a week. Now, Nurse, dear, I know I'm right, so kiss me in case I never come back. I *must* try if I can't save the people.'

'Well, if you must, you must,' said Nurse; 'but don't tear your clothes or get your feet wet.'

So off he went.

The Blue Bird sang more sweetly than ever, and the Butterfly shone more brightly, as Lionel once more carried the Book of Beasts out into the rose-garden, and opened it—very quickly, so that he might not be afraid and change his mind. The book fell open wide, almost in the middle, and there was written at the bottom of the page, 'The Hippogriff,' and before Lionel had time to see what the picture was, there was a fluttering of great wings and a stamping of hoofs, and a sweet, soft, friendly neighing; and there came out of the book a beautiful white horse with a long, long, white tail, and he had great wings like swan's wings, and the softest, kindest eyes in the world, and he stood there among the roses.

The Hippogriff rubbed its silky-soft, milky-white nose against the little King's shoulder, and the little King thought: 'But for the wings you are very like my poor, dear, lost Rocking-Horse.' And the Blue Bird's song was very loud and sweet.

Then suddenly the King saw coming through the sky the great straggling, sprawling, wicked shape of the Red Dragon. And he knew at once what he must do. He caught up the Book of Beasts and jumped on the back of the gentle, beautiful Hippogriff, and leaning down he whispered in the sharp white ear:

'Fly, dear Hippogriff, fly your very fastest to the Pebbly Waste.'

And when the Dragon saw them start, he turned and flew after them, with his great wings flapping like clouds at sunset, and the Hippogriff's wide wings were snowy as clouds at the moon-rising.

When the people in the town saw the Dragon fly off after the Hippogriff and the King they all came out of their houses to look, and when they saw the two disappear they made up their minds to the worst, and began to think what would be worn for Court mourning.

But the Dragon could not catch the Hippogriff. The red wings were bigger than the white ones, but they were not so strong, and so the white-winged horse flew away and away and away, with the Dragon pursuing, till he reached the very middle of the Pebbly Waste.

Now, the Pebbly Waste is just like the parts of the seaside where there is no sand—all round, loose, shifting stones, and there is no grass there and no tree within a hundred miles of it.

Lionel jumped off the white horse's back in the very middle of the Pebbly Waste, and he hurriedly unclasped the Book of Beasts and laid it open on the pebbles. Then he clattered among the pebbles in his haste to get back on to his white horse, and had just jumped on when up came the Dragon. He was flying very feebly, and looking round every where for a tree, for it was just on the stroke of twelve, the sun was shining like a gold guinea in the blue sky, and there was not a tree for a hundred miles.

The white-winged horse flew round and round the Dragon as he writhed on the dry pebbles. He was getting very hot: indeed, parts of him even had begun to smoke. He knew that he must certainly catch fire in another minute unless he could get under a tree. He made a snatch with his red claws at the King and Hippogriff, but he was too feeble to reach them, and besides, he did not dare to over-exert himself for fear he should get any hotter.

It was then that he saw the Book of Beasts lying on the pebbles, open at the page with 'Dragon' written at the bottom. He looked and he hesitated, and he looked again, and then, with one last squirm of rage, the Dragon wriggled himself back into the picture, and sat down under the palm tree, and the page was a little singed as he went in.

As soon as Lionel saw that the Dragon had really been obliged to go and sit under his own palm tree because it was the only tree there, he jumped off his horse and shut the book with a bang.

'Oh, hurrah!' he cried. 'Now we really *have* done it.'

And he clasped the book very tight with the turquoise and ruby clasps.

'Oh, my precious Hippogriff,' he cried, 'you are the bravest, dearest, most beautiful—'

'Hush,' whispered the Hippogriff, modestly. 'Don't you see that we are not alone?'

And indeed there was quite a crowd round them on the Pebbly Waste: the Prime Minister and the Parliament and the Football Players and the Orphanage and the Manticora and the Rocking-horse, and indeed everyone who had been eaten by the Dragon. You see, it was impossible for the Dragon to take them into the book with him—it was a tight fit even for one Dragon—so, of course, he had to leave them outside.

They all got home somehow, and lived happily ever after.

When the King asked the Manticora where he would like to live he begged to be allowed to go back into the book. 'I do not care for public life,' he said.

Of course he knew his way on to his own page, so there was no danger of his opening the book at the wrong page and letting out a Dragon or anything. So he got back into his picture, and has never come out since: that is why you will never see a Manticora as long as you live, except in a picture book. And of course he left the pussies outside, because there was no room for them in the book—and the milk-cans too.

Then the Rocking-Horse begged to be allowed to go and live on the Hippogriff's page of the book. 'I should like,' he said, 'to live somewhere where Dragons can't get at me.'

So the beautiful, white-winged Hippogriff showed him the way in, and there he stayed till the King had him taken out for his great-great-great-great-grandchildren to play with.

As for the Hippogriff, he accepted the position of the King's Own Rocking-Horse—a situation left vacant by the retirement of the wooden one. And the Blue Bird and the Butterfly sing and flutter among the Palace garden to this very day.

from

The Odyssey of Homer

Translated by Allen Mandelbaum

Homer wrote his epic poem *The Odyssey* some-
time between 800 and 600 B.C.E. The poem
recounts Greek hero Odysseus' long and dangerous journey home at the end of the Trojan War.
These verses show Odysseus and his men upon
their arrival in Aeáea, an island ruled by the
beautiful but devious enchantress Círcë.

We reached Aeáea, isle of fair-haired Círcë,
the awesome goddess with a human voice,
twin sister of the sinister Aeétës:
they both were born of Hélios—who brought
his light to men—and Pérsë Ocean's daughter.
In silence we put in to shore; the harbor
seemed safe; some gracious god had been our guide.
We stayed two days, two nights—fatigued and tried.

"But when, with fair-haired Dawn, the third day came,
with spear and sharpened sword in hand I climbed
up from the ship. I reached a rise from which
I hoped to see the signs of human work
and hear the sounds of men. And as I stood
upon that lookout point, up from wide fields
and through the forest and the underbrush,

smoke rose: it came from Círcë's house. The sight
of that black smoke inclined my heart and mind
to seek the source. But as I thought again,
another plan seemed best: I'd first go back
to my swift ship along the shore, find food
to feed my men, and then have them explore.

"But when I had already neared my ship,
some god took pity on my loneliness:
across my path he sent a tall-horned stag.
Down from his pasture in the forest, he—
responding to the sun's oppressive fury—
was heading to the riverbank to drink.
When he had quit the stream, I struck his back;
and right through his mid-spine, my bronze shaft passed.
He moaned; he fell into the dust; his life
took flight. I straddled him and tugged the shaft
out from the wound, then left it on the ground
and gathered lengths of brush and willow witches
to weave a rope two arm's-lengths long, twisted
from end to end. I tied that huge beast's feet
and slung him round my neck, then, trudging, leaned
my weight upon the spear that I'd retrieved.
That way I brought him back to the black ship:
one hand across one shoulder never could
have carried him—that stag was so immense.
I threw him down in front of our lithe ship
and gently urged my comrades, one by one:

"'O friends, however sad, let's not descend
to Hades' halls before our destined day.
No, just as long as there is food and drink
in our swift ship, forget your fears of starving!'

"These were my words. My men did not delay.
They'd hid their heads with cloaks in their despair,
but now they threw those wrappings off and stared:
they saw the stag along the shore: indeed
that beast was huge. And with their eyes appeased,
they washed their hands and readied the fine feast.

"All through that day we sat, until sunset:
we had much meat; the wine was honey-sweet.
But when the sun sank and the dark arrived,
we all stretched out and slept on the seaside.

"As soon as Dawn's rose fingers touched the sky,
I called my crew together, and I said:
"Despite your long ordeal, do hear me out:
my friends, we've lost all sense of where we are;
this island may lie east, it may lie west—
where sun, which brings men light, sinks to its rest
or where it's born again. Let's try at once
to see if we can find some better course.
I doubt it, for I climbed a rugged lookout:
we're on an island that is ringed about
by endless seas; so crowned, the isle lies low,
and at its center I saw curling smoke
that rose up through the forest and thick brush.'

"My words were done. And their dear hearts were torn,
recalling the fierce Laestrygónian,
Antíphatës, and the man-eating Cyclops.
Their groans were loud, their tears were many—yet
nothing was gained by weeping. So I split
my well-greaved men into two squads: each band
had its own chief. I headed one; the second
was led by the godlike Eurylochus.

Within a casque of bronze we mixed our lots
to see who would go off and spy the land.
The choice fill on the firm Eurylochus.
And he went off with two-and-twenty men;
both they who left and we who stayed then wept.

"Within a forest glen, they found the home
of Círcë, it was built of polished stone
and lay within a clearing. Round it roamed
the mountain wolves and lions she'd bewitched
with evil drugs. But they did not attack
my men; they circled them; their long tails wagged.
And just as dogs will fawn about their master
when he returns from feasts—they know that he
will offer them choice bits—just so, did these
lions and sharp-clawed wolves fawn on my men.
And yet those tough beasts terrified my friends.
They halted at the fair-haired Círcë's door;
within they heard the goddess' sweet voice sing
as she moved back and forth before her web—
imperishable, flawless, subtly-woven—
such work as only goddesses can fashion.

"Polítës, sturdy captain, the most dear
and trusted of my men, now told his friends:
'Someone inside is singing gracefully
as she weaves her great web. And what she sings
echoes throughout the house. Let's call to her.'

"These were his words. They did what he had asked.
She came at once. She opened her bright doors,
inviting them within; and—fools—they followed.
Eurylochus alone did not go in;
he had foreseen some snare. She led the way

and seated them on chairs and high-backed thrones.
She mixed cheese, barley meal, and yellow honey
with wine from Prámnos; and she then combined
malign drugs in that dish so they'd forget
all thoughts of their own homes. When they had drunk,
she struck them with her wand, then drove them off
to pen them in her sties. They'd taken on
the bodies—bristles, snouts—and grunts of hogs,
yet kept the human minds they had before.
So they were penned, in tears; and Círcë cast
before them acorns, dogwood berries, mast—
food fit for swine who wallow on the ground.

"Meanwhile Eurylochus rushed back to us
to let us know our comrades' shameful fate.
But he was speechless; though he longed for words,
his heart was struck with pain, tears filled his eyes;
nothing but lamentation filled his mind.
But when we—baffled—questioned him, at last
he told us what had happened to our friends:

"'Odysseus, we did follow your commands:
we crossed the underbrush and reached the glen.
We found a sheltered house with smooth, stone walls.
And there, intent on her great web, a goddess
or woman could be heard distinctly singing.
My comrades called to her; she opened wide
the gleaming doors. inviting them to enter.
They, unsuspecting, trailed along. But I
held back; I felt this was a trap. They dropped
from sight together. though I kept close watch—
I waited long—no comrade reappeared.'

"These were his words. Across my back I cast

my massive sword of bronze with silver studs,
and then I slung my bow; I ordered him
to lead me back along the path he'd taken.
But he, his arms about my knees, implored:

"'May you, whom Zeus has nurtured, leave me here;
don't force me to retrace my path. I know
that you will not return and not bring back
our men. With those we have let's sail away,
for we may still escape the evil day.'

"These were his words. I was compelled to say:
'Eurylochus you can stay here and eat
and drink beside the hollow black ship; I
Must go, however; I cannot forgo
a task so necessary—this I owe.'

"That said, I left the sea and ship behind.
But after I had crossed the sacred glades
and was about to reach the halls of Círcë,
the connoisseur of potions, I saw Hermes,
who bears the golden wand, approaching me.
He'd taken on the likeness of a youth
just come of age, blessed with a young man's grace.
He clasped my hands. These were his words to me:

"'Where are you wandering still, unlucky man,
alone along these slopes and ignorant
of this strange land? Círcë has locked your friends
like swine behind the tight fence of her pens.
And have you come to free them? On your own,
be sure, you never will return; you'll stay
together with the others in her sties.
But come, I'll save you from her snares, I'll thwart

her plans. Now, when you enter Círcë's halls,
don't leave behind this tutelary herb.
I'll tell you all her fatal stratagems:
She'll mix a potion for you; she'll add drugs
into that drink; but even with their force,
she can't bewitch you; for the noble herb
I'll give you now will baffle all her plots.
When Círcë touches you with her long wand,
draw out the sharp sword at your thigh, and head
for her as if you meant to strike her dead.
Shrinking, she'll ask you then to share her bed.
And do not, then or later, turn her down,
for she will free your friends and be of help
to you, her guest. But first force her to swear
the blessed gods' great, massive oath: She must
forgo all thought of any other plots—
when you are stripped and naked, she must not
deceive you, leave you feeble, impotent.'

"When that was said, he gave his herb to me;
he plucked it from the ground and showed what sort
of plant it was. Its root was black; its flower
was white as milk. It's *moly* for the gods;
for mortal men, the mandrake—very hard
to pluck; but nothing holds against the gods.

"Then Hermes crossed the wooded isle and left
for steep Olympus. And I took the path
to Círcë's house—most anxious as I went.
I stopped before the fair-haired goddess' door;
I halted, called aloud; she heard my voice.
At once she opened her bright doors and then
invited me to follow her. I went
with troubled heart. She led me to a chair,

robust and handsome, graced with silver studs;
a footrest stood below. And she poured out
in ample drink into a golden bowl.
With her conniving mind, she mixed her drugs
within that bowl, then offered it to me.
I drank it down. But I was not bewitched.
She struck me with her long wand. Then she said:
'Now to the sty, to wallow with your friends!'

"At that, out from its sheath along my thigh,
I drew my sword as if to have her die.
She howled. She clasped my knees and, as she wept,
with these winged words, made her appeal to me:

"'Who are you? From what family? What city?
You drank my drugs, but you were not entranced.
No other man has ever passed that test;
for once that potion's passed their teeth, the rest
have fallen prey: you have within your chest
a heart that can defeat my sorcery.
You surely are the man of many wiles,
Odysseus, he whom I was warned against
by Hermes of the golden wand: he said
that you would come from Troy in a black ship.
But now put back your blade within that sheath
and let us lie together on my bed:
in loving, we'll learn trust and confidence.'

"These were her words. And this was my reply:
'Círcë, how can you ask for tenderness,
you who have turned my comrades into swine
and now, insidiously, try to bind
me, too—for once I'm naked on your bed,
you'll snare me, leave me weak and impotent?

I will not share your bed unless you swear
the mighty oath, o goddess—to insure
that you'll forgo all thoughts of further plots.'

"These were my words. As I had asked, she swore
at once. And after that great oath was pledged,
I then climbed into Círcë's lovely bed.

"Meanwhile four girls were busy in the halls;
these maids were once dear daughters of the woods
and springs and seaward-flowing sacred streams.
Across the high-backed chairs, one handmaid first
draped linen cloth and then threw purple rugs.
The second drew up silver tables set
with golden baskets, while the third maid mixed
smooth honeyed wine in silver bowls and brought
fair golden cups. The fourth maid filled a tripod
with water and, beneath it, lit a fire;
and when it bubbled in the glowing bronze
caldron, she set me down inside a tub.
Over my head and shoulders she poured water—
gradually tempering its heat—
to free my limbs and soul from long fatigue.
And when that maid had bathed and, with rich oil,
had smoothed my body and about me cast
a tunic and a handsome cloak, she led
the way and sat me on a high-backed chair,
robust and handsome, graced with silver studs;
a footrest stood below. A servant brought
a lovely golden jug from which she poured
fresh water out into a silver bowl,
so I might wash my hands; then at my side
she placed a polished table. The old housewife
was generous; she drew on lavish stores,
inviting me to eat. But I was not

inclined to feed my frame: I sat and thought
of other things; my soul foresaw the worst.
Círcë, who saw me seated there denying
all food and filled with dark despair, drew near.
And, at my side, she called on these winged words:

"'Odysseus, do not sit there like some mute,
with tattered heart, not touching drink or food.
Do you suspect another trap? Forget
your fears. I swore the strongest oath there is:'

"These were her words. And this was my reply:
'Círcë, what man with justice in his mind
would think of food and drink before he freed
his comrades and could see them with his eyes?
If you indeed would have me drink and eat,
release my men, bring back my faithful friends.'

"These were my words. And Círcë—wand in hand—
now left the hall and, opening the pens,
drove out my men; they had the shape of fat
nine-year-old hogs. They faced her. She drew close.
Upon the flesh of each of them, she spread
another herb. At that, their bodies shed
the bristles that had grown when they'd gulped down
the deadly brew she'd offered them at first.
Now they were men again—and younger than
they were before, more handsome and more grand.
They knew me quickly; each man clasped my hand.
Their cries of joy were long and loud; throughout
the house a clamor rose. And Círcë, too,
was moved. Then she—the lovely goddess—urged:

'Odysseus, man of many wiles, divine
son of Laértës, go to your swift ship

along the shore and beach it on dry land.
First store your goods and all your gear in caves,
but then return with all your faithful friends.'

"These were her words. My proud soul was convinced:
I hurried to the shore and my swift ship.
And there I found my faithful crew in tears.
Even as calves upon a farm are glad
when cows return from pasture, having had
their fill of grass, and come back to their stalls;
and all the calves frisk round unchecked; no pen
can hold them as they race around their dams,
lowing again, again—so did my men,
when they caught sight of me, weep tears of joy:
they felt as if they'd touched their native land,
their rugged Ithaca, where they were bred
and born. In tears, they uttered these winged words:

"'You, whom Zeus nurtured, have come back; for us
this joy is like the joy that would erupt
on our return to Ithaca, our home.
But tell us now the fate of all the rest.'

"These were their words. I quietly replied:
'Come, let us beach our ship along dry land
and stow our goods and all our gear in caves.
Then, all of you be quick to follow me;
in Círcë's sacred halls you soon will see
your comrades eating, drinking; they can count
on never-ending stores.'

                              "My words were done.
At once they answered my commands. But one—
Eurylochus—did try to check their course:

"'My sorry friends, where are we heading now?
Why court catastrophe in Círcë's house?
She'll turn us into lions, wolves, or hogs—
and we'll be forced to guard her massive halls.
So did the Cyclops catch and trap our friends—
then, too, the rash Odysseus was with them.
They, too, died through the madness of this man.'

"I heard his words. I had a mind to draw
the sharp blade sheathed beside my sturdy thigh.
I'd have sliced off his head and flung it down
upon the ground—although Eurylochus
was kin of mine by marriage. But my men
drew near and checked me with these gentle words:

"'If you—one sprung from Zeus—prefer it so,
he can stay here and watch the ship. We'll go
with you: lead us to Círcë's sacred house.'

"That said, they left the ship and shore behind.
Eurylochus came, too. He did not stay:
my rage was ominous—he was afraid.

"Meanwhile, with kindness, Círcë, in her halls,
cared for my other men: she bathed them all,
and then she smoothed their skins with gleaming oil
and wrapped them in fine tunics and soft cloaks.
We found them feasting on abundant stores.
But when they all had recognized each other,
their tears and wails were loud throughout the halls.
Bright Círcë, standing at my side, advised:

"'Odysseus, man of many wiles, divine
son of Laértës, do not urge more tears.
I know indeed the many miseries

you have endured upon the fish-rich sea
and how, on land, you faced fierce enemies.
But eat this food and drink this wine—and find
the force you had when you first left behind
your homeland, rugged Ithaca. Your minds
can only think of bitter wanderings;
you're worn and weary, without joy or ease;
you've lived too long—too much—with grinding griefs.'

"These were her words. And our proud hearts agreed.
Day after day we stayed for one whole year:
we ate much meat; the wine was honey-sweet.

"But when the months that fill a year had passed,
and seasons had revolved, and once again
the long days reached their end, my comrades said:

'Wake from your trance, remember your own land,
if fate is yet to save you, if you can
still reach your high-walled house, your native isle:'

"These were their words. And my proud heart agreed.
Through all that day we sat, until sunset:
the meat was fine; the wine was honey-sweet.
But once the sun had gone and darkness won,
within the shadowed halls, my comrades slept.

"And I went off to Círcë's splendid bed.
I clasped her knees. She heard as I beseeched:
'Círcë, fulfill the promise made to me:
do let me leave for home. My men entreat,
and my own heart wants that. Whenever you
are out of hearing, all my men implore
again, again: they long to leave these shores!'

"The lovely goddess gave this quick reply:
'Odysseus, man of many wiles, divine
son of Laértës, do not spend more time
within my house if you will otherwise.
But you cannot reach home till you complete
another journey—to the house of Hades
and fierce Perséphonë. There you must seek
the soul of that blind seer, Tirésias
the Theban: he alone among the dead
preserves his wits and sober sense: this gift
Perséphonë has granted just to him,
for all the other dead are wandering shades.'

"My heart was broken as I heard her words.
Seated upon that bed, I cried: my soul
had lost its will to live, to see the light.
But when my need to weep and writhe was done,
these were the words with which I answered her:

'Círcë, who'll serve as pilot on that way?
No man has ever sailed in his black ship
to Hades' halls:'

                "And her reply was quick:
'Odysseus, man of many wiles, divine
son of Laértés, there's no need to fret
about a helmsman. After you have stepped
the mast and spread your white sail, you can sit:
the breath of Bórëas will guide your ship.
But when you've crossed the Ocean, you will see
the shore and forests of Perséphonë—
the towering poplars and the willow trees
whose fruits fall prematurely. Beach your ship
on that flat shore which lies on the abyss
of Ocean. Make your way on foot to Hades.

In those dank halls, the Pyripthégethon
together with a branch of Styx, Cocytus—
two roaring rivers—form one course and join
the Ácheron just there you'll find a rock.
Draw near that spot and, as I tell you, dig
a squared-off ditch—along each side, one cubit.
Three times pour offerings around that pit
for all the dead: pour milk and honey first,
then pour sweet wine; let water be the third.
And scatter over these white barley meal.
Then give the helpless dead your fervent pledge
that, when you come to Ithaca, you'll offer
as sacrifice your finest barren heifer
and heap her pyre high with handsome gifts.
But to Tirésias alone pledge this:
the finest jet-black ram that you possess.
And after you have called upon the famed
tribes of the dead, do sacrifice a ram
and black ewe: bend their heads toward Érebus,
but you must turn toward Ocean's streams. That done,
so many souls of men now dead will come.
For them, command your crew to flay and burn
the slaughtered sheep, throats slit by ruthless bronze;
and pray unto the gods, to mighty Hades
and fierce Perséphonë. Draw your sharp sword
out from the sheath that lies along your thigh:
keep close watch on the blood of sacrifice,
lest any of the helpless dead draw near
that pit before you meet Tirésias.
Soon he, the seer, leader of men, will come
to tell you what will be your path, how long
your homeward journey is to take, and how
you'll make your way across the fish-rich sea.'

"So Círcë said. Upon the throne of gold,
Dawn came straightway. The goddess Círcë clothed
my frame in cloak and tunic; she herself
put on a long and gleaming, gracious robe
of subtly-woven threads. She bound a belt
of gold around her waist; she veiled her head.
And I went through the house; with gentle words
I spurred my comrades, one by one. I urged:
'You've had enough sweet sleep. It's time to go.
Great Círcë told me all that we must know.'

"These were my words. And their proud hearts agreed.
But I was not to lead all of my men
away from Círcë's isle, one of my band,
our youngest man, Elpénor—not too brave
nor too alert—had lain alone, stretched out
along the roof of Círcë's house to find
some cooler air: he'd taken too much wine.
Then, when he heard the noise of our departure,
he jumped up suddenly, and so—forgetting
the long way down by ladder—off the roof
headfirst he fell. And from his spine, his neck
was broken off, his spirit went to Hades.

"But I, to those who followed me, now said:
'Though you may think that you are going home,
back to your own dear land, another road
is ours, for Círcë said we first must see
the hall of Hades and Perséphonë;
there we must meet Tirésias of Thebes.'

"My words broke their dear hearts. They sat and wept;
they tore their hair; but all of that lament

gained nothing for us. Still in tears, we went
back to the shore; alongside our black ship,
Círcë had tied a ram and jet black ewe,
but none of us had seen her go or come;
she passed us by so easily. How can
a man detect a god who comes and goes
if gods refuse to have their movements known?"

from

A Wizard of Earthsea

by Ursula K. Le Guin

Ursula K. Le Guin's (born 1929) father was an anthropologist and her mother was a writer. The family's house in Berkeley, California was filled with books and all kinds of interesting people, and Ursula grew up to write scores of books of fantasy. In this story we meet a young apprentice mage Ged on his way to study with the great Archmage on the island of Roke.

Ged slept that night aboard *Shadow*, and early in the morning parted with those first sea-comrades of his, they shouting good wishes cheerily after him as he went up the docks. The town of Thwil is not large, its high houses huddling close over a few steep narrow streets. To Ged, however, it seemed a city, and not knowing where to go he asked the first townsman of Thwil he met where he would find the Warder of the School on Roke. The man looked at him sidelong a while and said, "The wise don't need to ask, the fool asks in vain," and so went on along the street. Ged went uphill till he came out into a square, rimmed on three sides by the houses with their sharp slate roofs and on the fourth side by the wall of a great building whose few small windows were higher than the chimneytops of the houses: a fort or castle it seemed, built of mighty grey blocks of stone. In the square beneath it market-booths were set up and there was some coming and going of people. Ged asked his question of an old woman with a basket of mussels, and she replied, "You cannot always find the Warder where he is, but sometimes you find him where he is not," and went on crying her mussels to sell.

In the great building, near one corner, there was a mean little door of wood. Ged went to this and knocked loud. To the old man who opened the door he said, "I bear a letter from the Mage Ogion of Gont to the Warder of the School on this island. I want to find the Warder, but I will not hear more riddles and scoffing!"

"This is the School," the old man said mildly. "I am the doorkeeper. Enter if you can."

Ged stepped forward. It seemed to him that he had passed through the doorway: yet he stood outside on the pavement where he had stood before.

Once more he stepped forward, and once more he remained standing outside the door. The doorkeeper, inside, watched him with mild eyes.

Ged was not so much baffled as angry, for this seemed like a further mockery to him. With voice and hand he made the Opening spell which his aunt had taught him long ago; it was the prize among all her stock of spells, and he wove it well now. But it was only a witch's charm, and the power that held this doorway was not moved at all.

When that failed Ged stood a long while there on the pavement. At last he looked at the old man who waited inside. "I cannot enter," he said unwillingly, "unless you help me."

The doorkeeper answered, "Say your name."

Then again Ged stood still a while; for a man never speaks his own name aloud, until more than his life's safety is at stake.

"I am Ged," he said aloud. Stepping forward then he entered the open doorway. Yet it seemed to him that though the light was behind him, a shadow followed him in at his heels.

He saw also as he turned that the doorway through which he had come was not plain wood as he had thought, but ivory without joint or seam: it was cut, as he knew later, from a tooth of the Great Dragon. The door that the old man closed behind him was of polished horn, through which the daylight shone dimly, and on its inner face was carved the Thousand-Leaved Tree.

"Welcome to this house, lad," the doorkeeper said, and without saying more led him through halls and corridors to an open court far inside the walls of the building. The court was partly paved with stone, but was roofless, and on a grass-plot a fountain played under young trees in the sunlight. There Ged waited alone some while. He stood still, and his heart beat hard, for it seemed to him that he felt presences and powers at work unseen about him here, and he knew that this place was built not only of stone but of magic stronger than stone. He stood in the innermost room of the House of the Wise, and it was open to the sky. Then suddenly he was aware of a man clothed in white who watched him through the falling water of the fountain.

As their eyes met, a bird sang aloud in the branches of the tree. In that moment Ged understood the singing of the bird, and the language of the water falling in the basin of the fountain, and the shape of the clouds, and the beginning and end of the wind that stirred the leaves: it seemed to him that he himself was a word spoken by the sunlight.

Then that moment passed, and he and the world were as before, or almost as before. He went forward to kneel before the Archmage, holding out to him the letter written by Ogion.

The Archmage Nemmerle, Warder of Roke, was an old man, older it was said than any man then living. His voice quavered like the bird's voice when he spoke, welcoming Ged kindly. His hair and beard and robe were white, and he seemed as if all darkness and heaviness had been leached out of him by the slow usage of the years, leaving him white and worn as driftwood that has been a century adrift. "My eyes are old, I cannot read what your master writes," he said in his quavering voice. "Read me the letter, lad."

So Ged made out and read aloud the writing, which was in Hardic runes, and said no more than this: *Lord Nemmerle! I send you one who will be greatest of the wizards of Gont, if the wind blow true.* This was signed, not with Ogion's true name which Ged had never yet learned, but with Ogion's rune, the Closed Mouth.

"He who holds the earthquake on a leash has sent you, for which be doubly welcome. Young Ogion was dear to me, when he came here from Gont. Now tell me of the seas and portents of your voyage, lad."

"A fair passage, Lord, but for the storm yesterday."

"What ship brought you here?"

"*Shadow*, trading from the Andrades."

"Whose will sent you here?"

"My own."

The Archmage looked at Ged and looked away, and began to speak in a tongue that Ged did not understand, mumbling as will an old old man whose wits go wandering among the years and islands. Yet in among his mumbling there were words of what the bird had sung and what the water had said falling. He was not laying a spell and yet there was a power in his voice that moved Ged's mind so that the boy was bewildered, and for an instant seemed to behold himself standing in a strange vast desert place alone among shadows. Yet all along he was in the sunlit court, hearing the fountain fall.

A great black bird, a raven of Osskil, came walking over the stone terrace and the grass. It came to the hem of the Archmage's robe and stood there all black with its dagger beak and eyes like pebbles, staring sidelong at Ged. It pecked three times on the white staff Nemmerle leaned on, and the old wizard ceased his muttering, and smiled. "Run and play, lad," he said at last as to a little child. Ged knelt again on one knee to him. When he rose, the Archmage was gone. Only the raven stood eyeing him, its beak outstretched as if to peck the vanished staff.

It spoke, in what Ged guessed might be the speech of Osskil. "Terrenon ussbuk!" it said croaking. "Terrenon ussbuk orrek!" And it strutted off as it had come.

Ged turned to leave the courtyard, wondering where he should go. Under the archway he was met by a tall youth who greeted him very courteously, bowing his head. "I am called Jasper, Enwit's son of the Domain of Eolg on Havnor Isle. I am at your service today, to show you about the Great House and answer your questions as I can. How shall I call you, Sir?"

Now it seemed to Ged, a mountain villager who had never been among the sons of rich merchants and noblemen, that this fellow was scoffing at him with his "service" and his "Sir" and his bowing and scraping. He answered shortly, "Sparrowhawk, they call me."

The other waited a moment as if expecting some more mannerly response, and getting none straightened up and turned a little aside. He

was two or three years older than Ged, very tall, and he moved and carried himself with stiff grace, posing (Ged thought) like a dancer. He
wore a grey cloak with hood thrown back. The first place he took Ged
was the wardrobe room, where as a student of the school Ged might
find himself another such cloak that fitted him, and any other clothing
he might need. He put on the dark-grey cloak he had chosen, and
Jasper said, "Now you are one of us."

Jasper had a way of smiling faintly as he spoke which made Ged
look for a jeer hidden in his polite words. "Do clothes make the
mage?" he answered, sullen.

"No," said the older boy. "Though I have heard that manners make
the man.—Where now?"

"Where you will. I do not know the house."

Jasper took him down the corridors of the Great House showing
him the open courts and the roofed halls, the Room of Shelves where
the books of lore and rune-tomes were kept, the great Hearth Hall
where all the school gathered on festival days, and upstairs, in the towers and under the roofs, the small cells where the students and Masters
slept. Ged's was in the South Tower, with a window looking down over
the steep roofs of Thwil town to the sea. Like the other sleeping-cells it
had no furnishing but a straw-filled mattress in the corner. "We live
very plain here," said Jasper. "But I expect you won't mind that."

"I'm used to it." Presently, trying to show himself an equal of this
polite disdainful youth, he added, "I suppose you weren't, when you
first came."

Jasper looked at him, and his look said without words, "What could
you possibly know about what I, son of the Lord of the Domain of
Eolg on the Isle of Havnor, am or am not used to?" What Jasper said
aloud was simply, "Come on this way."

A gong had been rung while they were upstairs, and they came down
to eat the noon meal at the Long Table of the refectory, along with a
hundred or more boys and young men. Each waited on himself, joking
with the cooks through the window-hatches of the kitchen that opened
into the refectory, loading his plate from great bowls of food that
steamed on the sills, sitting where he pleased at the Long Table. "They

say," Jasper told Ged, "that no matter how many sit at this table, there is always room." Certainly there was room both for many noisy groups of boys talking and eating mightily, and for older fellows, their grey cloaks clasped with silver at the neck, who sat more quietly by pairs or alone, with grave, pondering faces, as if they had much to think about. Jasper took Ged to sit with a heavyset fellow called Vetch, who said nothing much but shovelled in his food with a will. He had the accent of the East Reach, and was very dark of skin, not red-brown like Ged and Jasper and most folk of the Archipelago, but black-brown. He was plain, and his manners were not polished. He grumbled about the dinner when he had finished it, but then turning to Ged said, "At least it's not illusion, like so much around here; it sticks to your ribs." Ged did not know what he meant, but he felt a certain liking for him, and was glad when after the meal he stayed with them.

They went down into the town, that Ged might learn his way about it. Few and short as were the streets of Thwil, they turned and twisted curiously among the high-roofed houses, and the way was easy to lose. It was a strange town, and strange also its people, fishermen and workmen and artisans like any others, but so used to the sorcery that is ever at play on the Isle of the Wise that they seemed half sorcerers themselves. They talked (as Ged had learned) in riddles, and not one of them would blink to see a boy turn into a fish or a house fly up into the air, but knowing it for a school-boy prank would go on cobbling shoes or cutting up mutton, unconcerned.

Coming up past the Back Door and around through the gardens of the Great House, the three boys crossed the clearrunning Thwilburn on a wooden bridge and went on northward among woods and pastures. The path climbed and wound. They passed oak-groves where shadows lay thick for all the brightness of the sun. There was one grove not far away to the left that Ged could never quite see plainly. The path never reached it, though it always seemed to be about to. He could not even make out what kind of trees they were. Vetch, seeing him gazing, said softly, "That is the Immanent Grove. We can't come there, yet. . . ."

In the hot sunlit pastures yellow flowers bloomed. "Sparkweed," said Jasper. "They grow where the wind dropped the ashes of burning

Ilien, when Erreth-Akbe defended the Inward Isles from the Firelord."
He blew on a withered flower-head, and the seeds shaken loose went
up on the wind like sparks of fire in the sun.

The path led them up and around the base of a great green hill, round
and treeless, the hill that Ged had seen from the ship as they entered the
charmed waters of Roke Island. On the hillside Jasper halted. "At home
in Havnor I heard much about Gontish wizardry, and always in praise, so
that I've wanted for a long time to see the manner of it. Here now we have
a Gontishman; and we stand on the slopes of Roke Knoll, whose roots go
down to the center of the earth. All spells are strong here. Play us a trick,
Sparrowhawk. Show us your style."

Ged, confused and taken aback, said nothing.

"Later on, Jasper," Vetch said in his plain way. "Let him be a while."

"He has either skill or power, or the doorkeeper wouldn't have let
him in. Why shouldn't he show it, now as well as later? Right,
Sparrowhawk?"

"I have both skill and power," Ged said. "Show me what kind of
thing you're talking about."

"Illusions, of course—tricks, games of seeming. Like this!"

Pointing his finger Jasper spoke a few strange words, and where he
pointed on the hillside among the green grasses a little thread of water
trickled, and grew, and now a spring gushed out and the water went running down the hill. Ged put his hand in the stream and it felt wet, drank
of it and it was cool. Yet for all that it would quench no thirst, being but
illusion. Jasper with another word stopped the water, and the grasses
waved dry in the sunlight. "Now you, Vetch, he said with his cool smile.

Vetch scratched his head and looked glum, but he took up a bit of
earth in his hand and began to sing tunelessly over it, molding it with
his dark fingers and shaping it, pressing it, stroking it: and suddenly it
was a small creature like a bumblebee or furry fly, that flew humming
off over Roke Knoll, and vanished.

Ged stood staring, crestfallen.What did he know but mete village
witchery, spells to call goats, cure warts, move loads or mend pots?

"I do no such tricks as these," he said. That was enough for Vetch,
who was for going on; but Jasper said, "Why don't you?"

"Sorcery is not a game. We Gontishmen do not play it for pleasure or praise," Ged answered haughtily.

"What do you play it for," Jasper inquired, "—money?"

"No!—" But he could not think of anything more to say that would hide his ignorance and save his pride. Jasper laughed, not ill-humoredly, and went on, leading them on around Roke Knoll. And Ged followed, sullen and sore-hearted, knowing he had behaved like a fool, and blaming Jasper for it.

That night as he lay wrapped in his cloak on the mattress in his cold unlit cell of stone, in the utter silence of the Great House of Roke, the strangeness of the place and the thought of all the spells and sorceries that had been worked there began to come over him heavily. Darkness surrounded him, dread filled him. He wished he were anywhere else but Roke. But Vetch came to the door, a little bluish ball of were-light nodding over his head to light the way, and asked if he could come in and talk a while. He asked Ged about Gont, and then spoke fondly of his own home isles of the East Reach, telling how the smoke of village hearthfires is blown across that quiet sea at evening between the small islands with funny names: Korp, Kopp, and Holp, Venway and Vemish, Iffish, Koppish, and Sneg. When he sketched the shapes of those lands on the stones of the floor with his finger to show Ged how they lay, the lines he drew shone dim as if drawn with a stick of silver for a while before they faded. Vetch had been three years at the School, and soon would be made Sorcerer; he thought no more of performing the lesser arts of magic than a bird thinks of flying. Yet a greater, unlearned skill he possessed, which was the art of kindness. That night, and always from then on, he offered and gave Ged friendship, a sure and open friendship which Ged could not help but return.

Yet Vetch was also friendly to Jasper, who had made Ged into a fool that first day on Roke Knoll. Ged would not forget this, nor, it seemed, would Jasper, who always spoke to him with a polite voice and a mocking smile. Ged's pride would not be slighted or condescended to. He swore to prove to Jasper, and to all the rest of them among whom Jasper was something of a leader, how great his power really was— some day. For none of them, for all their clever tricks, had saved a village by wizardry. Of none of them had Ogion written that he would be the greatest wizard of Gont.

So bolstering up his pride, he set all his strong will on the work they gave him, the lessons and crafts and histories and skills taught by the grey-cloaked Masters of Roke, who were called the Nine.

Part of each day he studied with the Master Chanter, learning the Deeds of heroes and the Lays of wisdom, beginning with the oldest of all songs, the *Creation of Éa*. Then with a dozen other lads he would practise with the Master Windkey at arts of wind and weather. Whole bright days of spring and early summer they spent out in Roke Bay in light catboats, practising steering by word, and stilling waves, and speaking to the world's wind, and raising up the magewind. These are very intricate skills, and frequently Ged's head got whacked by the swinging boom as the boat jibed under a wind suddenly blowing backwards, or his boat and another collided though they had the whole bay to navigate in, or all three boys in his boat went swimming unexpectedly as the boat was swamped by a huge, unintended wave. There were quieter expeditions ashore, other days, with the Master Herbal who taught the ways and properties of things that grow; and the Master Hand taught sleight and jugglery and the lesser arts of Changing.

At all these studies Ged was apt, and within a month was bettering lads who had been a year at Roke before him. Especially the tricks of illusion came to him so easily that it seemed he had been born knowing them and needed only to be reminded. The Master Hand was a gentle and light-hearted old man, who had endless delight in the wit and beauty of the crafts he taught; Ged soon felt no awe of him, but asked him for this spell and that spell, and always the Master smiled and showed him what he wanted. But one day, having it in mind to put Jasper to shame at last, Ged said to the Master Hand in the Court of Seeming, "Sir, all these charms are much the same; knowing one, you know them all. And as soon as the spell-weaving ceases, the illusion vanishes. Now if I make a pebble into a diamond—" and he did so with a word and a flick of his wrist—"what must I do to make that diamond remain diamond? How is the changing-spell locked, and made to last?"

The Master Hand looked at the jewel that glittered on Ged's palm, bright as the prize of a dragon's hoard. The old Master murmured one word, *"Tolk,"* and there lay the pebble, no jewel but a rough grey bit of rock. The Master took it and held it out on his own hand. "This is a rock; *tolk* in the True Speech," he said, looking mildly up at Ged now. "A bit of the stone of which Roke Isle is made, a little bit of the dry land on which men live. It is itself. It is part of the world. By the Illusion-Change you can make it look like a diamond—or a flower or a fly or an eye or a flame—" The rock flickered from shape to shape as he named them, and returned to rock. "But that is mere seeming. Illusion fools the beholder's senses; it makes him see and hear and feel that the thing is changed. But it does not change the thing. To change this rock into a jewel, you must change its true name. And to do that, my son, even to so small a scrap of the world, is to change the world. It can be done. Indeed it can be done. It is the art of the Master Changer, and you will learn it, when you are ready to learn it. But you must not change one thing, one pebble, one grain of sand, until you know what good and evil will follow on that act. The world is in balance, in Equilibrium. A wizard's power of Changing and of Summoning can shake the balance of the world. It is dangerous, that power. It is most perilous. It must follow knowledge, and serve need. To light a candle is to cast a shadow. . . . "

He looked down at the pebble again. "A rock is a good thing, too, you know," he said, speaking less gravely. "If the Isles of Earthsea were all made of diamond, we'd lead a hard life here. Enjoy illusions, lad, and let the rocks be rocks." He smiled, but Ged left dissatisfied. Press a mage for his secrets and he would always talk, like Ogion, about balance, and danger, and the dark. But surely a wizard, one who had gone past these childish tricks of illusion to the true arts of Summoning and Change, was powerful enough to do what he pleased, and balance the world as seemed best to him, and drive back darkness with his own light.

In the corridor he met Jasper, who, since Ged's accomplishments began to be praised about the School, spoke to him in a way that seemed more friendly, but was more scoffing. "You look gloomy, Sparrowhawk," he said now, "did your juggling-charms go wrong?"

Seeking as always to put himself on equal footing with Jasper, Ged answered the question ignoring its ironic tone. "I'm sick of juggling," he said, "sick of these illusion-tricks, fit only to amuse idle lords in their castles and Domains. The only true magic they've taught me yet on Roke is making werelight, and some weatherworking. The rest is mere foolery."

"Even foolery is dangerous," said Jasper, "in the hands of a fool."

At that Ged turned as if he had been slapped, and took a step towards Jasper; but the older boy smiled as if he had not intended any insult, nodded his head in his stiff, graceful way, and went on.

Standing there with rage in his heart, looking after Jasper, Ged swore to himself to outdo his rival, and not in some mere illusion-match but in a test of power. He would prove himself, and humiliate Jasper. He would not let the fellow stand there looking down at him, graceful, disdainful, hateful.

Ged did not stop to think why Jasper might hate him. He only knew why he hated Jasper. The other prentices had soon learned they could seldom match themselves against Ged either in sport or in earnest, and they said of him, some in praise and some in spite, "He's a wizard born, he'll never let you beat him." Jasper alone neither praised him nor avoided him, but simply looked down at him, smiling slightly. And therefore Jasper stood alone as his rival, who must be put to shame.

He did not see, or would not see, that in this rivalry, which he clung to and fostered as part of his own pride, there was anything of the danger, the darkness, of which the Master Hand had mildly warned him.

When he was not moved by pure rage, he knew very well that he was as yet no match for Jasper, or any of the older boys, and so he kept at his work and went on as usual. At the end of summer the work was slackened somewhat, so there was more time for sport: spell-boat races down in the harbor, feats of illusion in the courts of the Great House, and in the long evenings, in the groves, wild games of hide-and-seek where hiders and seeker were both invisible and only voices moved laughing and calling among the trees, following and dodging the quick, faint werelights. Then as autumn came they set to their tasks afresh, practising new magic. So Ged's first months at Roke went by fast, full of passions and wonders.

In winter it was different. He was sent with seven other boys across Roke Island to the farthest northmost cape, where stands the Isolate Tower. There by himself lived the Master Namer, who was called by a name that had no meaning in any language, Kurremkarmerruk. No farm or dwelling lay within miles of the Tower. Grim it stood above the northern cliffs, grey were the clouds over the seas of winter, endless the lists and ranks and rounds of names that the Namer's eight pupils must learn. Amongst them in the Tower's high room Kurremkarmerruk sat on a high seat, writing down lists of names that must be learned before the ink faded at midnight leaving the parchment blank again. It was cold and half-dark and always silent there except for the scratching of the Master's pen and the sighing, maybe, of a student who must learn before midnight the name of every cape, point, bay, sound, inlet, channel, harbor, shallows, reef and rock of the shores of Lossow, a little islet of the Pelnish Sea. If the student complained the Master might say nothing, but lengthen the list; or he might say, "He who would be Seamaster must know the true name of every drop of water in the sea."

Ged sighed sometimes, but he did not complain. He saw that in this dusty and fathomless matter of learning the true name of each place, thing, and being, the power he wanted lay like a jewel at the bottom of a dry well. For magic consists in this, the true naming of a thing. So Kurremkarmerruk had said to them, once, their first night in the Tower; he never repeated it, but Ged did not forget his words. "Many a mage of great power," he had said, "has spent his whole life to find out the name of one single thing—one single lost or hidden name. And still the lists are not finished. Nor will they be, till world's end. Listen, and you will see why. In the world under the sun, and in the other world that has no sun, there is much that has nothing to do with men and men's speech, and there are powers beyond our power. But magic, true magic, is worked only by those beings who speak the Hardic tongue of Earthsea, or the Old Speech from which it grew.

"That is the language dragons speak, and the language Segoy spoke who made the islands of the world, and the language of our lays and songs, spells, enchantments, and invocations. Its words lie hidden and changed among our Hardic words. We call the foam on waves *sukien*: that word is made from two words of the Old Speech, *suk*, feather, and *inien*, the sea. Feather of the sea, is foam. But you cannot charm the foam calling it *sukien*; you must use its own true name in the Old Speech, which is *essa*. Any witch knows a few of these words in the Old Speech, and a mage knows many. But there are many more, and some have been lost over the ages, and some have been hidden, and some are known only to dragons and to the Old Powers of Earth, and some are known to no living creature; and no man could learn them all. For there is no end to that language.

"Here is the reason. The sea's name is *inien*, well and good. But what we call the Inmost Sea has its own name also in the Old Speech. Since no thing can have two true names, *inien* can mean only 'all the sea except the Inmost Sea.' And of course it does not mean even that, for there are seas and bays and straits beyond counting that bear names of their own. So if some Mage-Seamaster were mad enough to try to lay a spell of storm or calm over all the ocean, his spell must say not only that word *inien*, but the name of every stretch and bit and part of the sea through all the Archipelago and all the Outer Reaches and beyond to where names cease. Thus, that which gives us the power to work magic, sets the limits of that power. A mage can control only what is near him, what he can name exactly and wholly. And this is well. If it were not so, the wickedness of the powerful or the folly of the wise would long ago have sought to change what cannot be changed, and Equilibrium would fall. The unbalanced sea would overwhelm the islands where we perilously dwell, and in the old silence all voices and all names would be lost."

Ged thought long on these words, and they went deep in his understanding. Yet the majesty of the task could not make the work of that long year in the Tower less hard and dry; and at the end of the year Kurremkarmerruk said to him, "You have made a good beginning." But no more. Wizards speak truth, and it was true that all the mastery of Names that Ged had toiled to win that year was the mere start of what he must go on learning all his life. He was let go from the Isolate Tower sooner than those who had come with him, for he had learned quicker; but that was all the praise he got.

The Velveteen Rabbit

by Margery Williams

Margery Williams (1881–1944) wrote 30 children's books. She was born in England and later divided her time between that country and the United States. The toys in this classic tale have a lot to teach one another and the little boy who loves them.

There was once a velveteen rabbit, and in the beginning he was really splendid. He was fat and bunchy, as a rabbit should be; his coat was spotted brown and white, he had real thread whiskers, and his ears were lined with pink sateen. On Christmas morning, when he sat wedged in the top of the Boy's stocking, with a sprig of holly between his paws, the effect was charming.

There were other things in the stocking, nuts and oranges and a toy engine, and chocolate almonds and a clockwork mouse, but the Rabbit was quite the best of all. For at least two hours the Boy loved him, and then Aunts and Uncles came to dinner, and there was a great rustling of tissue paper and unwrapping of parcels, and in the excitement of looking at all the new presents the Velveteen Rabbit was forgotten.

For a long time he lived in the toy cupboard or on the nursery floor, and no one thought very much about him. He was naturally shy, and being only made of velveteen, some of the more expensive toys quite snubbed him. The mechanical toys were very superior, and looked down upon every one else; they were full of modern ideas, and pretended they were real. The model boat, who had lived through two seasons and lost most of his paint, caught the tone from them and never missed an opportunity of referring to his rigging in technical terms. The Rabbit could not claim to be a model of anything, for he didn't know that real rabbits existed; he thought they were all stuffed with sawdust like himself, and he understood that sawdust was quite out-of-date and should never be mentioned in modern circles. Even Timothy, the jointed wooden lion, who was made by the disabled soldiers, and should have had broader views, put on airs and pretended he was connected with Government. Between them all the poor little Rabbit was made to feel himself very insignificant and commonplace, and the only person who was kind to him at all was the Skin Horse.

The Skin Horse had lived longer in the nursery than any of the others. He was so old that his brown coat was bald in patches and showed the seams underneath, and most of the hairs in his tail had been pulled out to string bead necklaces. He was wise, for he had seen a long succession of mechanical toys arrive to boast and swagger, and by-and-by break their mainsprings and pass away, and he knew that they were only toys, and would never turn into anything else. For nursery magic is very strange and wonderful, and only those playthings that are old and wise and experienced like the Skin Horse understand all about it.

"What is REAL?" asked the Rabbit one day, when they were lying side by side near the nursery fender, before Nana came to tidy the room. "Does it mean having things that buzz inside you and a stick-out handle?"

"Real isn't how you are made," said the Skin Horse. "It's a thing that happens to you. When a child loves you for a long, long time, not just to play with, but REALLY loves you, then you become Real."

"Does it hurt?" asked the Rabbit.

"Sometimes," said the Skin Horse, for he was always truthful. "When you are Real you don't mind being hurt."

"Does it happen all at once, like being wound up," he asked, "or bit by bit?"

"It doesn't happen all at once," said the Skin Horse. "You become. It takes a long time. That's why it doesn't happen often to people who break easily, or have sharp edges, or who have to be carefully kept. Generally, by the time you are Real, most of your hair has been loved off, and your eyes drop out and you get loose in your joints and very shabby. But these things don't matter at all, because once you are Real you can't be ugly, except to people who don't understand."

"I suppose *you* are real?" said the Rabbit. And then he wished he had not said it, for he thought the Skin Horse might be sensitive. But the Skin Horse only smiled.

"The Boy's Uncle made me Real," he said. "That was a great many years ago; but once you are Real you can't become unreal again. It lasts for always."

The Rabbit sighed. He thought it would be a long time before this magic called Real happened to him. He longed to become Real, to know what it felt like; and yet the idea of growing shabby and losing his eyes and whiskers was rather sad. He wished that he could become it without these uncomfortable things happening to him.

There was a person called Nana who ruled the nursery. Sometimes she took no notice of the playthings lying about, and sometimes, for no reason whatever, she went swooping about like a great wind and hustled them away in cupboards. She called this "tidying up," and the playthings all hated it, especially the tin ones. The Rabbit didn't mind it so much, for wherever he was thrown he came down soft.

One evening, when the Boy was going to bed, he couldn't find the china dog that always slept with him. Nana was in a hurry, and it was too much trouble to hunt for china dogs at bedtime, so she simply looked about her, and seeing that the toy cupboard stood open, she made a swoop.

"Here," she said, "take your old Bunny! He'll do to sleep with you!" And she dragged the Rabbit out by one ear, and put him into the Boy's arms.

That night, and for many nights after, the Velveteen Rabbit slept in the Boy's bed. At first he found it uncomfortable, for the Boy hugged him very tight, and sometimes he rolled over on him, and sometimes he pushed him so far under the pillow that the Rabbit could scarcely breathe. And he missed, too, those long moonlight hours in the nursery, when all the house was silent, and his talks with the Skin Horse. But very soon he grew to like it, for the Boy used to talk to him, and made nice tunnels for him under the bedclothes that he said were like the burrow the real rabbits lived in. And they had splendid games together, in whispers, when Nana had gone away to her supper and left the night-light burning on the mantelpiece. And when the Boy dropped off to sleep, the Rabbit would snuggle down close under his little warm chin and dream, with the Boy's hands clasped close round him all night long.

And so time went on, and the little Rabbit was very happy—so happy that he never noticed how his beautiful velveteen fur was getting shabbier and shabbier, and his tail becoming unsewn, and all the pink rubbed off his nose where the Boy had kissed him.

Spring came, and they had long days in the garden, for wherever the Boy went the Rabbit went too. He had rides in the wheelbarrow, and picnics on the grass, and lovely fairy huts built for him under the raspberry canes behind the flower border. And once, when the Boy was called away suddenly to go to tea, the Rabbit was left out on the lawn until long after dusk, and Nana had to come and look for him with the candle because the Boy couldn't go to sleep unless he was there. He was wet through with the dew and quite earthy from diving into the burrows the Boy had made for him in the flower bed, and Nana grumbled as she rubbed him off with a corner of her apron.

"You must have your old Bunny!" she said. "Fancy all that fuss for a toy!"

"Give me my Bunny!" he said. "You mustn't say that. He isn't a toy. He's REAL!"

When the little Rabbit heard that he was happy, for he knew what the Skin Horse had said was true at last. The nursery magic had happened to him, and he was a toy no longer. He was Real. The Boy himself had said it.

That night he was almost too happy to sleep, and so much love stirred in his little sawdust heart that it almost burst. And into his boot-button eyes, that had long ago lost their polish, there came a look of wisdom and beauty, so that even Nana noticed it next morning when she picked him up, and said, "I declare if that old Bunny hasn't got quite a knowing expression!"

That was a wonderful Summer!

Near the house where they lived there was a wood, and in the long June evening the Boy liked to go there after tea to play. He took the Velveteen Rabbit with him, and before he wandered off to pick flowers, or play at brigands among the trees, he always made the Rabbit a little nest somewhere among the bracken, where he would be quite cosy, for he was a kindhearted little boy and he liked Bunny to be comfortable. One evening, while the Rabbit was lying there alone, watching the ants that ran to and fro between his velvet paws in the grass, he saw two strange beings creep out of the tall bracken near him.

They were rabbits like himself, but quite furry and brand-new. They must have been very well made, for their seams didn't show at all, and they changed shape in a queer way when they moved; one minute they were long and thin and the next minute fat and bunchy, instead of always staying the same like he did. Their feet padded softly on the ground, and they crept quite close to him, twitching their noses, while the Rabbit stared hard to see which side the clockwork stuck out, for he knew that people who jump generally have some-thing to wind them up. But he couldn't see it. They were evidently a new kind of rabbit altogether.

They stared at him, and the little Rabbit stared back. And all the time their noses twitched.

"Why don't you get up and play with us?" one of them asked.

"I don't feel like it," said the Rabbit, for he didn't want to explain that he had no clockwork.

"Ho!" said the furry rabbit. "It's as easy as anything," And he gave a big hop sideways and stood on his hind legs.

"I don't believe you can!" he said.

"I can!" said the little Rabbit. "I can jump higher than anything." He meant when the Boy threw him, but of course he didn't want to say so.

"Can you hop on your hind legs?" asked the furry rabbit.

That was a dreadful question, for the Velveteen Rabbit had no hind legs at all! The back of him was made all in one piece, like a pincushion. He sat still in the bracken, and hoped that the other rabbit wouldn't notice.

"I don't want to!" he said again.

But the wild rabbits have very sharp eyes. And this one stretched out his neck and looked.

"He hasn't got any hind legs," he called out. "Fancy a rabbit without any hind legs" And he began to laugh.

"I have!" cried the little Rabbit. "I have got hind legs! I am sitting on them."

"Then stretch them out and show me, like this!" said the wild rabbit. And he began to whirl around and dance, till the little Rabbit got quite dizzy.

"I don't like dancing," he said. "I'd rather sit still!"

But all the while he was longing to dance, for a funny new tickly feeling ran through him, and he felt he would give anything in the world to be able to jump about like these rabbits did.

The strange rabbit stopped dancing, and came quite close. He came so close this time that his long whiskers brushed the Velveteen Rabbit's ear, and then he wrinkled his nose suddenly and flattened his ears and jumped backwards.

"He doesn't smell right!" he exclaimed. "He isn't a rabbit at all! He isn't real!"

"I am Real!" said the little Rabbit. "I am Real! The Boy said so!" And he nearly began to cry.

Just then there was a sound of footsteps, and the Boy ran past near them, and with a stamp of feet and a flash of white tails the two strange rabbits disappeared.

"Come back and play with me!" called the little Rabbit. "Oh, do come back! I *know* I am Real!"

But there was no answer, only the little ants ran to and fro, and the bracken swayed gently where the two strangers had passed. The Velveteen Rabbit was all alone.

"Oh, dear!" he thought. "Why did they run away like that? Why couldn't they stop and talk to me?"

For a long time he lay very still, watching the bracken, and hoping that they would come back. But they never returned, and presently the sun sank lower and the little white moths fluttered out, and the Boy came and carried him home.

Weeks passed, and the little Rabbit grew very old and shabby, but the Boy loved him just as much. He loved him so hard that he loved all his whiskers off, and the pink lining to his ears turned grey, and his brown spots faded. He even began to lose his shape, and he scarcely looked like a rabbit anymore, except to the Boy. To him he was always beautiful, and that was all that the little Rabbit cared about. He didn't mind how he looked to other people, because the nursery magic had made him Real, and when you are Real shabbiness doesn't matter.

And then, one day, the Boy was ill.

His face grew very flushed, and he talked in his sleep, and his little body was so hot that it burned the Rabbit when he held him close. Strange people came and went in the nursery, and a light burned all night and through it all the little Velveteen Rabbit lay there, hidden from sight under the bedclothes, and he never stirred, for he was afraid that if they found him someone might take him away, and he knew that the Boy needed him.

It was a long weary time, for the Boy was too ill to play, and the little Rabbit found it rather dull with nothing to do all day long. But he snuggled down patiently, and looked forward to the time when the Boy should be well again, and they would go out in the garden amongst the flowers and the butterflies and play splendid games in the raspberry thicket like they used to. All sorts of delightful things he planned, and while the Boy lay half asleep he crept up close to the pillow and whispered them in his ear. And presently the fever turned, and the Boy got better. He was able to sit up in bed and look at picture-books, while the little Rabbit cuddled close at his side. And one day, they let him get up and dress.

It was a bright, sunny morning, and the windows stood wide open. They had carried the Boy out on the balcony, wrapped in a shawl, and the little Rabbit lay tangled up among the bedclothes, thinking.

The Boy was going to the seaside to-morrow. Everything was arranged, and now it only remained to carry out the doctor's orders. They talked about it all, while the little Rabbit lay under the bedclothes, with just his head peeping out, and listened. The room was to be disinfected, and all the books and toys that the Boy had played with in bed must be burnt.

"Hurrah!" thought the little Rabbit. "To-morrow we shall go to the seaside!" For the boy had often talked of the seaside, and he wanted very much to see the big waves coming in, and the tiny crabs, and the sand castles.

Just then Nana caught sight of him.

"How about his old Bunny?" she asked.

"*That?*" said the doctor. "Why, it's a mass of scarlet fever germs!— Burn it at once. What? Nonsense! Get him a new one. He mustn't have that any more!"

And so the little Rabbit was put into a sack with the old picture-books and a lot of rubbish, and carried out to the end of the garden behind the fowl-house. That was a fine place to make a bonfire, only the gardener was too busy just then to attend to it. He had the potatoes to dig and the green peas to gather, but next morning he promised to come early and burn the whole lot.

That night the Boy slept in a different bedroom, and he had a new bunny to sleep with him. It was a splendid bunny, all white plush with real glass eyes, but the Boy was too excited to care very much about it. For to-morrow he was going to the seaside, and that in itself was such a wonderful thing that he could think of nothing else.

And while the Boy was asleep, dreaming of the seaside, the little Rabbit lay among the old picture-books in the corner behind the fowl-house, and he felt very lonely. The sack had been left untied, and so by wriggling a bit he was able to get his head through the opening and look out. He was shivering a little, for he had always been used to sleeping in a proper bed, and by this time his coat had worn so thin and threadbare from hugging that it was no longer any protection to him. Near by he could see the thicket of raspberry canes, growing tall and close like a tropical jungle, in whose shadow he had played with the Boy on bygone mornings. He thought of those long sunlit hours in the garden—how happy they were—and a great sadness came over him. He seemed to see them all pass before him, each more beautiful than the other, the fairy huts in the flower-bed, the quiet evenings in the wood when he lay in the bracken and the little ants ran over his paws; the wonderful day when he first knew that he was Real. He thought of the Skin Horse, so wise and gentle, and all that he had told him. Of what use was it to be loved and lose one's beauty and become Real if it all ended like this? And a tear, a real tear, trickled down his little shabby velvet nose and fell to the ground.

And then a strange thing happened. For where the tear had fallen a flower grew out of the ground, a mysterious flower, not at all like any that grew in the garden. It had slender green leaves the colour of emer-alds, and in the centre of the leaves a blossom like a golden cup. It was so beautiful that the little Rabbit forgot to cry, and just lay there watch-ing it. And presently the blossom opened, and out of it there stepped a fairy.

She was quite the loveliest fairy in the whole world. Her dress was of pearl and dew-drops, and there were flowers round her neck and in her hair, and her face was like the most perfect flower of all. And she came close to the little Rabbit and gathered him up in her arms and kissed him on his velveteen nose that was all damp from crying.

"Little Rabbit," she said, "don't you know who I am?"

The Rabbit looked up at her, and it seemed to him that he had seen her face before, but he couldn't think where.

"I am the nursery magic Fairy," she said. "I take care of all the playthings that the children have loved. When they are old and worn out, and the children don't need them any more, then I come and take them away with me and turn them into Real."

"Wasn't I Real before?" asked the little Rabbit.

"You were Real to the Boy," the Fairy said, "because he loved you. Now you shall be Real to every one."

And she held the little Rabbit close in her arms and flew with him into the wood.

It was light now, for the moon had risen. All the forest was beautiful, and the fronds of the bracken shone like frosted silver. In the open glade between the tree-trunks the wild rabbits danced with their shadows on the velvet grass, but when they saw the Fairy they all stopped dancing and stood round in a ring to stare at her.

"I've brought you a new playfellow," the Fairy said. "You must be very kind to him and teach him all he needs to know in Rabbit-land, for he is going to live with you for ever and ever!"

And she kissed the little Rabbit again and put him down on the grass.

"Run and play, little Rabbit!" she said.

But the little Rabbit sat quite still for a moment and never moved. For when he saw all the wild rabbits dancing around him he suddenly remembered about his hind legs, and he didn't want them to see that he was made all in one piece. He did not know that when the Fairy kissed him that last time she had changed him altogether. And he might have sat there a long time, too shy to move, if just then something hadn't tickled his nose, and before he thought what he was doing he lifted his hind toe to scratch it.

And he found that he actually had hind legs! Instead of dingy velveteen he had brown fur, soft and shiny, his ears twitched by themselves, and his whiskers were so long that they brushed the grass. He gave one leap and the joy of using those hind legs was so great that he went springing about the turf with them, jumping sideways and whirling round as the other did, and he grew so excited that when at last he did stop to look for the Fairy she had gone.

He was a Real Rabbit at last, at home with the other rabbits.

★ ★ ★

Autumn passed and Winter, and in the Spring, when the days grew warm and sunny, the Boy went out to play in the wood behind the house. And while he was playing, two rabbits crept out from the bracken and peeped at him. One of them was brown all over, but the other had strange markings under his fur, as though long ago he had been spotted, and the spots still showed through. And about his little soft nose and his round black eyes there was something familiar, so that the Boy thought to himself:

"Why, he looks just like my old Bunny that was lost when I had scarlet fever!"

But he never knew that it really was his own Bunny, come back to look at the child who had first helped him to be Real.

from

Alice's Adventures in
Wonderland

by Lewis Carroll

Mathematician Charles Lutwidge Dodgson (1832–1898) didn't want other professors to know about his children's books, so he published them under the name "Lewis Carroll". He wrote his quirky tale of young Alice's adventures down a rabbit hole for a young girl named Alice Liddell. The tea party Alice stumbles upon in this passage from the book is a strange one.

There was a table set out under a tree in front of the house, and the March Hare and the Hatter were having tea at it: a Dormouse was sitting between them, fast asleep, and the other two were using it as a cushion, resting their elbows on it, and talking over its head. "Very uncomfortable for the Dormouse," thought Alice; "only as it's asleep, I suppose it doesn't mind."

The table was a large one, but the three were all crowded together at one corner of it. "No room! No room!" they cried out when they saw Alice coming. "There's *plenty* of room!" said Alice indignantly, and she sat down in a large arm-chair at one end of the table.

"Have some wine," the March Hare said in an encouraging tone.

Alice looked all round the table, but there was nothing on it but tea. "I don't see any wine," she remarked.

"There isn't any," said the March Hare.

"Then it wasn't very civil of you to offer it," said Alice angrily.

"It wasn't very civil of you to sit down without being invited," said the March Hare.

"I didn't know it was *your* table," said Alice: "it's laid for a great many more than three."

"Your hair wants cutting," said the Hatter. He had been looking at Alice for some time with great curiosity, and this was his first speech.

"You should learn not to make personal remarks," Alice said with some severity: "it's very rude."

The Hatter opened his eyes very wide in hearing this; but all he *said* was "Why is a raven like a writing-deck?"

"Come, we shall have some fun now!" thought Alice. "I'm glad they've begun asking riddles—I believe I can guess that," she added aloud.

"Do you mean that you think you can find out the answer to it?" said the March Hare.

"Exactly so," said Alice.

"Then you should say what you mean," the March Hare went on.

"I do," Alice hastily replied; "at least—at least I mean what I say—that's the same thing, you know. "

"Not the same thing a bit!" said the Hatter. "Why, you might just as well say that 'I see what I eat' is the same thing as 'I eat what I see'!"

"You might just as well say," added the March Hare, "that 'I like what I get' is the same thing as 'I get what I like'!"

"You might just as well say," added the Dormouse, which seemed to be talking in its sleep, "that 'I breathe when I sleep' is the same thing as 'I sleep when I breathe'!"

"It *is* the same thing with you," said the Hatter, and here the conversation dropped, and the party sat silent for a minute, while Alice thought over all she could remember about ravens and writing-desks, which wasn't much.

The Hatter was the first to break the silence. "What day of the month is it?" he said, turning to Alice: he had taken his watch out of his pocket, and was looking at it uneasily, shaking it every now and then, and holding it to his ear.

Alice considered a little, and then said, "The fourth."

"Two days wrong!" sighed the Hatter. "I told you butter wouldn't suit the works!" he added, looking angrily at the March Hare.

"It was the *best* butter," the March Hare meekly replied.

"Yes, but some crumbs must have got in as well," the Hatter grumbled: "you shouldn't have put it in with the bread-knife."

The March Hare took the watch and looked at it gloomily: then he dipped it into his cup of tea, and looked at it again: but he could think of nothing better to say than his first remark, "it was the *best* butter, you know."

Alice had been looking over his shoulder with some curiosity. "What a funny watch!" she remarked. "It tells the day of the month, and doesn't tell what o'clock it is!"

"Why should it?" muttered the Hatter. "Does your watch tell you what year it is?"

"Of course not," Alice replied very readily: "but that's because it stays the same year for such a long time together."

"Which is just the case with *mine*," said the Hatter.

Alice felt dreadfully puzzled. The Hatter's remark seemed to her to have no sort of meaning in it, and yet it was certainly English. "I don't quite understand you," she said, as politely as she could.

"The Dormouse is asleep again," said the Hatter, and he poured a little hot tea upon its nose.

The Dormouse shook its head impatiently, and said, without opening its eyes, "Of course, of course: just what I was going to remark myself."

"Have you guessed the riddle yet?" the Hatter said, turning to Alice again.

"No, I give it up," Alice replied. "What's the answer?"

"I haven't the slightest idea," said the Hatter.

"Nor I," said the March Hare.

Alice sighed wearily. "I think you might do something better with the time," she said, "than wasting it in asking riddles that have no answers."

"If you knew Time as well as I do," said the Hatter, "you wouldn't talk about wasting *it*. It's *him*."

"I don't know what you mean," said Alice.

"Of course you don't!" the Hatter said, tossing his head contemptuously. "I dare say you never even spoke to Time!"

"Perhaps not," Alice cautiously replied; "but I know I have to beat time when I learn music."

"Ah! That accounts for it," said the Hatter. "He won't stand beating. Now, if you only kept on good terms with him, he'd do almost anything you liked with the clock. For instance, suppose it were nine o'clock in the morning, just time to begin lessons: you'd only have to whisper a hint to Time, and round goes the clock in a twinkling! Half-past one, time for dinner!"

("I only wish it was," the March Hare said to itself in a whisper.)

"That would be grand, certainly," said Alice thoughtfully; "but then—I shouldn't be hungry for it, you know."

"Not at first, perhaps," said the Hatter: "but you could keep it to half-past one as long as you liked."

"Is that the way *you* manage?" Alice asked.

The Hatter shook his head mournfully. "Not I!" he replied. "We quarreled last March—just before *he* went mad, you know—" (pointing with his teaspoon at the March Hare) "—it was at the great concert given by the Queen of Hearts, and I had to sing

    'Twinkle, twinkle, little bat!

    How I wonder what you're at!'

You know the song, perhaps?"

"I've heard something like it," said Alice.

"It goes on, you know," the Hatter continued, "in this way:—

    'Up above the world you fly,

    like a tea-tray in the sky.

    Twinkle, twinkle—'"

Here the Dormouse shook itself, and began singing in its sleep *"Twinkle, twinkle, twinkle, twinkle—"* and went on so long that they had to pinch it to make it stop.

"Well, I'd hardly finished the first verse," said the Hatter, "when the Queen bawled out 'He's murdering the time! Off with his head!'"

"How dreadfully savage!" exclaimed Alice.

"And ever since that," the Hatter went on in a mournful tone, "he won't do a thing I ask! It's always six o'clock now."

A bright idea came into Alice's head. "Is that the reason so many tea-things are put out here?" she asked.

"Yes, that's it," said the Hatter with a sigh: "it's always tea-time, and we've no time to wash the things between whiles."

"Then you keep moving round, I suppose?" said Alice.

"Exactly so," said the Hatter: "as the things get used up."

"But what happens when you come to the beginning again?" Alice ventured to ask.

"Suppose we change the subject," the March Hare interrupted, yawning. "I'm getting tired of this. I vote the young lady tells us a story."

"I'm afraid I don't know one," said Alice, rather alarmed at the proposal.

"Then the Dormouse shall!" they both cried. "Wake up, Dormouse!" And they pinched it on both sides at once.

The Dormouse slowly opened its eyes. "I wasn't asleep," it said in a hoarse, feeble voice, "I heard every word you fellows were saying."

"Tell us a story!" said the March Hare.

"Yes, please do!" pleaded Alice.

"And be quick about it," added the Hatter, "or you'll be asleep again before it's done."

"Once upon a time there were three little sisters," the Dormouse began in a great hurry; "and their names were Elsie, Lacie, and Tillie; and they lived at the bottom of a well—"

"What did they live on?" said Alice, who always took a great interest in questions of eating and drinking.

"They lived on treacle," said the Dormouse, after thinking a minute or two.

"They couldn't have done that, you know," Alice gently remarked. "They'd have been ill."

"So they were," said the Dormouse; "*very* ill."

Alice tried a little to fancy to herself what such an extraordinary way of living would be like, but it puzzled her too much: so she went on: "But why did they live at the bottom of a well?"

"Take some more tea," the March Hare said to Alice, very earnestly.

"I've had nothing yet," Alice replied in an offended tone: "so I can't take more."

"You mean you can't take *less*," said the Hatter: "it's very easy to take *more* than nothing."

"Nobody asked *your* opinion," said Alice.

"Who's making personal remarks now?" the Hatter asked triumphantly.

Alice did not quite know what to say to this: so she helped herself to some tea and bread-and-butter, and then turned to the Dormouse, and repeated her question. "Why did they live at the bottom of a well?"

The Dormouse again took a minute or two to think about it, and then said "It was a treacle well."

"There's no such thing!" Alice was beginning very angrily, but the Hatter and the March Hare went "Sh! Sh!" and the Dormouse sulkily remarked "If you can't be civil, you'd better finish the story for yourself."

"No, please go on!" Alice said very humbly. "I won't interrupt you again. I dare say there may be *one*."

"One, indeed!" said the Dormouse indignantly. However, he consented to go on. "And so these three little sisters—they were learning to draw, you know—"

"What did they draw?" said Alice, quite forgetting her promise.

"Treacle," said the Dormouse, without considering at all, this time.

"I want a clean cup," interrupted the Hatter: "let's all move one place on."

He moved on as he spoke, and the Dormouse followed him: the March Hare moved into the Dormouse's place, and Alice rather unwillingly took the place of the March Hare. The Hatter was the only one who got any advantage from the change; and Alice was a good deal worse off than before, as the March Hare had just upset the milk-jug into his plate.

Alice did not wish to offend the Dormouse again, so she began very cautiously: "But I don't understand. Where did they draw the treacle from?"

"You can draw water out of a water-well," said the Hatter; "so I should think you could draw treacle out of a treacle-well—eh, stupid?"

"But they were *in* the well," Alice said to the Dormouse, not choosing to notice this last remark.

"Of course they were," said the Dormouse; "well in."

This answer so confused poor Alice, that she let the Dormouse go on for some time without interrupting it.

"They were learning to draw," the Dormouse went on, yawning and rubbing its eyes, for it was getting very sleepy; "and they drew all manner of things—everything that begins with an M—"

"Why with an M?" said Alice.

"Why not?" said the March Hare.

Alice was silent.

The Dormouse had closed its eyes by this time, and was going off into a doze; but, on being pinched by the Hatter, it woke up again with a little shriek, and went on: "—that begins with an M, such as mousetraps, and the moon, and memory, and muchness—you know you say things are 'much of a muchness'—did you ever see such a thing as a drawing of a muchness?"

"Really, now you ask me," said Alice, very much confused, "I don't think—"

"Then you shouldn't talk," said the Hatter.

This piece of rudeness was more than Alice could bear: she got up in great disgust, and walked off: the Dormouse fell asleep instantly, and neither of the others took the least notice of her going, though she looked back once or twice, half hoping that they would call after her: the last time she saw them, they were trying to put the Dormouse into the teapot.

"At any rate I'll never go *there* again!" said Alice, as she picked her way through the wood.

"It's the stupidest tea-party I ever was at in all my life!"

Acknowledgements

Many people made this anthology.

At Thunder's Mouth Press and Avalon Publishing Group:
Neil Ortenberg and Susan Reich offered vital support and expertise.
Michael Walters designed a beautiful book. Maria Fernandez
cheerfully and skillfully oversaw production with the help of Paul
Paddock. Proofreader Fran Manushkin caught our slip-ups.
My gratitude is due to Will Balliett for his friendship and guidance.

At the Thomas Memorial Library in Cape Elizabeth, Maine:
Thanks to all the librarians, but especially to Susan Sandberg, for
working to find and borrow countless books from around the
country.

At the Writing Company:
Nate Hardcastle's artful conjuring helped this book to materialize in
a timely fashion.

At Shawneric.com:
Shawneric Hachey used his most powerful spells to secure permis-
sions for the selections in this book.

Among family and friends:
Jane Rosenberg and Bob Porter shared their extensive knowledge of
the literature of magic with me.
Clint Willis, a gifted writer and editor and my husband of 20 years,
encouraged and supported me as he always has done.
My sons Abner and Harper Willis inspire me every day.

Finally, I am grateful to the writers whose work appears in this book.

Bibliography

Anderson, Hans Christian. *The Snow Queen*. New York: Random House, 1985.

Burnett, Frances Hodgson. *The Secret Garden*. New York: Puffin Books, 1951.

Carroll, Lewis. *Alice's Adventures in Wonderland*. New York: MacMillian, 1865.

Dahl, Roald. *The Witches*. New York: Puffin Books, 1983.

Eager, Edward. *Half Magic*. New York: Harcourt Brace, 1985.

Gogol, Nicolai. "The Nose" London: Bibliomania.com

Heaney, Seamus (translator). *Beowulf: A New Verse Translation*. New York: W.W. Norton & Company, 2001.

Helprin, Mark. . New York: Harcourt, 1975. (*A Jew of Persia*)

LeGuin, Ursula. *The Wizard of Earthsea*. Berkeley, CA: Parnassus Press, 1968.

Lewis, C.S. *The Lion, The Witch and The Wardrobe*. New York: MacMillan, 1962.

Macdonald, George. *At The Back of the North Wind*. New York: MacMillan, 1964.

Mandelbaum, Allen (translator). *The Odyssey of Homer*. Berkeley, CA: University of California Press, 1990.

Nesbit, E. *Five Children and It*. London: Penguin UK, 1959.

Nesbit, E. *The Last of the Dragons*. New York: McGraw-Hill, 1980.

Pearce, A. Phillipa. *Tom's Midnight Garden*. New York: JB Lippincott, 1959.

White, T.H. *The Troll*. New York: GP Putnam's Sons, 1981.

White, T.H. *Once and Future King*. New York: GP Putnam's Sons, 1987.

Williams, Margery. *The Velveteen Rabbit*. New York: Doubleday, 1998.

Yolen, Jane. *Wizard's Hall*. New York: Puffin Books, 1973.